new aspects 2

studies in western europe
regional and thematic

WILLIAM MACNAMARA
BRIAN Ó CINNÉIDE

THE EDUCATIONAL COMPANY

First published 1987
This edition 1997
The Educational Company of Ireland
Ballymount Road
Walkinstown
Dublin 12

A trading unit of Smurfit Services Ltd

© William MacNamara, Brian Ó Cinnéide 1997

Editor: Aengus Carroll

Fact & photographic research: Nell Regan

Design and layout: Creative Inputs

Artwork: Daghda

Colour reproductions: Impress

Acknowledgements:
The authors and publishers would like to thank for their permission to reproduce copyright material:
Irish Co-Operative Organisation Society, Irish Department of Agriculture, Food and Forestry, Commission of European Communities, Embassies (all in Ireland), Norwegian Embassy, Swedish Embassy, Danish Embassy, Netherlands Embassy, Swiss Embassy, Italian Embassy, Spanish Embassy, Belgium Embassy, ICEP – Portuguese Trade and Tourism Board, French Commercial Counsellor.

The publishers would also like to thank the following for permission to reproduce photographic material:
Teagasc, IDA – Irish Development Authority, EPIC – European Public Information Centre, (Dublin), Netherlands Board of Tourism (London), Belgium National Tourism Office (London), Swiss National Tourism Office (London), Spanish National Tourism Office (London), Spanish Commercial Office (Dublin), Swedish Embassy (Dublin), French Government Tourism Office (Dublin), German-Irish Chamber of Commerce, ICEP - Portuguese Trade and Tourism Board (Dublin), Slide File.

If the publishers have inadvertently overlooked any copyright holders, they will be happy to make the appropriate arrangements at the earliest convenience.

Printed in the Republic of Ireland by
Smurfit Web Press, Dublin 9

6789

The paper used in this book comes from Managed Forests in Northern Europe. For every tree felled, at least one new tree is planted

contents

CHAPTER	PAGE
NORTHERN EUROPE	
norway	3
sweden	21
denmark	37
WESTERN AND CENTRAL EUROPE	
the netherlands	53
belgium	77
france	95
germany	123
switzerland	151
MEDITERRANEAN EUROPE	
italy	167
iberia	191
spain	195
portugal	213
EUROPEAN TOPICS	
core growth regions	224
the decline of coal	226
energy in the EU	228
the iron and steel industry	230
europe's environmental problems	233
the influence of the sea on europe's economy	237
european migration	239
aspects of tourism	242
common agriculture policy (CAP) & common fisheries policy (CFP)	248
economic & monetary union	252

northern europe

norway

sweden

denmark

chapter one
norway

INTRODUCTION

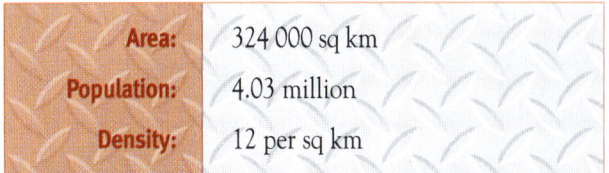

Area:	324 000 sq km
Population:	4.03 million
Density:	12 per sq km

Highest mountain: Glittertind 2470 m
Largest island: Hinnøy 2198 sq.km
Longest fjord: Sognefjorden 183 km
Longest river: Glåma 611 km
Largest city: Oslo 550,000 inhabitants
Minimum width: 6.3 km
Maximum width: 430 km

Fig. 1.1 Norway features

The Scandinavian peninsula consists of Norway and Sweden. It is the most northerly peninsula in western Europe. Norway is on the western side of this peninsula and stretches from 58°N to 71°N. In the extreme north it borders Finland and Russia. Well over one-third of the country lies within the Arctic circle and there is almost continuous daylight in this area from May to August. It is often called *The Land of the Midnight Sun* because of this. It has a long coastline of some 3 200 km but, if we include the inlets and fiords, the total length is over 20 000 km, about half the length of the equator. Norway is a sparsely settled country with a density of only 12 per sq km. It has one of the highest standards of living in western Europe.

Fig. 1.2 Norwegian Fiord

Norway is not a member of the EU. In 1972 and again in 1995, the Norwegian people voted not to join the Union. The anti-EU lobby was backed strongly by the small farmers who feared the competition from the bigger EU farmers and by the fishing industry, which did not want to open its fishing grounds to the other EU fleets.

Climate

The climate of Norway can be classified as cool temperate

maritime, but that of the north has deep winter cold. A number of factors play important roles in determining the climate. These are: the North Atlantic Drift (NAD), altitude, latitude, relief, and distance from the sea. The average temperature for summer along the south coast is about 16°C and this falls gradually to 10°C in the north. Here latitude is an important influencing factor. Inland the influence of relief is felt and temperatures again fall with altitude. Along the south and south-west coasts the winter temperatures are above freezing point, and while they fall below freezing point inside the Arctic circle, the winters are not as severe as one would expect for the latitude. Here the influence of the North Atlantic Drift is very strong and the ports remain ice-free throughout the winter. The upland interior suffers from the effects of distance from the sea and altitude, and temperatures fall to around –10°C in places.

Precipitation is evenly spread through the year and there is much snow in winter. Total precipitation amounts vary, as does the number of days of snow cover. The west coast and the mountains are directly in the path of the westerlies and the Atlantic depressions. Totals may reach as high as 2 000mm. On the other hand, sheltered rain shadow valleys may have as little as 500mm.

Natural Resources and Advantages

The economy of any country depends on the use of its resources, both physical and human. Norway has achieved a very high standard of living for its people and in recent years has cleared the national debt. This has been achieved through a diligent exploitation and careful management of the main resources:

> **Water power**
> **Fisheries**
> **North Sea oil and gas**
> **Forests**
> **Minerals.**

SAMPLE QUESTION

> Select three resources and show how the economy of Norway is dependant on the use of these resources.

1 WATER POWER

> Norway has the largest per capita production of hydro-electricity in the world. Except for small supplies of coal on Spitzbergen island, well inside the Arctic, Norway has no other power resources

Fig. 1.3 Climate

on land. The development of **hydro-electric power** (HEP) towards the end of the last century gave the country the power resources necessary to develop industry. Since then, the country has established hydro stations from the south to the far north. The widespread development of hydro power signalled the start of Norway's industrial revolution.

Hydro production is dependant on the physical characteristics of a country – high precipitation, mountains, steep falls – so it is obviously confined to countries with these characteristics. Norway has them in abundance.

Consider the following factors:

- It has high and well-distributed precipitation over a large catchment area. This feeds numerous rivers which come off the mountain slopes and create the steep falls, or **heads,** necessary for hydro production.
- The glaciated mountain lakes function as reservoirs to give a controlled flow of water.
- Much of the upland area is sparsely populated so there is little objection to the construction of dams, reservoirs and power plants.
- The fuel is free and guaranteed and the whole operation is pollution free.
- Technical advances have allowed for the transmission of electricity to even the most remote and less densely populated areas. Supply and demand no longer need to be closely located.

The south of Norway is the most favoured area for hydro production. It is also the area of greatest consumption. Many rivers fall west and south-west to the fiord coastline and provide excellent sites for power stations. To the north and west of Oslo the Glomma, Skien, Lagen and Begna rivers have been harnessed at numerous points along their courses. The Begna river alone has about 50 stations. The north of the country does not have the same advantages. The more severe winter weather freezes the rivers and the transmission lines. The heads are not as high or as powerful as

Fig. 1.4 Hydro Stations

in the south. Production and transmission costs are higher because of the scattered nature of the market. Most of the remaining potential – about 35% – lies within the Arctic circle, but the higher costs in this area, plus the availability of oil in the south for thermal stations, mean that this potential will probably never be realised to the full.

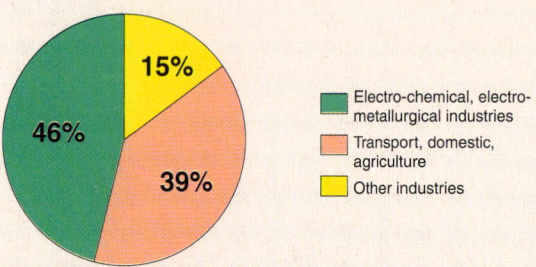

Fig. 1.5 Uses of Electricity

Aids to the Economy

Up to the discovery of North Sea oil and gas in the 1970s, Norway had no home-produced energy except HEP. The industrialisation of Norway in the earlier part of this century was aided by the growth of HEP. Most of the traditional industries of timber, pulp, paper, light engineering and fish processing developed and expanded by using cheap HEP.

Engineering and ship-building are heavy users of energy. In recent years the ports of Bergen and Stavanger have become major support ports for the North Sea, supplying pipes, rigs, platforms, tankers, etc. This was made possible in the early years by an abundance of cheap HEP.

Two groups of industries owe their very existence to the abundant supplies of cheap HEP – the electro-metallurgical and electro-chemical industries. These industries are energy hungry and would find it impossible to survive without HEP. These industries are widespread across Norway and many of the plants have their own power stations. Mo-i-rana has a large integrated steel mill, Sulitjelma has copper, Sarpsborg has lead and zinc and Ardal has aluminium. There are electro-chemical works at Rjukan, Glomfiord, Odda and Heroya.

The cheapness of HEP and the good transmission network, means the electricity is available to all homes. It has also helped the spread of industry, guaranteeing jobs and income, and creating a high standard of living.

Many stretches of the rail network are electrified thereby helping transport and the economy.

Finally, Norway exports electricity to Denmark and Sweden, earning valuable foreign currency.

2 FISHERIES

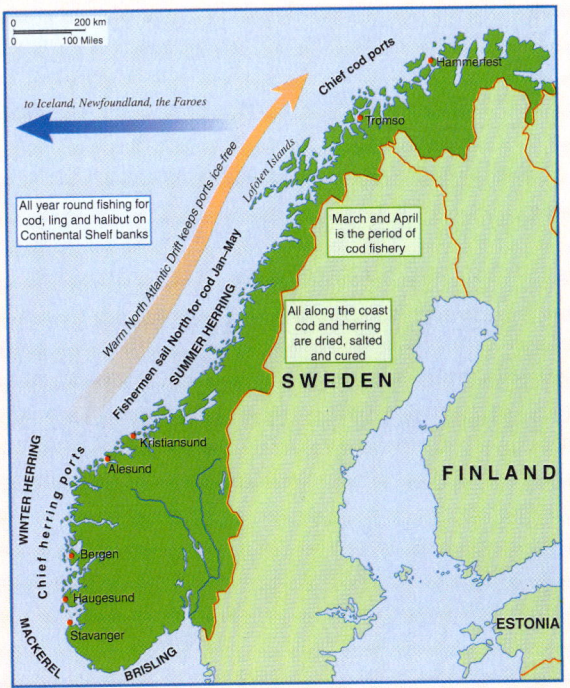

Fig. 1.6 Fisheries and ferry ports

Norway is one of the top six fishing countries in the world. Directly or indirectly, nearly 20% of the population is engaged either in fishing or in the processing and back-up service industries. Fish and fish products make up 10% of Norwegian exports.

Fishing can be a full-time or part-time occupation for many Norwegians. Part-time fishermen use the industry to supplement their income from farming or forestry. In the north of the country where there is little agriculture or forestry, fishing is often the only means of livelihood. The industry is well developed with modern trawlers, advanced equipment and good government support. Modern equipment and bigger boats mean that the total catch is well maintained, despite dwindling fish stocks. The annual catch is now in excess of 1.5 million tonnes.

Norway has a long association with the sea and, in a country with very limited land resources, the sea has provided both employment and food. Much of the farming in the north of Norway is part-time and subsistent in character, so naturally people turn to the sea for a living. Norway possesses many of the factors that enable a sea-fishing industry to be carried on successfully.

Consider the following:

- Norway has an extensive continental shelf which is rich in plankton (fish food). Where there is plankton there are fish.
- The mixing of the warm Atlantic waters with the cold Arctic waters off the coast of Norway adds to the variety of species of fish, with cod in the Arctic waters and mackerel, brisling and herring further south.
- The warm North Atlantic Drift provides ice-free harbours and allows fishing to be carried on all year.
- The deeply indented fiord coastline, protected by a string of islands (the Skerry Guard) provides safe harbours, rich fishing waters and good training grounds.
- The support industries of trawler building, marine engines, etc, is well developed, as is the processing industry.

- The shallow coastal waters are the spawning ground for many varieties of sea life.

Fishing Operation

While many of the fishing trawlers, with their factory ships, fish the North Atlantic, about 75% of the catch still comes from the coastal fishing grounds. Figure 1.6 shows the varieties, the peak seasons and the main fishing ports. Many of the fishing boats in the North are 2/3 man operations, involving small capital outlay and so are ideal for part-time fishermen. At the same time, half the fishing catch and over half the employment is in the north, and to protect this employment, the use of very large trawlers is restricted there.

The chief ports in the north are Hammerfest, Tromso, Vardo and Vadso. In the south-west are Alesund, Bergen and Stavanger. With a very small population, the home-market for fish is restricted. Only about 5% is consumed as fresh fish and the rest is processed. There is a growing demand for frozen fish and fish products worldwide, but still the bulk of the catch is converted to canned foods, fertilisers, margarine oils and medical oils. All of the ports named above have processing plants.

The Future for Fishing

Like the other European fishing states, Norway faces an uncertain future. After a boom period in the 1960s and 1970s, when the catch rose to 3 million tonnes, fishing in the North Sea went into a decline. The over-fishing of the 1970s meant that fish stocks could not regenerate quickly enough to maintain the level of catch of the 1970s. Many of the smaller boats went out of business to be replaced by large trawlers with sophisticated equipment and fewer men. Even still, the catch continued to fall to about 1.5 million tonnes in the 1990s. The number of fishermen has also fallen from 85 000 in 1950 to about 30 000 in 1997. The industry has become sophisticated, modern and efficient.

The more efficient fishing of the 1990s, with a regulated control of stocks, should ensure the survival of this industry (which is vital to the economy of the nation, particularly to that of the North Coastal zone). Control of the size and number of trawlers, regulation of mesh sizes, protection of spawning grounds and of the endangered species have all helped to maintain the industry.

Aquaculture

Fish farming can now be regarded as a major element in the fishing industry of Norway. The coast of Norway is considered an ideal location for fish farming. The sheltered waters within the fiords, the warm North Atlantic Drift, the ice-free harbours and the shallow, unpolluted waters provide the ideal setting for aquaculture. Norway was the pioneer of marine fish farming and is today the world leader. Salmon, sea trout, oysters, mussels and lobsters are the main varieties. Research into the rearing of other species is ongoing. There are about 700 hatcheries giving employment, directly or indirectly, to about 5 500 people. Most of the harvest (salmon 150 000 tonnes) is exported, earning valuable revenue for the economy.

Aids to the Economy

Employment is provided for about 30 000 fishermen. This employment is vital to the economy of northern Norway where many settlements depend almost entirely on fishing, fish processing and distribution.

The back-up services of boat-building, marine engines, repairs, net and box making, etc, depend entirely on fishing, so many land-based jobs are created and maintained by the fishing industry.

The processing sector is also dependant on the fishermen. About 90% of the catch is first processed and then exported. The processing creates jobs and gives an added value to the products. Fish and fish products amount to about 10% of total exports.

The marketing and transport of fish is another element in the whole industry.

3 NORTH SEA OIL AND GAS

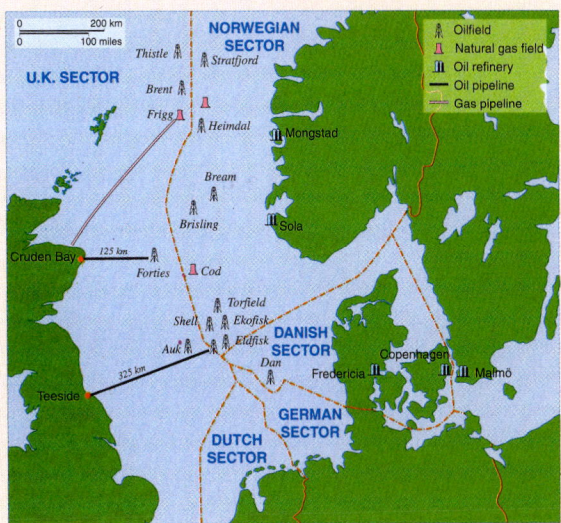

Fig. 1.7 North Sea

After the discovery of the enormous gas fields at Gröningen in the Netherlands in 1958, a renewed interest was taken in the North Sea where it was hoped to discover a continuation of the Dutch field. The breakthrough came in 1965 when British Petroleum discovered the first gas field about 80km off the Humber Mouth and this was the first of many gas finds in the southern section of the sea. Later in the decade, both Britain and Norway struck oil in the northern part of the sea.

The first major field was Ekofisk in the south-western corner of the Norwegian sector and this was followed by a string of smaller fields to the north of Ekofisk. The next major field to come on stream was Stratfiord. Frigg, and then Cod, were the first extensive gas finds. In the late 1980s the Sleipner field was discovered and this was followed by the giant Troll field, which is believed to be larger than the Groningen field in the Netherlands. Most of the exploration so far has been south of the line 62°N. North of this line, test drills have discovered extensive deposits of both gas and oil. There are difficulties of high seas, high winds and winter freezing to be surmounted, as well as distance from the market and the high risk to the very rich fishing grounds in the area. The state-owned oil company, Statoil, has a policy of moving slowly in the exploration to keep up the reserves for the future. Norway itself, with its small population and abundant HEP uses less than 20% of the oil and gas and is now the world's second largest oil exporter.

Exploitation

Exploitation of gas and oil presents many problems as the winter weather conditions are hazardous. Strong winds, high waves, frost and fog create difficulties for both the exploration and production rigs. In addition, the rigs are often cut off for days at a time because of the weather problems encountered by the ships and helicopters supplying them.

In the early days of production Norway encountered a major difficulty. There is a very deep marine trench between the fields and the south-west coast which prevented the laying of pipelines from the fields. Some of the oil was stored in underwater tanks and brought ashore by tankers. Pipelines brought the oil to Aberdeen and Teeside, and the gas to Peterhead or Emden in Germany. In the late 1980s new techniques allowed the building of pipelines across the trench, so that now both oil and gas can be brought ashore. This has created jobs in the refining and petro-chemical industries.

Fig. 1.8 Oil Rig, Norwegian Fields

Importance to Economy

The oil and gas make an important contribution to the economy of Norway, and in terms of production, Norway is as important as Kuwait or Nigeria. In Europe, it is the third largest producer of energy after Britain and the Netherlands. Over 80% of the yields are exported and this accounts for one third of the country's export earnings. The national debt has been cleared as a result of the oil and gas reserves.

The oil money is used by the state to develop the poorer regions of the country and much of the wealth is directed towards the Northern Provinces. Grants and subsidies have been paid to the farming and forestry sectors and the welfare system has been upgraded.

The industry has created about 8 000 offshore jobs and 50 000 land jobs. It has also led to the expansion of Stavanger and Bergen. Stavanger has developed as a major world centre in the design and construction of oil rigs, drilling platforms, tankers, tanks, pipes, etc. Bergen is the chief supply centre and service base for the Norwegian sector of the North Sea.

The future for Norway's economy looks good, with the fields in the North soon to come into production.

ASPECTS OF MANUFACTURING INDUSTRY

The manufacturing industry in Norway is firmly based on: (1) the availability of cheap HEP and (2) on the major natural resources of the country fish, timber, minerals and oil.

Norway did not have the coal measures that initiated the industrial revolution in Belgium or Britain. Political independence was gained only in 1905, and this provided the country with the incentive needed to develop its own industries. This early part of the century also saw the widespread development of HEP. In an effort to develop industrial and economic independence, the Norwegian government introduced an industrialisation programme using local resources. At present about 1 400 000 people are engaged in the manufacturing industry.

The **fish-processing** industries have been noted on page 8. **Timber** industries rely heavily on native resources and water power. The industry has been rationalised and is now concentrated around the Oslo fiord. Here the supplies of both timber and power are readily available and the coastal location of the mills facilitates the export of the products to the industrialised markets of north-west Europe. Sawn timber is used in the furniture and construction industries but little is exported. Processed timber products are much more important and there is a large export of pulp, paper, newsprint, cardboard and rayon fibre. The main processing plants are in Oslo, Sarpsborg, Drammen and Kristiansand.

Iron and **steel** mills, using both native and imported ore, are located at Mo-i-Rana, Stavanger, Arendal and Kragero. All have coastal locations to facilitate the import of ore and coke. The furnaces, however, use coke and electric power in combination. The steel is used in the shipbuilding yards of Oslo, Stavanger and Bergen. Other electro

Fig. 1.9 Electro Industries

metallurgical industries include **copper** at Sulitjelma and Lokken, **aluminium** at Glomfiord and Odda, and lead and zinc at Ardal.

The **electro-chemical** industries are also well developed and owe their success to the presence of cheap HEP. Products include fertilisers, ammonia, nitrates, acids and chlorates. The chief centres are Odda, Ardal, Heroya and Rjukan.

The availability of oil and gas by pipeline since the late 1980s has given a huge impetus to the **refining** and **petrochemical** industries. They have expanded since then, creating many more jobs at Oslo, Bergen and Stavanger.

SAMPLE QUESTION

As the core area of Norway, outline briefly the primary, secondary and tertiary activities of the Oslo lowlands.

If we apply the theory of core/periphery to Norway, then the Oslo lowlands comprise the core while the Northern Provinces of Nordland, Troms and Finnmark (collectively called Nordkalotten) make up the periphery. The Oslo lowlands include the area of lowland around the fiord, the coastal plains as far as Kristiansand in the south, and the river valleys stretching from the uplands to the head of the fiord. Numerous rivers drain the uplands, the chief of which are the Glomma, Lagen and Skien.

This core region has attracted the most investment over the years. Oslo, the capital, has been the focus point for the immigration of the rural workers who are leaving forestry, farming and fishing. Nearly half the population of Norway lives across these lowlands, providing both a labour force and market.

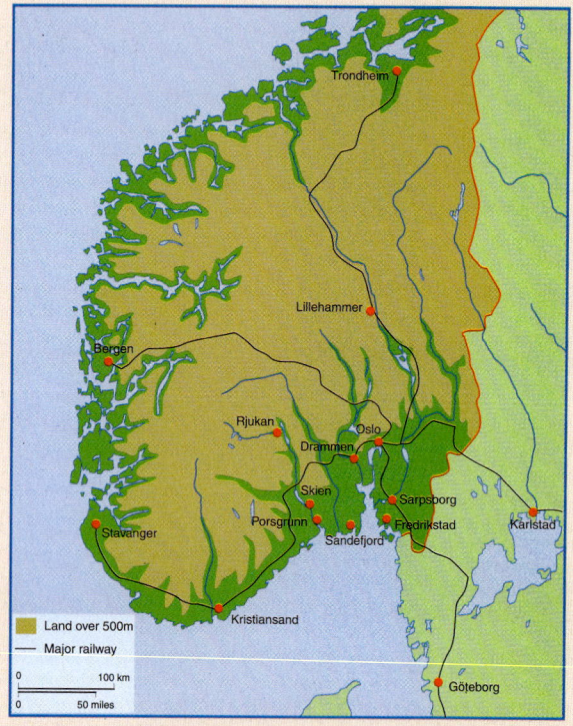

Fig. 1.10 Oslo Lowlands

The uplands are cut by numerous streams draining into the fiord and it is in these valleys and on the flood plains of the rivers that the main farming activities are carried on. The valleys are south-facing and enjoy the influence of the North Atlantic Drift. Consequently, the climate is warmer than in the rest of the country and this allows the cultivation of wheat, oats, barley and roots. Much of this produce is used in winter to feed the dairy herds which is the main pastoral activity. Market gardening is carried on around Oslo, and the large population across the lowlands provides a ready market for both fruit and vegetables and dairy produce. Agriculture has developed strongly over the last 30 years with yields up by 70% in that time. This advance has been achieved through farm amalgamation, mechanisation, the commercial use of home produced fertilizers and a more scientific approach to farming. The co-operative movement has also been extended.

The higher valley slopes and the north-facing ones are covered in forest. In more recent times the timber, pulp and paper industries have been revitalised and many of the smaller mills have been shut down to achieve economy of scale. Oslo has confirmed its position as the chief centre for the processing and manufacture of forest products. Oslo, Drammen, Skien and Larvik produce and export sawn timber, pulp, paper, newsprint, plastics, etc. The proximity of the forests, the availability of cheap HEP and the excellent facilities of Oslo harbour are the important factors.

The cheap HEP was also the influencing factor in establishing and expanding the electro-metallurgical refineries of iron, copper and zinc in the coastal towns. Electro chemicals are also important at Notodden, Rjukan and Heroya, again using the cheap HEP. Shipbuilding which supplies the fishing industry and the merchant navy is still important, as is engineering. Two new oil refineries, using North Sea oil, are in production in Oslo and these also supply the petro-chemical industry. As a capital city, Oslo has all the consumer industries associated with a capital – food, textiles, clothing, printing, furniture, etc.

Oslo is the focal point of all the valley routeways and is connected by road and rail, with the western coastal centres of Stavanger, Bergen and Trondheim and, through these points, to the north of the country. It has a safe, deep-water harbour and is home to one of the world's greatest merchant fleets. As capital, it has built a very large tertiary sector in administration, banking, law, health and education. It is the seat of government, home to the royal family and an attractive tourist focus.

NORTHERN NORWAY – PROBLEM REGION

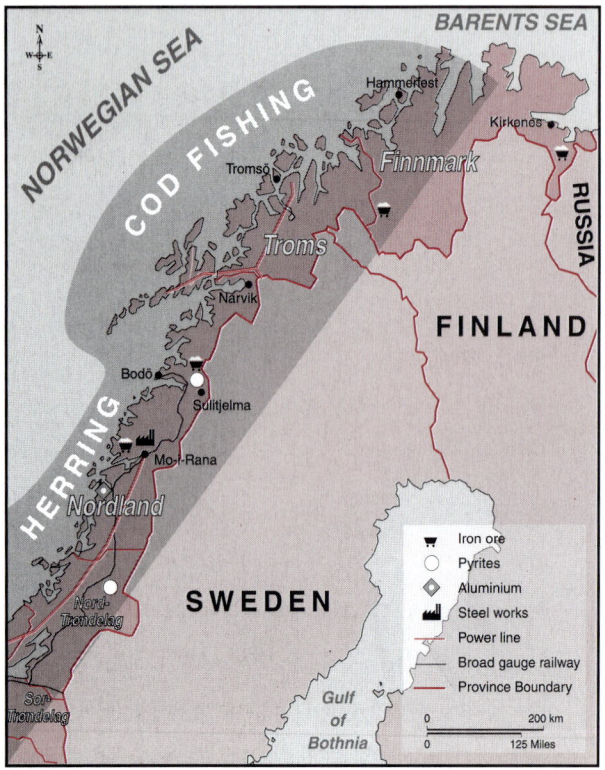

Fig. 1.11 Northern Provinces

SAMPLE QUESTION

Discuss the problems of northern Norway. How are they being tackled?

Beyond latitude 64°N lie the Norwegian provinces of Nordland, Troms and Finnmark which together constitute northern Norway. This area of the country stretches for 1 800km to the Barents Sea and varies in width from about 6km at Narvik to over 180km in the north of Finnmark. Together the provinces occupy about one-third of the total area but have only one-tenth of the population.

The coastline is deeply indented by fiords and is fringed by a string of islands, of which the Lofoten are the best known. Inland there is a very narrow coastal plain rising rapidly to the Kjolen mountains. The inhabitants live very close to the sea and an almost continuous line of small fishing settlements lies along the Atlantic coast. Almost 90% of the population lives within 8km of the sea. The density is very low, about 3 per km^2 along the coast, but much less away from it. Many parts of interior Finnmark have no inhabitants apart from nomadic Lapps tending their reindeer herds. Even these, attracted by the lifestyle in the towns, are abandoning their traditional way of life. A number of towns along the coast serve as market, service and industrial centres. They include Bodo, Narvik, Tromso, Hammerfest, Vardo and Mo-i-Rana.

The **problems** encountered in the north are many and varied, and include physical, social and economic ones.

- It is a peripheral area, removed from the core area of Oslo, which is the seat of government, the decision-making area and the economic pulse of the country.
- Farming is difficult because of the small amount of suitable flat land, the length and severity of the winter and the short growing season. For the most part, farming is of a subsistence nature and, on its own, is not an

economic proposition. Many farmers combine farming with forestry and fishing.

- Resources are limited and any development needs to be financed from outside the area. Unemployment, under-employment and seasonal employment are major problems.
- The population is small and scattered and communications are difficult to establish and maintain.
- It is difficult and costly to provide many of the social services taken for granted in the south. Added to the problem of providing such services is the ability to staff them. It is difficult to attract administration and professional people to this inhospitable area.
- As with the service industry, it is also difficult to attract manufacturing industry to the region. A plentiful supply of cheap HEP is the only attraction. The government must give major incentives to attract private industry, but private industry tends to leave once the incentives dry up.
- Similar to other European countries, there is a steady drift from the rural to the urban areas, and from the whole region to the south.

Employment

What are the chief means of livelihood for these northern people and what has the Norwegian government done to help them? We have seen that a large section of the population is engaged in primary activities such as fishing, forestry or mining. Fishing is the most developed of these activities. Proximity to the sea, lack of good land and tradition are the factors which determined the development of fishing. Over 10 000 people are engaged in fishing or fish-processing, working from the major fishing ports of Vardo, Vadso, Narvik, Hammerfest and Tromso.

There has been a sharp decline in the number of boats and fishermen in the small fishing villages. The industry has modernised and become more efficient with bigger, better equipped boats. But these boats have tended to locate in the larger ports, where the facilities for processing the fish and servicing the boats are located. The overfishing of the 1960s and 1970s has not helped.

Farming is of a subsistence nature. Cattle rearing is the chief activity but the herds are stall-fed for

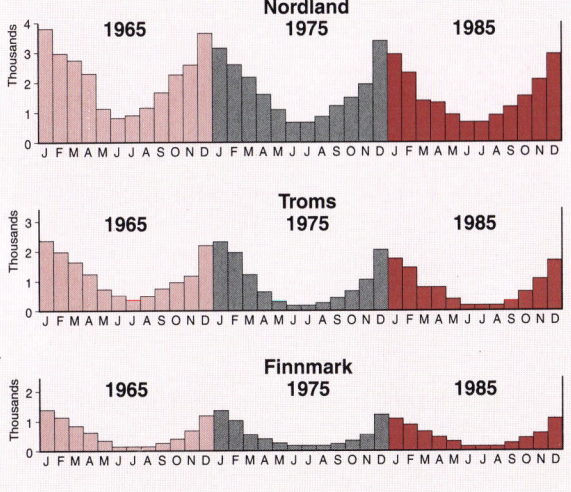

Fig. 1.12 Unemployment

seven or eight months and this means the introduction of feedstuffs from outside the region.

There are a number of mineral deposits unevenly distributed through the region. Iron ore is mined at Kirkenes and at Dunderland, and copper, lead and zinc at Sulitjelma.

A number of capital intensive industries have been established – integrated steel at Mo-i-rana, ammonia at Glomfiord and copper at Sulitjelma. There are a number of small scale industries and craft skills which are labour intensive.

Response to the Problems

The solutions to the north's problems are not easy to find. In 1952, and again in 1972, the Norwegian government invested, through the Northern Norway Scheme, large sums of money in the area. The transport infrastructure has been re-organised, with the railway being extended to Bodo and the E6 motorway to Kirkenes. Link roads have been improved, new bridges built, ferry services modernised and new small airports constructed. Money has been provided to improve the facilities at the fishing ports. Connecting transport to Oslo and the south-west is heavily subsidised.

Farms are being consolidated while subsidies and guaranteed farm prices have made farming less risky. Co-operatives have been established but still agriculture is of a subsistent nature, part-time in operation and marginal, economically.

The government has a policy of de-centralisation of industry and services, and to further this policy, generous grants, loans, subsidies and tax concessions are offered to companies locating within the area. Subsidies are also provided for existing fishing and farming jobs and for one-industry towns.

There is a potential for growth and jobs in the tourist and winter sports areas and money is being provided to improve facilities. Exploitation of the gas and oil reserves in the north of the North Sea could create onshore employment in this problem region.

There are some good results of the development programmes. Jobs have been created in both industry and services. As a result, the standard of living has risen, as has the per capita income. The population has stabilised as out-migration has slowed down. The feelings of remoteness and isolation have been reduced.

SAMPLE QUESTION

In the case of Norway draw a sketch map to divide it into regions. Explain your division by describing in detail three of the regions.

REGIONS OF NORWAY

1. Northern Territory (a problem region)
2. Oslo Lowlands
3. South West Coastlands
4. Interior Uplands

The regions of Norway are illustrated on the map below. Revise regions 1 and 2.

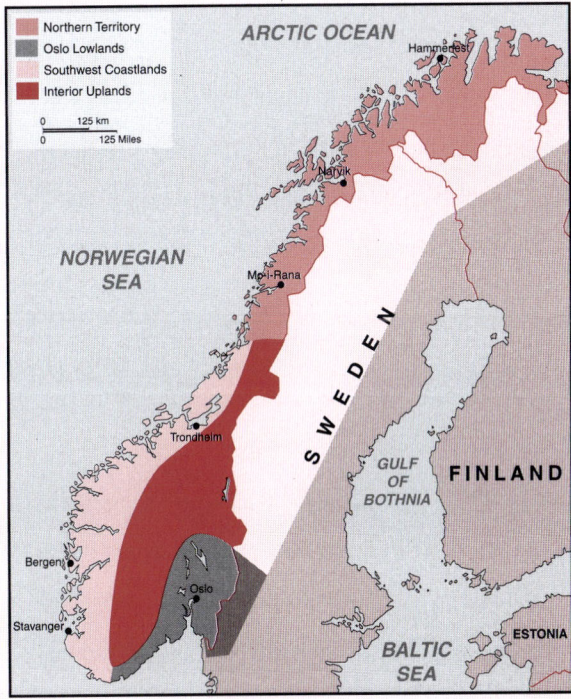

Fig. 1.13 Norway Regions

South West Coastlands

The south west coastlands stretch from the southern tip of Norway to the Trondheim Lowlands. In the very south there is a modest coastal plain but north of Stavanger the coastline is cut by a series of deeply penetrating fiords such as the Hardanger and

Fig. 1.14 Stavanger

the Sogne. The land rises steeply to the interior plateaus so that the only areas of flat land are at the heads of the fiords or near the mouths where marine erosion has cut small **beaches**. The only area of extensive lowland is around Trondheim. Off the coast is a series of islands – the Skerry Guard. The fiords allow settlement to penetrate far inland.

The region experiences the cool temperate maritime climate being influenced by both the rain bearing westerlies and the NAD (North Atlantic Drift). Winters are remarkably mild for the latitudes with Bergen and Trondheim at +2°C. Summer temperatures average about 16°C. There is abundant rainfall of about 1 500mm –

1 750mm. The NAD keeps the ports icefree during winter.

Agriculture is difficult because of the steep slopes, infertile soils and the moist climate. The growing of grass and hay is widespread but there is some cultivation of barley, oats and roots which can tolerate the cool moist conditions. Cattle and dairy rearing is important but winter feeding presents some difficulties and sometimes winter fodder has to be brought in from elsewhere. Transhumance is dying out as improved yields reduce its necessity.

After the Oslo lowlands the Trondheim lowlands are the most important agricultural area. This is an extensive lowland growing potatoes, oats and barley. Grass is important for the most important activity – dairy farming.

Fishing is important all along the coast with the fleets specialising in winter herring, brisling and mackerel. The chief ports are Stavanger, Bergen and Alesund. They all have large fleets, processing facilities and the support services of trawler building, marine engineering, etc. Even the smaller ports along this coast engage in fishing as a basic activity often combining it with farming. The fiords are important in the fishing industry providing safe harbours and good training grounds.

Industrially the main cities along the coast are expanding rapidly, supported by the North Sea oil and gas. Bergen, Stavanger and Sola now have major refineries and petro-chemical works. Stavanger has emerged as a world leader in the design and construction of rigs, platforms, tankers, pipelines, etc., while Bergen is the supply and service centre for the North Sea. Trondheim is the focus of railways from the south and south-east and across the mountains from Sweden. It is the service and market centre for the Trondheim lowlands. It has a wide range of industries – shipbuilding, chemicals, fish and timber processing and textiles. It is an important service and administrative centre.

The interiors of these coastlands have abundant supplies of HEP. This cheap power is the principal reason for the establishment of the electro-chemical and electro-metallurgical industries – aluminium at Hoyanger and Ardal, copper at Odda, aluminium at Sunndalsora and electro-chemicals at Porsgrunn.

This is a very scenic part of Norway with its massive fiords and high interior glaciated mountains. Both summer and winter tourism is expanding. The coastal steamer service between the settlements perched on the fiord sides is a tourist service unique to Norway.

URBAN SETTLEMENT

Fig. 1.15 View of Bergen

Bergen

Bergen is the second town and port of Norway with a population of about 275 000. The hinterland of the town is poor so, unsurprisingly, most of its activities are connected with the sea. It is the home port and administrative centre of the mercantile marine. It is also an important fishing port with fish-processing industries. There is varied manufacturing in the town including shipbuilding, marine engineering, chemicals and textiles. The discovery of North Sea oil and gas has given new life to the city which is now developing as a service centre and petro-chemical industrial base. Bergen has rail and road links with Oslo, but the road is often closed for long periods during the winter. It is however, an important starting point for tourists, with regular ferry services to Britain. Bergen is a university city with a world famous oceanographical research department.

Stavanger

Stavanger is only about half the size of Bergen and traditionally it has been an important fishing and canning town. The abundant supplies of HEP are used in the electro-metallurgical, engineering and shipbuilding industries. The last ten years have seen a huge growth in the importance of Stavanger as it has been selected as *the* service centre for North Sea oil and gas. It is now a busy port, designing and constructing rigs, platforms, supply ships, pipes and storage tanks, as well as servicing the offshore platforms and rigs. Refineries and chemical works have been added. Stavanger has road and rail links with Oslo.

Questions

1. The Oslo lowlands: Analyse the factors that have contributed towards the growth and development of settlement and industry in the above region. (L.C. Higher Level)

2. Explain why hydro-electric power is important in Norway. (L.C. Higher Level)

3. Discuss the extent to which the economy of Norway is dependant on the natural resources of the country. (L.C. Higher Level)

4. Examine the following statement in detail: The development of Norway has been strongly influenced by the sea. (L.C. Ordinary Level)

5. (a) Describe and account for the distribution of population in Norway.
   (b) Contrast the climates of Norway and Sweden.

(c) Describe the factors that have encouraged the people of Norway to look to the sea for a living. (L.C. Ordinary Level)

6 Write an explanatory note on the importance of the sea to Norway's economy. (L.C. Ordinary Level.)

7 The Oslo lowlands.
   (a) Name an important agricultural activity in the region.
   (b) What were the factors which favoured the development of the activity you have named? (L.C. Ordinary Level)

8 'The sea has greatly helped the economic development of Norway.' Discuss in relation to (a) fishing (b) oil.

9 Account for the influence of relief on agriculture in Norway.

10 Describe briefly the problems of communications in Norway.

11 Assess the importance of the North Sea oilfields to Norway.

12 Discuss the advantages that Norway possesses for the production of HEP. Explain the importance of HEP production to the country's economy.

13 'The importance of a port depends on the richness of its hinterland.' Discuss this statement with reference to Oslo.

14 Draw a sketch map to divide Norway into regions. Select three of the regions and deal with each under the headings: primary activities, secondary activities, tertiary activities. (L.C. Ordinary Level)

chapter two
sweden

INTRODUCTION

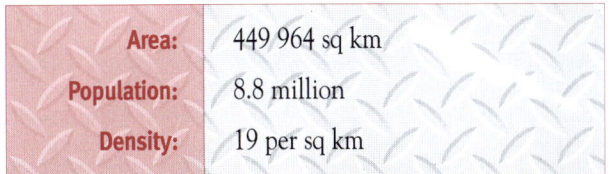

Area:	449 964 sq km
Population:	8.8 million
Density:	19 per sq km

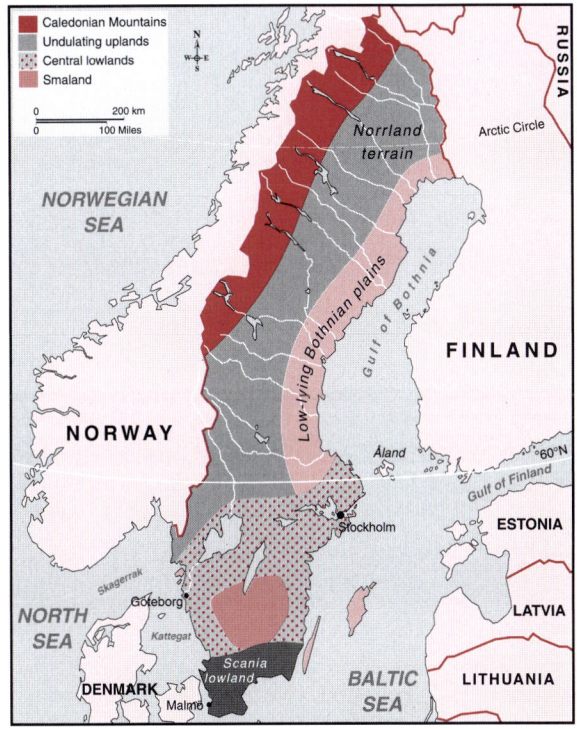

Fig. 2.1 Sweden's Physical Geography

Sweden is the largest, the most centrally located and the most prosperous of the Scandinavian countries. Its northern tip (69°N) lies well within the Arctic Circle. Its southern tip (55°N) is 1 600 km distant. Much of the north is mountainous, much of the south is flat and the coastline is dotted with thousands of islands. Almost all of Sweden was under ice during the Ice Age, so that many of the lowlands have been covered with glacial deposits, mainly of gravel and boulder clay.

CLIMATE

The climate is distinctly continental, with extremes of temperature. Summer brings long hours of sunshine, but winter brings snow and ice to many areas. Conditions vary from north to south. In the extreme north, the growing season lasts only three months, while in Scania, in the south, it lasts for seven months. Norrland has colder and longer winters than southern Sweden, where there is often rain interspersed with snowfall.

NATURAL RESOURCES

The chief resources of Sweden are:

Water power

Minerals

Forestry

Water Power

Water plays a double role in the economic life of Sweden. Its numerous and lengthy rivers are used to supply energy to a country that has very limited resources of coal and oil. The rivers are also used for transport in the lumber industry.

In Sweden, conditions for generating HEP are not as favourable as in Norway. The relief is more subdued, so high heads (steep falls) of water are not as frequent. The rainfall is lower and many rivers are frozen in winter.

However, the long rivers of Sweden ensure greater volumes of water than those of Norway. In addition, its many lakes

Fig. 2.2 Sweden's Electricity

The less favourable physical conditions for producing HEP – the high cost of transmission over lengthy distances from north to south and the harnessing of almost all the potential – have led Sweden to turn to other sources of power – nuclear power and imported oil. However, Sweden's HEP stations have played an important role in the development of its railways and industries, especially the electro-metallurgical and electro-chemical industries.

Minerals

Sweden is rich in mineral wealth. Its most important mineral is iron ore, but there are also significant deposits of lead, copper, zinc, silver and pyrites. The deposits of high-grade iron ore are among the largest in Europe.

have been made larger by building dams and have been turned into huge storage reservoirs. In this way, the flow of water can be regulated to give an even supply to the power stations throughout the year.

Sweden's HEP resources are unevenly distributed in **three** areas: (1) northern Sweden (Norrland) which produces 80% of the country's hydro-electric power from such rivers as the Indals and Lule; (2) the lake belt in central Sweden; (3) southern Sweden. Thus, while the greatest demand for power comes from the urban and industrial areas in central and southern Sweden, the major sources of power are in the north. A national grid transmits electricity from the north to the south and is also linked with the Danish and Norwegian grids, so that a shortage in one country can be filled from a surplus in another.

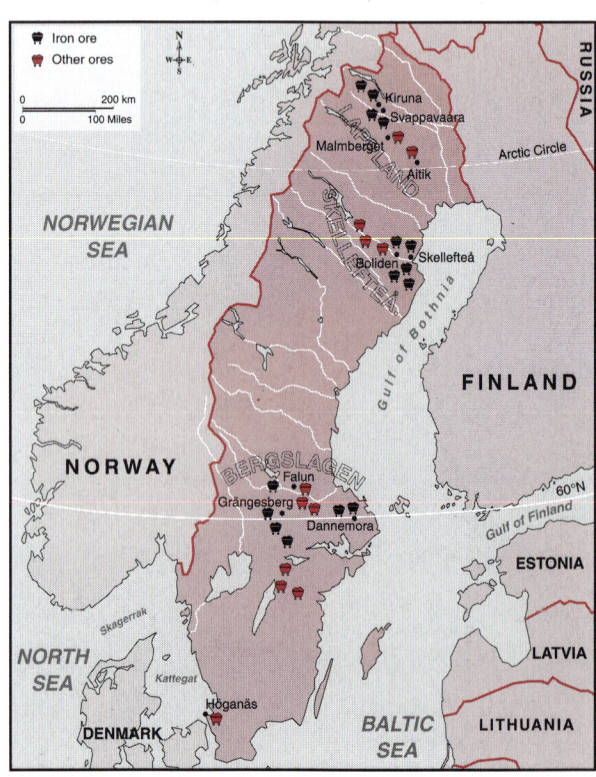

Fig. 2.3 Sweden's Minerals

Sweden is the largest exporter of iron ore in Europe. The main markets are indicated on the map below. Three major locations may be noted: the Lappland field, the Skelleftea field and the Bergslagen field. The earliest production of iron ore in Sweden was in the central lowlands as early as the 13th century. Here, there were abundant forests for charcoal and numerous waterfalls for power. By the 18th century, Sweden had become the world's leading producer of iron with over one third of world trade. But the Industrial Revolution ended that supremacy as new methods of smelting iron, using coke, were introduced in Britain, Belgium and Germany. Sweden had no coal and was unable to mass produce like its competitors. This led to a change in the industry, with Sweden concentrating on the production and export of high-grade steels. This trend has continued to the present day.

The Lappland iron ore field

Towards the end of the 19th century, a number of important developments took place.

It was well known that there were extensive deposits of iron ore in the north of Sweden around Kiruna and Gallivare, but distance from the market and a lack of power created difficulties. In addition, the iron ores had a high phosphorous content and were difficult to process.

A new method of smelting (the Gilchrist-Thomas process) was discovered which enabled the smelting of high phosphorous ores. Around the same time, hydro-electric power was developed and an electric railway was built across the Kjolen mountains to the ice-free port of Narvik in Norway. (The north of the Gulf of Bothnia is frozen for up to six months each year.) Today, 80% of the ore is still shipped through Narvik, the rest through Lulea. Some of the ore is used in the integrated steelworks at Lulea and Oxelosund. The railway, the mines and the town of Kiruna are powered from the HEP stations on the river Lule.

In recent years, Europe's biggest copper mine was opened near Gallivare and Sweden's biggest lead mine is worked in the west of Lappland, near the Norwegian border.

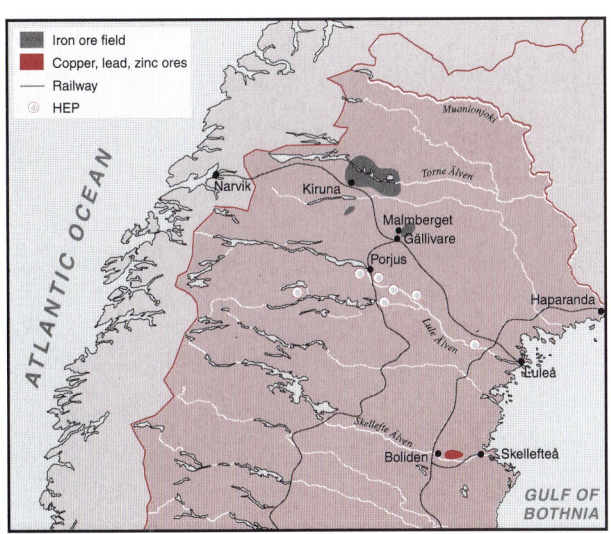

Fig. 2.4 Iron Ore Fields

Fig. 2.5 Underground Mining

The Skelleftea iron ore field

The Skelleftea iron ore field is a highly important mining region; it has the most diverse range of minerals in the world. It lies south of Lulea. Iron, copper, lead, zinc and nickel are mined here. Boliden is the chief mining centre from which the various ores are collected and brought for smelting and refining to Skelleftea. Because of the large range of minerals produced there, Skelleftea is able to withstand fluctuations in the world price of individual minerals.

The Bergslagen iron ore field

The Bergslagen region lies inland from the coastal town of Gavle. It is in central Sweden, just north of the lakes. It is a region rich in mineral ores. Iron, copper, lead and zinc have been mined in the area since the earliest stages of Sweden's industrialisation. The iron ore has a lower iron content but also a lower phosphorus content than that of the Lappland field. This haematite (low phosphorous) ore is mined around Dannemora and used locally in the production of high quality steel. The area of the Bergslagen around Grangesberg is the *Export Field* of magnetite ore, producing some 2.3 million tonnes annually. The ore is brought to the port of Oxelosund where one-fifth of it is used in the local steelwowrks. The remainder is exported.

With the reduction in demand for ore and steel in Europe, and with the competition from Australia and South America, many of the smaller mines in the Bergslagen region have closed. Further closure of mines and steel mills by the **ECSC** (European Coal and Steel Commission) are expected now that Sweden has joined the European Union.

Difficulties in development

The Lappland iron ore field is a sub-arctic area in the extreme north of Sweden. The climate is severe – long dark winters with continuous snow cover and unreliable summer rainfall. The landscape is monotonous, with endless coniferous forests on the lower slopes near the Baltic Sea and tundra vegetation on the higher areas. It is a remote and inhospitable region (see Norrland, p. 26). High wages and excellent amenities are necessary to attract workers from southern Sweden and abroad.

A world decline in demand for steel has resulted in less demand for iron ore. This has caused some unemployment in the Lappland ore region. The remoteness of the region makes it difficult to attract alternative industries.

Iron ore – Contribution to the economy

- It is a valuable native raw material supporting the steel, engineering, shipbuilding and car industries.
- It creates jobs in mining and the transport networks. Some 30 000 people are employed.
- It sustains jobs in all the engineering sectors.
- It is a valuable export earning foreign currency and it accounts directly for over 5% of Swedish exports.
- It helps in the country's balance of payments.
- It creates investment in research and development.

SAMPLE QUESTION

The impact of its HEP resources on Sweden's economy has been very great and may be summarised as follows:

Because of its limited resources of coal and oil, Sweden has relied heavily on its own hydro-stations to produce the electricity required for industrial and other uses. Hydro-electric power has contributed greatly to Sweden's industrial prosperity and, thus, to the high standard of living enjoyed by its people. Its power stations are among the largest in Europe. The use of HEP has helped Sweden to reduce its dependence on imported coal and oil.

The generation of HEP in Sweden is favoured by a number of factors:

1. A heavy and well-distributed precipitation, especially in the north, allows snow-melt to increase the river flow in spring and summer.
2. The length of the rivers ensures a high volume of water.
3. The hard crystalline rocks of the Baltic Shield provide ideal sites for dams.
4. The numerous lakes serve as storage reservoirs.

This high potential for HEP has now been fully exploited and Sweden's need for extra energy is met by nuclear power and imported oil. Because the greatest resources of HEP were in the north, while the areas of greatest demand were in the more industrialised south, it is no surprise that Sweden pioneered the long-distance transmission of electricity along a high-voltage national grid.

Sweden's origin as an industrial country dates back to the Middle Ages when wood-working and metal industries first harnessed running water as a source of power. In Europe's industrial revolution, Sweden was largely by-passed, because of its limited supplies of coal. Engineering, non-ferrous metal industries and the traditional industries of pulp, paper and glass are also important users of HEP.

The impact of its HEP resources on Sweden's industry has been very great and may be summarised as follows:

- Industry is widely dispersed throughout central and southern Sweden. The siting of industry has been made quite flexible with the transmission of electricity along the national grid. As a result, there are no industrial wastelands and little environmental pollution.
- Much of Sweden's railway network is electrified.
- Supplies of HEP have favoured the development of modern industries notably the electro-smelting and electro-chemical industries. The siting of these industries is

greatly influenced by the availability of a relatively cheap energy source – HEP.

- The saw mills and pulp plants of the timber industry and the mining plants in the north rely on HEP. By substituting hydro-electric power for thermal energy, and by adopting new smelting techniques, Sweden has become one of the few countries in the world to have an important steel industry without a base of native coal resources. Electro-smelting is used extensively in the Swedish steel industry; it uses hydro-electric power, requires less coke (which has to be imported) than other processes, and it favours the production of the high-grade steel needed by the metal industries of central Sweden. Engineering and non-ferrous metal industries are also important users of HEP.

- Despite the great transmission distances involved, 99% of Swedish homes use electricity. This has raised and maintained the high standard of living in Sweden.

- Hydro production provides jobs, particularly in the north where job opportunities are not as favourable as in the south.

- By providing cheap power to industry, HEP succeeds in making Sweden very competitive in industrial Europe.

FORESTS

Fig. 2.6 Forest Resources

Nature is not entirely hostile in Sweden. The climatic and soil conditions suit the development of one of the largest forest areas in Europe. The forests, which cover 55% of Sweden's land area, form one of its most important sources of wealth. They are Sweden's **Green Gold**. Although Sweden has only a tiny proportion of the world's supplies of timber, its forests have an economic value out of all proportion to their extent.

km²	Norway	Sweden
Arable	8 940 (2.9%)	28 870 (7.0%)
Pasture/Meadow	1 020 (0.3%)	5 600 (1.4%)
Forest	66 600 (21.8%)	227 420 (55.3%)
Unproductive	230 250 (75%)	149 040 (36.3%)

Of these forests, 84% are coniferous, mainly Norway spruce or Scots pine. In recent years Sitka spruce, Douglas fir and Canadian lodgepole have been introduced. Most of the original forest cover has disappeared and has been replaced by conifers.

The main coniferous forest belt is in Norrland. It dominates the landscape from the river Dal northwards to within the Arctic circle (fig. 2.6).

The most productive forest areas lie in central and southern Sweden where climatic conditions are more favourable for tree growth. Here the annual growth rate is three times greater than in Norrland.

However, much of the southern forest has been cleared to make way for agriculture, industry and settlement. Agriculture gives a much better return per hectare than forestry and is the preferred land use. The favourable climate and the fertile soils suit agriculture in the south.

The ownership of the forests is well distributed across all sectors of the population.

Forest area		227 420 km²	
State	5%	Forest Companies	5%
Public Companies	8%	Private	8%

Obviously, forestry is least profitable in the north of Sweden where it has to contend with a harsh climate, a shorter growing season, slow growth rate and distance from the markets. Here, the State owns 80% of the forests.

Much of the private forest area was managed in combination with part-time farming. The farming was largely subsistence farming and part-time forestry provided fuel, construction timber and wood for sale. Today, the specialisation of both farming and forestry has broken the link between the two, and fewer farmers are now forest owners. In addition, the whole industry has been re-organised, so that the big companies have their own forests, transport systems and manufacturing plants.

FOREST RESOURCES

SAMPLE QUESTIONS

> Write an account of Sweden's forest resources under the headings: (i) distribution, (ii) factors favouring development, (iii) difficulties relating to their development, (iv) management, (v) importance to Sweden.
>
> ### Distribution of forests
> Forests cover 55% of Sweden's land area. The main coniferous forest belt is in Norrland and extends from latitude 60°N to within the Arctic circle. Spruce and pine are the main trees of these coniferous softwoods. The forests in central and southern Sweden are often a mixture of deciduous and coniferous trees. The Norrland forests are the most extensive, but the central and southern forests are more productive. Here the climate

conditions give an annual tree growth rate that is three times faster than in the harsh Norrland region (50 years v 150 years).

Factors favouring development

The factors favouring the development of Sweden's forest resources may be stated briefly:

- Sweden is protected from the Atlantic storms by the Kjolen mountains and has a growing season of some 200 days.
- The Baltic Shield has extensive lowland plains of less than 200 metres suitable for forestry.
- Forests are accessible because of the many river valleys.
- Sweden is close to the affluent markets of Europe.
- The timber is commercially valuable.
- HEP stations supply the power for the saw mills and pulp mills.

Difficulties in development of forestry

We may note the following:

(a) Long-distance sulphur pollution is carried by prevailing winds from industrial Britain and the Ruhr. It is deposited in Sweden as acid rain or acid snow. Forests and fish life have been severely affected. Acid rain is destroying tree growth and the quality of the timber and is causing serious concern to the countries of northern Europe. Unfortunately, while these countries which are at the receiving end of acid rain possess a high degree of environmental concern, the industrialised countries to their south, where the sulphur dioxide originates, have comparatively lower standards.

(b) Tree growth in Norrland is much slower than that of the south, for climatic reasons. Hence, the productivity of the Norrland forests is less than those in the south.

(c) As already noted, forest land is being cleared in the south of Sweden for farming and building. This has resulted in reducing the most productive forest areas and in increasing Sweden's dependance on the Norrland forests.

(d) World demand for both sawn timber and paper has increased rapidly in recent years. Careful conservation and afforestation measures are needed to ensure that the forests are not depleted. Cutting rates are now strictly controlled and the native pines are gradually being replaced by the Canadian lodgepole which grows twice as fast.

(e) The expansion of Sweden's forest industries has also brought pollution problems. Some paper mills send sulphur gases into the atmosphere, and effluent from saw mills pollutes the rivers.

Management

Trees are a renewable resource, but only if there is

a proper management policy in place. Up to the late 1800s, forestry in Sweden was a resource that was exploited rather than managed. Since then, a strict management policy has been developed. About 250 000 hectares are cut annually. Of this, 70% is replanted with 500 million plants and the rest regenerates naturally. The policy is one of sustained yield and at present forest stocks are actually increasing. Drainage, fertilisation, insect and disease control have all contributed to the increasing yield.

The lumbering industry is now highly mechanised. Harvesters fell the trees, strip branches and bark, and cut them into standard lengths ready for transport. Road transport (67%) and rail transport (32%) have replaced the timber floating method, so that the logs arrive at the mills all year round and in a much better condition for processing.

There are still a number of problems with the industry. Acid rain from Britain, Germany and Poland has affected tree growth, the quality of the timber and the forest soil. Storm damage and insect attacks also cause problems.

Importance of forest resources

1. The timber industries have proved to be of decisive social and economic importance to Sweden. The efficient exploitation of the country's *Green Gold* has helped it to become one of the world's most prosperous countries. Timber products form almost 20% of Sweden's exports.

2. The chart below indicates the wide range of timber products. The **saw mills** and **pulp**

Fig. 2.7 Forestry in Sweden

Saw mills	Pulp mills
Sawn timber	Mechanical pulp
Plywood	(newsprint)
Furniture	Chemical pulp
Wallboard	(writing paper)
Safety matches	Packaging
Charcoal	Rayon (cellulose)
(used in the	Wood alcohol
manufacture	
of high-quality steels)	

mills are concentrated at the river mouths of the Norrland region, along the coast of the Gulf of Bothnia. The **paper mills** are in the south, with Norrkoping, Jonkoping and Göteborg as the chief centres.

3 The social importance of the forests must also be considered. In northern Sweden, particularly, the forests provide valuable permanent employment for forestry workers and saw mill operatives. In addition, government policy to convert uneconomic farmland to forest has led to many farmers becoming full-time forest workers. Even for those farmers for whom forestry is still only a part-time winter activity, it is interwoven with life on the farm. Up to 200 000 are employed full-time or part-time.

4 Timber provides a valuable raw material for both the sawn timber and processed timber mills. There are about 2 000 saw mills, 60 pulp mills and 50 paper mills. Sweden is the world's chief exporter of paper. At present, the rationalisation of the pulp and paper industry has meant fewer mills and workers, but increased productivity from larger mills.

5 Forests provide the raw material for the furniture and building industries with a large export trade to the EU.

6 Exports are an important earner of foreign currency and help with the country's balance of payments.

7 Sweden's forests are also a major recreational resource. They act as *Green Lungs* because they provide a breathing space for urban dwellers away from the traffic congestion and pollution of city life.

AGRICULTURE IN SCANIA

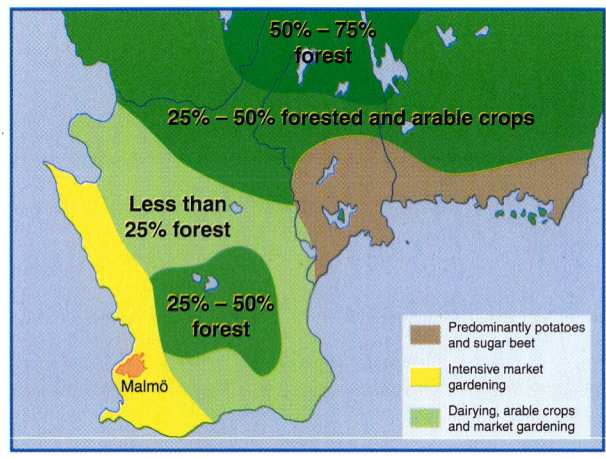

Fig. 2.8 Agriculture in Scania

Until the seventeenth century, Scania belonged to Denmark. Even today, with its rich productive farms, it looks like a section of Denmark transplanted on to forested Sweden. Although it occupies only a small area, Scania has an importance out of all proportion to its size. It has the highest density of rural population, it is Sweden's main farming area, and its urban centres along the coast are major industrial centres.

Relief, soils and climate combine to make Scania the richest and most productive farming region in Sweden. It is an area of level plains, broken only by small hills and ridges of sands, clays and pebbles deposited by glacial action long ago. The underlying chalk soils, covered with boulder clay, are the most fertile in the country. The climate also favours agriculture in this lowland peninsula. The southerly latitude provides Scania with a longer growing season (240 days), a milder winter, a more evenly distributed rainfall, higher summer temperatures (18°C), and more sunshine than the rest of Sweden. These factors result in an intensive and productive agriculture that has earned for Scania a reputation as *the Granary of Sweden*.

The natural vegetation of mixed forest has almost entirely disappeared in Scania and over 60% of the land is now under cultivation. The emphasis is on arable farming and productivity is high. Wheat, barley and oats are the chief cereals grown and sugar beet is the main root crop. Other crops grown are oilseeds, vegetables and orchard crops. Increased mechanisation, greater use of fertilisers and the introduction of fast-ripening strains of crops have helped to increase farm productivity.

Fig. 2.9 Farming in Scania

Scania is more open to the rain-bearing westerly winds and the N.A.D. than the rest of Sweden. As a result, its annual rainfall of 600mm is evenly distributed through the year. Thus, grass grows in most months and dairy farms are a feature of the region. Dairy farming has developed along the Danish pattern with co-ops playing a major role. Some of the milk is processed into butter and cheese, but much of it is sold daily to the urban areas of the region. The rearing of pigs and poultry has also increased steadily.

Not all the people of Scania work on farms. Increased mechanisation has resulted in less employment in agriculture. Many of the displaced farm workers are employed in the thriving market towns, and in industrial cities such as Malmo, Göteborg and Hälsingborg, along the coast. The food-processing industries in these towns and cities provide ready evidence of the prosperity and productivity of farming in Scania. These industries include brewing, margarine, flour milling, sugar-refining, vegetable-processing and fruit-preserving. As with Denmark, manufacturing industry supplies agri-chemicals, fertilisers and machinery to agriculture – a good example of the interdependence of the farming and industrial sectors.

THE INDUSTRIAL CORE – THE CENTRAL LOWLANDS

The central lakes lowland is the economic heart of Sweden – the most important industrial region and the most densely populated area in the country. Industry is widely dispersed throughout the central lowlands and the industrial towns are all well linked by railways, roads and inland waterways. Sweden's industrial development has been characterised by a natural talent for design, a high degree of craftsmanship, a genius for invention and a diversity of products.

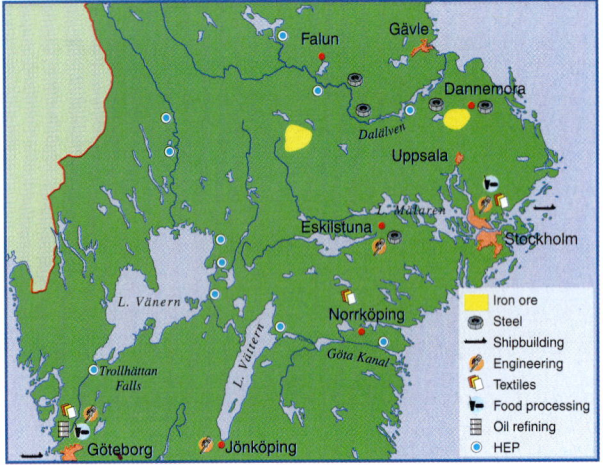

Fig. 2.10 Central Lakes Lowland

Several factors have contributed to the concentration of manufacturing industry in the central lowlands:

- The lowland relief favoured the development of **transport links** between the industrial towns.
- The Bergslagen area contains valuable **mineral ores** (iron, copper, lead, zinc).
- The agricultural prosperity of the region provides **raw materials** for food-processing industries.
- The proximity of **coniferous forests** has led to the development of paper-making industries.
- Two **major** ports, Stockholm and Göteborg, are located in the region.
- The availability of **HEP**.
- Proximity to European **markets**.

The major industrial centres are Stockholm, Eskilstuna, Jonkoping and Göteborg, but smaller centres are scattered throughout the region. This dispersal of industry is due to (1) the availability of electricity from HEP stations in the north and (2) the use of local resources such as minerals, timber and farming produce as raw materials for industry. Most Swedish industrial plants are relatively small and almost every town in the central lowlands has a specialised industry.

The traditional metalworking skills of the Bergslagen still flourish today, enhanced by modern technology. The production of high quality special steels is a feature of the Bergslagen output. This has resulted in a wide range of precision engineering products which are leaders in world markets – agricultural machinery (Alfa Laval), armaments (Bofors), ball bearings (SKF), telecommunication equipment (Eriksson) and cutlery. Transport vehicles (Volvo, Scania), surgical instruments and computers are other products of the Bergslagen factories.

Textile industries were originally based on local raw materials, but now use imported fibres. Norrkoping is the centre of the woollen industry. Cotton manufacture is centred around Göteborg, Boras and Norrkoping. Linen and jute are made in Göteborg and rayon in Boras. These textile factories supply the clothing industries in Göteborg and Stockholm.

Newsprint mills are located north of Stockholm and at Norrkoping.

More than 10% of Sweden's industrial output comes from its chemical industry. Pharmaceuticals have rapidly expanded and are strongly export-oriented. The basic chemical industry is owned mainly by foreign firms. On the other hand, Swedish-owned chemical firms, such as Nobel Industries, have merged with foreign firms, such as the Dutch firm Akzo NV, in order to survive in the European market.

Fig. 2.11 Stockholm, Riddacholmen and Gamla Stan

Two towns dominate the central lowlands region – Stockholm in the east and Goteborg in the west.

Stockholm is the capital and the main commercial and industrial centre of Sweden. It is located on a group of islands at the entrance to Lake Malaren and is often referred to as *The Venice of the North*. As a bridging point on Lake Malaren, it became an important route centre- west to the Bergslagen region and south-west to Göteborg. It is, thus, the natural outlet for the northern sector of the central lowlands. It is a major port, centrally placed on Sweden's Baltic coast and is kept open in winter by icebreakers. Its industries include shipbuilding, chemicals, engineering and consumer goods. As capital of Sweden, it has numerous tertiary industries – banking, transport, insurance, tourism.

Fig. 2.12 Sweden's vibrant ports

Göteborg is Sweden's second city. It is the premier port and is located on the deepwater estuary of the river Gota which flows into the Kattegat. It is ice-free and is the terminal for the Gotta canal, which links the port with lakes Vanern and Vattern and thus, with Stockholm. The canal, however, is of minor importance today because of its narrow width. The land-routes to and from Göteborg are of great importance in winter, when only Göteborg is open to ocean-going ships. In contrast to Stockholm, Göteborg faces west to the industrial markets of western Europe.

The port imports a variety of raw materials for the industrial centres of the central lowlands and has developed a varied industrial base including shipbuilding, oil refining, textiles, engineering and Volvo car manufacture.

NORRLAND – A PERIPHERAL REGION

The Norrland region of Sweden extends from 60°N to well

beyond the Arctic circle. It is a region of old crystalline rocks that have been extensively glaciated. The thin acid soils are mainly covered with coniferous forest. The Norrland plateau slopes to the south-east from the Scandinavian highlands in a series of steps to the gulf of Bothnia. It is a glaciated landscape of parallel rivers with steep-sided valleys and numerous ribbon lakes. These rivers (e.g. Lule, Angerman, Indals, Dal) are often broken by waterfalls in their middle and lower courses.

The climate is harsh. Summers are short and relatively cool. Winters are cold with temperatures well below freezing point. Much of the precipitation falls as snow which covers the region from October to April. Summer frosts, due to temperature inversion, are frequent.

Agriculture

These limitations of relief, soil, and climate in Norrland make farming very difficult. The long, harsh winter limits the growing season to about 150 days. The lower temperatures restrict the choice of crops to such as barley, rye and oats. Because of the poor soils, large areas of land are uncultivated. The farms are small and usually occupy forest clearings. Agriculture in Norrland is chiefly of the subsistence type, based on cattle pasture. Barley and rye are grown for fodder. Many farmers own some forest land and have part-time jobs in lumber camps or saw mills. Agriculture is mainly confined to the coastal plains of the Gulf of Bothnia.

Industry

Industrial development suffers from similar limitations. The isolation and remoteness of Norrland are unattractive to industrialists and workers alike. For industrialists, transport costs are high because of the great distances to the urban markets in southern Sweden and western Europe. The lack of amenities and the long cold winters make working conditions rather difficult.

Population

Population density is very low (1.0 per km^2). Settlements are rather isolated and are found either in the river valleys or at the mouths of rivers along the Bothnian coast. Limited agriculture and the disincentives to industrial development have resulted in the migration of many young people to the more attractive urban areas of central and southern Sweden. Norrland, despite its wealth of natural resources in forests, hydro-electric power and minerals, is Sweden's problem area today.

Problems

Norrland suffers from many of the problems found in the north of Norway. The harsh climate, the farming difficulties, the slow forest growth and the reluctance of industry to establish there, afford few opportunities for jobs and permanent employment. With the small scattered population, it is extremely difficult to establish staff and maintain social services.

The modernisation and rationalisation of the forestry and saw mill industries resulted in major job losses. The government responded by increasing grants to farming and industry, and by subsidising transport to central and southern Sweden. Money was also invested in education, healthcare and social services. But Norrland still remains the peripheral area of Sweden.

Questions

1 (a) Define the term *natural resource*.

   (b) Identify Sweden's main categories of natural resources.

   (c) Write an account of *two* of these categories under the headings: distribution; importance to Sweden; difficulties relating to their development (L.C. Higher Level)

2 The Scandinavian Northlands

   (a) State what are the problems facing the region.

   (b) Outline briefly the factors responsible for the growth of the problems in the region.

   (c) Outline the efforts being made to solve the problems. (L.C. Higher Level)

3 Use the information in the tables below to make a comparative study of Norway and Sweden. In your answer refer to density of population and agricultural production. (L.C. Higher Level)

Table 1: Land Utilisation (1970)

	Area Thousands of Km^2	Arable	Pasture	Forest	Waste Land
		As percentage of the total area			
Norway	324	3	–	26	71
Sweden	450	7	1	51	41

Table 2: Population and Employment Structure

	Population (Millions)	Agriculture Forestry Fishing	Mining Manufacture Construction	Commerce Transport Communications	Services
		Economically Active Population Percentage Distribution (1970)			
Norway	4.3	14	37	27	22
Sweden	8.32	9	40	23	28

4 In general, Norway and Sweden display a steady diminution of wealth and opportunity from south to north. Explain in terms of relief, climate and availability of natural resources the causes that may underline the above situation. (L.C. Higher Level)

5 Account for the economic importance of hydro-electric power in Scandinavia. (L.C. Higher Level)

6 Discuss the extent to which the economy of either Norway *or* Sweden is dependant on the natural resources of the country. (L.C. Higher Level)

7 'The Scandinavian countries of Norway and Sweden have many similarities and many contrasts'. Compare and contrast the two countries, using the following guidelines: (i) relief, (ii) effects of the sea, (iii) land use, (iv) population distribution. (L.C. Ordinary Level)

8 (a) What are the chief characteristics of the climate of Norway and Sweden? Explain their influence on the agriculture practiced in those countries.

   (b) Describe the distribution of population and settlements in the Scandinavian peninsula. Analyse the chief factors upon which this distribution depends. (L.C. Ordinary Level)

9 'Sweden's forest resources are basic to its industrial development.' Write an account of Sweden's forest resources under the headings:

   (i) favouring factors,

   (ii) importance, and

   (iii) problems/difficulties.

10 Examine the factors which have influenced the development of agriculture in Sweden. (L.C. Higher Level)

11 Sweden
   (i) Draw a sketch-map, showing a division of the country into regions.
   (ii) Describe and explain *three* reasons for your division of the country. (L.C. Ordinary Level)

12 'Forestry is a good use of poorer land.' Examine this statement with relation to Sweden.

13 Examine the economic development of Sweden under each of the following headings:

   primary activities

   secondary activities

   tertiary activities.

14 Select *one* important manufacturing region of Sweden;
   (i) Draw a sketch map to show:
      (a) the location of the region
      (b) the chief transport features
      (c) the chief towns.
   (ii) Explain why the region has attracted so much manufacturing industry.

chapter three
denmark

INTRODUCTION

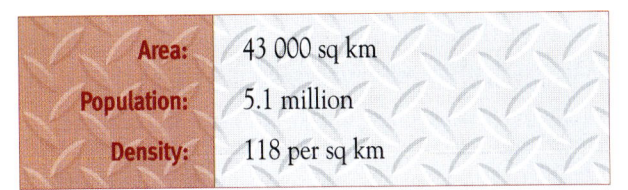

Area:	43 000 sq km
Population:	5.1 million
Density:	118 per sq km

Fig. 3.1 Denmark – Position in Europe

Denmark, with an area of 43 000 square km, is the smallest of the three Scandinavian countries that we study. It consists of the Jutland peninsula, four large islands – Zealand, Funen, Lolland and Falster, and over 400 smaller islands. Of the smaller islands, only about 100 are inhabited. The population is also small, at about five million people. However, the small size and small population should not lead us to believe that Denmark is of little importance. It is very strategically located between the North Sea and the Baltic Sea and so it is the land bridge between Europe and Scandinavia. Its capital, Copenhagen, controls the Sound – the entrance to the Baltic – and this control has had an enormous effect on the growth and commercial influence of Denmark.

Denmark is part of the north European plain and is almost totally lowland. The only relief feature is the north-south terminal moraine running through Jutland with the highest point only 175m above sea level. The Ice Age played a significant part in the formation of the country. The Jutland moraine is an important dividing line. It marks the limit of the advancing glaciers – the point where melting took place. To the west of it lie outwash plains of sand and gravels, giving rise to a heathland of poor unproductive soils. The east of the Jutland peninsula and the main islands have a mantle of high boulder clay spread by the retreating ice.

This clay forms the basis of a fairly rich soil. Much money has gone into improving both areas. The east of the moraine is mostly under cereals, while the west is devoted to pasture land with coniferous forest on the poorer areas.

CLIMATE

The climate of Denmark is truly transitional, lying between the maritime influences of the west and the continental ones of the east. The $0°C$ winter isotherm runs north-south through Jutland. In winter, places to the east of this line fall below freezing point, while those to the west are just above ($-2°C$ to $2°C$). Summer temperatures average about $17°C$ in all parts. The small extent of the

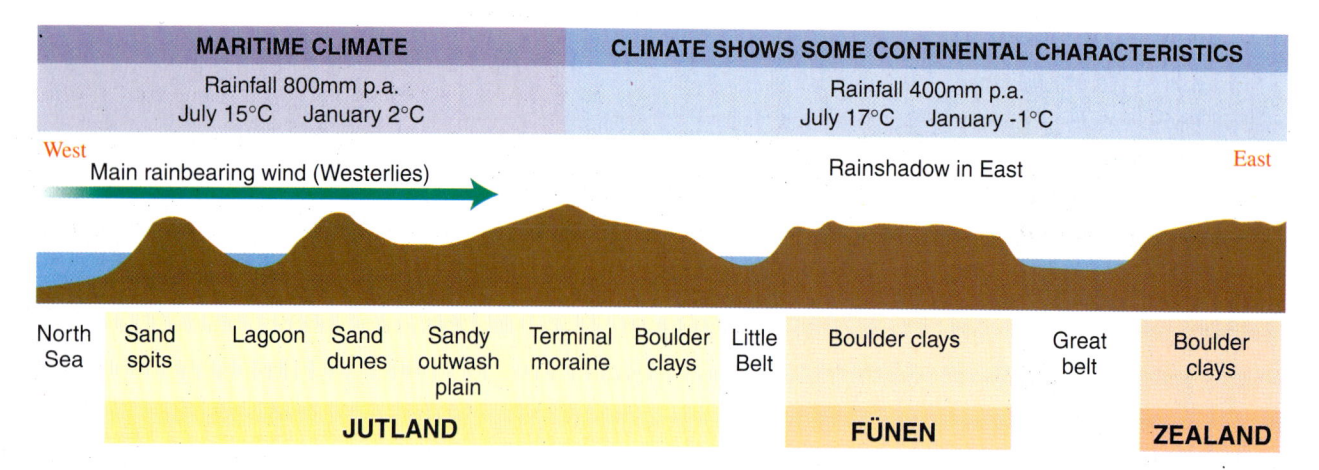

Fig 3.2 Climate and Soils

MARITIME CLIMATE
Rainfall 800mm p.a.
July 15°C January 2°C

CLIMATE SHOWS SOME CONTINENTAL CHARACTERISTICS
Rainfall 400mm p.a.
July 17°C January -1°C

West — Main rainbearing wind (Westerlies) → Rainshadow in East — East

JUTLAND: North Sea | Sand spits | Lagoon | Sand dunes | Sandy outwash plain | Terminal moraine | Boulder clays | Little Belt
FÜNEN: Boulder clays | Great belt
ZEALAND: Boulder clays

---

land area and proximity of all parts to the sea mean that the continental influence is not keenly felt. Rainfall is moderate, reaching a maximum of about 700mm. It is well spread throughout the year with a definite winter maximum. The major influences on the climate are:

- Position in north central Europe
- Depressions moving in from the Atlantic
- Cold winds blowing in from winter high pressure areas in eastern Europe.

Soils

The soils of Denmark form the basis on which the flourishing agricultural industry was founded. Two contrasting areas of landscape and soil may be distinguished, both the products of the Scandinavian ice sheets. To the west of the Jutland moraine (Fig 3.2) lies an outwash plain of sands and gravel stretching to the sand dunes of the North Sea. For centuries these lands were covered with moor and heath and so were agriculturally unproductive. The need for more food for the rapidly expanding population of Europe was the spur needed to start a massive reclamation scheme in this area.

Today most of the heathland has been reclaimed and transformed into modern productive farms (Fig. 3.3). The marsh areas along the west coast have been drained and reclaimed in the same way as the Dutch polders and this has increased the land bank. Both areas of reclamation are important to Denmark as they help compensate for the land lost to industry, communications and urbanisation in the rest of the country. Mixed farming is widespread in this region. This pattern is essentially an extension of the successful arable/livestock methods which have been developed over the last hundred years in the east of the country.

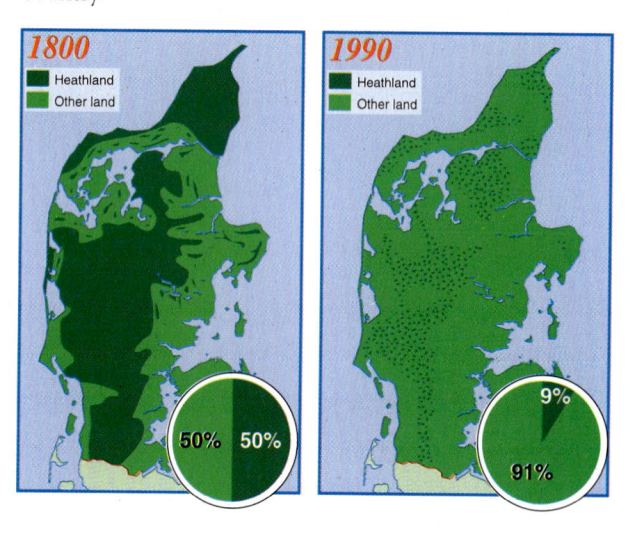

1800 — Heathland / Other land — 50% / 50%

1990 — Heathland / Other land — 9% / 91%

Fig. 3.3 Reclamation

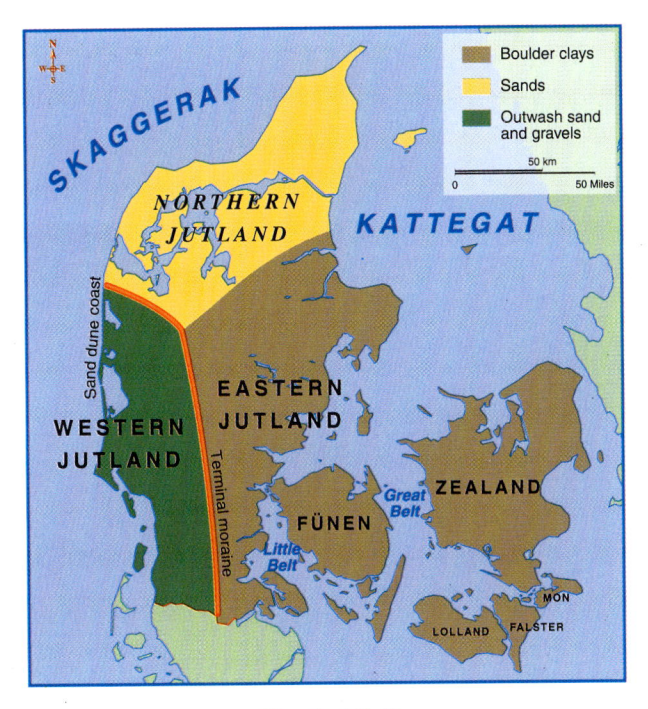

Fig. 3.4 Soils

On the east of the Jutland peninsula and on the islands the soils have developed on the boulder clay left by the retreating ice sheets. This is a fertile soil and has been enriched over the years by the addition of fertilisers and by a rotation system. A studied scientific approach to the use and conservation of soil has led to the emergence of a highly productive agricultural economy. The system of farming which yields the highest returns is that of livestock, fed from the fodder crops grown on this fertile boulder clay.

THE ECONOMY OF DENMARK

The three major pillars of the Danish economy are agriculture, fishing and the manufacturing industry, and because of their success the 5 million inhabitants have a high standard of living.

Agriculture

Denmark is renowned as an agricultural country, specialising in dairy products, and in the export of fresh and processed foods. Up to recently, its population has been mainly rural, working the land and living in small rural towns and villages. Agriculture was the mainstay of the economy attracting the most workers and accounting for well over 50% of total exports. In the course of this chapter we will note the changes that have taken place in the economy of Denmark over the years.

Fig. 3.5 Farming, South Jutland

SAMPLE QUESTION

Describe the main features of agriculture in Denmark and account for its development.

Even though agricultural exports are now less than industrial ones and allowing for the fact that agriculture only employs about 5% of the labour force, it is still a fact that agriculture is the major single industry and the base on which the economy is built. Over the last thirty years both agricultural yields and exports have grown despite the decrease of farm workers.

By any standards Denmark is a remarkable agricultural country. It is probably the most intensively developed agriculture in western Europe and it is interesting to trace its development.

Land Tenure

Up to the middle of the last century Denmark was a country of large estates and tenant farmers. This was not an ideal system of land holding as it gave the tenant farmers very little incentive to modernise and improve. As a result of government policy, the system gradually changed. The large estates were taken over, broken up and distributed to the farmers. Gradually a pattern of small family-owned farms emerged. This pattern of small farms persisted up to the middle of this century. From then to the present time there has been a gradual change.

km^2	
Arable	25 700 (60.79%)
Pasture/Meadow	2 170 (5.1%)
Forest	4 930 (11.6%)
Unproductive	9 590 (75%)

Consolidation and amalgamation, especially since entry to the EU in 1973, has led to an increase in farm sizes which now average over 25 hectares. This increase in farm size has, in turn, led to greater mechanisation but fewer farms and farm labourers.

From Cereals to Dairying

Concurrently with these changes came a change in the type of farming carried on. Up to 1880 Denmark was a cereal producing country. The climate of winter frosts and low summer rainfall suited grain production. Then, with the advent of steam ships, Europe became a *near market* for North American and Russian grains which could be delivered to the European markets much cheaper than Danish grain. Denmark soon realised that it could not compete but turned this apparent disadvantage to its own advantage.

It changed from cereal production to dairy farming as the best way of utilising its small land area and also of taking advantage of cheap imported grain to feed its cattle. It also realised that its proximity to the two great industrial nations of Britain and Germany, whose rising populations needed large quantities of food, was an added advantage.

It is surprising that Denmark is such a successful dairy country because it has really not got the ideal conditions for dairy farming. The climate is not the best for grass growing. The rainfall is low at about 600mms and spring is late arriving. These give a shorter grass growing season than in, for example, Ireland. Also, the winters are longer and colder. The table shows that very little land is devoted to grass.

Instead the land is devoted to the production of cereals – wheat, oats and barley – and root crops – beet, turnips, mangolds and potatoes. These are then converted to fodder for a long winter stall-feeding programme. In this way the Danes obtain the maximum feedstuffs from their limited land area. The stage has now been reached where the chief aim of arable farming is to supply feedstuffs for the dairy and beef herds. In fact, about 85% of the crops are used as animal feeds.

DEVELOPMENT OF DAIRY FARMING

Denmark is probably the most intensive and successful dairy farming country in the world. How has this been achieved? Consider the following factors:

1. A **scientific** approach to farming has had the support and co-operation of both farmers and governments. This has meant research into the best seeds, strains, breeds and fertilisers suited to the particular needs of the industry and the requirements of the market, e.g. selective breeding has produced the Danish Red dairy cow and the Landrace pig.

2. Nearly 85% of the animal feedstuffs are **home produced**.

3. The **co-operative movement** has been used very effectively to reduce costs on small farm units. Co-operatives cater for the total needs of the farmer. Seeds, fertilisers, feedstuffs and machinery are bought in bulk by the co-operative and the savings are passed on to the farmers. Co-operative dairies, bacon factories and egg-packing stations handle and market the produce. The co-operatives also handle research, records, marketing, finance and insurance and most farmers belong to a number of societies. The use of the co-operative system keeps down labour and administrative costs.

4. **Education** for farming and farm management is an essential element in the agricultural framework. Technical colleges, agricultural schools, folk schools and universities all play their part.

5. Danish farmers have always insisted on products of only the **highest standards** reaching the markets. This makes it relatively easy for a strong marketing board to sell these products worldwide.

6. There are rich **industrial markets** within easy reach by land or sea. South Sweden and Britain are just short sea journeys, and Belgium, France and Germany are readily accessible by road and rail.

Membership of the EU since 1973 has confirmed the traditional markets (Britain and Germany) and opened up new ones. Over 70% of agricultural products now go to EU member states. In addition, the EU has guaranteed fixed prices under CAP.

Farm Practices

Three elements may be distinguished in the farming industry.

Arable farming produces crops of wheat, barley, oats, beet, turnip, mangolds, etc. To maintain the high yields, there is heavy application of fertilisers and an intensive use of machinery. Barley is the dominant crop and accounts for about 90% of all cereals.

These crops are then processed into fodder and fed to the **dairy and beef herds**, the second sector. Milk yields are high (average annual yield of about 1 500 gallons per cow). With a small home market for immediate consumption most of the milk is converted to butter (60%) and cheese (15%). The remainder goes to the production of cream, yogurts, baby and invalid foods, milk powder, etc.

The third sector is the *factory farming* of pigs, poultry and eggs. Very little land is required for this valuable farming. The skimmed milk is returned to the farmers and is added to cereals and roots to provide food for the pigs. Special breeding has produced the very lean Landrace pig. Denmark has increased the number of pigs from 6 million to 10 million over the last 20 years and now supplies well over half the bacon that enters world trade. Pig rearing is becoming increasingly popular with many farmers.

Changes in Farm Practices

Changes are gradually taking place in farm practices in Denmark. The number of small farms is falling with a resulting increase in medium to large units. This has resulted in a sharp fall in the number of farmers and farm workers and an increase in mechanisation (Fig. 3.6).

Improvements in transport and the better use of that transport have led to a dramatic decline in the number of dairies leading to *economies of scale*. There are now about 120 dairies replacing the 1 350 in operation in 1960. Denmark, over the years, has lost a significant parcel of farmland to housing, factories, motorways, etc – from 3 094 000 hectares to 2 750 000 hectares. This has been compensated for in some way by an increasing use of fertilisers to obtain higher yields from the remaining land.

Difficulties in getting labour for a 7-day, twice-daily milking programme has forced many farmers to turn to pig rearing, beef cattle and cereal growing, as these activities are less labour intensive. Overproduction of milk and milk products is also encouraging changes from dairy farming.

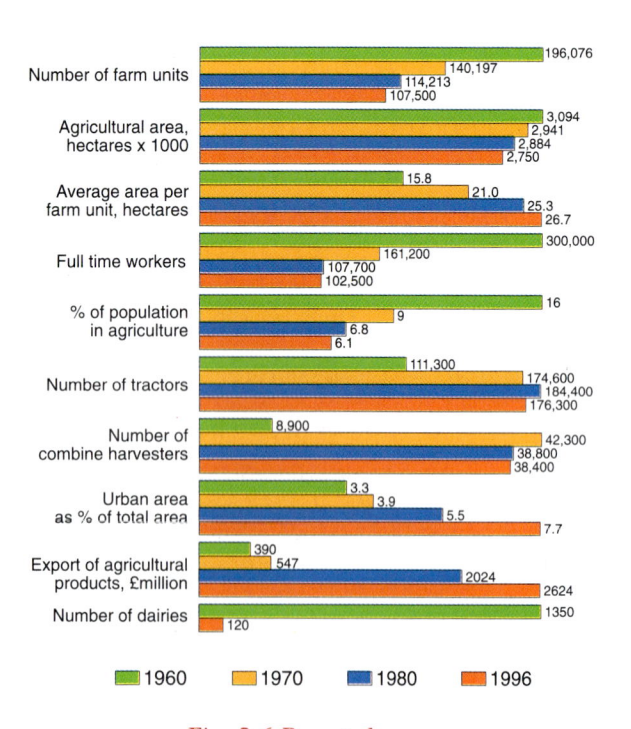

	1960	1970	1980	1996
Number of farm units	196,076	140,197	114,213	107,500
Agricultural area, hectares x 1000	3,094	2,941	2,884	2,750
Average area per farm unit, hectares	15.8	21.0	25.3	26.7
Full time workers	300,000	161,200	107,700	102,500
% of population in agriculture	16	9	6.8	6.1
Number of tractors	111,300	174,600	184,400	176,300
Number of combine harvesters	8,900	42,300	38,800	38,400
Urban area as % of total area	3.3	3.9	5.5	7.7
Export of agricultural products, £million	390	547	2024	2624
Number of dairies				1350 / 120

Fig. 3.6 Recent changes

Denmark's chief contribution to the EU over the years has been as a supplier of food, but the balance between agriculture and industry is changing, as the table below shows.

	Norway	Denmark
1960	1486	574
1970	2910	1200
1980	2470	1983
1988	1735	1963
1996	1700	1896

Fig. 3.8 Fish Landings '000

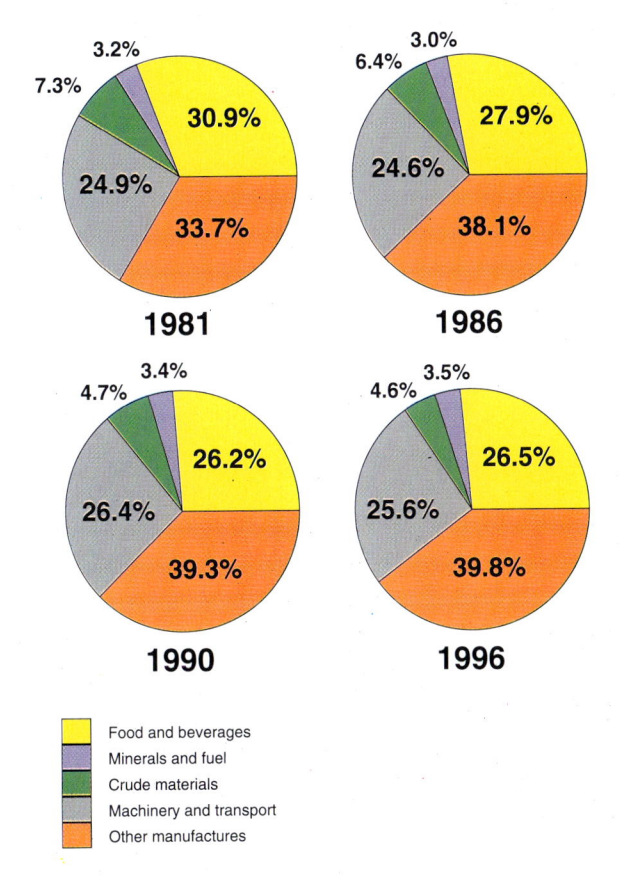

1981
- Food and beverages: 30.9%
- Minerals and fuel: 3.2%
- Crude materials: 7.3%
- Machinery and transport: 24.9%
- Other manufactures: 33.7%

1986
- Food and beverages: 27.9%
- Minerals and fuel: 3.0%
- Crude materials: 6.4%
- Machinery and transport: 24.6%
- Other manufactures: 38.1%

1990
- Food and beverages: 26.2%
- Minerals and fuel: 3.4%
- Crude materials: 4.7%
- Machinery and transport: 26.4%
- Other manufactures: 39.3%

1996
- Food and beverages: 26.5%
- Minerals and fuel: 3.5%
- Crude materials: 4.6%
- Machinery and transport: 25.6%
- Other manufactures: 39.8%

Fig. 3.7 Principal exports

SEA FISHING

The sea fishing industry is an important source of both employment and income in Denmark. It has grown rapidly over the last number of years with a large modern fleet and up to date processing facilities. In recent years the Danish catch has exceeded that of the Norwegians.

A number of factors have contributed to the growth of the industry;

- Denmark has a very long coastline in proportion to the size of the country. This has encouraged people to turn to the sea as a means of livelihood.
- There are good ports on the islands and on east Jutland.
- There is a long tradition of seafaring and fishing. Denmark was an important part of the Hanseatic League when the Sound was famous for its herring shoals.
- Denmark is near the rich fishing banks (Viking, Dodder) of the North Sea. This ensures both a good supply of fish and fast processing.
- Adjacent markets in Sweden, Germany, France and Britain ensure a quick sale.
- EU membership since 1973 has given Denmark access to additional fish stocks within European Community waters, bigger EU markets and guaranteed prices under the **Common Fisheries Policy** (CFP).

The chief fishing grounds are the North Sea and the rich fishing banks of Dodder and Viking where a wide variety of different species are to be found. The North Sea is also important as a breeding ground. All the coastal waters are fished with 70% of the catch taken in the North Sea and 15% in the Skaggerak. Cod, herring, haddock, plaice and sole are the chief varieties. As in Norway, much of the catch is reduced to fish meal, animal feeds, margarine oils and pharmaceutical oils. However, in recent years, a growing consumer demand for filletted and frozen fish products has meant that less fish is reduced. There are 400 fish-processing plants, employing 9 000 people.

Fig. 3.10 A Danish Fishing Port

Fig. 3.9 Fishermen in Frederikshavn

Denmark has about 10 000 fulltime fishermen and a small number of part-time ones. There are about 3 150 boats. There are also a large number of land-based jobs that owe their existence either directly or indirectly to fishing (transport, processing, boat building, etc). Like the other fishing countries in the EU, Denmark is facing a fishing crisis. Because of the small population and limited resources, fishing is central to the economy. The heavy overfishing of the 1970s (see Fig. 3.8) has depleted the fishing stocks and now the EU, through the CFP, has placed major restrictions on the number of boats and has introduced catch quotas for the major species – (**Total Allowable Catches** – TAC). The CFP is providing subsidies to maintain fish prices, to guarantee a livelihood to the fishermen and to compensate for withdrawal from the industry. The present quota system has only had partial success and in 1997 a further reduction of 30% of quotas to the end of 1999 has been proposed.

Fig. 3.11 Fisheries and ferry ports

The increased scale and efficiency of the industry (sonar, radar, factory ships) has put great pressure on existing stocks and Danish fishermen are now fishing further out into the Atlantic for new species.

The chief fishing ports are Esbjerg, Hirtshals, Skagen and Fredericshaven, all on the west or north coasts of Jutland, where commercial farming opportunities are weakest, but also adjacent to the richest fishing grounds. There are smaller fleets at Aarhus and Nyborg.

DENMARK INDUSTRIAL DEVELOPMENT

For many years Denmark was recognised as primarily an agricultural country with farm products forming the bulk of the exports, employing a large percentage of the work force and contributing the major share of export earnings. It took a long time for the country to realise its industrial potential and the first period of broad industrial growth did not come until the years between the wars. Danish agriculture was a model for the rest of Europe at the time and to many people the future lay in farming and food production. Since that time, however, the picture has changed. Industry has expanded, the industrial workforce has increased and industrial exports now dominate the economy.

At first sight Denmark does not appear to have any of the recognised (accepted) advantages for manufacturing.
- It has no basic raw materials - iron, lead, zinc, copper, timber.
- It has no rivers capable of being harnessed for HEP.
- It has no primary energy sources of coal, oil, gas. (Its small sector of the North Sea seems to have very little potential.)
- With only 5 million inhabitants it is dependant on export markets.

Despite these disadvantages and a late industrial start, Denmark has developed a dynamic and varied industrial economy and has emerged as one of the small but significant industrial countries of Europe.

Why?

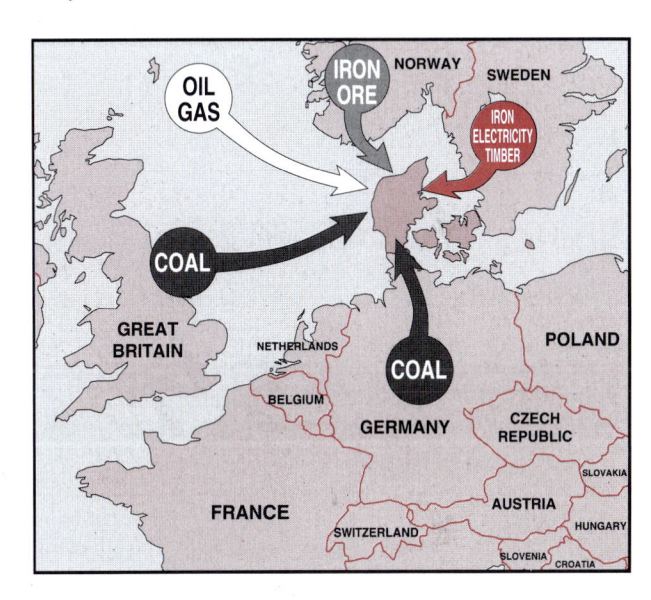

Fig. 3.12 Centre of Resource Basin

1. Its strategic geographical location means that it is at the centre of a rich resource basin. The map above shows its location in regard to supplies of iron, timber, electricity, coal, oil and gas. Its maritime tradition and merchant navy facilitates imports.
2. Denmark is on the edge of the industrial core of Europe. The affluent markets of the EU are within easy reach by land or sea.
3. The agricultural and fishing industries supply the raw materials for food processing.

4 Both farming and fishing create markets for the engineering and chemical industries – trawlers, marine engines, nets, farm machinery, fertilisers, pesticides, etc.
5 Denmark concentrates on activities where skill and technology are more important than the raw materials involved.

By international standards Danish industries are small. Of the 8 000 industrial companies, about 70% have only about 50 employees each, while only 3% have over 500.

However, the Danes use their research and marketing programmes to identify exploitable niches in the international commercial markets and have the expertise to fill these markets with quality products.

The chief enterprises are:
- Industries supplying and depending on agriculture and fishing (butter, cheese, brewing, distilling, bacon, fertilisers, chemicals, fish processing, shipbuilding).
- Shipbuilding, marine engineering, general engineering, cement and cement-making machinery.
- Quality industries which have developed from the old craft skills – silver, glass, porcelain, textiles and furniture.
- Modern electronics, computers, office equipment, etc. Both IBM and Commodore have their European Headquarters in Denmark.

Copenhagen is the chief centre of manufacturing activities. Other industrial towns include Aarhus, Aalborg, Odense and Randers.

Fig. 3.14 Pewter, a flourishing specialised industry

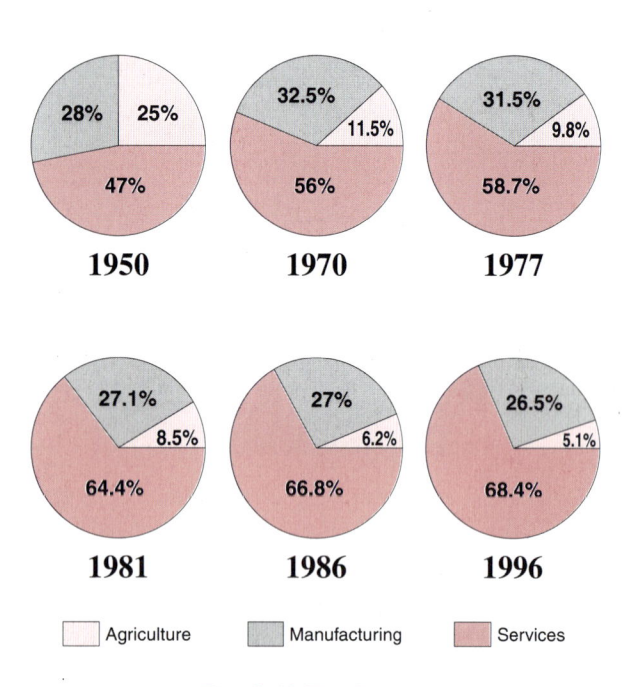

Fig. 3.13 Employment

Copenhagen

Copenhagen was the old central capital of southern Scandinavia and was built as a safe harbour between the island of Amager and the mainland. It controls the Sound – that narrow strait of water between the island of Zealand and southern Sweden. That control has aided the development of Copenhagen through the centuries. During the thirteenth and fourteenth centuries Copenhagen was a major port of the Hanseatic League and it continued to prosper from that time. Its strategic location cannot be over-emphasised, as it controlled the main sea route to the Baltic and was the capital and chief port of Denmark. Its expansion continued in line with the expansion of the Danish economy.

In 1895 the Kiel canal was opened across the neck of the Jutland peninsula to provide an alternative route to the Baltic. Copenhagen was threatened. It responded by creating Copenhagen Freeport – an entrepot at the northern end of the city to handle transit trade. The Kiel canal did not attract the business it hoped, but it unwittingly helped Copenhagen to expand. The increased trade and commerce generated by the entrepot initiated new industry.

Industrial and agricultural raw materials like oil, coal, ores, timber, fertilisers and oilseeds are imported and many are processed in Copenhagen. The fishing industry and mercantile marine gave the impetus to the shipbuilding trade, and marine engineering got a tremendous boost with the invention of the diesel engine which was patented at Copenhagen.

The expanding agricultural economy provided the basic raw materials for brewing, distilling and food processing and provided the market for fertilisers and agricultural machienry. The craft industries penetrated new world markets and so were also involved in this strong industrial growth. Large numbers of rural workers became redundant

Fig. 3.15 Main Industries

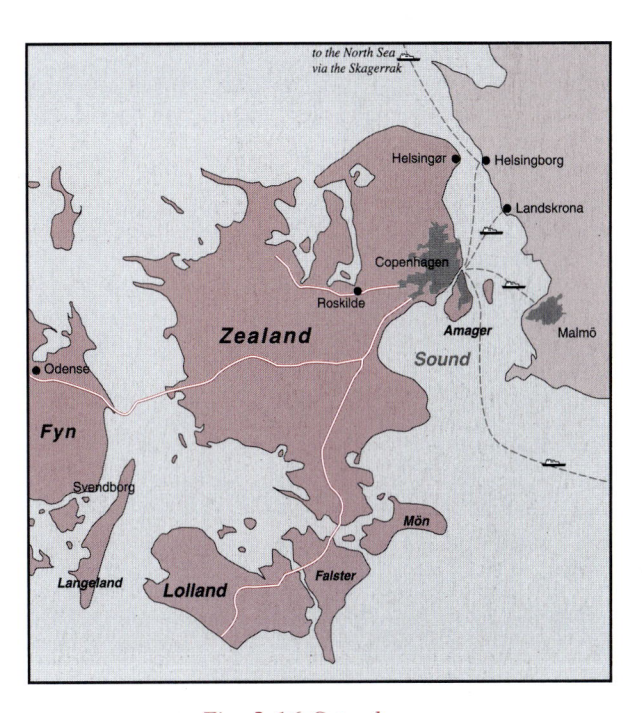

Fig. 3.16 Copenhagen

on the newly mechanised farms and moved to the capital. Copenhagen experienced phenomenal growth in the last 100 years, expanding from 200 000 to 1.5 million today. This expansion has given rise to a vibrant tertiary sector dealing with administration, finance, tourism and port activity. Even the loss of some of its hinterland after the last war has not reduced its importance.

Copenhagen's function as a centre of communications has led to further expansion of the city and the future looks assured. Plans are well advanced for important future projects including the following:

- A new bridge for road and rail will link Zealand, Funen and Jutland and thus open up the routes to the west of Europe.
- A bridge from Falster to Lolland to Fehmarn will provide a further link with Germany.
- A new bridge across the Sound (via the island of Saltholm) will provide road and rail links to Malmo in Sweden. This bridge will help to develop both sides of the Sound and could lead to the emergence of a major industrial conurbation from Malmo to Helsingborg to Helsingor to Copenhagen.

Copenhagen is thus the chief port of Denmark and the political, industrial, administrative and commercial capital.

Esbjerg

Esbjerg is the headquarters of the fishing industry. Over 600 boats use the five fishing docks. It is an artificial port built inside two great sand bars with a narrow channel leading to the sea. The docks area and the channel have to be constantly dredged. Esbjerg has grown from a small fishing hamlet in 1870 to an important port and thriving city of 100 000 people today. Much of this growth is due to its fishing fleet and associated industries.

Fig. 3.17 Postmen in Copenhagen

Questions

1. Discuss the factors which favour and hinder the development of manufacturing industry in Denmark. (L.C. Higher Level)
2. Describe the extent to which glaciation has influenced the pattern of agriculture in Denmark.
3. 'The Danish agricultural scene is characterised by the intensity and diversity of land use.' Discuss.
4. Danish agriculture is one of the most developed in western Europe. Describe its main characteristics.
5. Denmark is not one of the industrial giants of western Europe but it has made rapid progress in

industrialisation. Describe the major sectors of manufacturing industry.

6 Copenhagen
   (a) With the aid of a sketch map, identify the locational advantages of Copenhagen.
   (b) Explain *two* ways in which its economic activities show that it has a large hinterland. (L.C. Ordinary Level)

7 Denmark has three major natural resources – the soil, the sea and a strategic geographical location. Write an account of *two* of these resources.

8 Describe the influence of the sea on the economic development of Denmark.

9 What are the advantages and disadvantages of the Common Fisheries Policy (CFP) on the fishing industry of Denmark.

western and central europe

the netherlands

belgium

france

germany

switzerland

chapter four
the netherlands

INTRODUCTION

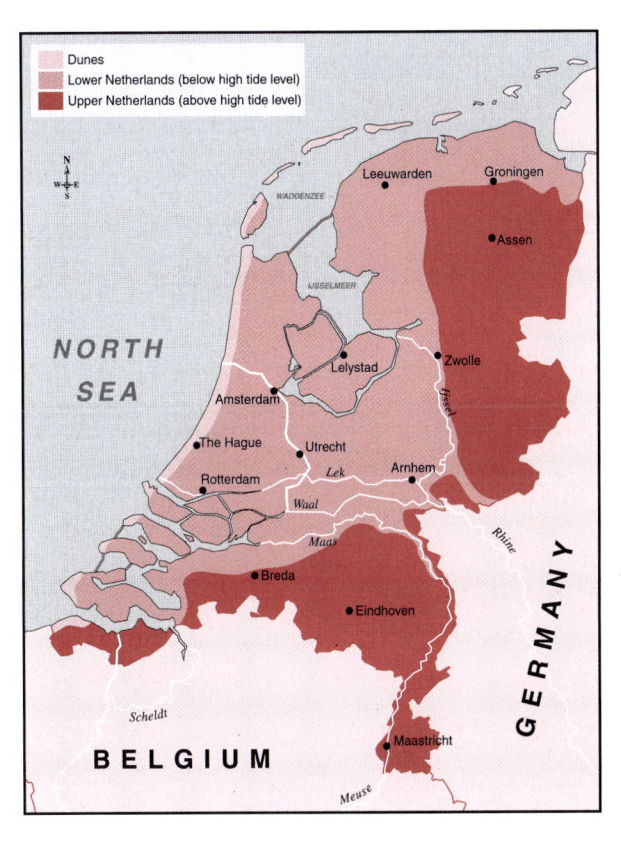

Area:	41 200 sq km
Population:	14.3 million
Density:	347 per sq km

Fig. 4.1 The Netherlands: features

The low countries of the Netherlands and Belgium lie to the north-west of Europe as the western extension of the great European plain. The Netherlands, frequently called Holland, consists mainly of the delta lands of the Scheldt, Maas and Rhine and the North Sea lowlands. The country is almost entirely flat, rising very gradually to the south and east with its highest point in Limburg, being less than 300 metres above sea level. To the west much of the land (of the whole country) is below sea level. Over the years the rivers have built up their beds by deposition so that in their lower courses they flow above the level of the surrounding land. Because of the danger of either permanent or temporary flooding both agriculture and settlement are dependent on the protection afforded by lines of dykes running from the German border and along the lower courses of the rivers.

The Netherlands is a small densely-populated country but its influence on the trade and commerce of Europe is immense. The Dutch, by the very nature and position of their country, have been involved with drainage, reclamation and the sea. Over the centuries they built up a

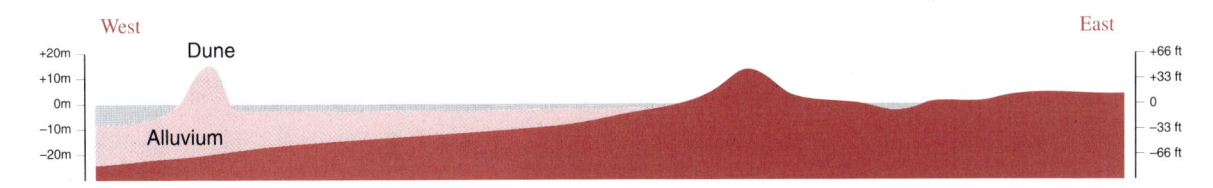

Fig. 4.2 The Netherlands: a cross-section

reputation and tradition for things maritime. During the seventeenth century in particular they developed their maritime tradition, expanded their overseas trade, acquired and utilised colonies and generally laid the foundations for today's trade, commerce and industry.

The struggle with the rivers and seas has been going on for 2 000 years. In that time the Dutch have won and lost many battles but have never fully mastered the water. History records disastrous floods in nearly every century up to the present time. The floods of 1953 proved to be the greatest disaster of all. A high tide, combined with 100 mph winds, piled up the sea water in the narrow neck at the southern end of the North Sea. The sea rose dramatically in a few hours and breached the dykes in sixty-seven places. Two thousand people were drowned, fertile farms flooded, cattle lost, communication links were torn apart and valuable property destroyed. This storm bred a determination in the Dutch not to suffer again at the hands of the sea. Dykes were reinforced along the coast and the Delta plan was put into operation.

CLIMATE

The Netherlands lies within the cool temperate maritime climate belt and so has mild winters, cool summers and moderate rainfall. Summer temperatures average 17°C along the coast with a slight rise to about 19°C to the east and south-east. Winter temperatures range from about 3°C along the coast to 1°C in the east where the continental influences begin to be felt. The number of days with frost increases eastwards from about thirty to eighty. Frequently drainage channels and canals freeze over.

Precipitation is well distributed throughout the year. The total varies from 600mm to 900mm and the wettest areas are the Veluwe and the province of Drenthe. The late summer/early autumn is the season of most rain.

Because of the small size of the country and the absence of high relief there are no great regional variations in climate. Climate plays a major part in the development of agriculture and accounts for the wide range of arable and pastoral activities. Cereals ripen in the warm sunny summers, an advantage also enjoyed by root and fodder crops. The climate is sufficiently warm and damp to encourage grass for grazing, hay and silage and this has led in turn to the expansion of the dairy and beef industries.

NATURAL RESOURCES AND ADVANTAGES

The Netherlands is a very small country (less than half the size of Ireland), with a very high density of people. The demand for land and resources is consequently high. Being a small country these resources are few and limited and the high population means that the resources are quickly utilised and consumed. Among its advantages we list the following:

> Geographical location
> Soils
> Natural gas and oil.

Geographical Location

The Netherlands is strategically placed on the western edge of the North European plain where the European highlands sweep down to meet the North Sea and the English Channel. Thus the country forms a major lowlands routeway in the northwest of Europe.

The occupation of the Netherlands during two world wars is a measure of its strategic location. It controls the English Channel, i.e. the entrance and exit to the North Sea. The spin-off from this traffic adds enormously to the trade and commerce of the country. The Netherlands also controls the mouth of the Rhine, Maas and Scheldt and consequently controls the movement of goods and freight along these rivers. The Rhine is the busiest waterway in Europe but the Maas and Scheldt also carry a large volume of traffic. As the meeting point of the rivers and seas, the Netherlands can be regarded as an entrepot for north France, Belgium, Germany and Switzerland, handling much of the imports and exports of these countries. The benefits of this traffic are not confined to commerce alone. Industry also benefits and many Dutch industries are based on the raw materials landed at Rotterdam.

A dense network of communications has developed across the flat land with road, rail and pipeline routes following the line of the rivers. Canals, canalised rivers and roadways carry about 90% of all freight between them. The Netherlands has no natural frontiers, so it is easy to extend the communications links right into the heart of Europe. A dense network of motorways focuses on Rotterdam. Most of these motorways have been built since the war and so are suited to modern motor transport. Pipelines carry oil, gas and chemicals. They are of prime importance to the Netherlands as they carry Groningen gas and the oil from Rotterdam into industrial Europe. Good routeways and good communications are the arteries of good trade.

The Netherlands is at the heart of the greatest concentration of industry and people in western Europe – west Germany, Britain, Belgium and France. This large market on its doorstep has encouraged industrial development and provides an outlet for the intensive agricultural activities of the Netherlands. The importance of the location of the Netherlands cannot be over-emphasised. It has led to the development of a prosperous and significant international trade.

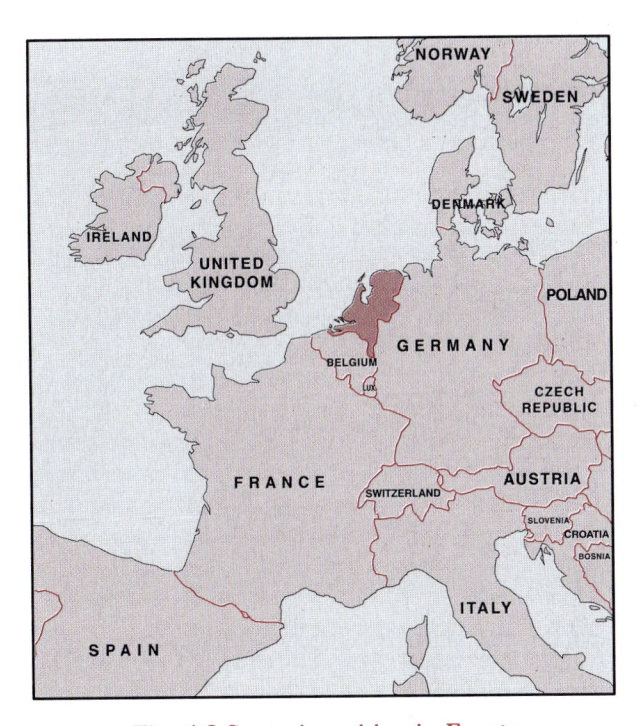

Fig. 4.3 Strategic position in Europe

Fig. 4.4 Rotterdam port

Fig. 4.5 Hot Banana

Note the following points in relation to the strategic location of the Netherlands:

- It borders the North Sea and English Channel which together form the busiest shipping route in the world.
- It is at the mouth of the river Rhine, which is the busiest river route in Europe.
- The Maas and Scheldt also enter the sea in the Netherlands and thus French and Belgian trade and commerce contribute to the economy of the Netherlands.
- The flatness of the land facilitates the building of roads, canals, railways and pipelines. This helps build up a good communications network.
- The Netherlands is at the heart of western Europe's great concentration of population and industry.

Soils

A line running due south from the Ijsselmeer would divide the country roughly into areas above and below sea level. It would also provide some guide to the soil divisions (see Fig. 4.6). The high land in the east and north of the country is heathland. Outwash sands and gravels cover much of this area, giving typical geest landscape similar to that in the north of Germany. In the south centre, within the bend of the Maas, is the province of North Brabant which has a similar type soil. This area is really an extension of the Kempen region of Belgium and is similar to it in most respects. The heathland soil is either sandy or peaty and of poor quality. A major reclamation scheme is being carried out. The peat cover has been removed (used as fuel), vast drainage schemes initiated and deep ploughing introduced. A heavy application of marl, lime

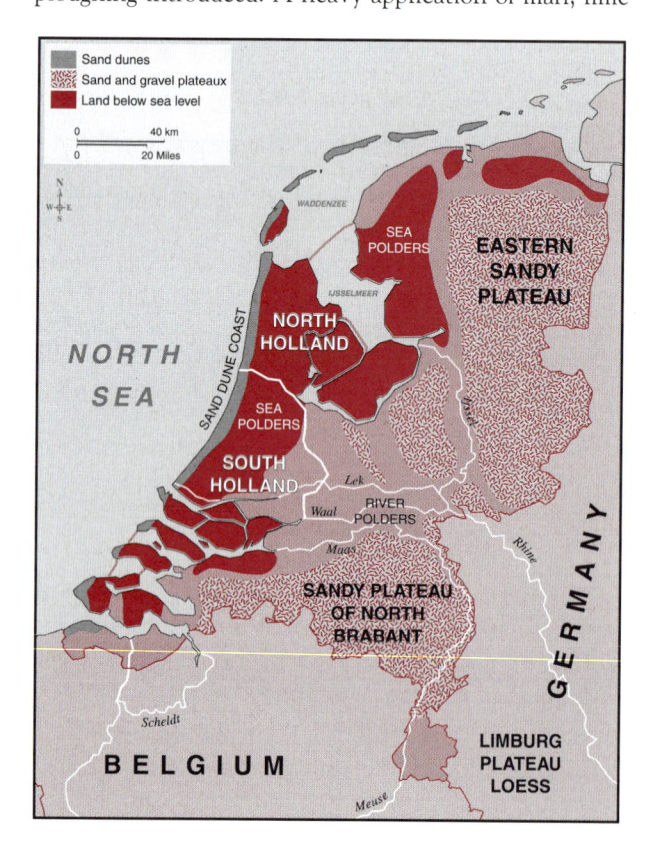

Fig. 4.6 The Netherlands: soil regions

and fertilisers has helped in the continued improvement of the land. Grazing is the primary land use, but root and fodder crops are gradually being introduced.

The western half of the soil line contains two soil regions – the sand dune region along the coast and the reclaimed polders stretching from inside the dunes to the rivers. The sand dunes run in an almost unbroken line along the coast and the sandy soil formed behind them is light, warm and rich in lime. Inside this belt lie the polder lands, i.e. land reclaimed, protected by dykes and artificially drained. Much of the polder land has been reclaimed from the sea so the soil is formed from marine clays. The lower flood plains of the rivers have also been reclaimed and protected and these riverine polders have alluvial clays which are not quite as fertile as the marine clays. The polders form the best land in the Netherlands and are intensively farmed. Arable farming is carried on in the drier lands because the damper clays are more suited to pastoralism. In the very south of the country, in the province of Limburg, are the richest soils of all. This is a loess covered region with soils similar to those of central Belgium or the Paris Basin. Mixed farming predominates here.

The soils are thus derived from a number of rocks and deposits and this has led to a variety of agricultural land uses. Improvements are being constantly carried out. The Dutch have very little land so what they have has to be fully utilised.

Energy

Up to the end of the 19th century it was thought that the Netherlands did not have any worthwhile natural resources. It was known that there was coal in Limburg but it was not exploited, as Limburg was regarded as a remote inaccessible part of the country. With an increase in industrial activity from 1900, new interest was shown in the coal-fields. Twelve mines were sunk to provide coal for the industrial and domestic markets. Some of the coal had a high gas content and proved ideal for the chemical industry.

A state chemical works was established in 1930 which has since grown into a chemical giant. As a result of rising production costs in the mines and the discovery of enormous reserves of natural gas in the north, the mines were gradually closed down between 1966 and 1975. The chemical industry has remained, now using oil and

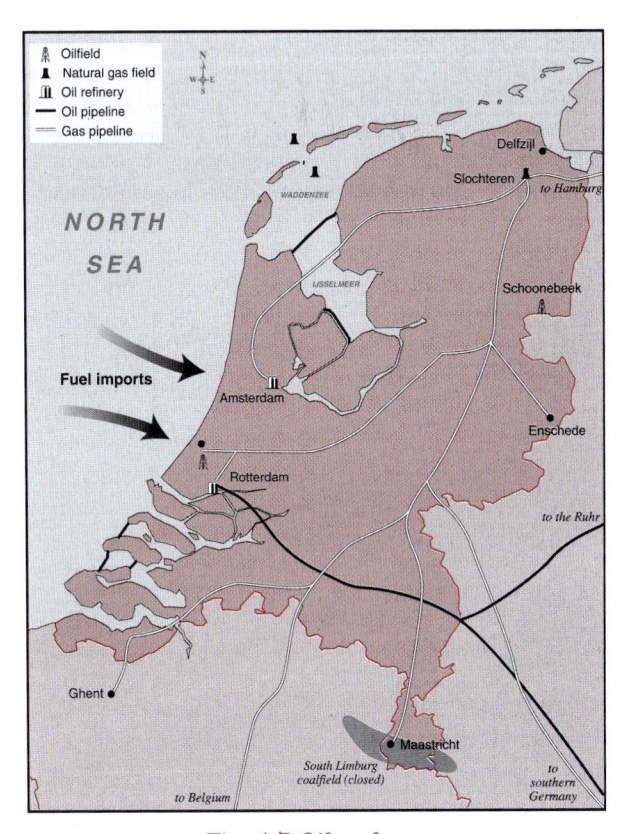

Fig. 4.7 Oil and gas

natural gas delivered by pipeline. This is a good example of geographical inertia.

In 1958 one of the world's largest gas fields was discovered in the province of Groningen, in the north of the country. This field was of major significance in a country with so few natural resources. Hundreds of wells were sunk and, in the 1960s, a whole network of pipelines was laid across the country bringing gas to most of the population for domestic use, to industries for power, to the petro-chemical works as a raw material, to power stations for electricity generation and to the glass houses for horticulture. In the early 1970s the pipeline network was extended across the border to Belgium, France, Germany, Switzerland and Italy. Further deposits were discovered during the 80s in the Wadden sea, the Frisian Islands and the southern part of the North Sea in the Dutch sector. The newer fields now account for about 50% of output, which in 1996 amounted to 84 billion M^3. Reserves are estimated at over 2 000 billion M^3. At present about 50% of the gas is exported.

Some oil is also found in Drenthe, around Rotterdam and in the North Sea. Quantities are small – about 8% of the needs – but exploration is still continuing in the North Sea.

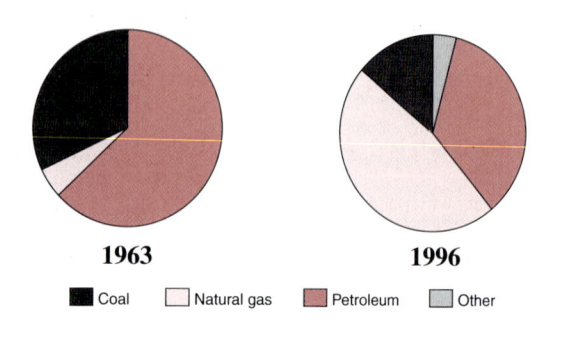

Fig. 4.8 Energy consumption

Benefits to the Economy

Fossil fuels make a major contribution to the economy of the Netherlands. It is now the fourth largest producer of natural gas in the world after Russia, USA and Canada. More significantly, however, is the contribution that the Netherlands makes to the European energy supply at a time when Europe is still trying to reduce its dependence on imported oil.

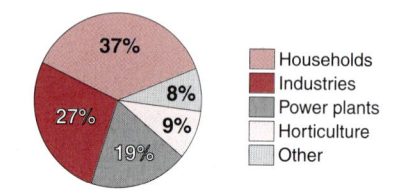

Fig. 4.9 Gas consumption

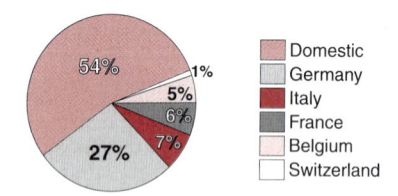

Fig. 4.10 Gas sales

Natural gas is a major earner of foreign currency and an aid to the balance of payments. It has significantly reduced the import of both coal and oil. Thousands of jobs have been created, industrial jobs have been maintained and a new market created in the shipbuilding industry, supplying rigs, production platforms, supply ships, pipelines, pumps, etc.

As a result of the benefits, more money can be diverted to industrial expansion and to investment in the less well developed provinces of the north and east. This takes some of the pressure off the Randstad and helps to correct the regional imbalance between west and east.

LAND RECLAMATION

On the map of the Netherlands we note two distinct relief regions – high and low Netherlands. Each occupies about half the country but the main concentration of population is in the low area which lies somewhere between 1 metre above and 6 metres below mean sea level and depends on the protection afforded by the sand dunes and dykes.

Fig. 4.11 Land Reclamation

Before examining the land reclamation schemes in the Netherlands it is helpful to have a very brief look at the processes that helped shape the landscape of the country. The ice sheets of the third great glacial period (Riss or Saale) extended as far south as the course of the present-day Rhine. In retreat these ice sheets spread ground moraine across the northern and eastern provinces. About this time the level of the sea rose and started to flood across the areas now termed the polder lands. The wind and sea piled up a line of sand dunes stretching from Dunkirk in France to the present German border. This line of dunes forms the first line of defence today for the Dutch. Mud and peats accumulated behind the dunes. Marshes developed where the sea bed had invaded the low-lying areas.

Over the last few thousand years the sea gradually gained on the land to the west and north, while to the south the rivers flooded regularly, thus depositing vast tracts of alluvium and building up their beds. During the Middle Ages a series of storms breached the dune line, forming an archipelago to the south through which the Rhine, Maas and Scheldt find their way to the sea. To the north the sweeping curve of the dune line was broken in many places to form the Frisian islands. The shallow mud flats behind were flooded. This resulted in the creation of the Wadden Sea which then penetrated deep inland to create the Zuider Zee.

The struggle against the sea and the rivers has gone on for 2 000 years and provides a prime example of a people's endeavour to control their environment. Up to the fourteenth century the Dutch struggled to keep out the water but from then onwards they also turned their attention to winning back the land lost to the sea.

Reclamation started in a small way in the twelfth and thirteenth centuries and there is historical evidence of land won back in the north-east and in Zeeland – but the sea still attacked. In 1421 much land was again lost in the delta region during the great floods of that year. Over seventy villages disappeared under the waves and 10% of the population was drowned. Still the struggle continued and many dams were built, as reflected in the place names Rotterdam, Schiedam, Amsterdam, Edam, Veendam. The problem was twofold. Defending the land from the seas and rivers was the first problem. Draining the water from low-lying enclosed land was the other.

In the sixteenth century a major step forward was achieved with the development of the windmill. By a careful location of the windmills (usually at different levels) it was possible to drain even the lowest land. During the following centuries much drainage was carried out, but major schemes became possible only when the windmill was replaced by the steam pumps of the nineteenth century and the diesel and electric pumps of the twentieth century. (Note Fig. 4.12 showing the rate of reclamation over the centuries.)

The fear of floods was probably the major factor in defence but many factors contributed to the desire to win back land. The development of the windmill coincided with the Dutch Golden Age when trade, commerce and colonisation prospered. Dutch towns grew, industry flourished, population increased and the need for land to feed this developing population was the stimulus needed for the effort to totally conquer the sea.

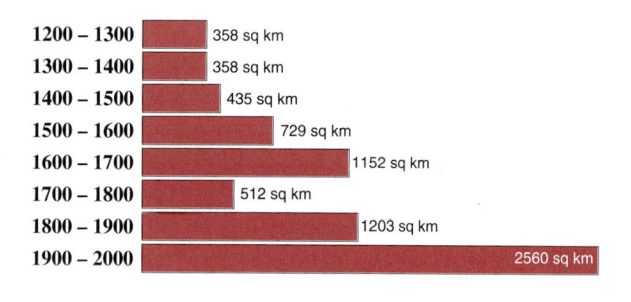

Period	Area
1200 – 1300	358 sq km
1300 – 1400	358 sq km
1400 – 1500	435 sq km
1500 – 1600	729 sq km
1600 – 1700	1152 sq km
1700 – 1800	512 sq km
1800 – 1900	1203 sq km
1900 – 2000	2560 sq km

Fig. 4.12 Land reclamation over the centuries

The Zuider Zee

Of all the Dutch projects the reclamation of the Zuider Zee is the one that most captured the admiration of the world. The Zuider Zee stretched far into the land and hundreds of kilometres of dykes were needed to protect the surrounding land. Many plans had been put forward over the centuries but nothing had come of them. A major flood in 1916 and food shortages during the 1914-18 war convinced the government of the necessity to reclaim part of the sea. Work commenced in 1927.

A major dam, with roads, was built from north Holland to Friesland across the mouth of the sea. This had the effect of cutting off the Zuider Zee from the Wadden Sea and turning it gradually into a much reduced fresh-water lake (fed by the Ijssel and other rivers). Five large areas of land on the edge of this lake were to be drained and dyked and so converted to polders (see Fig. 4.13). The Zuider Zee was now fresh water (Ijsselmeer) and the water could be used for agricultural, industrial and domestic purposes.

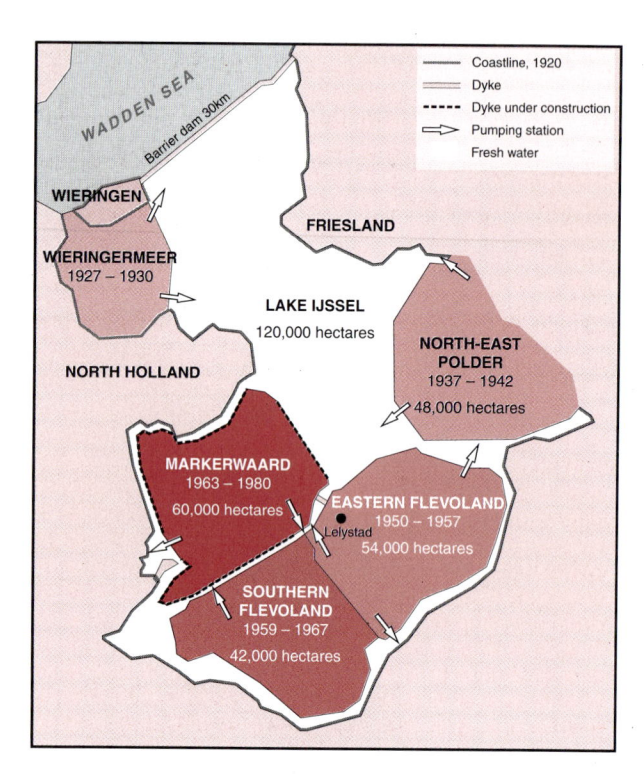

Fig. 4.13 The Netherlands: Zuider Zee polders

The first polder to be converted was the Wieringermeer in the north-west and the lessons learned here were used subsequently in the other four. Polderisation presented many problems and tasks. First the area had to be pumped dry. Then drainage channels and pipes were laid and the land enclosed with protective dykes. Pumping stations were established. The land was then treated with gypsum and other minerals to remove the salt. Several deep ploughings ensured a mixture of soils. Reeds were then planted to help dry out the land and consolidate it. The polders were now ready. Rye and kale were the first crops, but they were soon replaced by cereals, roots and grass as the land improved. All the polders have now been reclaimed and laid out. The objectives of the planning of the polders were to achieve a good arrangement of parcels of land, the optimum size of holding, good access by roads and canals and appropriate vegetation cover. During the first few years the state controlled the polders which were then leased or sold to farmers.

A number of villages and one or more centres were planned for each polder to provide market and service facilities and to act as social centres. Since 1986 the north-east polder, the two Flevopolders and Markerwaard have formed a new province called Flevoland. This province now has a population of nearly 300 000. Its capital is Lelystad (pop. 60 000), called after the engineer who drew up the plan. Almere takes the overflow from Amsterdam and has nearly 100 000 inhabitants.

It was intended originally that most of the land would be used for agriculture but in the 60s and 70s much of the land was re-designated for industrial, recreational and residential purposes. The proximity of these polders to the Randstad is the chief reason for this change in plan.

Fig. 4.14 The Oostersheldedam

Results of reclamation scheme

1. 500 000 acres of land were added to the land bank.
2. A 300 000 acre fresh-water lake provides water for a variety of purposes.
3. The old and new lands are protected from flood danger.
4. New roads on the dams have reduced travelling distances.
5. Control of water levels has increased farming efficiency and yields and reduced the dependence on rainfall.
6. Ijsselmeer is used for recreation and fresh-water fishing.
7. Sea fishing in the Zuider Zee is at an end. Locks in the barrier dam allow access to the Wadden sea and beyond.

The Delta Plan

The Delta Plan is included in this section on reclamation even though the primary aim of the plan was the protection of existing land rather than reclamation. The delta region was a mass of channels and islands protected by 1 100km of assorted dykes. Like the Zuider Zee, plans for its improvement were formulated and shelved for many years but the 1953 storm left no doubt in anyone's mind of the need to protect the region. The final plan accepted was bold and imaginative. All the sea inlets, except the New Waterway and the western Scheldt, were closed by a series of dykes running from island to island. This in effect closed off the sea and created freshwater lakes in the former sea inlets.

There were other important results from the implementation of the Delta Plan:

- The rich arable land of the delta region was rendered safe from flooding.
- Fresh-water lakes, formed from the rivers, provided water for agricultural, industrial and domestic use.
- The coastline was shortened by about 650km.
- The fresh-water lakes halted the seepage of salt water under the dykes.

- The delta region got a new improved road system built across the dykes.
- The once isolated delta region has been opened up and linked to the mainland.
- As a result of a new road system and link with the mainland, urbanisation has increased in the region.
- The eastern Scheldt is closed only when there is danger of flooding, so sea fishing can continue here.
- Other coastal fisheries of prawns, shrimps, oysters and mussels have disappeared.
- About 40 000 acres of new polder have been created.

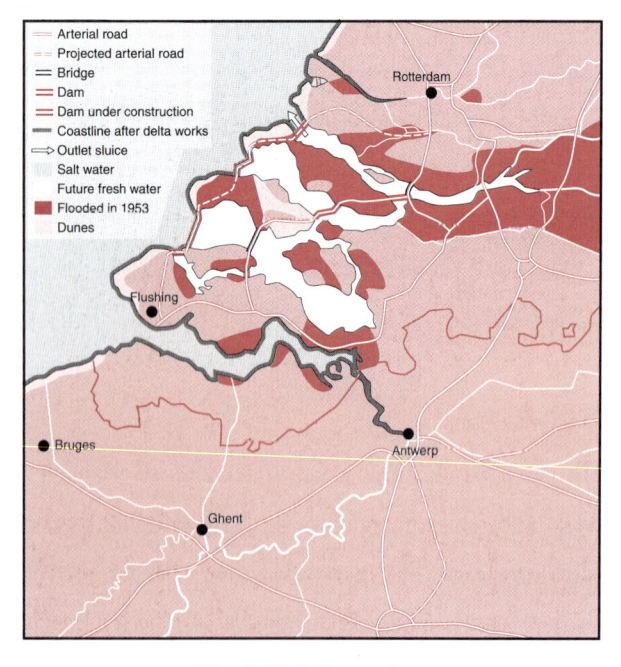

Fig 4.15 Delta region

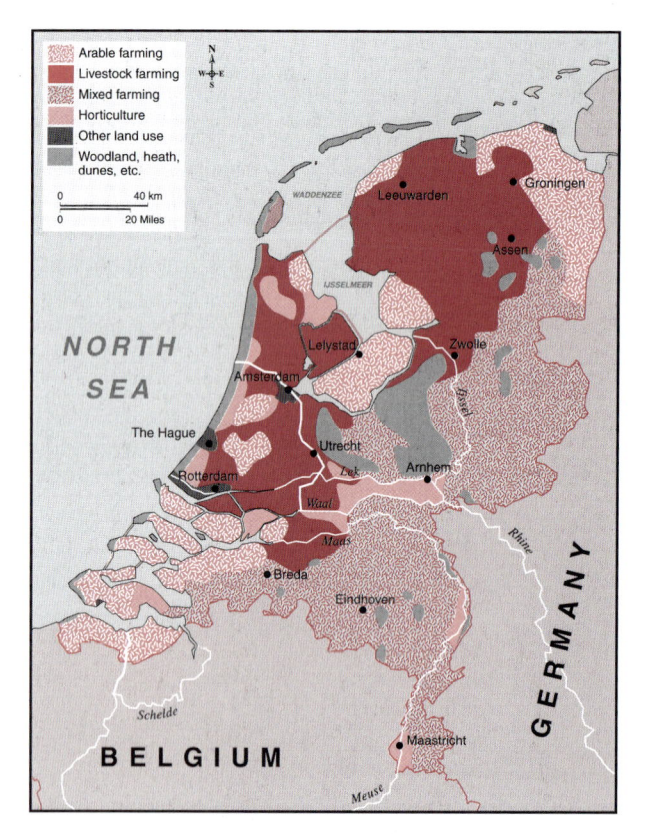

Fig. 4.16 Agriculture

AGRICULTURE IN THE NETHERLANDS

After the US and France, the Netherlands is the world's largest exporter of agricultural produce and food stuffs. This position has been achieved through the expertise of the farmers, the quality of the products and the high standards in the food processing industry.

The Netherlands is a small country but about two thirds of its land is suitable for farming. Dutch agricultural production is more intensive than in any other country in the world. It has to be. The small amount of land and the high costs of reclamation, drainage and protection demand high yields from the worked lands to make it profitable.

Most farming activities are carried on, and the variations in farm practices can be accounted for by reference to soil type, water supply and drainage. Arable farming is practised in the N.E., the S.W. delta lands and the Ijsselmeer. The soils here are fertile marine clays and the areas are well drained. Crops of cereals, sugar beet, fodder beet and potatoes are grown. In a land of traditionally small farms the arable farms are bigger than average – up to 40 ha. This makes mechanisation easier. Amalgamation and consolidation have reduced the number of Dutch arable farms but increased their size. Dutch cereals cannot meet the national demand but there is a major export of potatoes and seed potatoes.

About 35% of the land is pasture land and the rearing of beef and dairy cattle takes place on land which is considered too wet for arable farming. The main areas are the north and the provinces of north and south Holland. Here the high water table and the moderate climate ensure a good growth of grass.

Dairy farming is the more important end of the pastoral industry, but there is sufficient beef for the home market and a slight surplus for export. Milk is produced for two purposes. With 15 million people, there is a good demand for milk for immediate consumption but there is a huge market within the EU for processed milk – butter, cheese and other milk products.

Fig. 4.18 Dutch Farming

Mixed farming is carried on in the east and south of the country on the reclaimed heathlands. Cattle are usually stall fed during the winter months on locally grown feedstuffs. Maize is a favoured fodder crop.

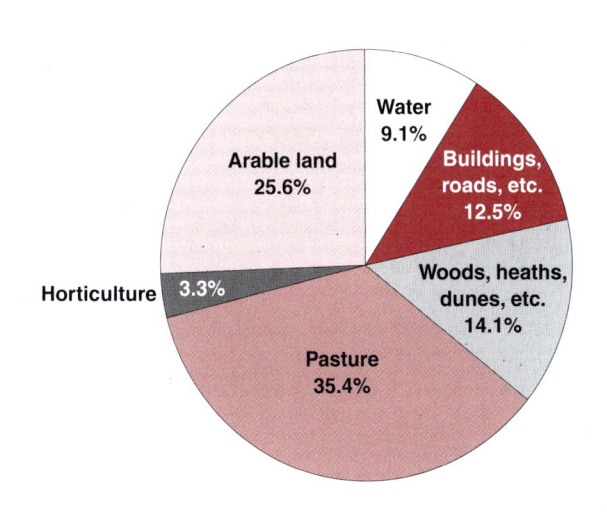

Fig. 4.17 Land use

More and more small farmers are concentrating on the *factory farming* of pigs, poultry and eggs. Little land is required and the controlled, scientific approach to production allows products of uniform quality. The pig population has increased 500% in the last thirty years to about 15 million animals now. Again the EU provides a large accessible market.

Market Gardening and Horticulture

Perhaps the best known farming activity of the Netherlands is that of market gardening and horticulture (see Fig. 4.16 for areas). The traditional bulb growing areas lie between Haarlem and Leiden in the shelter of the sand dunes. The millions of flowers are only a by-product, as the main farming is in the production of the bulbs. In recent years this form of horticulture has spread to north Holland and Friesland.

Salads are grown in the Westland region, south of The Hague, in heated glass houses. Cheap natural gas for heating and cheap home produced fertilisers aid production. Thousands of hectares of glass are found here and the enormous glasshouses are computerised to control heating and ventilation, watering and fertiliser systems. The success of the Westland area has led to the spread of glasshouse cultivation to other areas.

Vegetables and fruit are grown in many areas but the most productive region is the *Green Heart* at the centre of the Randstad. This is an area of intensive market gardening and horticulture and it accounts for about 40% of the country's agricultural income.

In line with all Dutch farming, the Dutch farmers are ignoring products which they can import cheaply and are concentrating more and more on products which are early or out of season, and so command high world prices.

Fig. 4.19 Market Gardening

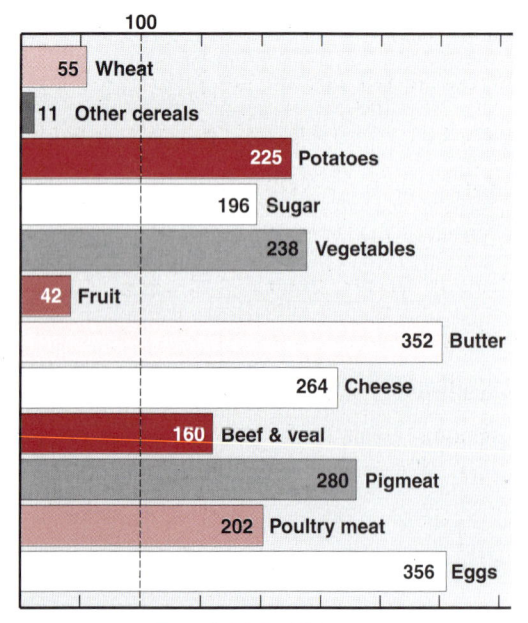

Product	Value
Wheat	55
Other cereals	11
Potatoes	225
Sugar	196
Vegetables	238
Fruit	42
Butter	352
Cheese	264
Beef & veal	160
Pigmeat	280
Poultry meat	202
Eggs	356

Fig. 4.20 Sufficiency

Glasshouse farmers are cultivating vegetables, flowers, pot plants and shrubs. These products attract a world-wide market, and with the aid of computers, are less labour intensive. The Netherlands accounts for 60% of the world's trade in cut flowers. Although only 5% of the population is engaged in farming, agriculture accounts for over 25% of exports. About 45% of all horticultural produce is exported.

What factors are responsible for the success of Dutch agriculture?

- The physical factors of soil and climate play their part. The land is flat and level with a good mixture of alluvial, reclaimed marine and sandy soils. The climate is equable, with adequate rainfall and early springs.
- The farms are generally small but specialised, leading to intensive farming of quality products. The high cost of the limited land area necessitates high yields and high prices.
- There is a large market at home and in nearby Europe and an expanding world market. Speed of delivery by air, road and rail is essential for perishable goods.
- There is a good back-up service of education, training, research and development supported by the government and the farmers' groups.
- There is an ongoing effort therefore to increase production both per hectare and per capita.
- A well developed co-operative system supports purchasing, credit, production and marketing.

THE RANDSTAD – PROBLEM REGION

SAMPLE QUESTION

> List the characteristics of the Randstad.
> Describe the main problems of this urbanised region.
> Discuss the efforts which have been made to solve the problems.

Throughout this text we identify and discuss problem regions in many countries such as the Norrlands of Scandinavia or the Mezzogiorno of Italy. In the Netherlands we also discover a problem region – the Randstad. But the Randstad is a problem region with a difference. It is the vibrant, prosperous city heart of the whole nation with enormous pressure on its limited land.

The main cities of western Netherlands have developed into a horseshoe shaped conurbation surrounding an agricultural green heart. Four main cities, Amsterdam, The Hague, Rotterdam and Utrecht, dominate this sprawling conurbation, but there are many other growth centres, e.g. Delft, Hilversum, Haarlem and Leiden. The Randstad opens to the south-east and is 100km from north to south and 80km from east to west. It houses half the country's population on 20% of the land.

Characteristics

1. The Randstad is not a Tokyo, London or Paris. It is a polycentric conurbation of many towns and cities, each retaining their own individual character and function.
2. **Amsterdam** is the financial and commercial capital of the Netherlands. It has finance, banking and commerce and is a major tourist focus. The North Sea Canal connects it to the open sea and there are two major industrial complexes associated with the canal. At Velsen there is a large integrated steel works using coke from the US and ore from Sweden. Zaandam lies nearer Amsterdam. It specialises in the processing of colonial raw materials and foodstuffs. Amsterdam is a thriving industrial port. **Utrecht**, in the centre of the country, is the major road and rail focus. As well as being the transport hub, Utrecht is characterised by service employment in banking and insurance. Over 500 international firms have been attracted to Utrecht including computer giants IBM and Digital. It is also the national centre for education, business services and conferences. **The Hague** is the seat of government and houses much of the political and administrative functions of the country. It is a service city and industry is only concerned with consumer industries – printing, clothing, footwear, food, etc. Over 75% of the workers are in the tertiary sector. (See **Rotterdam** – industrial city and port on page 73.)
3. The maritime tradition and trade of the Netherlands brought business, commerce and industry to this western area.
4. The Randstad is located where the great water routes (Rhine/North Sea) meet. The Randstad is at the heart of the core-axis of Europe (the Hot Banana on page 56). A massive infrastructure of roads, railways, canals, rivers and pipelines bring people, trade, industry and commerce to the Randstad.
5. The lack of natural resources in the eastern provinces started the movement towards the western cities where the opportunities for advancement were greatest.
6. Modern industry is footloose and people are mobile. This has led to a drift from the inner city to the suburbs creating ribbon development and urban sprawl – joining the towns, suburb to suburb, to create the conurbation.
7. During this century, there has been a remarkable growth in service industries. Most services seek city locations and this has led to an influx into the cities of the Randstad.

Problems

1. There are many problems within the Randstad and the chief one is the pressure on

land. Each sector wants its share and there is not enough to go round. Much of the inner city is being demolished to be replaced by car parks, office blocks, shopping centres and luxury apartments. Suburbs are growing with the demand for land increasing. It is estimated that Rotterdam alone needs 6 000 extra hectares each year.

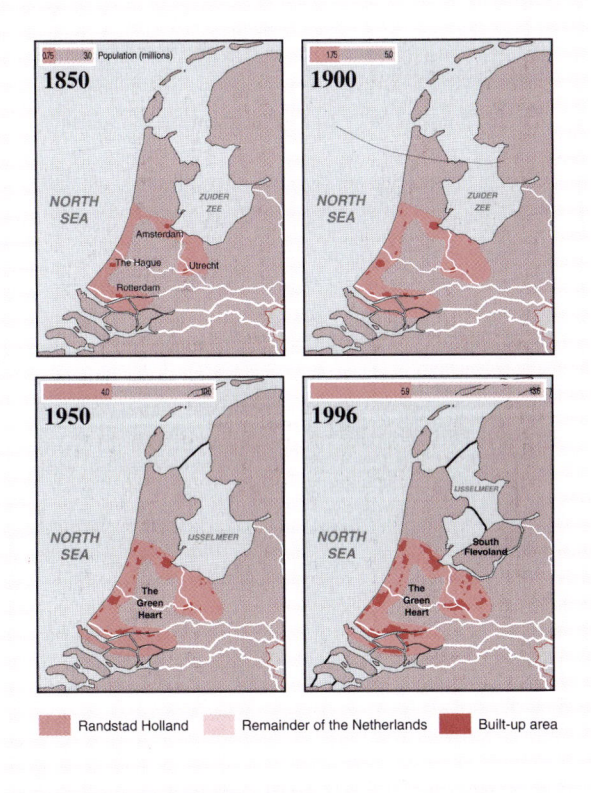

Fig. 4.21 The Netherlands: growth of the Randstad 1850-1996

2. Suburbanisation means more commuter traffic and more demand for better roads and rail links. Both eat into the land bank.
3. Increased traffic means more congestion, increased pollution and loss of man hours. Nearly two million cars converge on Rotterdam and Amsterdam daily.
4. The productive Green Heart is in danger.
5. Many MNCs have located their head offices and distribution centres in the Randstad to take advantage of the excellent communications network provided by Rotterdam, Amsterdam and Schiphol Airport. Schiphol now needs another airport. All this is choking the Randstad.
6. The Ruhr is growing westward and the Brussels-Antwerp axis extends to the north. There is a danger that a giant megalopolis might develop in this part of Europe stretching from Amsterdam to Bonn. However, by restricting the growth of the Randstad, there is the danger that the advantages which it enjoys might be lessened.

Responses to the Problems

The Dutch authorities are properly concerned about the Randstad. They must look at the present situation and the resources of the region, as well as to the future needs of housing, industry, transport and recreation. But the future of the Randstad cannot be looked at in isolation. It has to be planned in the context of overall planning for the entire country.

Dutch planners put forward a series of policies during the 70s and 80s to deal with the problems of growth. Development and investment were encouraged in the northern and eastern provinces. Grants, subsidies and tax concessions were put in place and this policy was helped by the availability of natural gas supplies. This took some of the pressure off the Randstad.

The preservation of the Green Heart was of prime concern as it was vital to the economy of the whole country. Severe restrictions were placed on future building but inevitably some of the land was lost to roads, railways and essential building. Buffer zones were developed between the towns and cities. Recreational and amenity areas were established in these zones. The Randstad was not allowed to grow inwards towards the Green Heart, so four corridors, or axes of growth, were designated as illustrated in the map below, Fig. 4.22.

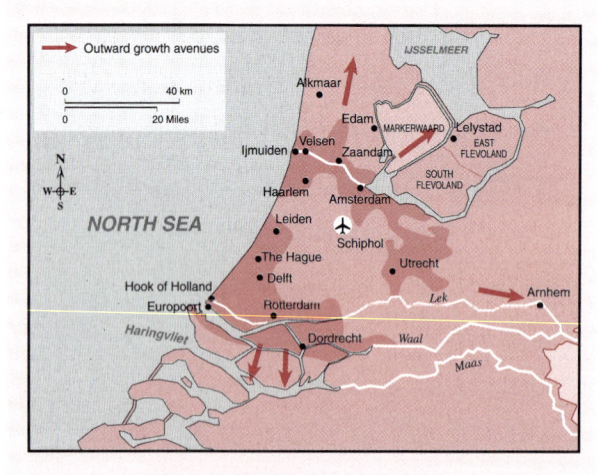

Fig. 4.22 The Netherlands: future growth axes of the Ranstad

The reclamation of the Zuider Zee and the development of the delta lands provided space along three of the axes. Utrecht had some space to the east.

One of the major problem areas was that of The Hague, as it could not expand to the north, south or west. A compromise was reached with the building of a new town, Zoetermeer, to the east. However, the growth of this town is planned and monitored to prevent any movement into the Green Heart.

The Dutch government is now satisfied that the situation has been brought under control without weakening the Randstad or neglecting the other provinces.

MANUFACTURING INDUSTRY

SAMPLE QUESTION

Write an account of manufacturing industry in the Netherlands under the headings:
1. Factors in the expansion of industry
2. Distribution of industry
3. Types of industry.

Manufacturing industry in the Netherlands did not develop on a wide scale until this century with the greatest expansion occurring after 1945.

The Netherlands lacked the coal and mineral resources that stimulated the industrial revolution in Britain, Belgium and Germany, as the Limburg coalfield was not developed until this century.

Industry in the Netherlands developed from a number of sources. Food processing and textiles were always present to supply the home market. During the seventeenth century the Netherlands enjoyed its *Golden Age*. Its mercantile and commercial life prospered. Two consequences of this should be noted. In the first instance, the shipbuilding industry flourished, providing the vessels for the commercial fleet. Secondly, industry was established to process the raw materials brought from the Baltic, the Mediterranean and the overseas colonies. The west coast ports became the centres for the processing and thus were laid the foundations for the industrial expansion of areas such as Amsterdam, Rotterdam, Dordrecht and Haarlem. A period of decline set in during the nineteenth century, but during the twentieth century rapid expansion occurred.

Dutch industry developed more because of the position of the Netherlands than because of any abundance of natural resources. In fact, the Netherlands had very few natural resources, so most of the materials for industry had to be imported. To achieve a balance of payments, many of the industrial products had to be exported. This gave rise to the Dutch emphasis on exports. A positive balance of payments was only achieved when natural gas came on stream and was exported to Europe.

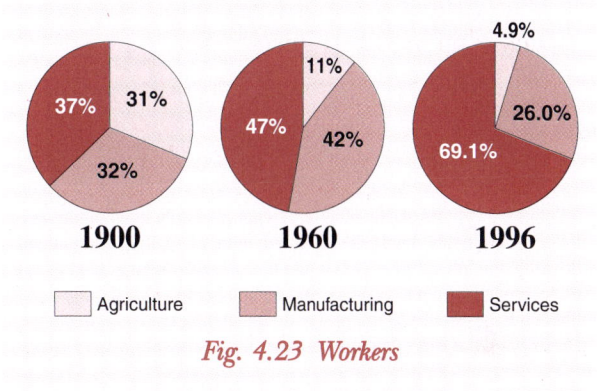

Fig. 4.23 Workers

The employment structure in the Netherlands is broadly similar to that of the other industrial countries of Europe. The agricultural and fishing sector has fallen from 31% in 1900 to 5% in 1996. Initially, the industrial sector rose to a high of 42% but has since dropped back to 26%.

Many factors have contributed to the expansion of the industrial sector but of critical importance is the strategic location of the Netherlands within the core axis of the EU supported by an impressive communications network.

Consider the following events which occurred this century:

- Pressure from a rising population – 9 million in 1900 to 15 million in 1996 – to create jobs.

Fig. 4.24 Parliament Buildings, The Hague

- Development of the Limburg coalfields in the early 1900s and the Groningen gas field in 1958 gave an impetus to manufacturing industry.
- The import of colonial raw materials and the expansion of home produced agricultural products.
- The strong Dutch merchant navy which facilitated the import of raw materials to Velsen, Amsterdam, Rotterdam and Dordrecht.
- The ease of communications across the Netherlands and into Europe.
- The strategic location on the Rhine and North Sea and the size of its hinterland with an ever increasing market.
- The recognition by major MNCs of the advantages of the Netherlands for manufacturing and particularly for distribution.

Distribution of Industry

The major expansion in industry took place after 1945. The economic post-war boom, the new developments in technology, the new consumer products and the huge demand in Europe were reflected in the industrial expansion in the Netherlands. In the 70s, 80s and 90s, with the expansion of the EU and the development of the Single Market, US and Japanese firms began to locate in Europe with 20% of Japanese investment going to the Netherlands. Traditionally industry located along the west, near the ports, and that tradition continues today. However, government assistance was provided to establish industry in the other provinces but industry developed there at a much slower pace. Limburg had a coal base and developed the early chemical industry. It still flourishes today but uses oil and gas. Many of the eastern and northern industries use native raw materials in textiles and food processing. Even today, despite the government's efforts, the west and south still predominate. Study the chart alongside.

Industry accounts for 70% of exports and employs about 26% of the labour force. Manufacturing is characterised by the high quality of the products and the high level of labour productivity. This is based on mechanisation, automation and a highly skilled workforce. There is an high annual investment in education, research and development. Dutch industry has penetrated the

North	East	West	South	Netherlands
79,200	179,720	318,600	269,490	**847,010**
9.4%	21.2%	37.6%	31.8%	**100%**

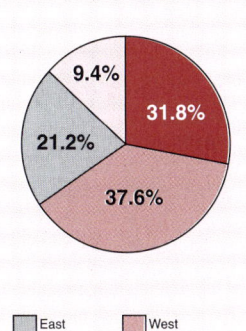

Fig. 4.25 Employees

world market with factories and sales offices all around the world. At the same time foreign firms employ 200 000 of the 1.1 million industrial workers.

Four industries and three MNCs – Shell, Philips and Unilever – dominate the industrial scene:

- Iron, steel, engineering and electricals
- Food, drink and tobacco
- Textiles
- Chemicals and petro-chemicals.

Iron, Steel, Engineering and Electricals

Iron and steel is now a major industry in the Netherlands. There are small works at Rotterdam, Dordrecht and Haarlem but the country's chief plant is at Velsen, at the mouth of the North Sea Canal, where a large integrated steel works uses imported ores and coal. The coastal location is ideal for the import of both. Engineering, which uses the local steel, is very well developed. The range of products is extensive and includes cars, agricultural machinery, dairy equipment, machines, tools, pumps and drainage equipment. The biggest steel user is shipbuilding. There are yards at Rotterdam, Amsterdam and Dordrecht.

Dutch shipyards concentrate on building medium sized and small ships with half of all orders coming from abroad. With their experience in drainage and flood control, pontoons and dredgers feature highly. Specialist ships, such as factory ships for fishing, container ships, etc., are also built. There is a growing market in exploration platforms, rigs, etc.

Philips is the dominant figure in the electrical field with 44 000 employed at Eindhoven. It produces domestic appliances, electronics, lighting equipment, medical systems and communications systems, etc. There are varied engineering works in all the major cities. An interesting statistic is that 50% of EU and 80% of world greenhouses come from the Netherlands.

Food Processing

Two branches of this industry should be noted. The section along the west coast had its origins in the colonial days when cheap raw materials were imported from the colonies. Even though the colonies have been lost, the supply routes and the trade still continue. The former colonies provide the raw materials for a wide range of food industries – grain, sugar, spices, vegetable oils, tea, coffee and tobacco. The expanding agricultural climate at home added to the supply of raw materials and promoted new branches of the trade. Chief centres are at Rotterdam, Amsterdam, Delft, Schiedam and Dordrecht.

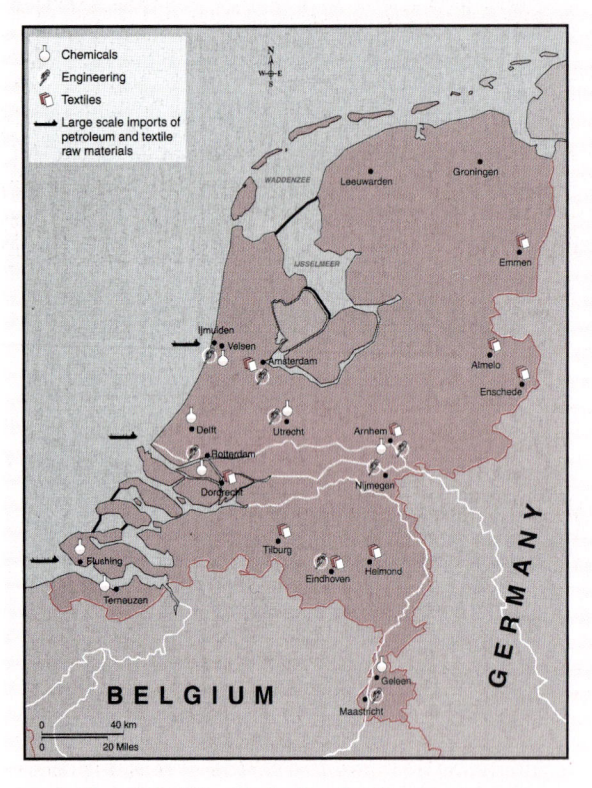

Fig. 4.26 The Netherlands: distribution of engineering, textile and chemical industries

The second branch of this industry is found in the eastern provinces and is based mainly on the processing of local raw materials. Grain milling, sugar beet, cheese, butter, milk products, brewing and distilling form the major industries at centres such as Leeuwarden, Groningen, Arnhem, Edam, Emmen and Oss.

Food processing is the country's biggest industry, employing 155 000 people and accounting for 26% of industrial exports.

Textiles

This was a typical cottage industry which gradually progressed through the years to a factory-based one. The early industry was a feature of life in the south and east, where local supplies of wool and the soft water were establishing factors. It is still found here (geographical inertia), even though traditional textiles have suffered a decline. Cheap imports from the Far East and the emergence of synthetics are responsible for the decline. Enschede is the main cotton centre. Tilburg is noted for woollens and Eindhoven for linen. Synthetics are developing rapidly, in response to demand, both in the traditional textile areas and in other centres, where oil and gas-based raw materials are available, e.g. Emmen, Arnhem and Dordrecht.

Chemicals and petro-chemicals

As in other European countries, the chemical industry has made remarkable progress since World War 2.

Many factors have contributed to the growth of the chemical industry:

- Good transport routes – canals, pipelines, road and rail – which facilitate the easy

movement of raw materials and finished products.
- An affluent market at home and within the EU.
- Native supplies of gas and salt.
- The position of Rotterdam as the oil port of Europe.

The oil-based industries are at Rotterdam, Amsterdam and Velsen. In the south the Geleen chemical industries were based on local coal but now use oil and gas brought in by pipeline.

Hengelo and Enschede use local salt while the Gröningen and Delfzijl chemicals are based on the local natural gas. The industry produces both light and heavy chemicals and the products include acids, sodas, fertilisers, plastics, synthetic fibres, pharmaceuticals and photographic chemicals.
The industry has over 100 000 workers in about 300 concerns.

The range and spread of Dutch industry is quite impressive and includes all the usual consumer goods.

Rotterdam

Fig. 4.27 Rotterdam

The city of Rotterdam is situated on the river Rotta, a small tributary of the Maas about 18km from the open sea, to which it is connected by the ship canal, the New Waterway. The port of Rotterdam stretches from the Hook of Holland to the city along the New Waterway and hence along the Maas and Waal to Dordrecht. It is the busiest port in the world.

Three distinct stages may be noted in the development of Rotterdam:

1. It started life as a small fishing village connected to the sea by a long winding channel. The growth of Rotterdam matched that of the Dutch colonial power. At the end of the eighteenth century it was second only to Amsterdam with a population of about 50 000. The great drawback to its further expansion at this stage was the winding channel to the sea.

2. In 1872 a canal, the New Waterway, was opened connecting the city to the open sea. This canal is wide and lock-free and gives easy access to deeper coastal waters where large ships can dock. The opening of the canal coincided with two major developments. The age of steam had arrived and with it the need for wide channels and deep harbours. Secondly, this period marked the great expansion of industry and trade in Europe. New waterways and roads were constructed and Rotterdam became the focal point for much of that trade. Even at this time Rotterdam was not much busier than Amsterdam or Antwerp. Its main dock areas were along the south bank of the New Waterway at Maashaven, Waalhaven, etc.

3. Rapid expansion has taken place since the end of the last war with the economic boom in Europe. The New Waterway has been deepened to take even the largest carriers.

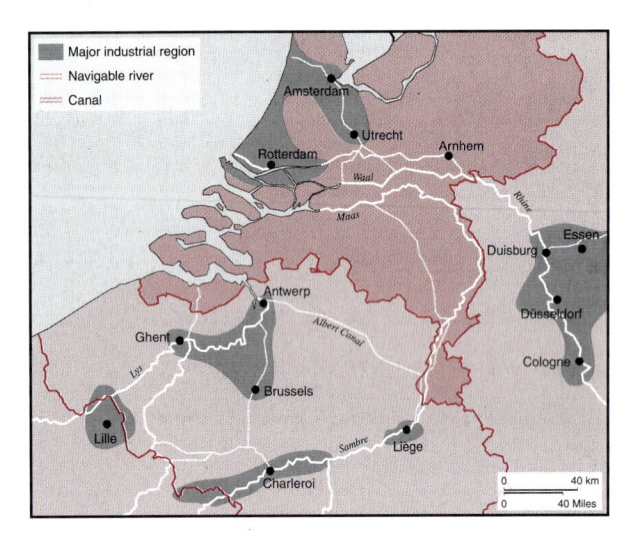

Fig. 4.28 Rotterdam: hinterland

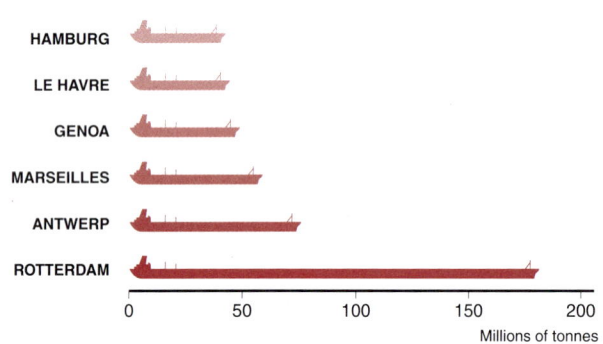

Fig. 4.29 Total traffic in European ports

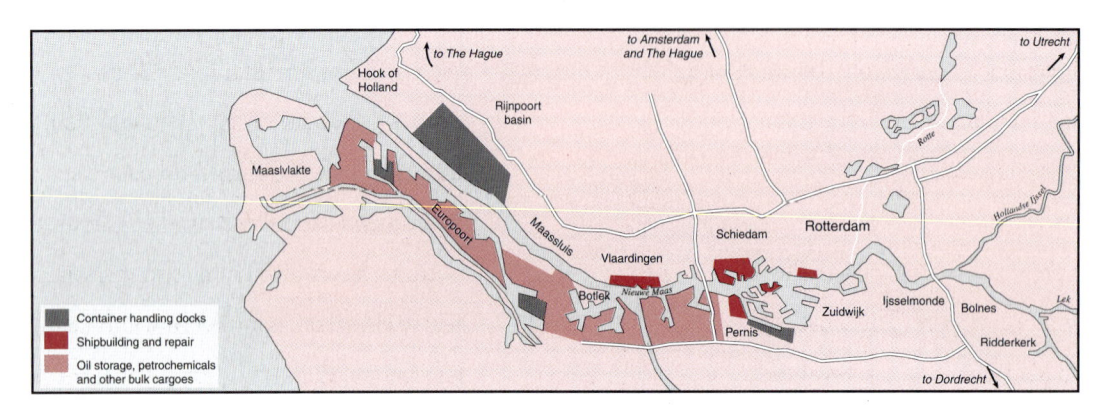

Fig. 4.30 Rotterdam-Europort

Obviously the original dock facilities along the New Waterway were insufficient to meet the growing demands of the port trade. The deeper waters downstream from the city have been developed and each port and dock area has a particular function. Pernis was the first to be developed for oil and chemicals and this was followed by Botlek, Maassluis and Rijnpoort. Europoort, opposite the Hook of Holland, was completed in the 70s and is used to accommodate the giant oil tankers and grain carriers. It can handle oil tankers of 300 000 tonnes. Recently completed is the reclamation of Maasvlakte where another 7 500 acres is available for port works and docks.

We see Rotterdam then as the busiest port in the world and the most significant industrial centre in the Netherlands. But the city has its problems. The chief problem at present is pollution. Water pollution is particularly serious, with this stretch of the Rhine often referred to as the sewer of Europe. The oil refineries, chemical and fertiliser factories cause air pollution, creating problems for the residential areas. There is also the problem of land usage similar to that experienced in other parts of the Randstad.

There are constant worries about housing and recreation – both related to the competition for land. At times industrial considerations have often outweighed any others. This has resulted in some outmigration from the port and industrial areas.

A further problem is the strong challenge to Rotterdam's supremacy as an oil port. This challenge will come from Genoa and Marseilles in the years ahead.

Questions

1. Randstad Holland.
   (a) What are the main problems of this region? What are the causes of these problems?
   (b) Discuss the efforts which have been made and other measures which you suggest should be adopted to help solve the problems of the region. (L.C. Higher Level)

2. Account for the economic importance of land reclamation in the Netherlands. (LC. Higher Level)

3. 'Water is both friend and enemy to the Dutch.' Discuss.

4. Discuss the role of (a) the Rhine, (b) the polders and (c) natural gas, in the industrial development of the Netherlands.

5. (a) Account for the high concentration of the population in the western Netherlands.
   (b) Comment on recent changes in the pattern of population distribution in the Netherlands. (L.C. Ordinary Level)

6. Write geographical notes on each of the following:
   (a) The Zuider Zee Project.
   (b) The development of Rotterdam-Europoort as a major port.
   (c) Horticulture in the Netherlands.

7. 'Despite the high density of population, there is no question of the Netherlands being over-populated in an economic sense; but one may speak of territorial overpopulation, which is reflected in problems of recreation, space, traffic and environmental pollution.'
   (a) By referring to particular areas within the Netherlands, examine the causes of these

problems, and the measures proposed by Dutch planners to control or lessen them.

(b) Explain the main features of the Delta Project. Describe briefly four of the main results.

(L.C. Ordinary Level)

8 Contrast the east and west of the Netherlands in terms of (a) population density, (b) industrial development and (c) environment.

9 With the aid of a sketch map describe the location of Rotterdam. Give a brief account of the traffic through the port under the headings (a) cargoes, (b) origins or sources, (c) destinations. (L.C. Ordinary Level)

10 Much of the Netherlands consists of the delta of the Rhine and its distributaries. What are the advantages and disadvantages?

11 Discuss the importance of the strategic location of the Netherlands within the EU.

12 Outline the chief characteristics of Dutch farming.

13 In the case of the Netherlands, identify and explain some of the factors which have influenced: (a) development of agriculture, (b) development of manufacturing industry. (L.C. Ordinary Level)

14 The Netherlands is now seen as an attractive base for many MNCs. Explain the advantages which the Netherlands has for these firms.

15 With reference to Rotterdam, examine the ways in which the development of transport links has encouraged economic growth.

chapter five
belgium

INTRODUCTION

Area:	30 520 sq km
Population:	9.85 million
Density:	323 per sq km

Like the Netherlands, Belgium occupies a central position in north-west Europe and forms a meeting point for trade routes from the Baltic, the North European Plain and the French lowlands. In history, it has been the cockpit of Europe, a battleground for rival armies and a buffer state between France and Germany. Today it is a densely populated, highly urbanised country, criss-crossed by important transport systems.

Although a small country, Belgium presents interesting geographical contrasts – of relief, landscape and culture. The wooded hill slopes of the Ardennes (500m) in the south-east are in striking contrast to the flat polders and fertile undulating lowlands (100m) of the north-west (Flanders Plain, Central Low Plateau). Throughout the country, intensively cultivated and densely populated farmlands lie alongside industrial towns and the distinction between rural and urban areas is often blurred.

As in the Netherlands, empty space is very scarce. Competition for land is very strong and the Belgians have had their own battles with the sea along the coast of Flanders.

CLIMATE

The climate type (cool temperate oceanic) is the same as that of Ireland and the Netherlands. Maritime influences are dominant and result in mild winters, cool summers and a moderate, well-distributed rainfall. The marked contrast between the climate in the northern half of the country (low Belgium) and south of the Sambre-Meuse Valley (high Belgium) reflects the influence of altitude and increasing distance from the sea. The northern lowland region has an average annual rainfall of 770mm, with mean monthly temperatures ranging from 2°C in January to 17°C in July. In the south, rainfall is heavier (1 200mm) and winter temperatures are often below freezing point, especially in the Ardennes region.

Fig. 5.1 View of Brussels

Natural resources and advantages

Location

Coal

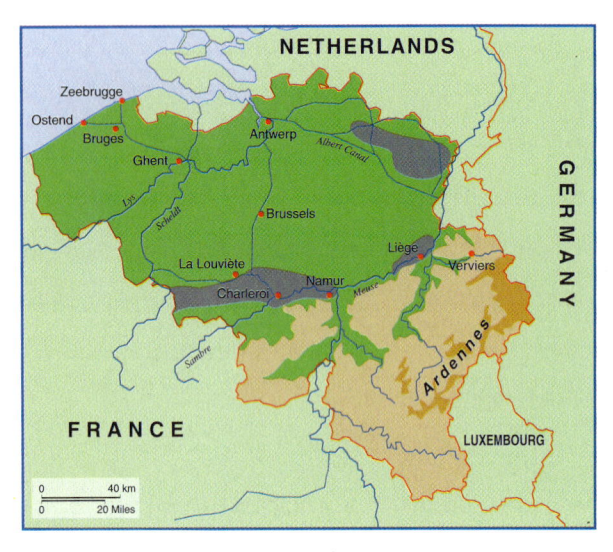

Fig. 5.2 Location

Location

Belgium shares with its neighbours a strategic location in north-west Europe that is a very positive natural resource because of the many advantages it confers on them. The elements of this strategic location may be summarised as follows:

1. Belgium is situated where the North European Plain narrows sharply between the Hercynian Uplands and the North Sea. Its location on this important lowland route between the uplands and the sea has been of great economic advantage. All through history the lowland area has been a meeting point for trade routes from northern France and Germany.

2. Two of Europe's most important rivers, the Meuse and the Rhine, flow through Belgium and the Netherlands and deposit their deltas in the North Sea. These rivers serve an extensive and highly productive hinterland.

3. Such a favourable location in relation to France, Britain and Germany has provided Belgium with valuable markets for its farming and industrial products.

4. It has also proved of immense benefit to the ports of Antwerp, Rotterdam and Amsterdam through which is funnelled much of the industrial output of northern France and Germany.

5. Commercial activities and international trade are therefore the economic lifeline of Belgium and the Netherlands and have played a major part in their prosperity.

6. However, the very importance of such a strategic location has resulted in the invasion, occupation and devastation of Belgium and the Netherlands by foreign armies in two world wars.

Coal

Belgium had two coalfields, the Sambre-Meuse in the south and the Campine in the north-east. The Sambre-Meuse coalfield is a continuation of the Nord coalfield of France. It is long and narrow and extends for 160km along the northern flanks of the Ardennes. This was the birthplace of Belgium's industrial revolution in the nineteenth century. A continuous zone of industrial towns – Mons, La Louviere, Charleroi, Namur, Liege – developed along the coalfield.

Decline of the Sambre-Meuse coalfield

Today, however, the Sambre-Meuse coalfield and industrial region is in decline. Coal-mining has now disappeared and the resulting unemployment has devastated the whole region.

The causes of this decline may be summarised thus:

1. The coalfield was developed early in the nineteenth century and most of the accessible coal has been mined.

2. The remaining coal seams are very deep and steeply faulted. This makes it very difficult, dangerous and expensive to mine.

3. Many of the companies mining the coalfield were too small to compete with the giant coal producers of Europe.

4. Competition from foreign energy sources, in particular oil and natural gas, led to a declining demand for Sambre-Meuse coal. Cheaper oil meant that coal prices had to be reduced, but this was impossible because of the increasing costs of coal production. In addition, the major oil refineries were located near the ports in the north of Belgium – the country's developing industrial region.

5. Attempts by the European Coal and Steel Community (ECSC) to prop up the ailing coalfield concentrated on closing many uneconomic mines, retraining miners for other industrial jobs and assisting miners to move to other areas in Belgium where jobs were available.

6. The decline was most intense in the Borinage and Centre coalfields which were largely dependent on mining and lacked other compensating industries.

The Campine coalfield

The Campine coalfield is located in the northern heathland and its development dates from 1917. Coal mining has now ceased in this region also. The last mine closed in 1992.

	Sambre-Meuse		Campine	
	Production (million tonnes)	Number of Pits	Production (million tonnes)	Number of Pits
1961	11.9	47	9.6	7
1981	0.3	1	5.8	5
1993	Nil	Nil	Nil	Nil

Fig. 5.3 Coal production in the Sambre-Meuse and Campine coalfields

SAMPLE QUESTION

Divide Belgium into its regions and show that division on a sketch map. Select three of the regions and describe their main characteristics under the headings

    1   Physical geography
    2   Agriculture
    3   Industry.

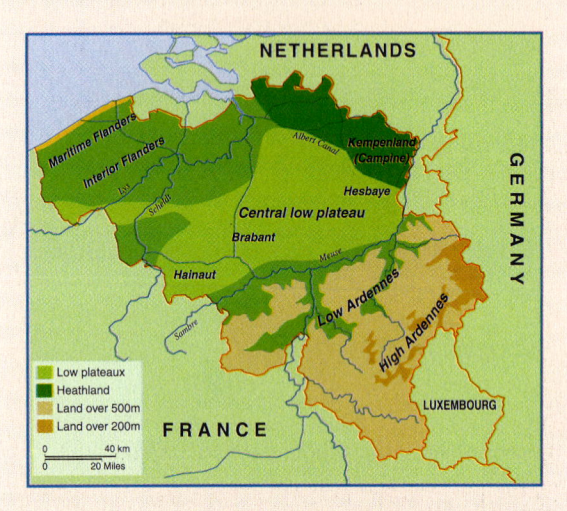

Fig. 5.4 Physical regions

Belgium consists of six major regions, numbered 1 - 6 on the map above, Fig. 5.4. They are:

1   Maritime Flanders
2   Interior Flanders
3   Central Low Plateaus
4   Sambre-Meuse valley
5   Ardennes
6   Campine.

Interior Flanders

Interior Flanders is a gently rolling plain, with an average height of about 50m. The rivers Lys, Scheldt and Dender flow slowly to the Scheldt estuary across rich alluvial valleys. The north has light sandy soils and the south is covered in heavy damp loams. The climate is typical cool temperate maritime with warm summers (17°C), mild winters (3°C) and rainfall of 800mm well distributed throughout the year.

The farmers of Interior Flanders were in the forefront of the agricultural revolution, introducing heavy manuring and crop rotation. For centuries this has been an area of intensive farming and dense settlement.

The farms are small with an average size of five hectares and the worker-peasant system is characteristic of the region. Farms in the north of the plain are often worked entirely by hand while those in the south are bigger and have some degree of mechanisation. The main cereals grown are barley, oats and wheat for milling and winter fodder. The production of industrial crops such as sugar beet, hops, tobacco, chicory and flax is an important aspect of agriculture in Interior Flanders. Flax is a specialised crop grown on the damp clay soils of the Lys-Escaut valley. These crops provide the raw materials for some of the region's industries – another example of the close link between rural and urban Belgium.

Almost every farm carries a few dairy cows which supply milk, cheese and butter to local urban markets. Around the larger urban centres of the plain there is an emphasis on market gardening.

There is also considerable industrial development in Flanders. This is the traditional home of the textile industry, which dates back to the Middle Ages. The woollen and linen industries were the first to be developed, using local wool and flax. Cotton was later introduced and in this century there was a change to synthetics. Cotton and synthetics now dominate the industry at Ghent, Tournai and Courtrai.

With the rationalisation of the steel industry, new integrated steel mills have been established at Zelgate on the coast, using imported ores from Sweden and Mauretania and coal from the USA. The Zelgate works supply the shipbuilding industry in Antwerp and the many engineering firms across the region. Car assembly, electronics and electricals are prominent.

Food processing is another major industry located at many centres. The industry uses local produce to supply the main urban centres and as a raw material for brewing, distilling, flour, sugar, etc.

The manufacture of agricultural machinery, fertilisers, chemicals, etc., is an important sector supporting agriculture.

Ghent is a major route focus as it lies at the confluence of the Lys and Scheldt, and is connected by canal to Bruges, Ostend and Antwerp. The main motorways from the coast pass through Ghent. Textiles remain the major industry, but shipbuilding, engineering, chemicals, petro-chemicals and glassware are also important.

Antwerp, on the Scheldt, lies on the edge of Interior Flanders. It is the major city of the region and the focus point for Flanders and much of Belgium. It is connected by canal with Brussels, Charleroi and Liege. Motorways fan out from Antwerp to the rest of Belgium and into industrial Europe.

Antwerp is the gateway to the core axis of Europe. Its varied industries include shipbuilding, oil refining, chemicals, petro-chemicals, food processing (home and imported products), car assembly, electronics, etc.

Central Low Plateaus

The Central Low Plateaus lie between the rivers Scheldt and Meuse. This is a region of gently rolling low plateaus and wide river valleys. They lie between 60m and 150m in height. Most of the region is covered in limon (loess) with alluvial soils on the lower flood plains of the rivers. The damp heavy clays of Flanders extend to the south and west of this region, while to the north the plateaus merge with the Campine, where the soils developed on sands and gravels are not very fertile. Many small tributaries (e.g. the Senne and Demer) drain to the Scheldt. The climate is similar to that of Flanders with summers 1°C or 2°C warmer. Rainfall is adequate – about 800mms – for most agricultural activities.

The limon soils give rise to a rich and diverse agricultural economy. Although highly intensive, the structure and type of farming contrast with that of Interior Flanders. Farms are much larger than in Flanders and much more mechanised. As a result, there is high productivity and the prosperous farmhouses are evidence of a high standard of living. This is Belgium's major cereal-growing region, with wheat the chief crop. Sugar beet is also important. In Brabant, intensive market gardening is a feature of agriculture. The area near Brussels has a large concentration of glasshouses, specialising in the production of table grapes, vegetables and salads.

Manufacturing industry is spread widely across the region. The textile industry has spread east from Flanders and is well established in Brussels and Anderlecht. Engineering industries in many centres are fed from a large integrated steelworks at Clabecq on the Brussels-Charleroi canal. The manufacture of agricultural machinery is particularly important. Louvain is a noted centre.

The rich agricultural lands provide the raw material for the food processing industry, of which a section is located in most of the smaller towns. Brewing, distilling, flour, sugar, vegetable freezing and canning are all important. Agriculture is supported by the fertiliser and chemical concerns. **Brussels**, on the river Senne, dominates the region. For over 1 000 years it has been one of the great cities of Europe. It is a port and a focus point for road, rail and canal routes. The great motorways to Paris, Amsterdam, Cologne, etc., run through Brussels. It is a major industrial centre with chemicals, pharmaceuticals, engineering, clothing, food processing, etc.

Above all, Brussels is a tertiary city as national capital and administrative centre of the EU. It is the centre of government, finance, administration and insurance.

The Ardennes

From the lowlands of the Sambre-Meuse valley rises the only upland region in Belgium – the Ardennes. This upland has an average height of 350m. The surface is one of undulating plateaus with peaks emerging to 500m. Rivers flow to the north and west towards the Meuse in deep winding valleys. The Semois, Ourthe, Ambleve and Vesdre are the chief tributaries. Peat and heath cover much of the land and there are extensive plantations of spruce and pine on the hill slopes.

Fig. 5.5 Dairy farming in the lower hill slopes of the Ardennes

The climate is more severe than in the rest of Belgium, with winter temperatures below 0°C and snow for up to two months. Summer temperatures average 18°C. Precipitation is well distributed throughout the year, but with a winter maximum. Total precipitation is 1 400mm – the highest in Belgium.

The Ardennes is a zone of marginal farming because of the relief, heavy rainfall and thin infertile soils. Farms are small and are mainly in pasture, with some oats, rye, barley, potatoes and beet. Cattle are reared but are sent north for fattening. Some dairying is practised in the sheltered valleys on the lower hill slopes. A speciality of the Semois valley is the cultivation of tobacco. Forestry is an important land use and timber is a major resource. Farms are being abandoned as there is a persistent out-migration of young people to the more advantaged north. This is the least densely populated region of Belgium with a total population of 200 000.

There are a number of small towns in the region, mainly located at junction or crossing points or on the rivers. These towns – Marche, Bastogne, La Roche, St. Vith – serve as market and service centres for the farming population. Some small food processing concerns and timber mills operate in the region, but the scale of industry is small.

Tourism is a thriving service industry, as the Ardennes is a region of outstanding scenic beauty which has escaped large-scale industrialisation. Tourism utilises the resources of woodland, slopes, forest walks, attractive valleys and picturesque villages. The many towns involved include Spa (the original Spa town), Dinant, La Roche, Bouillon. Many Belgians have a second home (weekend cottage) in the Ardennes. This brings commerce and trade and helps reduce the out-migration.

With modern transport the northern Ardennes region is now within commuting distance of the built-up areas of the Meuse, Middle Rhine and Luxembourg. Many of the northern and north-eastern towns – Spa, Barvaux, Theux – are now dormitory towns.

Population changes in Belgium (%)					
	1875	1958	1970	1984	1994
Flemish north	47	51	56	60	62
Walloon south	42	34	32	30	28
Brussels (bilingual)	11	15	12	10	10

THE NORTH-SOUTH CONTRAST

Although Belgium is a small country, it displays a number of striking contrasts on many levels – physical, religious, linguistic, cultural, political and economic. The contrast is between the north (Flanders) and the south (Wallonia) and the main differences may be noted as follows:

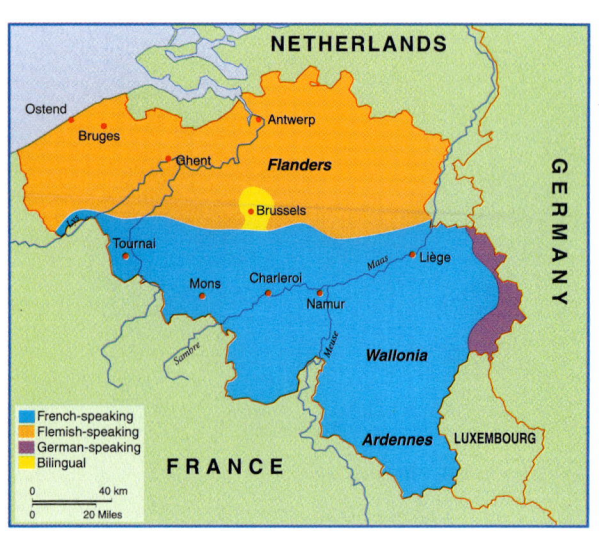

Fig. 5.6 Linguistic divide

	North (Flanders)		South (Wallonia)
1	Flanders is a low-lying extension of the North European Plain with a variety of productive soils. Agriculture is highly **intensive** with the emphasis on arable farming and market gardening.	1	The south is more elevated, especially in the south-east (Ardennes). Soils are poorer and the range of farming activities is **extensive.** Forestry is the main land-use in the Ardennes.
2	The Flemish are descended from **Germanic** tribes. They speak Flemish, a dialect of Dutch. They are strongly Catholic and conservative in outlook.	2	The Walloons are of **Celtic** origin. They speak French and are mainly Catholic. Their outlook is liberal and socialist.
3	For much of the nineteenth century, Flanders had mainly an **agricultural** economy. Rural Flanders was relatively under-developed.	3	Since Belgium gained independence in 1830, Wallonia was the most urbanised, **industrialised** and economically progressive part of Belgium.
4	The Flemish were regarded as socially inferior and were a **minority** of the population.	4	The Walloons were in a **majority** and were a prosperous and cultural elite. French was the official language of schools and of government.

North (Flanders)	South (Wallonia)
5 Today the Flemish comprise 60% of the population and their birthrate is higher than that of the Walloons. The economic axis of the country has now moved northwards to the new **growth areas** within Flanders, the Brussels-Ghent-Antwerp industrial triangle and the Campine area.	5 Walloons are now in a minority of the population, with a declining birth-rate. The dramatic decline in coal production from the Sambre-Meuse coalfield has been mirrored in the **decline** of Wallonia's traditional industries. Many of these industries have had to be restructured and rationalised.
6 A wave of **prosperity** has moved through the north with the development of modern industries and the injection of large-scale investment.	6 Wallonia is now a problem region. **Unemployment** is higher than elsewhere in Belgium.
7 With greater prosperity, the Flemish are now demanding more political and **economic power.**	7 The Walloons are very conscious of their minor position in Belgium today. They fear domination by Flemish politicians and seek greater **government investment** is their region.

Area of conflict

The language issue affects all aspects of daily life in Belgium. Walloons and Flemings live in their own parts of the country without making much contact. They attend their own schools, colleges and universities, marry within their own language group, and choose their shops and activities on the criterion of language – French or Flemish. They do not often visit each other's region. A law of 1932 established the *language line* (see Fig. 5.6). To the north of it Flemish placenames are the official form; to the south the placenames are in French. In places, the two forms of placenames are given. In the more militant linguistic areas, placenames are given in the one language only. Thus in some Flemish areas, roadsigns on important routeways point to cities that foreign motorists have never heard of: Rijsel for Lille, Luik for Liege and Bergen for Mons. Similarly in Wallonia the unfortunate foreigner is confused by Gand for Ghent, Anvers for Antwerp and Aix-la-Chapelle for Aachen.

The capital city, Brussels, lies at the centre of the language problem. Although it lies in the heart of the Flemish province of Brabant, it has been a predominantly French-speaking city for some 450 years and nearly 85% of its present population are French-speakers. Like all capitals it has continually expanded into the surrounding villages which of course are Flemish. To add to the problem, thousands of migrants from industrially depressed Wallonia have moved into these outer areas of Brussels and are demanding equal rights facilities for their language (French). In addition, these migrants have poured an environmental fuel on the language fire which now rages fiercely in these outer areas of Brussels. They have built their houses in a rather haphazard, unplanned fashion in their new Walloon villages and have thus destroyed the rural nature of the countryside in the south of Brabant. Brussels itself is officially a bilingual city and has many foreign residents. They are there because of NATO, the EU and foreign commercial and industrial firms. They do not see the language problem with the same intensity as do the Flemish and Walloons. To most of them, French is the language of diplomacy and trade throughout the world.

The linguistic cauldron that is constantly on the boil within Belgium is just one aspect of the political and economic differences between the two cultures – Flemish and Walloon. Until a solution is found, Belgium, small though it is, will remain a divided country.

INDUSTRIAL REGIONS

Belgium is one of the most industrialised countries in Europe and has a long tradition of industrial activity. Three major industrial regions form the core of Belgium's modern industrial development.

The Sambre-Meuse valley

Traditionally the location of Belgium's heavy industries, the region still remains the centre of the **steel industry**, which is concentrated around Liege and Charleroi. Local supplies of coking coal have been exhausted. Today coking coal comes from the Ruhr. High-grade ores are imported

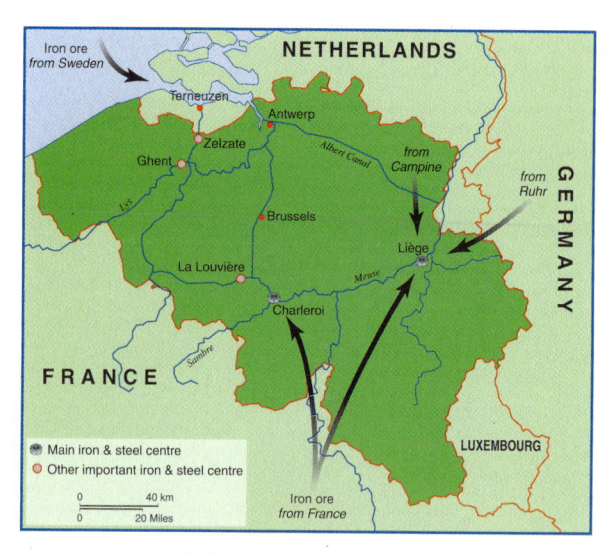

Fig. 5.7 Iron and steel industries

from Sweden, Lorraine and Luxembourg. Inland waterway transport of the bulky production materials is a vital factor. Charleroi is connected with Brussels and Antwerp by canal and Liege is linked to Antwerp by the Albert canal.

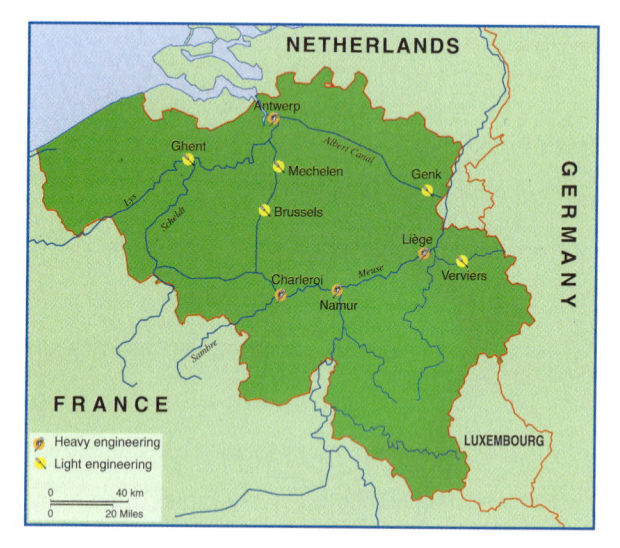

Fig. 5.8 Engineering

The **engineering industries** of the region provide a huge market for the steel products. In spite of recent problems in the Sambre-Meuse region, the steel and heavy engineering industries survive. This tendency of an industry to survive in its original location, even when the factors which favoured its location there no longer apply, is known as **industrial inertia**.

Liege is the cultural and industrial capital of Wallonia. Its economy is based on heavy industry. Belgium's major steelworks is located there and its metal manufacturing industries include zinc smelting, aircraft and heavy electrical machinery. Chemicals and glassworks are other important industries. Liege has adapted well to the decline in coalmining. Large industrial estates producing computers, electronic equipment, clothing and ceramics lie on the outskirts of the city, close to the modern motorways which link Liege to northern Belgium, France and west Germany. The Meuse river forms important communication links and the city can be reached by ocean-going ships from Antwerp. But in recent years, the Sambre-Meuse region has gone into decline.

Causes of the decline

1. The coalfields in the Sambre-Meuse valley were a major source of energy and a basis for industrial development in the nineteenth century. At one time there were 250 pits producing coal. The region's coal industry has now closed down. Its collapse has affected the traditional smokestack industries (iron and steel, engineering, chemicals). The reasons for the decline in coal production have been noted on page 79 of this chapter.
2. For a long time, Wallonia produced most of Belgium's steel. As in other west European countries, the steel industry was traditionally located near the coalfields. Coal supplied the energy and the coal-bearing strata also contained iron ore and limestone, the raw materials for the industry. Coalfields thus provided an unrivalled location for the steel industry. This was true of the Nord in northern France and the Ruhr in west Germany. Today the centre of gravity of the European steel industry has moved from the old industrial areas and steelmaking has moved from the coalfields to coastal locations. With the decline in cheap coal and with increasing competition from other countries, it became more economic to build modern, integrated steelmills in other parts of Belgium.
3. Other associated industries – engineering and chemicals – have also declined. The engineering industries obtained their steel from local steelmills and their energy from local coal. These are now less plentiful and so there is less reason for these industries to remain in Wallonia. In addition, the engineering industry had a local market. It provided many of the machines for the established industries of the region – glassmaking, metal smelting and chemicals. This market has now declined. Newer engineering factories elsewhere in Belgium are now making the machines for the modern industries.
4. The chemical industry of Wallonia, as elsewhere in western Europe, was based on coal. Changing energy sources, notably from coal to oil, and new technology led to the growth of petro-chemicals. The old chemical locations retained their importance, but have been overshadowed since oil became a major raw material, and therefore oil-importing ports became a major factor in the location of petro-chemical industries.
5. The decline of its major industries resulted in a decline of the construction industry in Wallonia. There is less

construction of new factories and houses. Much of the construction industry has moved to the dynamic and developing north, especially around Antwerp and Brussels.

Fig. 5.9 Major Motorways

6. The infrastructure of Wallonia is more suited to a nineteenth century industrial environment. Its communication system had been based largely on rail and canal transport, which was well suited to the heavy industry then developing in the region. Modern industry, with its greater variety and its emphasis on consumer goods, relies more heavily on a good network of motorways and canals that are deep enough to take the larger boats of today.

Fig. 5.10 Ghent

Revitalising Wallonia

The problems of the Sambre-Meuse region were not merely industrial. They were also intensely political, since Wallonia is the centre of Walloon culture. Early development policy aroused much anger because it favoured the Flemish north much more than the French-speaking south. Recent development has been much more favourable to Wallonia.

Huge amounts of ECSC and Belgian government funds have been invested in Wallonia to retrain unemployed miners, encourage native and foreign investment and attract new industries. Many new factories have been built, with the emphasis on clean growth industries – telecommunications, electronics, consumer goods and light industries. A number of industrial estates have been established throughout the region and have provided a much needed diversity and variety in Wallonia's industrial revitalisation. The basic infrastructure, notably in transport, has been improved and has contributed to a healthier economic outlook.

The Brussels-Antwerp-Ghent axis

This is the most rapidly expanding and densely populated region of Belgium. Its development is due to the increasing importance of Antwerp as an international port, the dynamic growth of Brussels as a national capital and the administrative centre of the EU and the development of an industrial region along the Ghent-Terneuzen canal.

Antwerp (800 000) has developed into an international port for three main reasons.

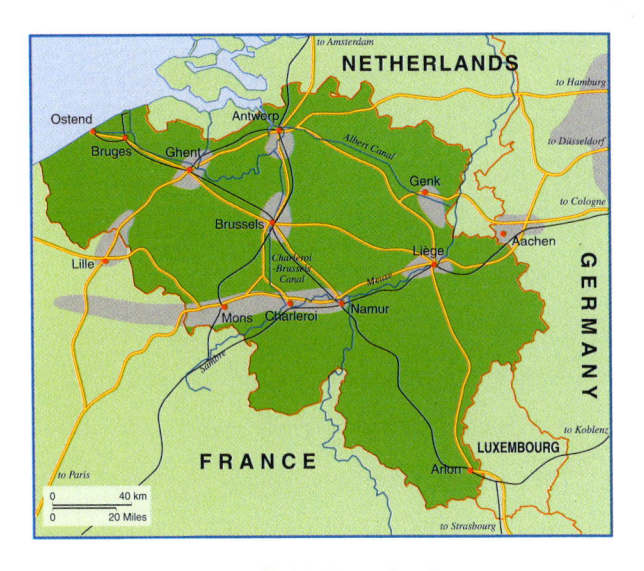

Fig. 5.11 Hinterland

1. Foreign trade is of vital importance to Belgium. Antwerp became a prosperous trading centre for clothing and spices in medieval times and later for the import of copper, diamonds and tropical products from the former Belgian colony of Zaire. These *colonial* imports still continue and form the basis of flourishing industries.
2. Antwerp is a gateway to the major industrial areas of western Europe. Not only does it serve a large industrial hinterland, handling much of Belgium's and Luxembourg's trade (64%) but its wider hinterland extends to north-east France, west Germany and the southern Netherlands. The Albert Canal links Antwerp to the Sambre-Meuse valley and the Campine. Motorway links are important, in particular the Antwerp-Brussels route and the Antwerp-Liege-Aachen route.
3. Large tracts of land were available at Antwerp for the extension of the docks and for industrial development. New docks have been built and connected to the Albert Canal along the east bank of the River Scheldt. Road tunnels under the river lead to modern industrial development on the west bank. But the most important port development has been the specialisation in container traffic. The number of containers handled has increased ten-fold over the past twenty years.

Antwerp is also a major industrial city. Dockside industries include oil refining, heavy chemicals, petro-chemicals, shipbuilding, car assembly and the processing of imported tropical foodstuffs. Factories along the banks of the Willebroek Canal (Antwerp to Brussels), produce ceramics, textiles and cement. Within the city, a wide range of precision and consumer goods are manufactured – radio, electronics, diamond-cutting, etc.

Brussels, an old walled city, with a population of over one million, stands as a bilingual island in the Flemish-speaking part of Belgium. It is the national capital and main industrial centre of Belgium and is also a major route

Fig. 5.12 The Atomium, Brussels

centre. Linked to Antwerp by the Willebroek Canal and to Charleroi by the Brussels-Charleroi Canal it is an important inland port. Its varied industries derive from its status as a port and the capital of Belgium. They include such port industries as chemicals, tobacco processing, timber and heavy engineering. Consumer industries range from printing, pharmaceuticals and cosmetics to furniture and electrical goods.

Brussels is also the administrative capital of the EU. The European Union functions from the Berlaymont Building and so, in effect, Brussels is the political capital of western Europe. Thus, on both a national and EU level, Brussels generates a huge demand for goods and services. This, in turn, creates valuable employment in the city's consumer and tertiary industries. Per capita income in Brussels is the highest in Belgium and the city is the most prosperous in the EU.

Ghent

Ghent is connected by ship canal to Terneuzen on the Scheldt estuary and to Bruges, a river port 14km from sea. An industrial region stretches along the canal to Terneuzen, with textile industries, oil refineries, shipbuilding yards, steel plants and chemical plants. The city is linked to Ostend and Brussels by motorway.

The Antwerp-Genk axis

A third region of industrial development lies along the Antwerp-Genk axis initiated by the huge coal deposits of the Campine, formerly a neglected area of heathland, sand dunes and marshland.

A number of factors have stimulated the growth of industry in the region:

- The coalfield initially provided the energy source for the chemical, metal refining and glassmaking industries which are still thriving here.
- A huge area of level land is available on the heathlands for the siting of factories and of housing estates for workers.
- The Albert Canal (Antwerp-Genk-Liege) provides cheap transport for the movement of raw materials and manufactured goods in both directions.
- The comparative isolation and low population density of the region has favoured the siting of dangerous and noxious industries, e.g. explosives and chemicals.
- Government grants have encouraged the development of industries in the Campine.

The Campine is now a flourishing industrial region. Its mining and industrial activities are located in a rural setting that provides a striking contrast to the drab and built-up environment of the Sambre-Meuse valley. Many of the large, modern plants are located along the banks of the Albert Canal, which is now one of Europe's busiest waterways. The varied industries of this thriving axis include chemicals, glassmaking, the refining of zinc and copper, car assembly, electronic goods and engineering.

SAMPLE QUESTION

Describe some of the socio-economic problems caused by the decline in the coal industry. Name some of the strategies used to combat these problems.

Problems

1. The closure of mines leads to a general decline in the area. Associated industries (engineering, chemicals) move to other, more attractive locations. Unemployment soars.
2. Unsightly spoil heaps, empty factories and deteriorating housing create a landscape that is uninviting and neglected in appearance.
3. Younger people tend to move out of the area because of the lack of jobs.
4. The population pyramid of the area becomes unbalanced, with a majority of elderly people and relatively few children.
5. With fewer factories and fewer people, the area's decline gathers pace. Money is lacking to rebuild roads, to remove unsightly spoil-heaps and to create a pleasant environment.
6. The social fabric of the area disintegrates. There are fewer shops, fewer schools and fewer entertainment facilities.
7. The State faces loss of revenue from workers now unemployed and has to pay out huge amounts in unemployment benefits.
8. Political unrest often results because of the perceived inability of the government to solve the unemployment problem.

Strategies

1. EU and government funds are used to retrain unemployed miners.
2. Native and foreign industries are encouraged to locate in the area.
3. Firms setting up factories receive direct grants, low-interest loans, and low rates of taxation.
4. Special incentives, e.g., 10 years tax-free, are available for foreign investors.
5. Industrial estates are established with the emphasis on consumer and light industries – pharmaceuticals, electronics, telecommunications, etc.
6. The transport infrastructure is improved by the construction of new motorways, widening of canals and the introduction of fast electrified rail links with other towns within and outside the region.

POPULATION IN BELGIUM AND THE NETHERLANDS

Belgium and the Netherlands form the most densely populated part of Europe, with the Netherlands (347 per sq km) and Belgium (323 per sq km) ranking respectively first and second in the world. The following features may be noted on the map of population distribution of Belgium and the Netherlands.

1. There are a number of major concentrations of population: Randstad, Gröningen, Eindhoven (Netherlands) and Antwerp, Brussels, Ghent, Charleroi, Liege (Belgium).
2. The rural areas all support a moderate population. There are many large villages or small towns. The Netherlands is the more highly urbanised country,

with 88% of the population in urban areas compared to Belgium (67%) and Luxembourg (68%).
3 These countries contain some of Europe's oldest established towns – Ghent, Amsterdam, Brussels.

Population distribution in the Netherlands

The population of the Netherlands is not evenly distributed over the country. Studies show that the three western provinces of north Holland, south Holland, and Utrecht have only 20% of the land but nearly half the population. The remaining 80% of the land houses 55% of the people.

The reasons for this imbalance are mainly economic ones. The western provinces are situated on the sea and the rivers, i.e. at the junction of the water routes. Ports, industry and commerce grew here and the western provinces were seen as the regions which presented the best opportunities. There was a constant out-migration from the agricultural areas in the north and east. This led to the extraordinary growth of the Randstad cities. Some other areas also have a dense population. The natural gas at Gröningen has attracted industry and settlement, and Eindhoven is a good example of a modern industrial city. Unlike Belgium, the Netherlands has a large number of medium to large cities of 30 000 to 100 000 people. They are mainly in the west and south and are continuing to expand. The areas of smallest population density are the Veluwe, Drente and Overijssel.

Changes in the distribution of population are taking place. Government policy is to decentralise industry and therefore settlement. Attractive financial packages are offered to industrialists establishing in the north and east. The completion of the delta works and the Zuider Zee plan has made both areas more accessible and desirable to the people of the Randstad. A quiet rural environment seems more attractive after the congestion and pollution of city life. Government policies seem to be working, since both the northern and eastern provinces are now experiencing an in-migration.

Population distribution in Belgium

Fig. 5.13 Population

Dense urban areas. A high proportion of Belgium's population lives in three areas:

(a) Brussels region
(b) Antwerp, Ghent, Bruges region
(c) Liege-Charleroi region.

Brussels, with a population of over one million, is linked to Antwerp and Charleroi by canals. It is the political and commercial centre of the country as well as having important industries. It is also the administrative centre of the EU. Antwerp, Ghent and Bruges are all ports, with canals connecting Ghent and Bruges to the coast. All three towns have important industrial functions.

Liege and Charleroi are the most important of a number of industrial towns in the Sambre-Meuse valley where Belgium's steel, metal-working, chemical and engineering industries are concentrated.

Dense rural areas. Two rural areas show a high density of population: (a) the Central Plain; (b) Flanders.

The Central Plain is gently undulating and covered with fertile limon soils. Farming is intensive and highly productive with the emphasis on wheat, barley, sugar beet and market gardening. Farms are larger and more mechanised than elsewhere in Belgium. There are numerous prosperous farming villages and many thriving towns throughout the Central Plain.

Flanders is also a region of small towns and intensive cultivation. Some of the crops are used in local factories.

Sparse rural areas. (a) The Campine; (b) the Ardennes. The Campine consists of coarse infertile sands. Population density is low. Heathland and pine trees occupy much of the landscape.

The Ardennes form an upland region deeply dissected by rivers. The poor, thin soils and raw climate limit agriculture. Much of the plateau is wooded and farming is found only in the more sheltered areas.

Questions

	1950	1960	1970	1977	1981	1993
Campine	8.1	9.4	7.1	6.3	5.8	NIL
Sambre-Meuse	19.2	13.1	4.3	0.8	0.3	NIL
	27.3	22.5	11.4	7.1	6.1	NIL

Fig. 5.14 Coal output (million tonnes): Belgium 1950-1993.

1. Study the information above and answer the following questions:
   (a) Describe briefly the major changes in Belgium's coal production in the period 1950-1993.
   (b) Describe the effects of these changes on industrial development in Belgium.
   (c) On a sketch map locate and name the Campine and Sambre-Meuse regions. Also show and name: Antwerp, Brussels, the Albert Canal.
   (d) Account for the growth of Antwerp as a major port. (L.C. Higher Level)
2. Discuss the extent to which agriculture and industry are closely linked in Belgium. Note the chief advantages and disadvantages of such linkage.
3. Describe the importance of Belgium's geographical location.

4 With the aid of a sketch map suggest a division of Belgium into its major physical divisions (at least five). Select two of these regions and in each case analyse the influence of the physical environment on the economy of the region. (L.C. Higher Level)

5 Write an account of population density in Belgium.

6 The Sambre-Meuse is a region of declining traditional industry. Discuss (a) the causes of the decline, (b) the social and economic effects and (c) the measures taken to revitalise the region.

7 Discuss the physical, social and industrial contrasts that exist between the North and South in Belgium.

8 With the aid of a sketch map describe the locational advantages of the port of Antwerp. Explain two ways in which its economic activities show that it has a large hinterland. (LC. Ordinary Level)

9 Write geographical notes on each of the following:
(a) The Antwerp-Genk Industrial Axis
(b) The main features of Belgian agriculture.
(c) Brussels – a regional, national and European capital.
(d) The iron and steel industry in Belgium.

10 Compare the Brussels-Antwerp industrial axis with that of the Sambre-Meuse under any four of the following headings: (i) location, (ii) accessibility, (iii) availability of raw materials, (iv) products, (v) markets. (L.C. Higher Level)

11 In the case of Belgium, identify and explain some of the factors which have influenced (i) development of agriculture, (ii) development of manufacturing industry. (L.C. Ordinary Level).

12 Select two of the following statements and examine them in detail;
(a) The language issue threatens national unity in Belgium.
(b) Brussels is the capital of Europe.
(c) Flanders is a region of intensive agriculture.

13 Describe some of the socio-economic problems caused by the decline in the coal industry and the strategies used to combat them. (L.C. Higher Level)

14 Draw a sketch map to show how you would divide Belgium into regions. Select any two of these regions and in the case of each, describe its main characteristics, using the following headings: physical geography, agriculture, manufacturing industry. (L.C. Ordinary Level)

15 Examine some of the problems encountered in a multi-lingual country.

16 Examine some of the factors which have influenced the development of manufacturing industry in Belgium.

17 Brussels:
(i) Describe its location with the aid of a sketch map.
(ii) Explain any three factors which led to its growth and development. (L.C. Ordinary Level)

18 European cities are places of opportunity, but also have many problems. Explain this statement, referring to European cities you have studied.

19 Select one important manufacturing region in Belgium.
(i) Draw a sketch map to show (a) the location of the region, (b) the chief transport features, (c) the chief towns.
(ii) Examine in detail why the region has attracted so much manufacturing industry.

chapter six
france

INTRODUCTION

Area:	550 000 sq km
Population:	58.3 million
Density:	105 per sq km

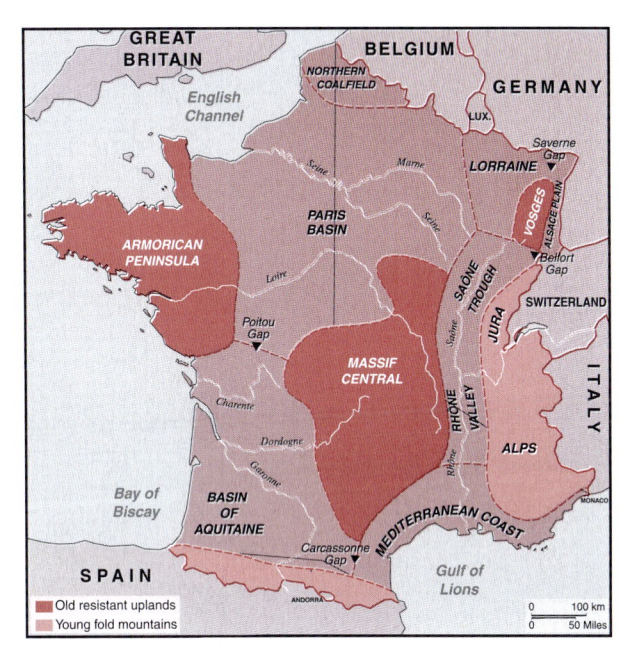

Fig. 6.1 Regions

Fig. 6.2 The Louvre, Paris

France is the largest country in western Europe. It is at once a compact and a very complex country. Its geographical boundaries are very definite – the mountain frontiers of the Pyrénées, Alps and Jura and the coastlines along the Atlantic and Mediterranean. Yet within these rigid physical boundaries there exists a considerable variety of relief, soils, climates, resources and cultures. France is a country of rich historic overtones and deep cultural traditions. It is also a major industrial country and a world nuclear power. The following observations on France are worth noting:

1. France has direct access by land and sea to its EU neighbours. To the north, the English Channel provides a vital trade artery to northern Europe. Within France itself, major valleys and gaps form natural routeways for roads and railways that link it to its European trading partners. In the east, the Saverne Gap links the Paris basin with the upper Rhineland and southern Germany, and the Belfort Gap lies between the Rhine, the Rhône-Saône valley and the Paris basin. The Rhône-Saône valley, one of the great corridors of movement down through the ages, links the political and economic core of Paris with the trading ports of the Mediterranean. In the south, the narrow Gate of Carcassonne controls the routeway from the Atlantic to the Mediterranean.

2   The diversity of physical resources allows for a variety of development throughout France. The rich and fertile soils of the Paris basin make it the focus of cereal growing on a large scale, while the climatic and scenic conditions of some mountain zones, especially in the Alps, provide a more prosperous way of life through tourism than would be possible by farming.

3   Natural resources for industrial development are spaced in a rather irregular manner throughout France. Supplies of coal and mineral ores, for example, are located in areas of limited access along the edge of the Massif Central or in frontier zones such as the Nord and Lorraine, where coal and iron deposits are shared with neighbouring countries.

4   Important cultural differences still exist in France. The culture, customs and dialects of one region differ from those of another. The Bretons, Burgundians, Basques and others are strongly aware and intensely proud of their regional culture and way of life. In general, much of western and southern France is a rural agricultural society often suspicious and envious of the urban industrial lifestyle of northern and eastern France.

5   Modern France therefore is a country with striking regional contrasts. Yet these very contrasts of landscape, cultures and lifestyles have all been fused together to form a country that is sometimes erratic, but always unique – *la belle France*.

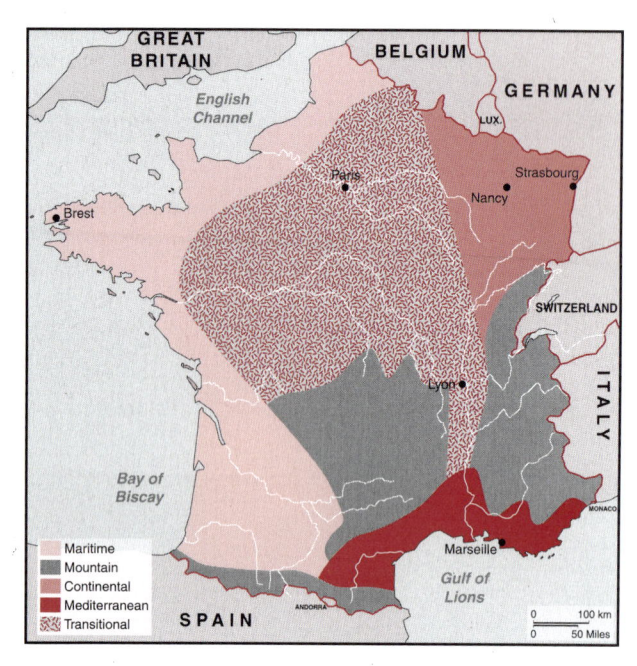

Fig. 6.3 Climatic regions

CLIMATE

Because of the range of latitude (42°N to 51°N), longitude and altitude in France, there is a similar range of climatic types. Three main climatic regions may be identified:

1   Cool temperate oceanic (maritime) climate in the north-west and west. The prevailing winds are the westerlies, which bring a succession of low-pressure systems (depressions) from the Atlantic throughout the year. Well-distributed rainfall, moderate conditions, small temperature range, mild winters and considerable cloud cover in coastal areas are the chief characteristics of the climate. The mild temperatures and absence of frost encourage specialised farming, e.g. in Brittany, the growing of *primeurs* (early vegetables).

2   Continental type climate in the centre and east of France. Summers are warmer and winters colder than

in the maritime region. Rainfall shows a distinct summer maximum, with much of the rain coming in heavy thunderstorms. In mountain areas, especially, the annual precipitation is over 1 200mm, much of it falling as snow.

3 Mediterranean climate along the south coast. Summers are dominated by high-pressure systems (anti-cyclones) which result in hot, dry, sunny summers. Rainfall maximum is in winter, which is mild.

SOILS

Variety is the key word as regards the soils of France. The various rock structures and the many shades of difference in the three main climatic types have resulted in a bewildering variety of soils. Not all of the soils, of course, are fertile or productive. Many others have been improved over the centuries by drainage and the application of fertilisers. But the fertility and productive quality of many French soils is emphasised not only by the variety of farming produce on display in the weekly market of any French country town, but also by France's self-sufficiency in many temperate foodstuffs.

The most fertile soils are found in the north of France. Here the chalk and limestone plains are overlain with a thin covering of **limon** (loess), the fertile and humus-rich deposits of fine dust which were carried by the wind from the edge of the retreating ice sheet. Much of the Paris basin has a limon covering and this fertile region (the granary of France) produces most of the country's cereals. The **alluvial** soils in the major river valleys of the lower Seine, the Rhône-Saône, the Garonne and the middle Loire (the garden of France) are also highly productive.

Over the centuries, French farmers have worked and improved infertile soils in many areas. They have terraced the steep, sunny, south-facing slopes and built stone walls to prevent soil erosion and retain the precious soil. In Britanny they have applied seaweed to sweeten and add humus to the acid soils. They have reclaimed the marshlands of the Rhône delta and irrigated the dry soils of Languedoc.

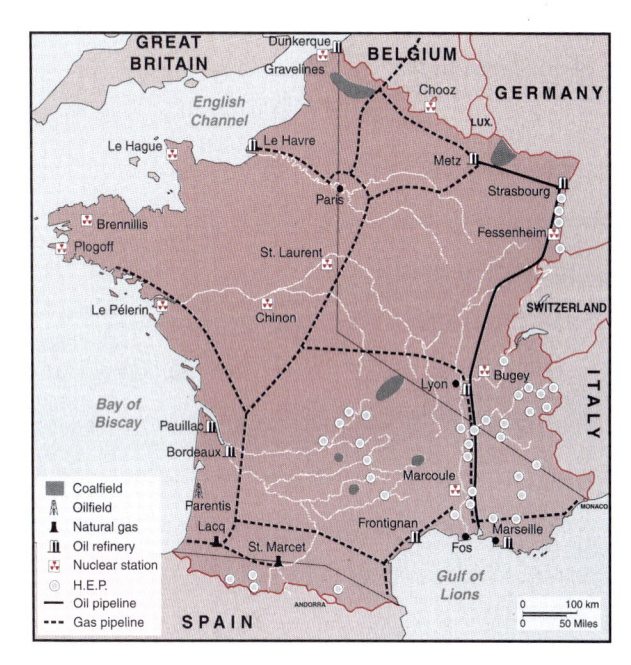

Fig. 6.4 Sources of Power.

ENERGY AND MINERAL RESOURCES

Coal

At one time, the Nord coalfield was one of the great coalfields of France. An extension of the Sambre-Meuse in Belgium, the Nord was the home of the French Industrial Revolution. On it developed a major industrial region with steel, engineering and textiles. However, as the better coal

Production figures 1986-1993 (in millions of tonnes)		
	1986	1993
Lorraine	9.4	7.4
Massif Central	2.6	1.2
Nord	1.9	NIL

Coalfield production

seams ran out, the whole region went into decline. The last coal pits closed in 1991.

Lorraine coalfield

The Lorraine coalfield is an extension of the Saar coalfield of west Germany. The coal seams are thick and productivity is high. The annual output of 7.4 million tonnes is of great value because of its proximity to the Lorraine iron-ore field. Although the coal is not of good coking quality, modern processes make it suitable for use in the region's steel industry. The Lorraine coalfield is now France's largest producer.

The Massif Central coalfields

The Massif Central coalfields are small and scattered and are gradually being phased out.

Oil

France's major oilfields are centred around Parentis in the Landes region. Some small oilfields are located south-east of Paris. Production from all these domestic fields is slightly more than 1% of France's energy requirements, so oil for energy has to be imported. The Landes oil is brought by pipeline to the refinery at Bordeaux. Oil refineries, using imported oil, are mainly on the coast, e.g., Fos and Sète on the Mediterranean, Le Havre at the mouth of the Seine and Pauillac on the Gironde estuary. Inland refineries, e.g., Lyon and Strasbourg, are fed by oil pipelines from the coast.

Natural gas

Natural gas fields on the flanks of the Pyrénées at Lacq and St Marcet have proved more important than the oil finds. The discovery of natural gas has not only helped in the generation of power, but it has stimulated the development of metallurgical and chemical industries in the region. The high sulphur content of the Lacq gas caused initial problems, but the sulphur is now an important by-product and France is a leading European supplier. Gas pipelines distribute the gas across the country. Imported gas from Algeria comes to the Mediterranean port of Fos and then by pipeline to Lyon. Gas is also imported from the Netherlands.

Fig. 6.5 Harnessing water in the Pyrénées

Hydro-electric power

France has relatively abundant supplies of water power. Hydro-electricity provides a significant 15% of the country's total electricity. Rivers and mountains have played a notable part in the development of France's HEP network. Dams and barrages have been constructed in five main areas:

1. **French Alps**
2. **Rhône Valley**
3. **Massif Central**
4. **Pyrénées**
5. **Rhine Valley.**

Major rivers like the Rhône and Rhine have been harnessed to generate electricity. But HEP production is concentrated in the Alpine and Pyrénéean regions. France's Alpine region, in particular, possesses a number of advantages for the generation of hydro-electricity.

Note the following:

(a) Heavy precipitation (1500mm per annum) occurs in the Alps.
(b) Snowfields and glaciers in the Alps store water over a long period. When the snow melts in spring and early summer, a huge volume of water surges into the Rhône and its tributaries.
(c) Lake Geneva, on the Rhône, and high-level lakes elsewhere act as reservoirs and control the flow of water.
(d) Steep gradients provide high heads of water.
(e) The gorges in the upper courses of the Rhône and its tributaries provide excellent sites for dams and barrages.

Nuclear energy

France was one of the first European countries to see nuclear energy as the long-term energy source of the future. Its major advantage is that the fuel, uranium, is needed in relatively small quantities and can be easily transported.

France now leads Europe in the production of nuclear energy. 37% of all energy used in the country is generated in sixty nuclear power stations located all over France. These produce 75% of the electricity used.

The uranium used to produce this level of nuclear energy has saved France the equivalent of 40 million tonnes of oil and 8 million tonnes of coal each year.

Nuclear power plants are located in coastal areas or near major rivers to ensure a plentiful and regular supply of water for cooling the nuclear reactors. They are also located far away from major population centres because of the risks of a nuclear accident such as occurred at Chernobyl in 1986.

Despite major world concerns about the dangers of nuclear accidents, the disposal of nuclear waste and the dispersal of radioactivity, France remains committed to the use of nuclear energy and plans to have more nuclear power plants in operation by the year 2000.

Mineral resources of Alsace-Lorraine

The most important minerals mined in France are bauxite, iron ore, potash and salt. Bauxite is the chief ore of aluminium, which is used in alloy form in the manufacture of aircraft and transport vehicles. Most of France's bauxite is in the south-east from where it is sent to processing plants which remove impurities until a white powdery substance (alumina) remains. The alumina is then sent to aluminium smelters powered by HEP in the Alpine valleys. Most of France's iron ore comes from the Lorraine orefield, one of the largest in the world. Much of the ore is extracted by opencast mining. There are extensive deposits of potash in Alsace (Mulhouse) and of salt in Lorraine (Dombasle and Sarralbe). These deposits form the basis of fertiliser and other chemical industries in France.

Hydro-electric power

SAMPLE QUESTION

Explain the importance of hydro-electric power in France.

The production of HEP in France is important for many reasons:

- It contributes significantly (15%) to the country's total electricity output.
- It reduces the dependence on the import of other energy sources – coal, oil, natural gas.
- The transmission of electricity throughout France has helped to make industry more footloose and independent of location. It has brought industry to regions that were formerly by-passed by industrialists.
- The supply of cheap power has also helped in the expansion of existing industry. For example, small market towns in the Jura have become minor industrial centres providing alternative employment for farmers and their families in food-processing industries such as brewing, liqueur-making and the making of chocolate.
- The construction and maintenance of HEP plants has provided employment in areas that would otherwise be neglected.
- HEP schemes not only provide electricity. They are often multi-purpose developments that have initiated developments in flood control, irrigation schemes (e.g. the lower

Rhône), navigation improvement (e.g. the lower Rhône between Lyon and Arles).

- The impact of France's HEP resources may be noted particularly in the development and location of the electro-chemical and electro-metallurgical industries which require huge quantities of electricity. Thus electro-smelters are mainly located near HEP plants, often in remote and isolated areas.

ASPECTS OF FRENCH AGRICULTURE

- Agriculture is an important sector of the French economy. It has the largest agricultural production in the EU, emphasising its large area of farmland 30.2 million hectares (Ireland has 4.4 million). Its production of **cereals,** the highest in the EU, has earned it the title of the *Granary of Europe*.
- Its surplus **food products**, which are exported, include cereals, wine, cheese, fruit and vegetables.
- The number of people working on the land has declined sharply from 4.4 million in 1958 to 1.2 million in 1993. Increased **mechanisation,** irrigation, fertilisers and improved crop strains have resulted in a marked reduction in the amount of land and labour needed to maintain and even increase productivity.
- Many of the farms are too small, with one-third of them less than 10 hectares (25 acres), and are difficult to work for profit. Thus there is insufficient capital for investment in farm machinery and fertilisers. In addition, many of these holdings consist of a number of scattered fields. This **fragmentation,** a legacy of the medieval open-field system, makes irrigation and crop sowing very difficult.
- Many of these small farms, especially in Brittany, Aquitaine and the south are worked by **elderly farmers** for whom farming is more a way of life than an economic investment. They are slow to adapt to modern farming and marketing techniques.
- Another significant factor in French agriculture over the past three decades has been **rural-urban migration** which has drastically reduced the agricultural workforce. Some mountain areas of marginal farming (Jura, Vosges, Massif Central) are in danger of becoming depopulated.
- The French government, with EU funding, has introduced a number of **reforms** aimed at promoting a balanced agricultural system;

1. Government agencies buy land to consolidate fragmented farms into bigger and more compact farm units.
2. Elderly farmers are encouraged to retire.
3. People leaving the land are retrained for other employment.
4. Hill farmers are given bonuses to increase their cattle herds and grants are given to young farmers who will settle in areas with population below the minimum desirable level (11 people per km^2).
5. EU funding is available for dairy processing, fruit and vegetable processing plants.

- **Variety** is the keynote of France's agriculture. It derives from the differences in soils, climate and landscape to be found within the country. This variety is shown in three ways: (a) the various types of farming landscape, from the *bocage* of Brittany to the **open fields** of the Paris basin, (b) the farming methods which vary from the conservative pastoral farming of Brittany to the modern irrigation farming of Languedoc, and (c) the diversity of products – cereals, fruits, vegetables, beef, cheese, milk, sugar beet and wine.

Principal agricultural products of France	
Sugar beet	1st in the EU, 2nd in the world
Cereals	1st in the EU, 8th in the world
Oilseeds	1st in the EU
Beef and veal	1st in the EU, 6th in the world
Milk	2nd in the EU, 5th in the world
Wine	2nd in the EU, 2nd in the world

Fig. 6.5 Crop growing

Brittany

The peninsula lies in north-west France. Its comparative isolation from the rest of the country has bred a spirit of independence and conservatism in the Bretons and made them a people apart. Brittany is a province where 'the past is preserved in the present'. The maritime climate is marked by the mildness of its winters. The early springs and absence of frosts make this an ideal location for the production of primeurs (early vegetables and fruits). The sheltered *rias* along the rugged coast are dotted with small fishing harbours, which support a thriving and important fishing industry. The fish and early vegetables find a ready market in the industrial north, Paris and Britain. Rapid rail and sea links make these areas very accessible to Brittany. Inland from the coast the soils are thin, but pastoral farming is important, with both beef and dairy cattle.

Aquitaine

This region, in the south-west of France, consists of the valleys of the Charente, Garonne and Adour rivers. The climate is essentially maritime with mild winters as in Brittany, but summers are warmer because of the more southerly latitude. The Aquitaine basin is one of the major farming regions of France for several reasons:

1. The warm summers and mild winters allow all year-round growth for crops and outdoor grazing of cattle.
2. Rainfall is moderate and well distributed.
3. The gently undulating landscape assists mechanisation and drainage.
4. The area has a wide variety of soils – limestones, sandstones and clays. Especially useful for farming are

the river terraces which are covered with fine silts and often with limon.

The **Garonne valley** is the heartland of Aquitaine, with a rich and varied pattern of agriculture. More than half the land is under cereals, mainly wheat and maize. Market gardens are cultivated intensively on the river terraces, and orchards and vineyards are widespread. Throughout Aquitaine, dairy and beef cattle are reared.

Massif Central

This is the problem region of French agriculture. The soils are thin and acidic and the upland relief of the region gives low temperatures and high rainfall. All combine to make farming difficult. Nevertheless, the variety of relief, climate and soils in the region has allowed for the development of various types of farming.

The uplands: livestock farming is dominant. On the Charollais and Limousin uplands these famous breeds of beef cattle are reared. They are then sent to the Paris Basin for fattening.

The interior basins: these produce a variety of crops, including cereals, fodder and market gardening.

The south: many of the valleys in the warmer area are sheltered. Vines, olives and mulberries are grown on the terraced slopes. For years, young migrants have left the Massif Central to seek better jobs elsewhere. New regional plans aim to develop agriculture. Notable developments include the following: cattle breeding stations to raise the quality of the livestock; growing irrigated fodder crops in the Allier valley; draining highland pastures; afforestation of unproductive upland areas.

Agriculture in the Paris basin

The Paris basin is the largest physical unit in France. It occupies almost 25% of the country. It extends for 420km from west to east and for 320km from north to south. It is thus a bigger unit than all Ireland. It is the most productive farming region in the country and its agricultural prosperity has been an important factor in the economic growth of the area.

Structurally, it is a broad shallow downfold consisting of layers of sedimentary rock, one inside the other, and may be described as a series of stacked saucers. In the centre are sandstones and limestones, which are surrounded by successive belts of chalk, clay and older limestone. In the east and south-east, the edges of the chalk and limestone stand out prominently. Erosion has exposed the various sedimentary rocks and has produced a landscape of alternate scarps and vales. Much of the bedrock is covered with limon (loess), the fertile fine-grained deposit carried by the wind at the end of the Ice Age. The variety of relief, soils and drainage within the Paris basin has produced a number of well-defined physical regions (pays), each with a distinctive character as regards land use and settlement.

The climate is very favourable to agriculture, with warm summers (20°C). Rainfall is well distributed throughout the year. Western areas are affected by maritime influences while continental influences are noticeable in the east of the basin.

In summary, the following factors favour agriculture in the Paris basin:

- Climate – warm summers, mild winters, well-distributed rainfall.
- Soils – a variety of soils.
- Drainage – well-drained soils.
- Large areas of level land – favours mechanisation.
- Markets – presence of Paris in the centre of the Basin, the proximity of the urban and industrial centres of the EU.

The Paris Basin

Region	Comment	Type of farming and crops
Ile de France	The central region of the Paris basin. Its varied rocks (limestone, clay, sandstone) are mostly covered with fertile limon soils and divided into distinctive pays by the tributaries of the Seine. Two notable and contrasting *pays* are Beauce and Brie.	Overall emphasis on cereal production. Market gardening is important near Paris.
	Beauce: Fertile limon soils cover limestone on the relatively level andscape. A very dry region.	Intensive cultivation of cereals – wheat and barley – and sugar beet. Large farms, over 200 acres. A high degree of mechanisation and efficiency. The granary of France.
	Brie: Clay bands on the limestone plateau. The heavy damp clay soils favour pastoral farming.	Smaller farms, with emphasis on dairy farming and fodder crops. Much of the milk is processed into the famous Brie cheese. Dairy products for the Paris market. On the better drained soils, cereals are grown.
Falaise	A limestone scarp which extends in a great semicircle from the river Oise to the river Seine. It marks the northern limit of the vine. The scarp slopes are sheltered and sunny.	This is a region of vineyards, famous for Champagne, Reims and Epernay are the market centres of the wine industry.

Region	Comment	Type of farming and crops
Champagne Pouilleuse (Dry Champagne)	Thin infertile chalk soils. Sheep rearing was the main farming activity until recently.	Extensive use of fertilisers has now created a prosperous mixed farming economy. Wheat is grown on large farm units.
Champagne Humide (Wet Champagne)	Heavy clay soils favour pastoral farming.	Dairy farming on the valley floors. Arable farming on the lower slopes.
Picardy and Artois	An undulating region of numerous streams and wide flood plains.	Cereals, sugar beet and fodder crops. Dairy farming also practised. Intensive market gardening around Amiens.
Upper Normandy	The north-western rim of the Paris basin.	Large scale arable farming. Wheat and sugar beet. Dairy farming is emphasised around Caen.

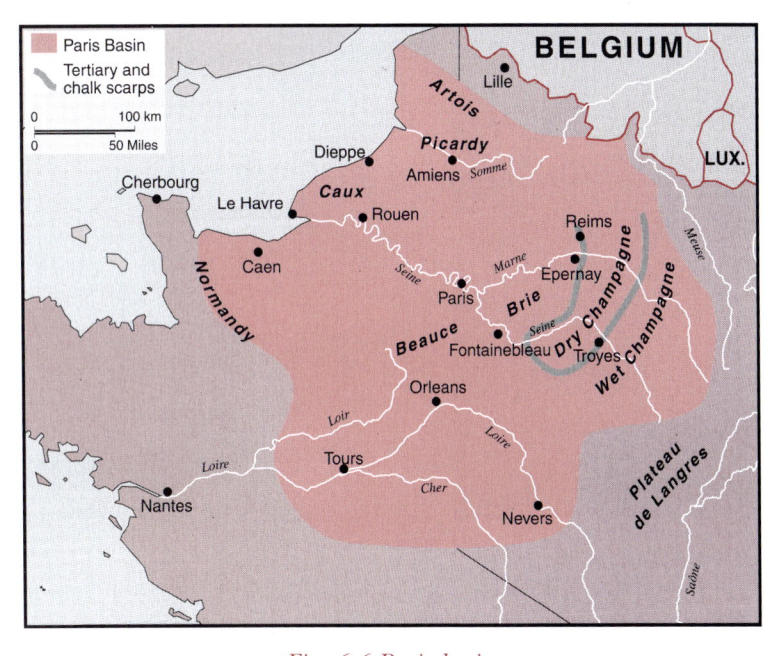

Fig. 6.6 Paris basin

WINE PRODUCTION IN FRANCE

- Wine is the most famous product of France. It is a major export earner and is important to the economy of many regions
- While Italy is Europe's largest producer of wine, France is the most important producer in terms of the **quality and variety** of its wine
- The type of wine produced depends on the vine best suited to the region's soils and weather
- Most vineyards are small (5 acres) and are intensively cultivated.

Geographical controls

- **Well-drained soils.** Rich soils are not necessary and the vine often thrives on soils that are useless for other crops
- **Slope.** Slopes provide good drainage and are sheltered by the hills behind
- **Rainfall.** Moderate, gentle rainfall in spring and early summer helps to swell the grapes, but excess moisture gives a thin, watery wine
- **Aspect.** South-facing slopes trap the maximum amount of sunshine during the summer and autumn. The quality and flavour of the wine largely depend on the amount of warmth and sunshine between the setting of the grape and its final ripening
- **Temperatures.** Cold short winters which strengthen root and stem growth and reduce pests. Frosts in May are disastrous. Summers need to be warm (over 20°C) and sunny to increase the sugar content of the grapes.

Wine production regions

The vine is grown south of a line from the mouth of the Loire to the eastern edge of the Paris basin (Fig. 6.6). The main production regions are:

1	Loire valley	6	Rhône valley
2	Aquitaine	7	Beaujolais
3	Armagnac	8	Burgundy
4	Languedoc	9	Champagne
5	Provence	10	Alsace.

- **Aquitaine** region produces 25% of France's wine output and some of the country's finest wines. Many of the vineyards are located on south-facing slopes in the valleys of the region's major rivers – the lower Dordogne (clarets), the Garonne (white wines), the Charente (brandy).

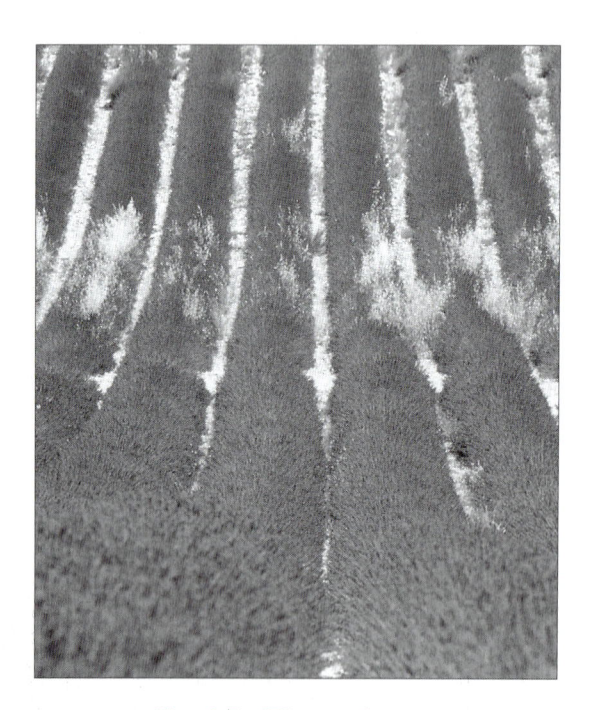

Fig. 6.7 Wine production

- **Languedoc** region is the wine factory of France, with some 70 000 vine growers. Most of the wine is *vin ordinaire* and there is serious over-production.

- **Burgundy** region produces superb red and white wines. An important factor is the age-old tradition of skills which go back to Roman times. This is combined with a quality control system that guarantees the quality of the wines.

- **Champagne** is the most northerly wine-producing region. It lies along the eastern edge of the Paris basin. Expertise in fermentation techniques and in blending has given the white bubbly wines of Champagne an international reputation. Only wine made in the Champagne region can use the famous name.

Markets

Much of the wine produced in the Mediterranean region of France is *vin ordinaire*, a rather inferior wine used for domestic consumption. The northern vineyards – Burgundy, Aquitaine, Loire valley, Bordeaux – give lower yields, but wines of a higher quality. These are the special or **prestige** wines which are mainly for export. Over-production of lower-quality wines within the EU has resulted in a wine lake. The Common Agricultural Policy aims at reducing exports of *vin ordinaire* and encouraging the production of high-quality wines.

Wine production – its importance to the economy

- The cultivation of vines is a valuable land use in many areas that would otherwise be non-productive in agriculture
- Many farms have their own small vineyards and produce wine for local sale
- Wine production creates employment in 10 regions throughout France
- The chemical industry benefits from the sale of fertilisers, insecticides and pesticides to the vineyards
- Spin-off industries are created locally in the manufacture of corks and casks and in the transport of the wine to wine-merchants
- Wine is a major French export earner.

ASPECTS OF FRENCH INDUSTRY

- France is one of the leading industrial countries in the EU.
- Industrial products generate twice the wealth created by agriculture, forestry and fishing in almost every region.
- Nuclear energy is of increasing importance in providing electricity for industry. France has 60 nuclear power stations, the highest number in the EU.
- In common with other EU countries, France has experienced a steady decline in such traditional industries as iron and steel, shipbuilding and textiles.

Fig 6.8 Aerial industrial view

Coal mining has declined from 17 million tonnes in 1986 to 4 million tonnes in 1993.
- To offset the unemployment created by the decline of traditional industries, **footloose industries** have been encouraged to set up factories in these regions. Footloose industries are those which are not tied to a particular region for raw materials or for local supplies of energy, e.g., car manufacturing, electronics and pharmaceuticals.
- The French government has encouraged the building of **science parks**, areas where university research departments can develop new products in low-cost surroundings.
- In the 1990s, the main aim of the French government was to balance growth between Paris and the regions. **Decentralisation** has been the aim, but it has been more successful in moving industrial jobs than service industries.

High-tech industries

In France, as in other EU countries, including Ireland, high-technology industries are in the forefront of industrial development. They have become increasingly important and make a significant contribution to the economy in terms of employment and export earnings. Products include electronics, computers, lasers, robotics, pharmaceuticals, telecommunication systems and medical equipment. But other industries such as the car and aerospace industries depend to a high degree on technology developed by high-tech industries. High-tech industries have a number of common characteristics:

- They are located in Science or Technology parks
- The workforce is highly qualified and consists mainly of professional engineers, technicians and scientists
- Their products are technologically advanced and innovative
- They are usually linked with American or Japanese multinational corporations.

Science parks/Technology parks

Science parks are a key influence on the location and success of high-tech industries. In France and Germany, particularly, they have had considerable success in providing alternative employment in areas where traditional industries of coalmining and iron and steel were in decline.

- Science parks are usually located on greenfield sites in pleasant, out-of-town surroundings
- They have formal links with a university or research centre
- There are high inputs of R&D (Research and Development)
- They help the local economy through direct and indirect employment, diversify local industry and attract investment.

Leading Industrial Sectors in France

- Construction and civil engineering
- Agri-foodstuffs (meat and dairy production, cereals, confectionery, soft and alcoholic drinks)
- Chemicals and plastics
- Pharmaceuticals
- Cars
- Metal processing

- Telecommunications
- Shipbuilding, aircraft and railway industries.

Industrial regions of France

The Nord. Historically the Nord has been one of the great industrial regions of France. It was the birthplace of the French Industrial Revolution. Its manufacturing industry was based on its rich coalfield. Iron ore from nearby Lorraine, used with the coal, laid the foundation for steel and engineering industries. Its textile industry was initially based on local wool and flax supplies. Cotton was later introduced and in the second half of this century synthetics became the predominant textile. As late as the 1960s, coal, steel and textiles employed over half the industrial workforce in the Nord – about 350 000 people.

During the last 25 years, the Nord has mirrored the Sambre-Meuse in its industrial economy and is now an industrial region in decline. The better coal seams became exhausted, production costs rose, output fell from 27 million tonnes in 1961 to 2 million tonnes in 1986 to total closure in 1991. As the coal industry declined, so also did the traditional steel and engineering industries in centres such as Douai, Valenciennes, Arras and Cambrai. Many of the mills were small, with old antiquated machinery. They closed one by one when a new integrated plant was established on the coast at Dunkirk. This Usinor plant utilises the excellent port facilities to import both ore and coal. It has the capacity to produce almost half of French steel. There is still a small steel output from the Nord from plants which have re-organised and amalgamated.

Textile manufacturing is the oldest industry in France, as it dates back to the Middle Ages. It was also the first to be factory-based. The main centres are Lille, Roubaix, Tourcoing and Armentiere, with small-scale operations in many of the rural towns. This industry also has suffered from many factors – obsolete machinery, antiquated production methods and competition from the cheap labour products of the Far East. Small firms vanished and the bigger ones amalgamated. This resulted in a slimmed-down industry which concentrated on skilled high-quality products and synthetics.

The whole environment of the Nord is run-down, polluted and in some decay. The infrastructure and housing is old and unattractive. The whole region requires urgent renewal. New science parks specialising in high-tech industries such as electronics and aerospace have been introduced. New *clean industries* (cars, plastics, electricals) are being encouraged to establish in the region. A major programme of renewal and house building is ongoing.

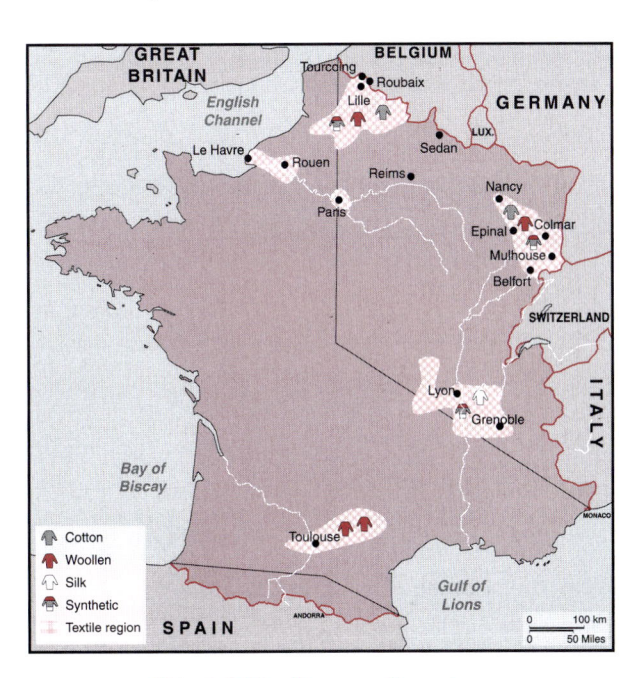

Fig. 6.9 Textile manufacturing

Efforts are being made to clean up the landscape and environment.

The Nord still retains some important advantages because of its location. It is in the centre of the Paris-Brussels axis, is adjacent to the huge affluent EU market and has a good workforce which is being retrained. The old canal system has been upgraded, with connections from Dunkirk to Lille and Paris. New motorways and rail connections to the coast, Paris, the Ruhr and the Netherlands are in place and there is a direct link to the Channel Tunnel.

Lorraine

Lorraine was a latecomer to the industrial scene in France. It had one of the biggest ore fields in the world, but the ore was low-grade with a high phosphorous content. The technology to use this type of ore only became available at the end of the nineteenth century. At this stage the Ruhr, Nord and Sambre-Meuse were well established as steel centres. Lorraine had other problems as well. Its coal deposits were of poor quality, so initially coal had to be imported. As a result, Lorraine developed as a steel centre on the **ore fields** rather than on the coal fields. The chief centres were Nancy, Longwy, Thionville and Metz. A further problem was that Lorraine was on the eastern border, remote from the French markets, and with poor water transport.

Nevertheless a major industrial region was established on its three main **resources** – coal, iron-ore and salt. Up to the 1970s Lorraine was producing over half the finished steel and two-thirds of the crude steel in France. After that, the industry went into decline as the new plants were located at coastal locations (Dunkirk and Fos). These plants use imported ores which are cheaper to transport and give a higher return (more iron per tonne carried).

As a result, Lorraine's share of the steel market fell dramatically. Around the same time, the ECSC began to fix quotas and remove State subsidies. Small firms in Lorraine had to close while the bigger firms began to merge. Employment has fallen over the last fifteen years with Lorraine losing some 25 000 steel jobs. Steel is now a small-scale employer. The state designated Lorraine as a target for other development and pressurised State-run industries to locate there. In addition, it persuaded Renault and Peugeot-Citroen, among others, to set up plants in Lorraine. The much smaller steel industry now specialises in the production of **special steels.** Other industries include electricals, light engineering, electronics, chemicals and cars.

Salt was the basis of a major chemical industry located at Dombasle, Sarralbe and Nancy. This industry is still important and has expanded over the years. Heavy and light chemicals are now manufactured.

Lorraine is compensating for the loss of jobs in the coal and steel industries by introducing new *clean* high-tech industries. More than 320 companies of 18 different nationalities have set up industrial operations there in recent years, attracted by generous government subsidies and the outstanding rail, road and air links to the rest of Europe.

Paris – an industrial centre

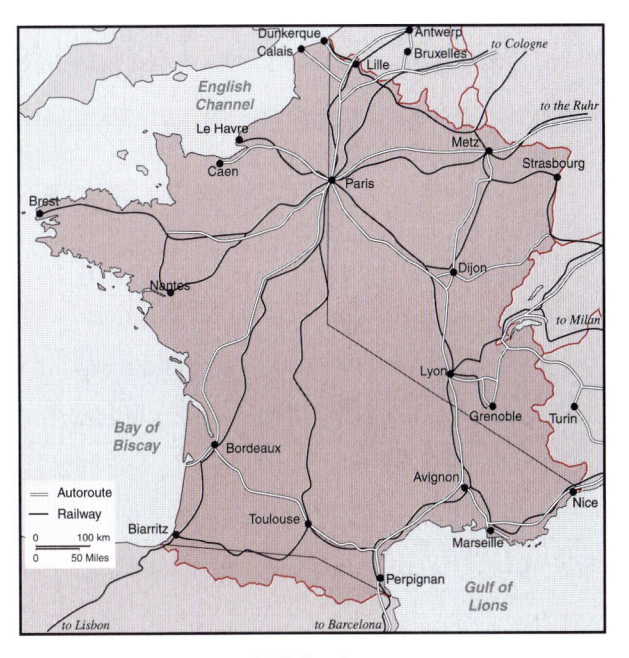

Fig. 6.10 Paris routes

The economy of France is centred on Paris and its conurbation, Ile de France. From its long history, Paris has assumed an unique role in the life of France. It is the political, commercial, administrative, cultural and communications centre of the country. All aspects of the economy converge on Paris.

Fig. 6.11 Port de Grenelle, Paris

Among the factors which favoured the supremacy of Paris as the industrial centre of France we may note the following:

- Paris is the centre of an important inland waterway system. It is connected by canal and canalised rivers to the Plain of Flanders, the Rhine, the Loire and Saône rivers and to the sea at Le Havre. Few people think of Paris as a port, since it is some 160km from the sea. It is, in fact, an extremely busy inland port. The quays along the Seine handle the industrial products of the Nord region, the farming produce of the Paris basin, the foreign imports which come upriver from Le Havre and Rouen and the industrial products of the Paris region itself.

- Paris is the focus of the French road and rail networks. The central position of the city within the saucer-shaped depression of the Paris basin syncline makes it the natural focus of routes using the valleys which breach the encircling chalk and limestone escarpments. The present system of *routes nationales* was initiated by Napoleon. It links the major provincial cities with Paris. The railway network emphasises even more strongly the dominance of Paris in the country's communications network. The airports of Orly and de Gaulle serve the capital.

- The huge population of the Paris region (over 10 million) provides both a labour force for industry and a market for the goods manufactured in the region.

- The proximity of Paris both to the industrialised Nord and the fertile Paris basin stimulated the development of a wide variety of industries.

- Its role as the commercial centre of France and its unequalled infrastructure of roads, railways, rivers and canals has attracted industry to Paris. For industrialists, it is the most favoured location in France.

- The service industries, in turn, have thrived on the central position of Paris in commerce, administration, tourism and culture. 25% of the doctors, 40% of the higher civil servants and 80% of the newspaper sales of France are in Paris.

Types of industries

Craft industries are usually located in the older parts of the city and include the manufacture of luxury goods such as jewellery, porcelain, perfumes, glassware, leather goods and fashion clothes. Printing and food-processing are other long-established industries.

Heavy industry is concentrated in the north-east suburbs. The factories are usually located on level land along a canal or railway line, to provide easy access for imports of bulky materials (coal, iron ore, ores). Products include a wide range of engineering goods, Renault and Citroen cars, machine tools, rolling stock for French railway system.

Port industries along the Seine and its canals process imported raw materials (petro-chemicals, chemicals, vegetable oils). Power and gas stations and the oil refineries are also situated along the Seine, west of Paris.

Modern industries are located in the outer suburbs and satellite towns. Their location is generally in relation to roads rather than canal or river transport. Such industries include electronics, pharmaceuticals, car components, food-processing, consumer appliances.

Problems

Paris. Overcrowding, poor housing, congestion of traffic and buildings and an inadequate transport system are the result of the city's ever-growing importance in the industrial and economic life of France.

Paris region. The growth of Paris as an industrial centre over the past century has to an extent stifled the development, and the economy, of the various regional centres.

Many of the industries in the Paris region were dependent on the Paris market, e.g. textiles, food-processing, building materials and semi-finished goods. Some of these industries, such as textiles, are reducing the workforce because of improved technology. Thus, the economic development of the hinterland of Paris has been restricted.

Responses

- The re-development of the inner city

- The creation of a number of new suburban areas and the restoration of existing ones around the city centre e.g. La Defense, Rungis, Creteil, Bobigny (Fig. 6.12)

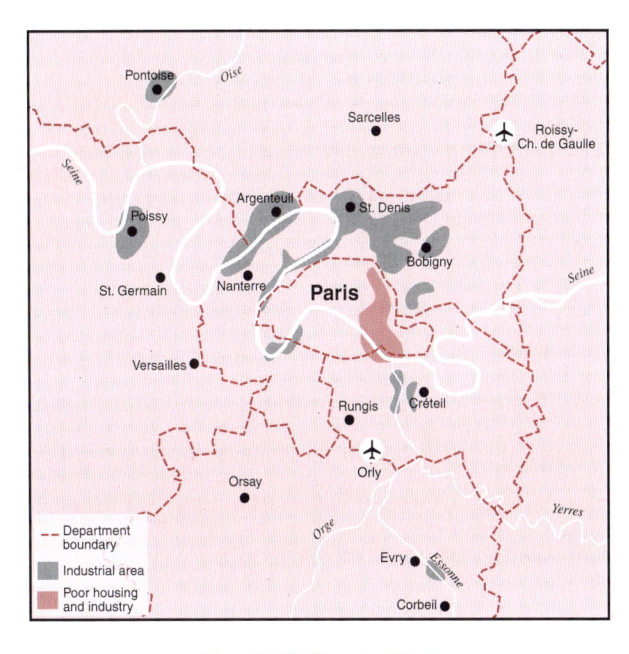

Fig. 6.12 Greater Paris

- Decentralisation of population, industry and tertiary activities to six new towns along two proposed axes north and south of the river Seine. This linear pattern of growth will preserve the open land along the Seine while providing for six new towns

- A balanced growth plan has been adopted for the region. Four support zones have been designated

- The development plan for these zones aims at the creation of new towns, new industries and new routeways. In this way, it is hoped to revitalise the regional centres (Rouen, Orleans, Reims, etc).

Languedoc – a problem region

The problems of Languedoc mirror those of the Mediterranean coastal areas (the Midi). In the past, the region suffered problems in agriculture, lack of industrial development and neglect of tourism.

PROBLEMS IN AGRICULTURE

The plains of Languedoc were once the granaries of imperial Rome, but today the cultivation of wheat is confined to the western sector of the province. Monoculture of vines has dominated farming until recent years. Almost two-thirds of farming land consisted of vineyards, which produced a poor quality *vin ordinaire*. This monoculture farming economy has suffered a series of problems from time to time.

Fig. 6.13 Rural landscape

The biting Mistral wind has often destroyed the season's crop of vines. Vine disease destroyed the vineyards in the last century. Cheap wines from Algeria posed a serious threat to the wines of Languedoc. The emphasis on wine production throughout France and Italy resulted in huge surpluses – the notorious wine lakes – and reduced prices for farmers in Languedoc. In addition, agriculture was essentially a small-scale operation. The farms were too small and fragmentation was common. Much of the farming, in effect, was subsistence farming, full of hazards and with very little reward.

Development. In 1955, as part of France's ambitious programme to modernise agriculture and redistribute industry, a semi-state development company (CNABRL) was formed with the aim of developing the Languedoc region on three fronts – agriculture, industry and tourism. Its achievements in relation to agriculture have been impressive.

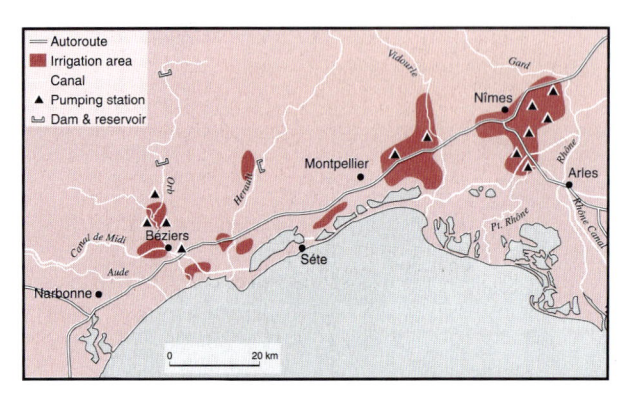

Fig. 6.14 Irrigation projects in Languedoc

Irrigation has been the keynote of the plan to modernise agriculture. Much of eastern Languedoc is now irrigated by water from the *Canal de Languedoc*, which runs from the Rhône above Arles to the river Aude, and by a series of feeder channels leading from it. The western sector is irrigated by a network of canals from the rivers Aude, Orb and Hérault, which flow from the Massif Central.

These irrigation schemes have transformed agriculture in Languedoc, especially in the east. Crops are now produced all year round. The monoculture of the vine has been replaced by a varied and valuable range of fruit crops (apples, peaches) and early vegetables (primeurs). The area under vines has been reduced and the emphasis is now on the production of high-quality wines. This emphasis became more urgent with the entry of Spain to the EU in 1986. Spain has more vineyards than any other country in the world and its entry posed a serious challenge to France's wine markets in general and to Languedoc in particular. Overall, the extension of irrigation into areas that were exclusively devoted to the vine has revolutionised farming practices in Languedoc. Commercial farming has replaced subsistence farming and farmers now enjoy a stable income and a higher standard of living. Co-operative marketing schemes, pest eradication programmes and afforestation projects have also played their part in revitalising the farming economy of Languedoc.

Lack of industrial development

Until the arrival of CNABRL, much of Languedoc was an industrial backwater, due to the concentration on agriculture. The relative isolation of the province and the limited energy sources available did not attract industry.

Development. Industrial development was a major objective in CNABRL's co-ordinated plan for Languedoc. Hydro-electricity from the great barrages of the Rhône development scheme and oil imported through the port of Sète provide power for a wide range of new industries. **Sète** is the centre of the region's industrial activity. It is a busy Mediterranean port, importing oil, phosphates, sulphur and wool from Algeria. It is also a canal port, as it is the terminus of the Canal du Midi and the Canal du Rhône-Sète. Its industries include oil refining, fertilisers and metal-working.

Farm-linked industries throughout Languedoc have been given a new lease of life. Co-operatives run canning factories and food-processing plants; they also manufacture farm equipment. **Nîmes** is the main centre for food-processing. Other industrial towns are Béziers, Narbonne and Montpelier. Bauxite is mined in the valley of the river Hérault and sent for smelting to the Alpine smelters. A new motorway links Languedoc with the Rhône corridor and has benefited both industry and tourism.

TOURISM

The coastline of Languedoc, west of the Rhône delta, was a complete contrast to that of the congested and prosperous Côte d'Azur. The lovely sandy beaches, ringed with mosquito-infested lagoons and swamps, were neglected and unknown. The decision by the French government to develop tourism in this region was based on a number of factors:

1. With the worldwide tourist boom of the 1960s, France had fallen behind in accommodation and facilities for foreign visitors and for the French population itself.

2. The Côte d'Azur had become highly congested and expensive for most tourists.

3. The promotion of tourism in the Languedoc region would do much to stimulate the local economy, afflicted with a chronic monoculture, an undeveloped infrastructure and a high unemployment rate.

Fig. 6.15 St. Tropez

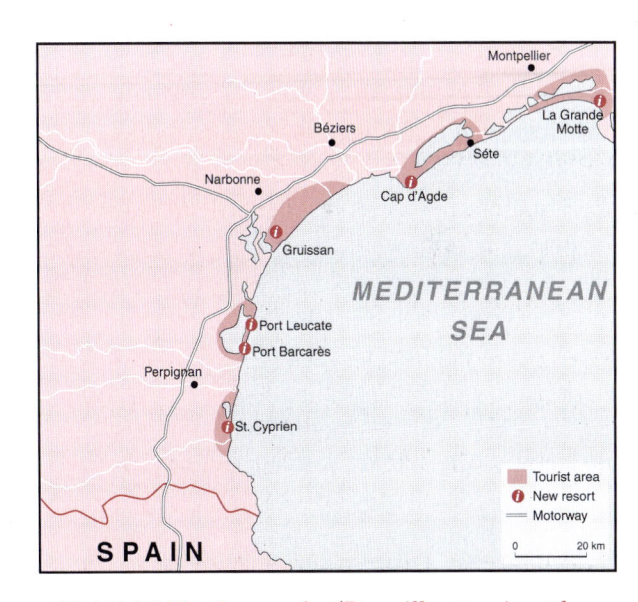

Fig. 6.16 The Languedoc/Roussillon tourism plans

Development. The development of tourism in Languedoc-Roussillon is seen as a classic example of using tourism to stimulate the economy in a rural and backward region. A whole new holiday coast has been created in Languedoc. It consists of six new tourist complexes, each independent of the other, with hotels, apartments, yachting marinas and entertainment facilities. The mosquito-infested swamps have been drained. The tourist units are linked by spurs to the main inland motorway. To date, the project, which caters for nearly 400 000 tourists, has greatly benefited not only Languedoc but also the French economy.

Tourism in Mediterranean France
SAMPLE QUESTION

Fig. 6.17 The French Riviera

Describe the development of tourism in Mediterranean France.

France has long been a favourite country for tourists. Paris, with its wealth of cultural, artistic and historical attractions, is the country's greatest tourist centre. But France indeed offers the tourist a wide range of choices from the rugged coastline of Brittany to the grandeur of the Alps, from the scenic beauty of the Loire Valley to the reflective quiet of the shrine at Lourdes, from the volcanic landscape of the Auvergne to the sun-drenched beaches of the Mediterranean.

Tourism in Mediterranean France presents a striking contrast between the well-established tourist industry of the Côte d'Azur (Riviera) and the modern development in Languedoc-Rousillon.

The Côte d'Azur. The French Riviera in Provence has been an important tourist area since the mid-nineteenth century, when it attracted wealthy English tourists with their discovery of Nice as a winter resort. The completion of the Paris-Nice railway in 1865 helped to popularise the Riviera coast even further and made it accessible to a wider range of tourists. The rapid development and 'democratisation' of international tourism in the years since World War Two have created a major growth area along the whole of the Riviera coastline from Menton on the Italian frontier westwards towards Marseilles. For generations, this sun-kissed south-eastern corner of France has won superlatives from tourists and travel brochures. It has been called the *Playground of Europe* and the *Jet-Setters' Paradise*. What factors have favoured the development of tourism here?

- The Mediterranean climate of hot, dry summers and abundant sunshine is the main attraction for the summer visitors. The mild and sunny winters also attract their quota of visitors. The coastal region is protected by the Maritime Alps from the cold Mistral wind which blows down the Rhône corridor in winter.

- The scenic beauty of the Riviera coastline is extremely attractive with granite and limestone cliffs overlooking magnificent sandy beaches. The warm waters of the Mediterranean, sheltered by numerous headlands, offer a variety of water sports – sailing, swimming, water-skiing, etc.

- Within easy reach of the coastal resorts lie the old Roman cities of Arles and Nîmes and the medieval cities of Avignon and Aix-en-Provence, with their cultural and historic attractions. Roman sites like the aqueduct at Pont du Gard and the Roman settlement of Vaison are other attractions. The Maritime Alps, not far from the coast, offer a glimpse of fascinating Alpine scenery. They are reached by spectacular mountain roads, with frequent hairpin bends.

- Communications have played an important part in the development of the Côte d'Azur. Excellent rail and motorway links from the Channel coast, Paris and elsewhere move through the Rhône corridor to the coastal resorts which include St Tropez, Cannes, Nice and Monte Carlo. The airport at Nice is another important means of access.

In recent years, the traditional hotel accommodation on the Riviera has been supplemented by caravan sites and holiday camps. Over two million tourists visit the area during the summer months. Congestion of people and traffic has become acute on the crowded Riviera coast.

URBAN SETTLEMENT

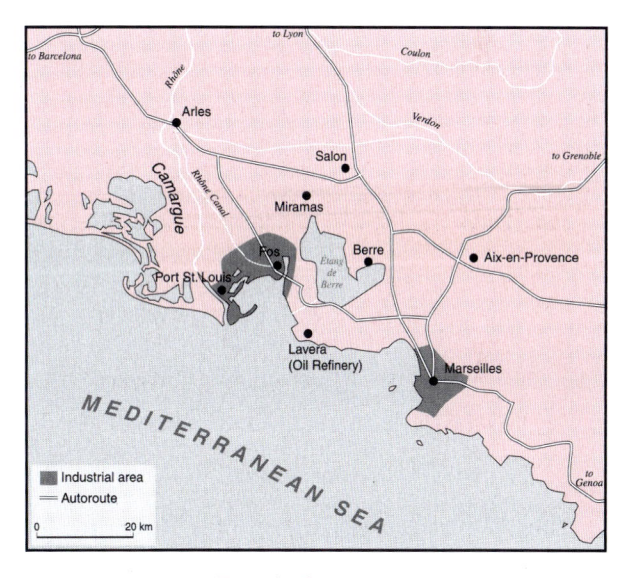

Fig. 6.18 Marseilles

Marseilles was an important port in the time of the ancient Greeks. Today it is France's premier port and a leading industrial centre. Several factors have led to its supremacy as a Mediterranean city:

- It is located to the east of the Rhône delta and is silt-free because the east-west movement of longshore drift carries the silt away from Marseilles.

- In the nineteenth century the opening of the Suez Canal increased its importance as a port for trading with the Far East. The expansion of French colonies in north Africa added to its trade and established it as France's major colonial port. Its early industries developed from its colonial imports of foodstuffs, (coffee, spices) and raw materials (rubber, silk, vegetable oils).

- Its location at the Mediterranean end of the Rhône-Saône corridor gives it access to a large and important hinterland. To the west, the Etang de Berre and Gulf of Fos provide deep-water access for oil tankers and bulk ore carriers.

- Marseilles' importance today stems from its four major functions:

  1. As an outlet for the prosperous Rhône-Saône valley
  2. As the Mediterranean port of France
  3. As an industrial conurbation
  4. As the link between the Mediterranean and industrial north-west Europe.

Modern developments

As part of a government industrial decentralisation plan Marseilles has been developed as a major growth area for the Mediterranean region of France. These developments may be summarised thus:

- The port facilities at Marseilles have been improved and extended.

- The Etang de Berre and the Gulf of Fos have been linked to Marseilles by a canal. A new port has been constructed at Fos, which is now capable of handling the largest oil tankers. Oil refineries, chemical plants, steelworks and car plants are some of the new industries established in Fos, which has become the *Europoort* of the Mediterranean and the southern gateway for the EU countries. From Lavera, on the Etang de Berre, the south European oil pipeline (S.E.P.) brings oil to Lyons, Basle and Karlsruhe.

- The industrial and port area of the expanded port complex of Marseilles has thus revitalised the south of France, which was for long one of France's economic deserts, created by the concentration of people and industry in Paris.

Lyons

Lyons is now the second city of France and the regional capital for much of the south-east. Established as a fortress town by the Romans, its nodal position along the Rhône-

Fig. 6.19 Vieux Lyon

Saône corridor at the confluence of these rivers has led to its development as a major communications and industrial centre. It is now the largest industrial centre outside of Paris.

In general, its industries benefit from the presence of the nearby St Etienne coalfield and the HEP generated in the French Alps and on the Rhône. Major industries include chemicals, metallurgy and engineering. Petro-chemicals are manufactured in the huge Rhône-Poulenc plant which is supplied with oil by pipeline from Marseilles. The famous silk industry, established in the Middle Ages, is now only a minor part of a diversified textile industry. Food-processing is a major industry, based on the thriving agriculture of the Rhône-Saône valley.

Bordeaux

Bordeaux developed at the lowest bridging point of the Garonne, at the head of the Gironde estuary. It is 96km from the sea and thus the larger ships are serviced by its outports, Pauillac and Le Verdon. It is the chief port of the south-west and the regional capital of Aquitaine, but its importance as a port and industrial centre has suffered from its relatively remote location in the south-west of France and its distance from the major market outlets of Paris and the north.

Bordeaux is the chief wine centre of France. It blends, bottles and markets the quality wines of Aquitaine. Many of its other industries are related to its imports (sugar cane, rum, coffee, oil seeds, cocoa and tropical timber).

Le Havre

Le Havre lies on the northern side of the Seine estuary. It is the second port of France and is the main outlet for the Paris basin. It is France's main port for the Atlantic trade and can take the largest tankers and bulk carriers. It is a major importer of fuels (oil, coal), cotton, timber and chemicals.

A major industrial area has developed at Le Havre as part of the development plan for the lower Seine valley. The aim is to create a French Europoort at the mouth of the Seine facing the Atlantic and Channel sea routes, as well as to attract industries from Paris.

Toulouse

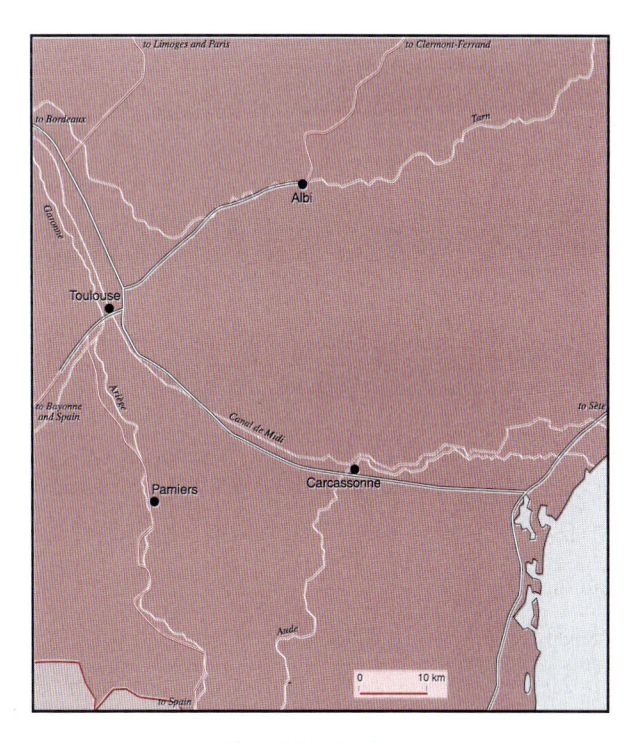

Fig. 6.20 Toulouse

Toulouse, just below the confluence of the rivers Ariege and Garonne, is a natural focus of routes between the Atlantic and the Mediterranean via the Garonne and the Carcassonne Gap. It is linked to Bordeaux by canal and to Sète on the Mediterranean by the Canal du Midi. It is also a focal point for routes from the north to the south-east (Mediterranean coast) and south-west (Bayonne and Spain).

Toulouse is the chief industrial town of Aquitaine and was chosen as a growth centre for the south-east. Industries, based on agriculture, process the varied produce of Aquitaine, the Massif Central and the Mediterranean coast. They include flour milling, tobacco and leather goods. HEP from the Pyrénées and natural gas from Lacq have helped the development of chemical industries. Toulouse is also the major centre of France's aircraft industry. Concorde, the supersonic aircraft, is manufactured here.

Questions

1. Write an account explaining how the population densities of France vary internally.
2. Explain what you understand by the term region. Illustrate your answer by referring to examples drawn from your study of France. (L.C. Higher Level)
3. 'Modern France is a country with striking regional contrasts.' Write an account of two contrasting regions under the headings (a) physical features, (b) agriculture, (c) industry.
4. The wine industry of France.
   (a) With the aid of a sketch map identify four major production areas.
   (b) Describe the factors which favour the cultivation of the vine.
5. Explain how both the main characteristics of France's agriculture and also its general regional pattern have been influenced by five of the following factors:
   (a) climate,
   (b) relief,
   (c) soils,
   (d) markets,
   (e) historical and social factors,
   (f) government and EU policy. (L.C. Higher Level)
6. Analyse the factors that have contributed towards the growth and development of settlement and industry in the Mediterranean coastlands of France (Midi). (L.C. Higher Level)

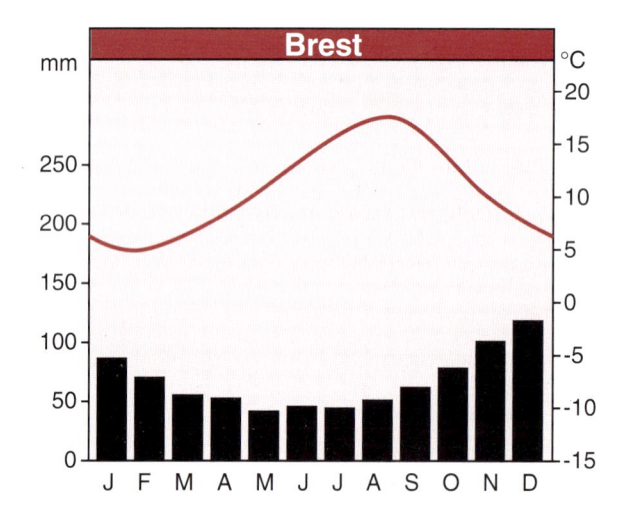

Fig. 6.27 Brest Climate

7. Study the climatic graph for Brest (Brittany, N.W. France) and answer the following questions:
   (a) Describe the main features of the climate.
   (b) Describe the main influences which determine the climate of Brest.
   (c) Explain why the temperature never drops below freezing.
   (d) Describe the other factors which contribute

towards making Brittany one of the important agricultural regions of France. (L.C. Ordinary Level)

8. Write geographical notes on each of the following:
   (a) The problems of the Massif Central region and the measures taken to overcome these problems.
   (b) The development of the Rhône.
   (c) The relocation of manufacturing industry in France.

9. Write an account of the tourist industry in Mediterranean France.

10. 'There is a great difference between Paris and the provinces in terms of job opportunity and other aspects of economic and social life.'
    (a) Give reasons for this inequality. Refer in particular to the area of France west of the Le Havre-Marseilles line.
    (b) Discuss the measures that have been taken to reduce this inequality.

11.
Arable land	30%
Pasture	25%
Forestry	21%
Built-up and Waste Land	24%

Examine the table above which gives details of the land use pattern in France.
   (a) In the case of any two regions state how the land use of those regions compares and contrasts with the land use pattern given above.
   (b) In each case account for the similarities/contrasts described. (L.C. Higher Level)

12. Choose two contrasting regions in France.
    (a) Draw a simple annotated sketch map to show the relative position of the two areas you select.
    (b) Account for the contrasts between the two regions.
    (c) What do you understand by a *problem region*?
    (d) Name one problem region in France and indicate why it might be classified as such. (L.C. Ordinary Level)

13. 'Paris dominates France.'
    (a) Discuss the role of Paris as a communications centre.
    (b) Describe its importance as an industrial centre.
    (c) Note the problems that have followed its development as a highly centralised conurbation.

14. Write brief notes on each of the following;
    (a) Afforestation in the Landes.
    (b) The Mistral.
    (c) The motor vehicle industry in France.
    (d) The iron and steel industry of Lorraine.

15. Languedoc is one of France's problem regions.
    (a) Name the chief problems of the region.
    (b) Outline the developments undertaken to overcome the problems.

16. Using a sketch map identify the locational advantages of Marseilles. Explain *two* ways in which its economic activities show that it has a large hinterland. (L.C. Ordinary Level)

17. (a) Draw a sketch map to show how you would divide the whole country into two or more regions.
    (b) Select *two* of these regions and, in the case of **each,** describe its main characteristics using the following headings:
    Physical geography
    Agriculture

Manufacturing industry and services.
(L.C. Ordinary Level)

18 Examine in detail the economic development of France, under each of these headings:
Primary activities
Secondary activities
Tertiary activities.
(L.C. Higher Level)

19 **Paris**
(a) Describe its location with the aid of a sketch map.
(b) Explain any *three* factors which led to its growth and development. (L.C. Ordinary Level)

20 **France**
Select *one* important manufacturing region.
(a) Draw a sketch map to show (i) the location of the region, (ii) the chief transport features, (iii) the chief towns.
(b) Explain in detail why the region has attracted so much manufacturing industry. (L.C. Higher Level)

21 **Farming in the Paris basin/Wine production in France**
Select one of the above and explain how its development has been influenced by: physical geography; markets; government and EU policy.
(L.C. Ordinary Level).

22 Name *one* region in Europe which has declined from its former industrial prosperity.
(a) Examine in detail the causes of its present problems.
(b) Indicate briefly the measures being taken to reduce these problems.

23 'Some regions of western Europe are clearly identifiable as **core** regions, while other regions are more marginal.'
Assess the validity of this statement, with reference to any two countries of your choice. (L.C. Higher Level)

24 'There are positive and negative aspects to nuclear power as a source of energy in Europe today.' Discuss this statement in detail. (L.C. Ordinary Level)

25 Describe some of the problems associated with major European cities.

26 'Tourism can have a negative impact on an area.'
Explain *three* reasons why this is so. (L.C. Ordinary Level)

27 Explain with the aid of a sketch map how Marseilles developed as an important port.

chapter seven
germany

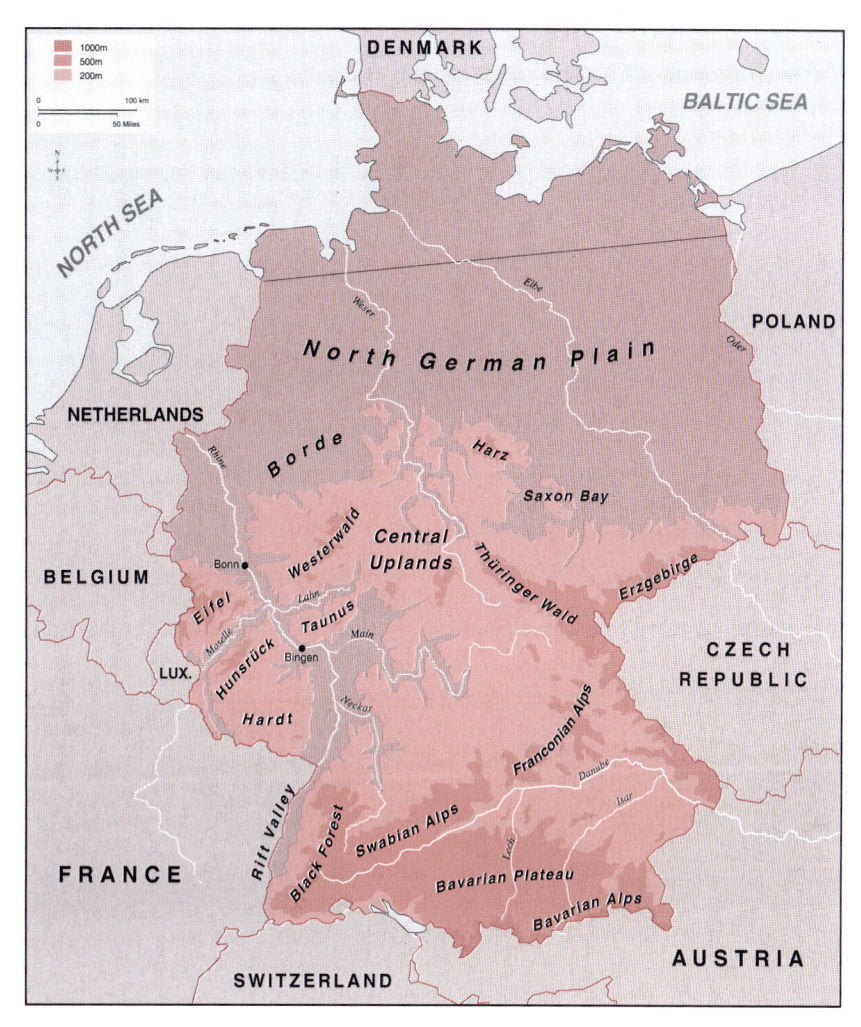

Fig. 7.1 Germany; physical

INTRODUCTION

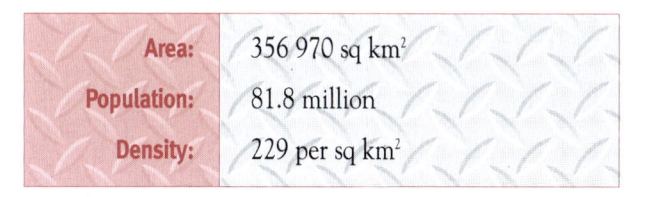

Area:	356 970 sq km²
Population:	81.8 million
Density:	229 per sq km²

At the end of World War 2 in 1945, Germany was occupied by troops from Britain, France, USA and the then USSR (Union of Soviet Socialist Republics). In 1949 the country was divided into East Germany (Communist) and West Germany (democratic). Rapid economic development followed in West Germany which became one of the six founder members of the EU in 1958. On 3 October 1990, Germany was reunited as the Federal Republic of Germany.

Germany has a variety of charming landscapes. Low and high mountain ranges intermingle with upland plains, hills and lakes as well as wide open lowlands. The country may be divided into three main physical regions: (1) the North German Plain, (2) the Central Uplands and (3) the Southern Mountains. Each of these three regions is markedly different in its origins, structure and landscape.

CLIMATE

Latitude, altitude and distance from the sea are the main climatic controls in Germany. North-west Germany has a maritime climate, mild and wet. Average winter temperatures are above 0°C, periods of severe weather are short and there is little snow. Southern and eastern areas of the country experience a continental climate, with cold winters, heavy frosts and often severe snowfalls. Summer temperatures are high, averaging up to 20°C, creating heavy thunderstorms and a high summer rainfall total.

SOILS

With some notable exceptions, the soils are not naturally fertile. In the north, extensive areas along the low-lying coastlands form a level, treeless, boggy moorland. To the south are the geestlands, vast expanses of higher land of gravel and sand, with peat bogs in surface depressions. The largest area of geestland lies between the Weser and the Elbe. The geestlands (infertile land) form sterile and useless agricultural land.

Between the geestlands and the Central Uplands lies the Borde, a region of well-drained, undulating lowlands with rich loess soils which is one of the most fertile agricultural regions in Germany. In the Central Uplands soils are generally poor while those in the Alpine region are thin, stony mountain soils. Soils in the Rhine Rift Valley and the Danube Valley are fertile alluvial soils, among the most productive in Germany.

ENERGY/MINERALS

Germany is the world's tenth largest producer and fifth largest consumer of energy. Its main energy resources are:

    Coal

    Lignite

    Oil

    Natural gas

Coal

1 Coal is Germany's most important natural resource. But the decline of coal as a source of energy throughout the EU and competition from newer sources of energy, especially oil, have had an impact on the industry in terms of employment, technology and rationalisation.

2

Coalfield	1974	1994	Comment
Ruhr	120.3	51.5	14 collieries
Saar	16.0	9.1	3 collieries
Coalfield's production (million tonnes)			

3 The German government, as a member of the ECSC (European Coal and Steel Community) moved swiftly to meet the challenge posed by the new importance given to oil as an energy source. The various coalmining companies in the Ruhr were amalgamated into a single company – Ruhrkohle. The smaller and unproductive collieries were closed to create fewer but more efficient units. The entire coal industry was

modernised and mechanised. Grants were given for re-housing and re-training redundant miners.

4. Thermal power stations were built near the collieries, thus reducing transport costs. The very quality of the environment in the Ruhr and other coal-mining areas was improved. Green fields, nature parks and leisure areas now cover much of what was once a grimy landscape of spoil heaps and abandoned collieries.

5. The oil crises of the 1970s marked a turning point for Germany and other industrial countries. The cost of imported oil soared and its supply became uncertain. OPEC's use of oil for political ends exposed the dangers of dependence on imported oil. Germany moved to reduce the consumption of oil by the energy industry. Laws were passed to phase out or reduce the use of oil in power stations. Coal returned to favour as a source of energy.

6. Although coal will never recapture its pre-war importance in Germany, output has stabilised and coal is now a more efficient and competitive source of energy.

Lignite

Germany's reserves of lignite (brown coal) are the largest in the EU. Lignite produces less heat than coal but it is easier to mine. It is thus a cheaper form of energy and is used in power stations and chemical plants. The most important lignite areas are around Cologne in the west and Leipzig and Cottbus in the east. Several power stations are located on the lignite fields.

Oil

Germany is very limited in its oil resources. A small oilfield near Ems on the Dutch border provides less than 4% of the country's oil needs. Oil pipelines carry imported oil from Wilhelmshaven and from the Netherlands, France and Italy to oil refineries throughout Germany. In recent years oil and gas reserves found originally in the North Sea and Netherlands have been found to extend into north-west Germany. The network of pipelines has been extended to collect these new resources.

Natural Gas

Germany has a number of natural gas fields. The most important are those in the Ems estuary and in the area between the rivers Ems and Weser. The output is quite significant and supplies 15% of the country's energy requirements. In addition, a well-developed pipeline network distributes domestic and imported gas to the chemical and iron and steel industries throughout the country.

As resources of coal, oil and natural gas decline and prices increase, the use of nuclear energy in the generation of electricity for industry has expanded throughout western Europe. Since the production of nuclear power requires plentiful supplies of water and plenty of space, nuclear plants are located on the coast or near large rivers. Because of radiation hazards they are situated away from major population centres.

Germany now has 23 reactors in operation. However, resistance to the use of nuclear energy with its appalling threat to human life and the environment for generations to come is very strong in Germany. The Greens and CND groups have vigorously opposed the government's plans to increase the number of nuclear plants. The accident at the nuclear plant in Chernobyl (USSR) in April 1986 and the resulting radioactivity over much of north and western Europe have strengthened the anti-nuclear lobby in Germany and elsewhere. In 1992 the German government closed all the nuclear stations in the former East Germany in response to safety fears, as the safety standards in these stations were poor.

HEP

A number of hydro-electric power stations are located along the Rhine border with Switzerland.

Minerals

The reserves of mineral resources are not very plentiful. The iron ore deposits of the Salzgitter-Peine area in Lower Saxony are the most important, but the iron content is low and high quality ores are imported from Africa and Sweden. Deposits of salt and potash in the Hanover and Brunswick areas form the basis of important chemical industries, especially the manufacture of fertilisers.

ASPECTS OF AGRICULTURE

1. Reunification in 1990 has restored to Germany large and fertile farming areas in the east which were the granaries of pre-war Germany.

2. About 3% of the workforce is engaged in the agricultural sector, compared to 25% in 1950. Attracted by the prospect of higher incomes, many farmers have left the land to work in industry and services.

3. The physical environment of Germany is not very suitable for a thriving and productive farming industry. Infertile soils, climate variations and large areas of upland all limit farming productivity.

4. Small family farms still dominate the farming economy. The average farm size is around 10 hectares (25 acres). Many of these small holdings are fragmented into scattered strips of land. Thus, farming is uneconomic because mechanisation is not practical, time is wasted in working the scattered parcels of land and the small-scale operation is generally inefficient. In the former East Germany, most of the land was worked in collective (State) farms. Because of lack of investment, farm yields were not very high. With reunification in 1990, farmland was returned to private ownership. As in other EU countries, the German government has initiated a policy of amalgamation and consolidation to make its agricultural sector more competitive in the EU market.

Fig. 7.2 German dairy farming

5 Even though many farm workers have left the land, too many people are still employed in agriculture and the income of the peasant farmer is in striking contrast to that of the industrial worker.

6 Although agriculture is still the weak link of the German economy, the impact of the EU has resulted in greater productivity in both cereals and livestock.

Agricultural regions

FLOOD PLAIN — Pasture (dairying) and woodland on poorer gravel soils

LOWER SLOPES — Wheat, sugar beet, maize, vegetables, hops, tobacco

UPPER SLOPES — Vines dominate (3/4 German wine production); also fruit orchards – Mediterranean and temperate fruits

BLACK FOREST — Large areas remain forested; pasture in clearings and some fodder crops; dairying important

Fertile Loess soils in many places | Thin infertile soil; heavy rainfall

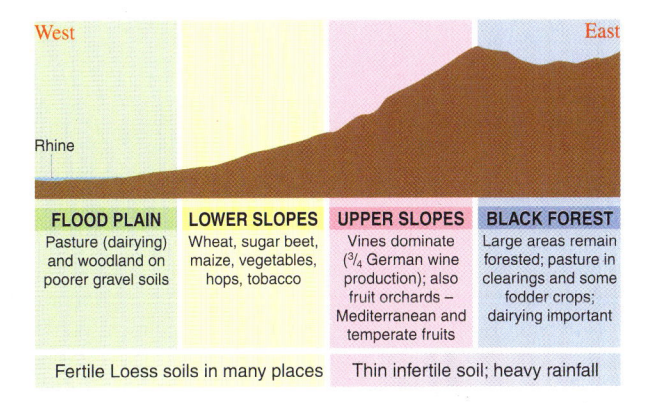

Fig. 7.3 Rhine Rift Valley

The Rhine Rift Valley

The Rhine leaves Switzerland at Basle and flows north to Mainz through a prosperous rift valley about 320km long and 45km wide. This valley is bordered by the Vosges and Hardt mountains on the French side and by the Black Forest and Odenwald on the German side.

In the first section of the valley, it forms the boundary between these two countries. It is joined here on its right bank by two significant tributaries – the Neckar at Mannheim and the Main at Mainz.

This is a rich, productive and diverse farming region – one of the most important agricultural regions in Germany. It has many advantages for farming, notably its soils. Alongside the river lowlands are heavy alluvial soils which have been drained and support water meadows. This is the centre of the pastoral farming with dairy herds particularly important. The lower slopes of the uplands are covered in very fertile loess soils. We find here intensive cultivation of wheat, maize, sugar beet, tobacco and hops. The middle slopes are often terraced and are covered in vines and orchards. The south-facing slopes are particularly important. This is the centre of the German wine trade, producing much of the country's output.

Fig. 7.4 The German Wine-growing regions around Mosel

The rift valley is well sheltered and has more sunshine and higher temperatures than any other agricultural area in Germany. Winter frosts are not severe and spring arrives early. There is a well-developed transport infrastructure, and because of the richness of the agriculture the whole region is densely settled with many large villages, towns and cities, many of them dating back to medieval times.

The early wealth of this middle Rhine region was based on the prosperity of the agriculture in the valley.

The Borde

Along the southern edge of the North German Plain, at the border of the Central Uplands lies the Borde, the most fertile and intensively farmed region in Germany. Highly mechanised arable farming produces rich harvests of wheat, barley and sugar beet from the deep loess soils. Population density is very high. The typical settlement is a nucleated village of up to 2 000 people. The beet supplies the raw material for the numerous sugar factories in the area while the beet waste is used for animal fodder. Market gardening is concentrated near the cities – Cologne, Hanover, Brunswick.

Fig. 7.5 Main Industrial Areas

MANUFACTURING INDUSTRY

Germany is one of the world's major industrial nations. Its economy has the third largest gross domestic product (GDP) in the world, behind only Japan and the USA. The main driving force in the economy is manufacturing industry, employing 37% of the workforce.

Aspects of manufacturing industry

1. Germany is the most highly industrialised country in western Europe. Manufacturing is its lifeblood. It employs 37% of the workforce and contributes very significantly to the country's prosperity.

2. The abundant reserves of coal were the basis of industrial development in Germany. The earliest industrial cities developed around the coalfields in the Ruhr, Saar and Aachen regions.

3. The central location of Germany in Europe and its superb communications network of Rhine, inland waterways, railways and roads have provided easy access to raw materials and to the vast markets of the EU for its industrial products.

4. Germany's industrial economy consists of two very different patterns:
   - heavy capital-intensive industries
   - light industries.

Heavy capital-intensive, basic industries which often use coal either as a power source or a raw material, e.g. coalmining, iron and steel, heavy engineering, heavy chemicals. These industries are generally located near the coalfields or have access to inland ports or pipelines for the import of raw materials.

The use of oil, natural gas and electricity as alternative energy sources has made industrial location much more flexible than before, since these new sources can be transported with comparative ease across a country.

Despite this, the type of industries noted above tend to remain where they were first established, even though local power sources or raw materials have declined – an example of geographical inertia. This is the process whereby industry remains in an area because of such factors as a skilled workforce, linkages with other industries, the capital invested in the plant, a large regional market or a long tradition of quality products.

Light industries which use varied raw materials and produce highly processed goods. They may cater for a local market, e.g. Hildesheim, in the loess region of the north, manufactures agricultural machinery. Or a factory industry may have evolved from a craft trade, as in the manufacture of cutlery in Solingen. Many of these light industries are *footloose*. They are not tied to a particular type of location by raw materials or power source. For these industries, the market determines the location. Many of the modern industries, using high technology and aimed at the consumer market, e.g. electronics and cars, are located in the south of the country, far away from the traditional centres of industry.

5   Manufacturing industry is widely dispersed throughout Germany. The Ruhr, despite its relative decline, is still the most important industrial region. It is part of the *Hot Banana,* Europe's core area for industry and services. As in other EU countries, a significant development has been the growth of industrial cities such as Frankfurt, Leipzig, Dresden, Munich, Stuttgart, Nuremberg, Karlsruhe, Hanover and Brunswick.

6   In the field of advanced technology, Germany has led in western Europe, particularly in the petro-chemical and electronic engineering industries. Adaptation has been German industry's answer to the challenges of every decade – in technology, in raw materials, in location and in markets.

7   Germany's industrial strength is shown in the following table.

Rank in EU	Company	Country	Activity
3	Daimler Benz	Germany	Motor vehicles
5	Volkswagen	Germany	Motor vehicles
6	Siemens	Germany	Electrical engineering
9	VEBA	Germany	Electrical, Chemicals
12	Deutsche Telekom	Germany	Telecommunications
17	Hoechst	Germany	Chemicals
19	BASF	Germany	Chemicals
20	RWE	Germany	Energy production

Top 20 Manufacturing Groups in the EU

SAMPLE QUESTION

Fig. 7.6 Main Industrial Areas

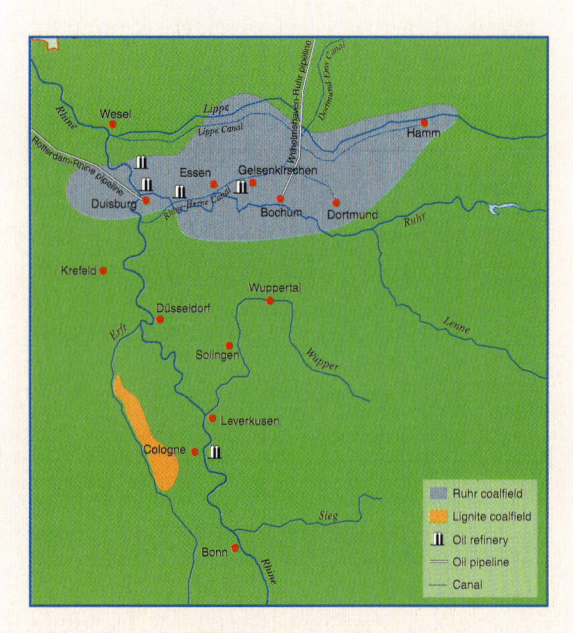

Fig. 7.7 The Rhine - a superb water transport system

(i) Draw a sketch-map to show the major industrial regions of Germany, **(ii)** Select *four* regions and discuss their importance.

Rhine-Ruhr industrial region

The Rhine-Ruhr region is one of the most concentrated industrial and urbanised areas in the world. Over eleven million people live in an area one-sixth the size of Ireland, in a conurbation of twenty-two cities headed by Cologne and including Essen, Düsseldorf, Duisburg and Dortmund. This is the largest conurbation in Europe.

For over 100 years, the region has been the powerhouse of Germany industry. Its great industrial significance is shown by its resilience in twice recovering after many of its factories had been either destroyed or dismantled as a result of the two World Wars. Today it plays a major role in the industrial prosperity of Germany and is the apex of the *Heavy Industrial Triangle* of the EU.

Note the following factors which account for the importance of the Rhine-Ruhr industrial region:

Location. The development of the region began in the eleventh century. The medieval cities of Cologne, Duisburg and Dortmund originated as market and trading centres along the Hellweg, the ancient *east-west* trade and migration route from the east. The Rhine has long been a major *north-south* route axis, not only for river transport, but for the roads and railways which converge on or follow it.

The Rhine-Ruhr region is thus located at the crossroads of two major routeways, the Hellweg and the Rhine. The importance of its location is further emphasised by its position at the heart of the EU Industrial Triangle.

Coal. The region's industries were based on coal. Although affected by the general decline in the coal economy of the EU, which resulted in a reduced workforce and fewer coalmines, the Ruhr coalfield is still the most productive in the EU. It contains a variety of coals, but it is noted for the quality of its coking coal, used in the steel industry. Mechanisation and high technology are important factors in the efficiency of its coal industry.

Skills. Over a century of intense industrial development has established a tradition of high industrial skills in the labour force, especially in the steel and engineering sectors.

Adaptation. In its major industries – coal, steel, engineering, chemicals – the region has successfully adapted to the challenge of modern technology. The survival of the steel and engineering plants despite the disappearance of the original advantages of location shows the strength of German industry.

Rhine-Ruhr industries and cities

Iron and steel. The coal and iron and steel industries are the twin pillars of the region's industrial might. As with coal, the iron and steel industry has had to adapt to economic pressures and new technology. It has done so in three ways: (a) there has been considerable investment in new plant; (b) the Rhine and its canals are used for the large-scale import of iron ore from Sweden and west Africa; (c) steel production is now concentrated at waterside locations – Dortmund and Duisburg. The steel plants of the Ruhr produce 75% of Germany's steel.

Engineering. Engineering industries are widespread throughout the Rhine-Ruhr region. Towns formerly engaged in steel production now concentrate on heavy and light engineering products. Bochum, Essen and Dortmund are noted engineering centres.

Chemicals. The availability of coal as a fuel and a raw material stimulated the pre-war chemical industry in the region. Today, coal has been replaced to a large extent by oil and natural gas, fed into the region by pipeline. In addition, the Rhine waterway carries bulk raw materials into the region from Rotterdam and is used in the distribution of the finished chemical products. The Bayer plant at Leverkusen employs 30 000 workers. Cologne is noted for cosmetics and pharmaceuticals. Düsseldorf has the largest detergent works in Germany.

Outside the mining area, the proximity of the Rhine waterway has stimulated a wide variety of industries.

The southern or Rhineland part of the Rhine-Ruhr region has major cities with many-sided developments, based on service industries as well as a diversity of manufacturing industries. It thus contrasts with the Ruhr cities, which depend very much on manufacturing and mining. This Rhineland section is a major growth area and it is dominated by three cities – Düsseldorf, Cologne and Bonn.

Textile industries are concentrated around Wuppertal to the east of the Rhine and around Krefeld to the west. In the lower Wupper valley, the towns of Solingen and Remscheid are noted for their special steels, used in the manufacture of cutlery, machine tools and precision instruments.

Düsseldorf is the administrative capital of the Rhine-Ruhr region. It is the financial, banking and commercial centre of the region and home to the company headquarters of many of Germany's major firms, such as Krupp, Siemens and Thyssen, as well as those of multi-national corporations such as IBM and the Chase Manhattan Bank. Its impressive high-rise buildings and elegant streets are a striking image of Germany's economic success. Although service industries provide much of the city's employment, it also has a varied industrial base, including fashions, engineering and chemicals.

Cologne has been an important route centre since medieval times. With the coming of the railways, it expanded rapidly as a trading and industrial centre. Today it is a focal point for the roads and railways that converge on the Rhine valley. It is an inland port and a major commercial and service centre. Its many industries range from oil refining and petro-chemicals to food processing and a wide range of consumer goods including cosmetics, chocolate, clothing and leather.

Bonn is situated at the point where the Rhine emerges from its narrow gorge. It had been the capital of West Germany since 1949. However, since unification in 1990, Berlin has been restored as capital. It is a relatively small city of medieval origins with some light industries.

The Ruhr: Problems and Responses
Although the Ruhr is the leading industrial region in the EU it is not without its problems.

Problems
As already noted, the decline of coal as an energy source has had a catastrophic effect on the coal industry. The smaller, shallower mines have been exhausted and closed. Mining has moved northwards to the deeper (1 000m) mines along the Lippe valley. This migration has resulted in

higher costs at a time when there is increasing competition from cheaper imported coal and other cheaper, cleaner energy sources such as oil, natural gas. In addition, the Ruhr steel industry, which was a major consumer of Ruhr coal, fell into decline because of the move to coastal steel plants which use imported iron ore. New technology in steel production made many of the Ruhr steel plants out of date.

Closures at Ruhr coalmines, steelworks and textile factories led to the loss of hundreds of thousands of jobs. In the coal industry alone, the number of miners fell from 500 000 in 1950 to 70 000 in 1993. The unemployment rate soared from 1% in 1970 to 15% in 1988. Over 550 000 people migrated out of the Ruhr, leaving behind a derelict, blighted landscape and a polluted environment.

Responses

The structural re-organisation which followed the closure of mines and the large-scale re-organisation of the industry has resulted in a remarkable rise in productivity. Ruhrkohle AG now controls 95% of total coal production in the region and has diversified into engineering, environmental technology and building construction.

The Ruhr steel industry is now concentrated at waterside locations along the Rhine to the west and along the Dortmund-Ems and Rhine-Herne canals to the east. Duisburg is Germany's major steel producing centre and the world's largest inland port. A new planning authority for the region, the KVR, an association of local authorities, has actively worked to improve the quality of the environment. Green areas, nature parks, new housing and new urban areas now cover much of the former industrial wasteland.

Faced with the problem of creating a 'new' Ruhr industrially and environmentally, with 'a blue sky over the Ruhr', the Federal and State governments have attracted new light industries – electrical engineering, cars, food processing, etc. – into industrial estates in the region. New industries have been developed, especially in environmental industries (water management, waste management, air cleaning, noise abatement) and technology centres. Industrial jobs in the region are often more high-tech than unskilled. The service sector in the region now employs 55% of the workforce.

Re-training facilities for unemployed miners, steelworkers and others have been introduced and subsidised by the Federal and State governments. All these developments are now creating a more balanced industrial structure, a cleaner industrial sector and a pleasant, healthier environment.

MIDDLE RHINELANDS

The Middle Rhinelands (Rift Valley) is a focus of routes that (i) link the North Sea with the Alpine passes and the Mediterranean and (ii) link France with southern Germany and Austria. These routeways have been used since the Middle Ages and now the railways and autobahns follow these ancient lines. The Rift Valley, and the rest of the Rhine, is the centre of the economic axis of the EU (*The Hot Banana*) and so industry, trade and commerce converge on the area.

The wealth of the agriculture, the density of population and the convergence of routes have also laid the foundations of a thriving industrial economy. The Rift Valley is the second most important industrial area of Germany. The main concentration lies between the Neckar valley and the Frankfurt-Mainz complex to the north.

Stuttgart lies on the river Neckar, a major tributary of the Rhine. It is a major route link between the east and south, to the Rhine in the west. It is also the rail focus for south Germany. The Middle Rhinelands lacks raw materials, but compensates by specialising in high quality products that require little raw material. Stuttgart is the chief manufacturing centre and industry has spread from there to the surrounding towns. It is a major centre for the car industry. Daimler, Mercedes, Porsche and Audi have major plants there. Other industries include machine tools, engineering, electricals, chemicals, textiles and food processing.

Karlsruhe, on the Rhine, is a city vital to the needs of all industry in the Rhine Rift Valley. It is the terminus for the south European pipeline from Marseilles, and of the central European and trans-Alpine pipelines via Ingolstadt. It has major refining and chemical plants and is the distribution centre for oil throughout the Rift Valley.

The twin towns of **Ludwigshaven/Mannheim** lie to the north of Karlsruhe. These are the most important inland ports in the area, as they can be reached by 5 000 tonne barges. In addition to the Rhine transport there are rail, road and pipeline networks. This ease of transport has influenced the development of chemicals, petrochemicals, synthetic fibres and pharmaceuticals. The major German chemical firms are located here. The BASF operation at Ludwigshaven is the largest chemical complex in Europe.

At the northern end of the Rift Valley lies the major industrial triangle of Frankfurt/Mainz/Darmstadt. Each town lies within 30km of the other. The towns were settled over a long period, as Mainz was an old Roman defence town, Frankfurt a crossing point to southern Europe and Darmstadt the capital of the old kingdom of Hesse. All three towns are *route foci*.

Frankfurt has engineering, rolling stock, rail works, motor, electricals and chemical industries. It is a rail focus and has one of the busiest airports in Europe. Above all, it is a financial and commercial centre. It houses the German Bundesbank, and the European Monetary Institute as well as over 400 German and foreign banks. It has the largest Stock Exchange in Europe and is the centre for numerous fairs and international gatherings, of which the Book Fair is the most notable.

Darmstadt has renowned chemical and pharmaceutical works, with both Hoechst and Merck established there. Early computers were first assembled in Darmstadt, which also has a famous agricultural research centre.

A mini-conurbation has developed in this area as Frankfurt extends west to Hoechst, Russelsheim, Wiesbaden and Mainz and south to Darmstadt. Hoechst has chemicals, textiles and dyes; Russelsheim is the Opel headquarters; Wiesbaden is famous for paper and printing; and Mainz is an important river port with a variety of industries including cars, engineering and electricals.

Fig. 7.8 Industrial complex

The whole region from Mannheim to Mainz is one of the major growth areas of the EU. Industry concentrates on light engineering rather than the heavy-type industry of the Ruhr. Its development can be traced to the convergence of routes, the river and canal transport of raw materials and finished products, the ready availability of oil, the area's centrality and the dense settlement across the whole valley which provides a workforce and a market.

Bavaria – an area of industrial growth

Throughout this text we have noted certain traditional industrial areas which are now in decline, e.g. Sambre-Meuse in Belgium and the Nord in France. In this section we see the rise of an industrial region which up to the last forty years had very little industrialisation.

Bavaria is the largest federal state in area and up to 1950 its economy was based on agriculture. Farming and forestry are still important, but Bavaria's economy is changing. Its industrial development is growing at a faster rate than any other region.

Up to the post-war era, Bavaria was deficient in many of the then requirements for industry:

- It had no coalfield.
- HEP was the only local energy source.
- It had few of the basic raw materials for industry.
- It was remote from the traditional industrial areas of Germany.
- Because of the poor physical environment, it had a low density of population.
- The transport infrastructure was poorly developed and because of this and its remoteness, the cost of importing raw materials was high.

As a result, industry was small-scale, specialised and widely dispersed, relying on local timber and agricultural produce.

The large-scale industries of the Ruhr were absent, but instead, the Bavarians used their traditional skills to produce quality textiles, toys, wooden ornaments, glass, porcelain, ceramics, beer and wine.

Among the factors which have aided the economic transformation of Bavaria, we may note the following:

- The change in energy sources from coal to oil stimulated industrial development throughout Bavaria. Pipelines from Trieste, Genoa and Lavera brought oil to the region, with Ingolstadt as the major oil refining centre. Oil refining led to associated chemical industries (See pages 139). The coming of the oil pipelines acted as a major stimulus to industry throughout Bavaria.

- Improvements in the transport infrastructure – canalisation of the river Main, construction of autobahns and the electrification of the rail system in the region – have helped to reduce the remoteness of Bavaria from the rest of the country.

- Refugees from East Germany brought with them traditional craft skills and set up small specialised industries – glass, jewellery, textiles.

- The central government policy after the war was to decentralise new industry so as to achieve a balance between the richer traditional industrial areas and the less advantaged areas like Bavaria. At that time agriculture was being re-organised in Bavaria and so a large surplus labour force was available which migrated to the cities. Many German firms which were in the process of expanding began to locate on greenfield sites in Bavaria, away from the traditional industrial areas which were not attractive to the newer *cleaner* industries.

TOURISM

Bavaria has a year round tourist industry. It owes its great tourist appeal both to its rich cultural and historical heritage and the charm of its scenic landscape. It spends £40 million annually in preserving its cultural heritage. The Bayreuth Festival commemorates the works of composer Richard Wagner. Since 1634, the Oberammergau Passion Play has been presented every ten years. The next performance of this world famous play is scheduled for the year 2000.

The magnificence of the Alps, the beautiful lakes in the Alpine foreland and the serenity of the Bavarian Forest attract thousands of tourists. Forest walks, hill trails, fishing and watersports all entice the tourist. Bavaria has many extensive parks and magnificent palaces but above all, it has a clean and healthy environment in vivid contrast to the old industrial areas.

Fig. 7.9 Bavaria's tourist industry

Munich

Munich is the third largest city of Germany. Situated in the valley of the river Isar, it is at the intersection of the north-south trans-Alpine route and the east-west route from Paris to Vienna. Munich developed rapidly since it was selected as the capital of Bavaria in 1806. It became the administrative centre of southern Germany. But at the end of World War Two Munich lay in ruins. Yet by the 1970s it had grown into one of the country's most prosperous cities and hosted the 1972 Olympic Games. Its post-war development has been an advantage in that, unlike older industrial regions such as the Ruhr, it has avoided the problems of pollution and dereliction and concentrated on the cleaner high-technology sections of industry. It is now an important rail and road centre. It is also a major industrial centre with electronics, food processing, textiles, chemicals, brewing, cars (BMW), optical instruments and cameras (Agfa), Siemens electricals and electronics. It is also the centre of Germany's film industry. It has a number of historic buildings and art museums, one of which – the Deutsches Museum – houses the world's largest collection devoted to the history of Science and Technology.

Fig. 7.10 BMW headquarters in Munich

Nuremberg The National Museum of German Culture is located here.

Guestworkers in Munich

Two world wars within twenty-five years left Germany with a serious demographic problem, a great shortage of male workers. The solution has been to import foreign labour. Seventeen per cent of the population of Munich is made up of guestworkers. They are most heavily concentrated in older areas around the CBD (central business district). They come from Yugoslavia, Greece, Turkey and Italy. They are generally employed in jobs which are unpopular with native German workers. These include the less skilled jobs, as in the construction industry; dangerous jobs, as in mining and asbestos works; menial jobs such as street cleaning; poorly paid jobs as in catering; and labour-shortage activities such as agriculture. The guestworkers, however, are much better off than at home and send money back home to support their families.

In 1990 Germans thought that unification would mean another economic miracle like that from the mid-1950s to the mid-1970s, when unemployment never rose above half a million. But the cost of unification has been high. DM 800 billion has flowed from west to east since 1990, mainly the proceeds of higher taxation in the west. Unemployment has soared to 4.7 million, the highest for over 60 years. This has lead to demands for the repatriation of the guestworkers.

In recent years, Germany has been deeply shocked by a series of brutal attacks on foreign workers. Arson attacks on hostels for guestworkers have become so common that they make headlines only when someone is killed.

SAXONY

On 3 October 1990, the two Germanies were reunited and the former East Germany brought 108 000 km² and 16.5 million people into the new Germany. It also brought many problems with it – environmental, industrial and social. Saxony had been part of the former East Germany.

Saxony's extensive deposits of lignite (brown coal) were used to generate electricity, to power the railways, and as a domestic fuel. Thermal power stations using lignite lacked pollution control equipment, resulting in regular smogs and heavy concentrations of acid rain. The environmental damage thus created was enormous. For four decades the land, air and water suffered from absolute neglect. Little or no effort was made to protect the environment.

Industry suffered from similar neglect. Energy costs were high, labour efficiency and output were low, the infrastructure was poor. Because industries were protected under the state-controlled system and the market was confined more or less to the Comecon (Communist countries) group, there was no competition from the western economies. For the most part, exports consisted of equipment and machinery while imports included a high proportion of energy and raw materials.

The standard of living was well below that of West Germany – fewer cars, TVs, telephones, poorer housing and health services, inefficient public transport and widespread environmental degradation.

With unification came rationalisation. Overmanning in industry was huge. Companies were closed, sold off or re-organised. Unemployment rose dramatically in industry and the services sector. Grants and loans were allocated to the eastern provinces (including Saxony) by the Federal government and the EU.

The state of Saxony had a long tradition of industry and a moderate infrastructure, so the major initial investment took place here. State-controlled factories were sold off, mainly to industrialists, investors and banks from the former West Germany who brought capital, technology, skills and access to markets with them.

The **chemical industry** has long been established in Saxony and government policy is to retain the core of the industry there. Lignite (brown coal) provides the raw material for much of the chemical industry there. Over 60 billion tonnes of lignite are still available for use in Saxony. Over 40 000 workers are employed in the industry mainly in Dresden, Chemnitz and Leipzig. All the plants are being redeveloped and brought up to modern pollution control standards. Within the chemical industry there is on-going research into environmental protection and methods of repairing the damage already done. Government environmental agencies rigorously enforce three principles – co-operation, prevention and 'the polluter must pay'.

Automobile production is an important industry in Saxony. Zwickau was a pre-World War Two car manufacturing centre. State-controlled factories produced the Trabant model, whose unreliability and out-dated style was a legend internationally. After unification Volkswagen bought the factory and promptly closed it, transferring its workers to a new site at Mosel. Volkswagen are also in Chemnitz. Car components are manufactured at Chemnitz, Leipzig, Zwickau and Mosel. Many of the large car manufacturers from western Germany have opened assembly lines in Saxony, investing about 15 billion DM. At the end of 1996 some 350 000 cars per year were rolling off the assembly lines – almost twice as many as before unification.

Electrical engineering is an important industry. Siemens, the biggest single employer in Germany, have established new electrical engineering and electronics plants in Dresden and Chemnitz. Factories involved in the supply of plant and production equipment for the major industries are located throughout the state. The world's first CFC-free refrigerator was designed and built at Leipzig. Chemnitz specialises in tool making and textile machinery. The world famous Meissen and Dresden china and porcelain factories are now back to full production, exporting to Europe and North America. Before World War Two, this area was noted for its craftwork and that tradition still survives with the production of finely crafted toys and optical instruments. It is the most important economic sector and employs 1.5 million people.

With 4.9 million people Saxony is the most densely populated of the new German Lander (states) apart from Berlin. The triangle of Dresden, Leipzig, Chemnitz was one of Germany's major industrial regions before the war. It suffered immense damage from aerial bombing during the final days of the war. Today its industries are a skilful blend of the traditional and the high-tech. It has a rich cultural heritage which is mirrored in its churches, palaces and museums and which attracts tourists in ever-increasing numbers. More than 5 million tourists visited Dresden in 1996. The Leipzig fairs have been in existence for 800 years. The city is a noted centre for publishing and printing and its world renowned Book Fair has been restored. The whole region is attracting financial and administrative services as well as international banking institutions.

Chemical production regions

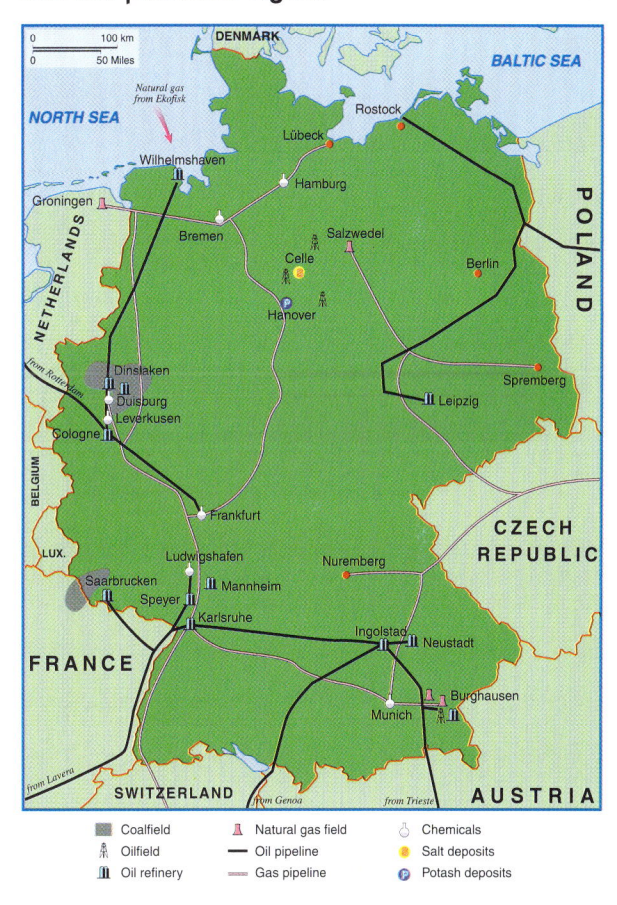

Fig. 7.11 Chemical industries

There are *five* main production regions, two of which are in the densely-populated Rhine valley. The major chemical companies in Germany are Hoechst, BASF and Bayer, each of which produces a wide range of chemical products.

The Rhine-Ruhr region. The availability of coal as a fuel and a raw material stimulated the pre-war chemical industry in the region. Today, coal has been replaced to a large extent by oil and natural gas, fed into the region by pipeline. In addition, the Rhine waterway carries bulk raw materials into the region from Rotterdam and is used for the distribution of the finished chemical products. The Bayer plant at Leverkusen employs 30 000 workers. Cologne is noted for cosmetics and pharmaceuticals. Düsseldorf has the largest detergent works in Germany.

Middle Rhine region. The excellent import and distribution links provided by the rivers Rhine and Main were important factors in the development of the region into a major chemical region. At Ludwigshafen the giant BASF plant lines the banks of the Rhine and employs 45 000 people. The main products are fertilisers, dyes, acids and plastics.

Bavaria. The chemical industry in Bavaria developed in the Alpine foreland, using local limestone and salt deposits, local HEP and imported Ruhr coal to produce insecticides and fertilisers in a number of small towns around Burghausen, east of Munich. Ingolstadt, with five large oil refineries supplied by the South European pipeline from Lavera and the trans-Alpine pipeline from Trieste, is now the major petro-chemical centre of Bavaria.

Lower Saxony. Hanover is the chemical centre of the region. Local supplies of potash form the basis of the industry.

North Sea Ports. Modern chemical plants require large areas of level land. The North Sea ports provide ideal sites for such plants which are serviced by oil pipelines. The import of salts and pyrites gives a wide base to the industry.

Saxony. Centred around Dresden and Leipzig, using lignite.

The chemical industry

SAMPLE QUESTION

> **Write a description of the chemical industry in Germany.**
>
> Germany is the leading producer of chemicals in the EU, with a workforce of over 580 000. Its modern technology and emphasis on research have placed it among the world's leaders. This applies especially to its three giant MNCs – Bayer, BASF and Hoechst. There is also a large number of small and medium-sized companies. 56% of the industry's output is exported. Major oil companies have played an important part in the development of the industry.
>
> ### Chemical products
>
> The chemical industry is analytical and synthetical. It separates raw materials into their basic elements and re-arranges them to form new products. It thus plays a leading role in providing a wide range of raw materials for many industries. In this way, it is a key industry in the whole industrial economy. It supplies bleaches, synthetic fibres and dyes to the textile industry; rubber,

plastic, tanning materials to the footwear industry; fertilisers and chemicals for crop protection to the agricultural sector; medicines and cosmetics to the pharmaceutical industry; acids to the heavy chemical industry. The chemical industry, in one way or another, touches on most aspects of modern living, urban and rural. It supplies our needs from petrol to plastic, from fibres to fertilisers.

Requirements for location

In Germany we find all the factors which influence the location of the chemical industry. They are:

> Availability of raw materials
> Proximity of market for the product
> Availability of power supplies
> Proximity to waterway sites.

Availability of raw materials. Organic chemicals (now using coal, oil, natural gas) were first produced in large quantities from coal. Hence the earliest chemical plants were located on the coalfields, e.g. the Ruhr. Although oil and natural gas have now to a large extent replaced coal as a raw material, the chemical plants still operate on the coalfield sites, although the raw materials have changed. Deposits of salt, potash, limestone have also stimulated a chemical industry, e.g. lower Saxony, Bavaria.

Proximity of market. The development of a network of oil and natural gas pipelines has led to the location of oil refineries and chemical plants in areas where there is a large demand. This location factor may be noted in the Rhine-Ruhr, Middle Rhine and Bavarian chemical industries.

Availability of power supplies This factor applied to the early coalfield locations. Cheap and plentiful supplies of HEP attract electro-chemical industries in particular. The traditional sector of the chemical industry in Bavaria uses the abundant HEP of the Alpine foreland.

Proximity to waterway site. Coastal and inland waterway locations offer an attractive location for chemical plants because of the ease of supply of fuel and raw materials. Such sites are also important because of the abundance of water available for cooling purposes and because the soluble chemical waste can be conveniently deposited. Thus in the Rhine-Ruhr and Middle Rhine we find the importance of the Rhine emphasised in the number of chemical plants that line the banks of the waterway.

Problems for chemical industry

The chemical industry is one of the leading sectors of the Germany economy. It covers a wide range of goods from industrial raw materials to finished products. Inevitably, the sheer size and the very nature of the industry cause problems, both for the industry itself and for the environment.

1. A modern chemical plant requires an extensive area of land as a site. Such a site is both expensive and difficult to find near traditional chemical manufacturing locations in major urban areas. Hence existing plants are unable to expand.

2. The chemical industry has a bad reputation for pollution of air and water. Many of the chemical plants which line the banks of the Rhine discharge highly toxic chemical waste into the river.

3. Despite the emphasis on automation and fail-safe systems in petro-chemical plants, there is always the danger of explosion and/or the release of deadly chemicals into the air. The fears of environmentalists have been further increased by the fact that the major chemical corporations are building their own nuclear power stations to provide cheaper power. Rigorous pollution control measures are now in force. Many Chernobyl-style nuclear power stations in the former East Germany have been closed as have many chemical plants. The use of lignite, a major polluter, by chemical plants has been severely restricted.

4. Since the transport of the main raw material, oil, is comparatively easy by pipeline and since expansion of existing smaller plants is uneconomic, it would seem that for the future, the chemical industry will concentrate on the development of a few large complexes, located where plenty of land is available.

Fig. 7.12 The Rhine

THE RHINE

The Rhine, 1200km long, is Europe's most important waterway. Indeed, it is one of the most important in the world. From its source in the Swiss Alps to its mouth at Rotterdam on the North Sea, it borders or flows through six countries – Switzerland, Liechtenstein, Austria, Germany, France, Netherlands.

The Rhine waterway is central not only to the German economy, but also to that of the EU. The mineral resources, industrial zones, urban centres and network of waterways and other communications that are focused on the Rhine provide the major growth axis of the EU.

Importance of the Rhine

- The Rhine is a major north-south **routeway** in western Europe. With its tributaries and linking canals, the Rhine provides a superb water transport system. Its major tributaries – Moselle, Main, Neckar – are linked with other great European rivers and provide a water network between the North Sea, the Black Sea and the Mediterranean. In effect, the Rhine is the central artery of a vast economic circulatory system that reaches an immense hinterland and is vital to the industrial health of western Europe.

- The Rhine is **navigable** by 2 000 tonne barges as far as Rheinfelden, slightly upstream from Basle. The upstream journey from Rotterdam to Basle takes 4-5 days. Sea-going vessels can travel from Rotterdam to the inland port of Cologne. Navigation on the Rhine has been greatly improved by canalisation, especially in the Rift valley section (Basle to Bingen) where the river once meandered across a marshy floodplain and meltwater from Alpine glaciers caused flooding in early summer. The Grand Canal d'Alsace now bypasses this difficult section.

In the narrow Rhine gorge (Bingen to Bonn), the river slices through uplands in a narrow valley set between steep sides. The gorge provides the vital communication link between Germany's two great industrial areas – the Rhine-Ruhr and the Rift valley.

- The Rhine is an unique trading artery. It is the world's busiest river and its seaport, Rotterdam, is the world's greatest. Much of the traffic is carried by barges, often linked together in trains. The Rhine serves as an industrial conveyor belt of raw materials upstream from Rotterdam for industry. In particular, it services western Europe's major industrial region, the Ruhr.

The largest volume of traffic on the Rhine is carried between Rotterdam and Duisburg, the port of the Ruhr. Upstream ships and barges carry iron ore, oil, grain and other raw materials. Steel and other manufactured products are brought downstream. There is also heavy traffic between the different Rhine ports. The intense trading and traffic along the Rhine may be gauged from the annual traffic volume of the major ports (in million tonnes): Duisburg 46, Mannheim 17, Cologne 14, Strasbourg 12, Karlsruhe 8. In addition, the Rhine valley carries the major north-south road and rail links and pipelines.

- The impact of the Rhine on **industry** can be clearly noted in the growth of industrial cities along its banks and those of its tributaries – Strasbourg, Mannheim, Stuttgart, Mainz, Frankfurt, Cologne and Duisburg. The growth of industry and cities has been directly affected by the Rhine acting as a converging point. Port industries have developed in all these cities, with an emphasis on engineering and chemicals.

Berlin

Since 3 October 1990 Berlin has once again become the German capital. By the year 2 000 it will be the seat of Federal Government. Huge construction programmes to improve the standard of housing in the eastern half of the reunited city are underway and its transport systems are being improved and redeveloped.

Since its foundation as a trading settlement in 1232, Berlin has had a rich and varied history. It has long been the cultural metropolis of Germany, the home of many of the country's most famous writers, painters and architects. It boasts three Opera Houses, several major orchestras (including the world famous Berlin Philharmonic Orchestra), dozens of theatres and internationally renowned museums.

Berlin today is a vibrant resourceful capital. Emphasis is being placed not only on its traditional manufacturing industries of electrical and mechanical engineering, printing, chemicals and food processing but also increasingly on the service sector – financial services, software development, marketing, engineering services, etc. Siemens, AEG and IBM are major electronics firms in the city.

As an international conference centre, Berlin ranks sixth in the world. Its International Audio and Video Fair is the world's largest fair for consumer electronics. The Berlin Film Festival ranks alongside Cannes as Europe's most important film festival. Well over three million visitors come to Berlin every year to sample the city's wealth of cultural offerings.

THE NORTH SEA PORTS

Hamburg

Hamburg is Germany's second largest city, its principal seaport and the country's largest overseas trade centre. 150 firms from China, 135 from Japan, 65 from Taiwan and 25 from Hong Kong have offices there. All in all, more than 3 000 firms are engaged in import and export business in Hamburg.

As a result of reunification and the opening up of Eastern Europe the port of Hamburg has regained its old hinterland and is once again becoming the centre of trade, communications and services between East and West. The port area, one of the largest in the world, spreads out over 75km^2 and occupies one-tenth of the city area. In terms of container trans-shipment volume, Hamburg ranks second in Europe after Rotterdam.

Hamburg is Germany's second largest **industrial centre.** Four groups of industries may be noted:

1. **Port industries:** shipbuilding, marine engineering, refineries.
2. **Processing industries:** raw materials from abroad are processed – oil refining, chemicals, grain, rubber.
3. **Consumer industries:** brewing, food processing, tobacco, printing.
4. **Service industries:** banking, insurance, media industries. Hamburg is the centre of the German media industry. More than 3 300 firms are active in this sector and employ a workforce of 50 000. In recent years, the media sector has been the city's most rapidly expanding economic sector. Major television and

radio stations, advertising agencies and magazine publishers are located there. The city is also Germany's centre for the production of CDs, music cassettes and records.

Fig. 7.13 Shipbuilding in Hamburg

Hamburg is a city with a rich cultural tradition. Germany's first permanent Opera House was established here in 1678 and Handel's first opera *Almira* was staged there. Bach, Telemann, Brahms and Mendelssohn were born there. Four state theatres and forty private theatres enhance the city's cultural profile. It was in Hamburg that the Beatles embarked on their international career in the early 1960s. And finally – Hamburg is celebrated in the Guinness Book of Records as the city with the most bridges in Europe – more than London, Venice and Amsterdam combined!

Bremen

Bremen is situated on the river Weser, 64 km from the sea. It is the country's second largest port and the largest passenger port. Shipping, international trading and high-quality industrial products are the foundations of Bremen's economic life. Like Hamburg, its dominant industries are shipbuilding and the processing of imported raw materials. Bremen is also one of the centres of the German food, luxury food and beverage industries. Coffee, chocolate, milk products, spices and beer are the best-known products. The aerospace industry plays an important role in Bremen's economy. Key components for rockets, satellites and the Airbus are developed and built in Bremen.

Electricals, electronics and high-tech industries likewise play a prominent part in the city's economy. Bremen is also a noted centre for marine research. It houses the Institute of Shipping Economics, the Centre for Tropical Marine Ecology, the Institute for Polar and Marine Research. It is also home to the Bremen Free Market, one of Germany's largest fairs, and to the annual Bremen Music Festival.

Much of the modern expansion of Bremen has centred on its outport, Bremerhaven, which has ferry and container terminals and a variety of light industries. The Kusten canal links the Weser to the Ems and thus provides a valuable trading link with the Ruhr.

THE NEW GERMANY

At the end of World War Two, the victorious powers – USA, France, Russia and U.K. – assumed complete authority in Germany. They were determined that Germany would never again dominate Europe and hence they divided Germany into four occupation zones.

Russia quickly established control in its own zone to the east and a Soviet-style government was put in place.

Berlin, the old capital, was also divided into four sectors. East Berlin was confirmed as capital of the new **east Germany,** the German Democratic Republic (GDR). By 1948, the other allies had agreed to the formation of a new **west Germany,** the Federal Republic of Germany (FRG), with Bonn as its capital. In east Germany, west Berlin was an island of democracy linked economically to the FRG.

Fig. 7.14 Berlin

This situation obtained up to the end of the 80s. The GDR was a Communist dictatorship, with collective farms, state-controlled industry, little freedom and a ban on movement to the West. But the collapse of Communism in eastern Europe and the opening of the Berlin Wall in November 1989 led to the resignation of the GDR administration and in October 1990, the five *Lander* (states) of east Germany and east Berlin were incorporated into the Federal Republic of Germany. The unification of Germany was complete.

But unification was not a simple matter of new territory, larger area, bigger population and new eastern borders. It brought with it enormous economic and social problems. The highly productive, internationally competitive economy of the west was now faced with the unprofitable, unproductive, centrally-planned economic structures of the east. Almost all aspects of the East's economy have had to be reformed and restructured, at huge financial cost. To date, over DM800 billion of Federal Government and of private investment have been spent in transforming the former east Germany. EU funds have also helped.

The first initiative was the agreement to make the old less valuable FRG mark equal in value to the Deutschmark. This was essentially a massive subsidy to the eastern Lander. It marked the beginning of the complete restructuring of the GDR economy in all its aspects.

Industry. Production plant and machinery in the factories of the GDR were obsolete, productivity was less than 30% of the level in west Germany and energy consumption was twice as high as in the west. Industries, formerly state owned, had to be privatised wherever possible. Many companies were either restructured or closed. Generous grants and tax incentives were made available to encourage industries and services to establish in the eastern Lander. A number of the privatised companies were taken over by foreign investors from France, Japan, Netherlands and the U.S.A., e.g. the French oil company Elf Aquitaine which has taken over the former petrol stations chain Minol. Markets established in the Communist era in the old COMECON countries were maintained, thus giving the new Germany new business opportunities in Eastern Europe.

Retraining. The retraining of the east German workforce was an important element in the economic reform plan.

Retraining grants and schemes were introduced. Of particular importance was the reconstruction of an efficient small and medium-sized business sector, which had been almost completely wiped out during the GDR era. Today there are again some 500 000 small and medium-sized businesses and independent professionals employing a total of 3.4 million people. Unemployment in the eastern Lander declined noticeably in 1995. But in 1996 unemployment had increased again to a total of 1.2 million.

Agriculture. The agricultural sector in eastern Germany, formerly devoted to collective state-controlled farming, has been radically altered. The collective farms have been broken up and replaced by private farms run on an individual or group basis. As a result, the number of people employed in farming has been halved and almost a million hectares of arable farmland have been taken out of production.

Energy. A major challenge for the Federal government is to reduce dependence on the east's supplies of lignite (brown coal) although it is certain that it will continue to play an important role in Germany's energy supply. Improving energy efficiency in the east will require not only substantial investment in new technology but an emphasis on an **energy conservation** policy in urban and rural development schemes. All nuclear plants were closed because they were considered unsafe.

Environment. The critical environmental situation in east Germany also required immediate action. **Air pollution** was the most serious issue, due to the long-term neglect of environmental precautions in the east. As a result, east Germany had the highest emissions of sulphur dioxide in Europe and of carbon monoxide levels in the world at the time of reunification in 1990. The effects on the population were frightening. One out of every two east German children suffered from respiratory diseases and one child in three suffered from eczema. In addition, the high levels of air pollution created mainly by outdated lignite power stations have badly damaged German forests.

Water pollution is a further problem in the east. It was caused by the over-use of pesticides in farming and by uncontrolled dumping of toxic wastes and also by acid rain. Environmental conservation is now a feature of rural policy in the east. Since 1990, 67 new national and nature parks have been established there.

Urban Modernisation. Many of east Germany's historic town centres had been allowed to deteriorate considerably in the forty years of Communist rule. Sizeable funds have been allocated for urban improvements in the towns and cities of the east. The projects include the conservation of historic city centres, control of building development and the improvement of living, shopping and office facilities. Improving **transport links** between the east and west of Germany is also a high priority. Heavy investment in road and rail links is making movement between the new and old Lander (states) easy. Priority is given to improving transport links between Berlin and the major western cities and linking the Saxony industrial region to the Rhine-Ruhr and Rhine-Main industries.

Unification therefore has had its benefits and its problems for both sides of the formerly divided Germany. Difficulties still remain as regards jobs, housing and social security. Nevertheless, the new Germany now has a sense of strong national identity. It is now the largest country in the EU, it has the biggest population and it accounts for 25% of the EU's industrial and agricultural output.

Questions

1. 'Manufacturing is Germany's lifeblood.' Write an account of either the iron and steel industry or the chemical industry in Germany.

2. With the aid of a sketch map, name and locate the following: (a) the Rhine and three tributaries, (b) the Black Forest, (c) the Bavarian Alps, (d) the Ruhr coalfield, (e) the Lignite Triangle, (f) Berlin, (g) Munich, (h) Frankfurt, (i) Cologne, (j) Hamburg.

3. Write geographical notes on each of the following:
   (a) The role played by waterways in the economic development of Germany.
   (b) The industrial development of Bavaria.
   (c) Agriculture in the Rhine Rift Valley.

4. The river **Rhine** is the major water artery through Germany. Along its course is the agricultural Rift Valley and the industrial Rhine-Ruhr complex.
   (a) With the aid of an annotated sketch map show the location of these areas in relation to the rest of Germany and to each other.
   (b) In the case of any one of the above areas choose four appropriate headings from the following to describe the economy of the area: (i) relief, (ii) climate, (iii) historical development, (iv) soils, (v) accessibility, (vi) presence of raw materials, (vii) geographical inertia, (viii) markets. (L.C. Ordinary Level)

5. (a) Why is Germany the largest manufacturing producer in western Europe?
   (b) Examine briefly the development and problems of a major industrial region in Germany. (L.C. Higher Level)

6. Describe and explain the growth and development of Hamburg.

7. (a) Account for the decline in coal production in western Europe during the period 1955-75.
   (b) Discuss the changing geography of coal-mining in Germany and also the impact of decline on the coalfield areas concerned. (L.C. Higher Level)

8. Account for the importance of the Rhine to the German economy. What environmental problems are associated with it?

9. Account for the growth of the Ruhr basin into a major industrial area. (L.C. Higher Level)

10. 'Rotterdam is Germany's leading seaport.' Discuss.

11. Write a geographical account of the Ruhr region under the headings: (a) effects of the decline of coal, (b) environmental problems.

12. Coal, iron ore, salt, potash, petroleum, natural gas are all important minerals associated with Germany.
    (a) For each of the minerals mentioned name and locate an important producing area in that country.
    (b) Choose *three* of the minerals and write an account of the production and utilisation of each one in the area in which you have located it. (L.C. Higher Level)

13. Write an account of the chemical industry in Germany under the headings (i) location factors, (ii) products, (iii) problems.
14. What are the chief differences between the ports of Bremen and Hamburg? Refer to communications and hinterland in your answer.
15. Name the factors that have helped to create industrial regions in the south of Germany and have challenged the supremacy of the Ruhr. Give an account of *one* such industrial region.
16. Write an account of Germany's iron and steel industry.
17. 'Oil has helped to decentralise manufacturing industry throughout Germany.' Discuss.
18. Explain why the ECSC (European Coal and Steel Community) is closing down some coal pits and expanding others. What are the effects of these changes on the coalmining industry?
19. Draw a sketch map of the course of the Rhine and name and locate on it the following: (a) the neighbouring countries, (b) the major cities and industrial regions along its banks, (c) the major tributaries and relief features. Indicate also the type of products transported up river and down river.
20. Analyse the role played by the exploitation of natural resources in the economic development of Germany.
21. 'EU policies have been successful in many respects, but some notable problems remain to be overcome.'
    Examine this statement with reference to (i) agriculture or (ii) fishing.
22. Within a European country of your choice, select *one* important manufacturing region.
    (i) Draw a sketch map to show:
       (a) the location of the region
       (b) the chief transport features
       (c) the chief towns.
    (ii) Explain in detail why the region has attracted so much manufacturing industry. (L.C. Higher Level)
23. The distribution of manufacturing industry has changed over time. Older industries are still to be found concentrated in particular regions, while newer industries are more dispersed. (L.C. Higher Level)
24. (i) Name *one* core region within the EU.
    (ii) Explain some of the reasons for its success.
    (iii) This success has often led to problems within the core region itself. Examine briefly some of these problems.

chapter eight
switzerland

INTRODUCTION

Area:	41 300 sq km
Population:	6.9 million
Density:	168 per sq km

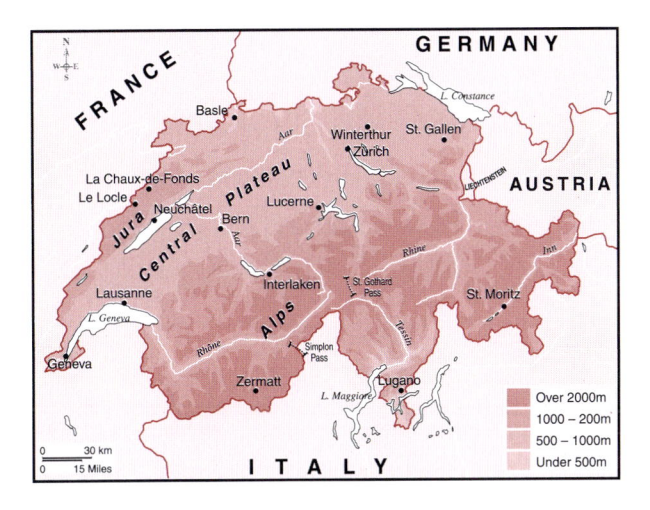

Fig. 8.1 Switzerland

Switzerland is one of the smallest countries of western Europe, landlocked between France, Germany, Austria and Italy. It has natural frontiers on all sides – the Rhine to the east and north, the Jura mountains to the north-west and Lake Geneva and the mighty Alps to the south. It occupies the main watershed of western Europe where the Rhine begins its journey to the North Sea, the Rhône to the Mediterranean, the Inn to the Danube and the Ticino to the Po and the Adriatic Sea.

It is a country of twenty-three cantons with a Federal government in Berne. Each canton has a large degree of self-government but the Federal authority controls national defence, power supply and communications. Neutrality is the keystone of the Swiss constitution. It is not a member of the United Nations nor of the EU.

Probably no other nation has made quite such a business out of neutrality as the Swiss. Ever since 1864, when the International Red Cross was started there, Switzerland has become the headquarters of such international organisations as the World Health Organisation (WHO), the World Wildlife Fund, the World Council of Churches, the International Labour Organisation (ILO) and the General Agreement on Trade and Tariffs (GATT).

There is no Swiss language by which to identify Swiss people. Four different languages are spoken and all are recognised officially. The most widespread is German. French speakers occupy the south-west, a smaller group of Italian speakers are in the Ticino valley, while in the remoter valleys of the south-east a few speak Romansch.

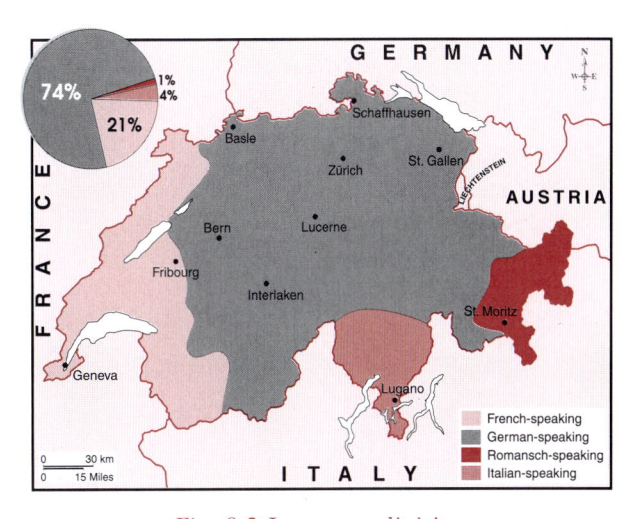

Fig. 8.2 Language divisions

Fig 8.3 Aerial valley view

CLIMATE

Much of Switzerland has a continental type climate (warm summers, cold winters), but the valleys south of the Alps experience much of the sunshine and high temperatures of the Mediterranean lands. A number of factors play an important part in the climate of different regions.

Altitude affects temperatures and precipitation.

Aspect is very important and determines land use. South-facing slopes (adrets) have much longer sunshine hours than north-facing slopes (ubacs), resulting in higher temperatures and a longer growing season. Distance from the sea increases summer temperatures but lowers them in winter.

Natural resources and advantages
Water power
Landscape
Forests

Water power

Switzerland is not rich in natural resources. It has no coal, oil, natural gas or iron. It has few metal ores. Only 27% of the land is suitable for agriculture. But it does have a wealth of water power which is of immense economic value and has provided the stimulus for the country's increasing industrialisation.

Thousands of HEP stations are scattered along the mountain valleys and produce electricity which is carried by high tension grid to all parts of Switzerland and used by the railways, factories and the domestic consumer. HEP now provides 75% of Switzerland's electricity.

Most of the HEP plants are located (a) in the Alps and (b) in the valleys of the Rhône, Rhine and Aar. As in Scandinavia, the harsh physical environment has contributed greatly to the development of hydro-electric power, especially in the Alpine areas – the heavy precipitation, the deep valleys, the steep gradients, the storage capacity of the snowfields and glacial lakes. Water is stored in high-level lakes and reservoirs and sent by the pumping stations to the power stations in the valleys. The problems of low water flow in March (water locked up by the winter freeze) and high water flow in early summer (flood water from the melting snowfields) have been solved by the construction of dams which hold back huge reservoirs and thus control the seasonal flow of water. Almost all the potential HEP resources have now been harnessed to provide electricity for industry, the railways and the domestic consumer.

Importance of HEP to the economy of Switzerland

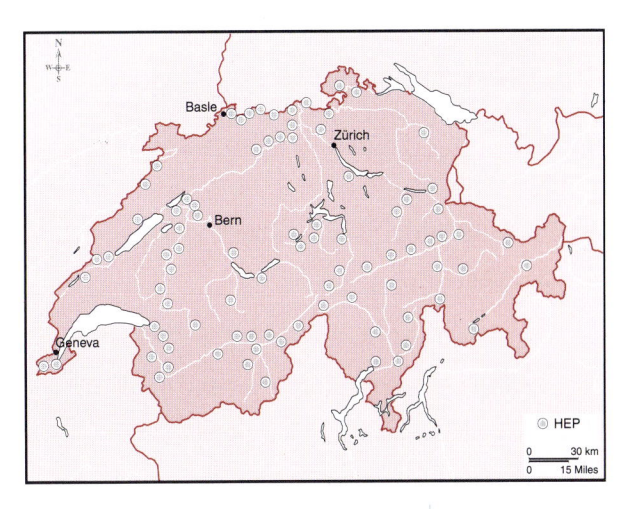

Fig. 8.4 HEP plants

- HEP provides Switzerland's only native source of energy and thus reduces its dependence on imported fossil fuels.
- It is a relatively cheap source of energy.
- The widespread use of HEP has contributed to the non-pollution of the environment by Swiss industry.
- The Swiss railway system is powered by electricity from the HEP stations.
- Hydro-electricity is used extensively in the country's steel plants, and in the engineering and metallurgical industries.
- The widespread location of HEP plants throughout the country has led to the dispersal of Swiss industry and a resulting spread of employment. Many of the power stations are small and serve only local domestic and industrial consumers, but they emphasise the gradual penetration of industry into the Alpine region.
- The construction of storage reservoirs for HEP stations has proved an effective measure of flood control in dealing with the problem of melting snow.

Landscape

Switzerland is a mosaic of mountains, lakes, valleys and forests. The Swiss Alps consist of two main ranges, each running from south-west to north-east and divided by the great east-west longitudinal trough, in which flow the Rhône and the Rhine. The northern range (Bernese Oberland and Glarus Alps) is formed mainly of limestone rock. The southern range (Pennine Alps, St Gotthard Massif, Rhaetic Alps) is composed of older crystalline rocks. The Jura mountains form a series of parallel limestone ridges and valleys.

The mountain slopes of the Jura and Alps are covered in coniferous forest up to 1 800m. In the Alps, meadows extend above the forests to the snowline and provide valuable summer pastures for the valley farms. Glaciation has had a profound impact on the landscape of Switzerland. Glaciers and snowfields are a feature of the higher Alps. Hanging valleys with cascading streams and spectacular gorges contrast with the serene beauty of the glacial lakes. The unrivalled scenery and the facilities for

Fig. 8.5 Switzerland's abundant water supply

winter sports have encouraged tourism both in summer and winter. The tourist industry has been of great benefit to the Swiss economy. The practical Swiss have maximised the attractions of an otherwise forbidding mountainous terrain into an important tourist asset.

THE ALPS

SAMPLE QUESTION

> Discuss the influence of the Alps on (a) agriculture in the Alpine region and (b) the economic development of Switzerland.

Influence on agriculture

The physical environment of the Alpine region (high altitude, cool temperatures, long snow cover and poor soils) ensures that pastoral farming dominates the farming system. The emphasis is on dairy farming, and transhumance plays an important role in the farming system. It is the most efficient way of using the available pastures at different seasons of the year. In winter, the cattle are stall-fed in the farm dwellings near the valley floor. In early summer, the cattle are driven from the lowland pastures to the lower slopes of the mountains (*moyenne*). As the snow thaws higher up along the mountain, the cattle are moved to the higher pastures above the forests (*alps*). During these summer months the valley lowlands and sides are used to grow hay and fodder crops. In autumn, the herds move down the mountains from pasture to pasture until by winter they are back in their stalls once more to feed on the hay and fodder crops harvested during the summer.

The milk produced on the summer pastures is brought by pipeline (*pipelait*) from the alps to the creameries in the valleys. Much of the milk is sold in the cities and tourist resorts. The rest is processed into butter, cheese and chocolate. As may be seen from Fig 8.6, maximum use is made of south-facing slopes for fodder crops and vineyards. Here too in the valleys the Alpine population is concentrated in the sheltered sunny settlements.

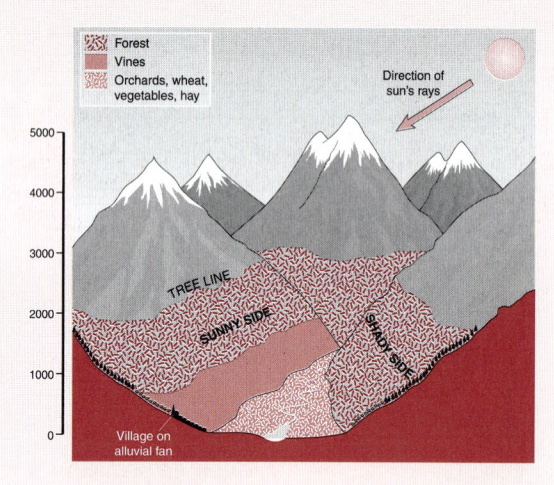

Fig. 8.6 Land use zones in Swiss Alps

The Föhn wind is a characteristic feature of the Alpine climate. When a depression moves across the north of Switzerland, it draws warm moist air from the Mediterranean. This air is dried and warmed even more as it descends the northern slopes of the Alps. The Föhn wind raises the temperature by 10°C or more in a few hours. The Föhn usually blows in spring and melts the snow rapidly. Thus the pastures are cleared on the mountain slopes and cultivation begins on the lowland farms. However, the rapid melting of the snow often results in avalanches and flooding.

TOURISM IN SWITZERLAND

Fig. 8.7 Dramatic landscape

Tourism is one of the cornerstones of the Swiss economy. This invisible export earns about 10% of all currency receipts. It is an industry for which Switzerland has an international reputation and is highly regarded as the great training school for the industry. Tourism in Switzerland combines the physical resources of weather, scenery, mountains, lakes and centrality with the human resources of education, training, communications and amenities.

- Tourism is one of Switzerland's older industries, with roots that go back about 200 years to a time when the tourist season was limited to summer only.

- The Swiss tourist industry is now year-round. Many of the tourist centres cater for both summer and winter tourists. The disadvantages of high mountains and winter snow have been turned to advantage by providing magnificent settings for winter sports. Many Alpine communities now depend almost entirely on tourism.

- The appeal of Switzerland is in its central location within Europe, its proximity to affluent markets, the climate, the variety of scenery and its rich and varied culture. Contributing factors are its role as an international trade centre, and the number of international organisations and conferences to which it plays host.

- A highly efficient road and rail transport system brings easy access even to remote Alpine villages. Small regional airports make the resorts very accessible. In the mountains, the provision of ski lifts and funicular railways facilitate the activities of the tourists.

- High standards of accommodation and catering facilities have earned an international reputation for Swiss hotels and guesthouses. The Swiss training schools in hotel management and cuisine are renowned for their excellence.

- 25% of Switzerland's foreign tourists come from outside Europe, mainly from North America.

Tourism and the economy

The effects of tourism on the economy of Switzerland.

- Tourism is a major source of foreign revenue. Each year, some 13 million visitors spend 5 000 million dollars.

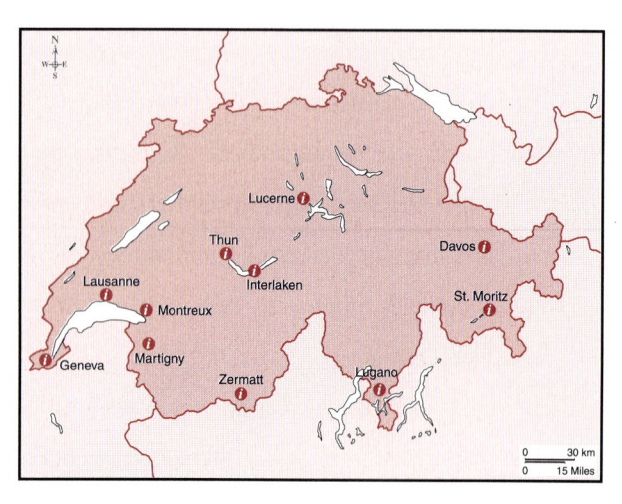

Fig. 8.8 Tourism centres

- Tourism creates 180 000 jobs directly and another 180 000 indirectly.
- In the many mountain areas, where manufacturing industry is largely impossible, tourism provides practically the only employment. Apart from the hotels and guesthouses, there are jobs as ski instructors, ski-lift operators, in the rescue services or in the manufacture and supply of ski equipment and clothing. Transport and construction jobs are also created.
- Tourism has halted the out-migration from the Alpine villages.
- Winter sports are an important element in the economy of the Alps, because they utilise both land and people at a time when they would otherwise be under-employed.
- High unemployment and low incomes have been traditional in the Alpine region. Tourism has helped to correct the imbalance between the Alps and the Central Plateau.
- The major problem has been that of providing the necessary amenities for the tourists while preserving an environment that attracted tourists in the first place. Strict planning controls relating to industry and the environment have preserved Switzerland from the environmental pollution affecting much of western Europe.

SAMPLE QUESTION

Switzerland
(a) Draw a sketch map to show how you would divide the whole country into its regions.
(b) Select one of these regions and describe its main characteristics using the following headings:
- Physical geography
- Agriculture
- Manufacturing industry and services.

(a) Three regions: (1) Jura Mountains, (2) Central Plateau, (3) Alps.

(b) The Central Plateau
   (i) Physical geography. Stretching in a wedge shape between the Jura Mountains and the Rhine to the north, and the Alps to the south, lies the Central Plateau. It is an undulating landscape ranging from 1 200m at the Alps, to 300m along the Rhine Valley, where that river forms the boundary with Germany.

   The Plateau is drained to the north by the Aar, Reuss and their tributaries. A number of moraine-dammed lakes – Geneva, Neuchatel, Thun, Lucerne, Zurich, etc. – lie across the Plateau. See Water Power, p. 154. The area is covered by glacial soils and alluvial deposits. The Central Plateau is the core area of Switzerland. It contains two-thirds of the population, the best soils, most of the industrial towns, the capital Berne and the only port Basle, a river port on the Rhine. It embraces the principal primary, secondary and tertiary activities of Switzerland.

(ii) Agriculture. Mixed farming predominates. About half the area is intensively cultivated with crops of grass, cereals, fodder and sugar beet. Much of this produce is used to provide winter fodder for the dairy herds, as dairying is the chief pastoral activity. Much of the milk is used for immediate consumption in the cities and holiday resorts. The rest goes to the production of high-quality dairy products – butter, cheese (Gruyere, Emmanthaler), baby and invalid foods (Glaxo) and chocolate products (Nestle, Tobler).

Beef cattle are also reared. Some transhumance is still carried on in order to free the lowland areas for summer crops. Increased yields from modern farming methods lessen the need for transhumance. A considerable area of land is now devoted to orchard farming (apples, pears, cherries). The south-facing slopes of the Jura and around Lake Geneva are devoted to vines. Market gardening is important around all the major towns.

(iii) Manufacturing industry and services. Despite a lack of coal and raw materials, no direct access to the sea and a small home market, the Central Plateau is a significant manufacturing region. The abundance of cheap HEP is of primary importance in accounting for the range and spread of industry across the Plateau. Industry is not tied to either a raw material or a power resource.

Switzerland compensates for its lack of raw materials by processing and enriching imported raw materials to a very high standard.

As the core area of Switzerland, the Central Plateau industries:
- are highly specialised
- concentrate on producing goods of low-bulk material with a high input of technology and skill, which command high prices.

- are often aimed at the affluent quality market, rather than the mass market.
- rank among the leaders in a variety of industrial sectors (see chart below).

Products include: diesel engines, turbines and electricity generating equipment (based on HEP experience), electronics, computers, audio equipment, cameras, lenses, medical and dental equipment, watches and precision scientific goods. High quality foods and textiles also feature, as do chemicals.

The chief industrial towns of the Central Plateau are Zurich, Geneva, Basle, Berne and St. Gallen.

The plateau also has a vibrant services sector. Tourism is of prime importance with resorts along all the lakes and at the foot of the Alps and Jura. An excellent infrastructure of airports, roads, railways and hotels adds the human resources to the physical ones of scenery, lakes and mountains.

International banking, insurance and financial services are located in the major cities of the Plateau and are an important part of an impressive services sector.

Year	1970	1980	1995
Primary	8.6	7.2	5.5
Secondary	47.1	39.8	34.4
Tertiary	5.5	34.4	60.1

% employed 1970-1995

The most important of a wide range of service industries are:
- Tourism
- Banks
- Commerce
- Insurance.

THE SWISS ECONOMY

Switzerland is in many ways a country of contrasts. Perhaps the greatest contrast of all is that between its physical environment and its prosperous thriving economy. Consider briefly the disadvantages of its location and physical environment.

1. Switzerland has one of the harshest physical environments in western Europe. Much of its surface land is mountainous. Snowfields, lakes and forest limit land use and settlement.
2. It has very few mineral ores and no fossil fuels, the traditional launching pads of industrial prosperity.
3. It is a landlocked country, far from the sea and from ports of import and export. Its only outlet is via the inland port of Basle on the river Rhine and thence to the sea at Rotterdam.

4   Transport is difficult and costly over the mountainous terrain.
5   It is a country of two cultures (German in the north, Mediterranean in the south); four languages (German, French, Italian, Romansch) and two major religions (Catholic and Protestant).

Despite these obstacles to industrial and social progress, Switzerland has achieved a high standard of living for its population and a highly successful industrial economy. Switzerland is an outstanding example of unity in diversity. The very limitations imposed by location, terrain and nature have been used by the Swiss to mould their country into a model of prosperity and stability.

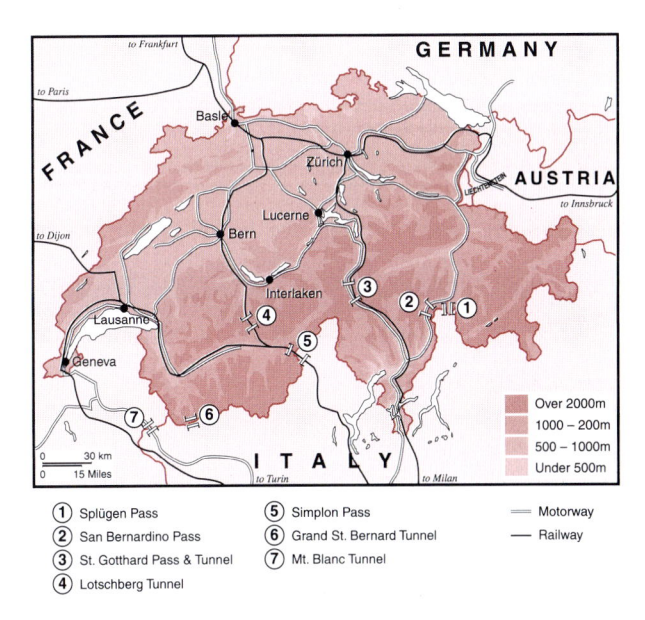

Fig. 8.9 Alpine passes and routes

① Splügen Pass
② San Bernardino Pass
③ St. Gotthard Pass & Tunnel
④ Lotschberg Tunnel
⑤ Simplon Pass
⑥ Grand St. Bernard Tunnel
⑦ Mt. Blanc Tunnel

Consider the factors that have contributed to this development:

- Switzerland is located at the crossroads of western Europe. It controls the international north/south road and rail routes through such central Alpine passes as the St Gotthard and Simplon (Fig 8.9) and the east/west routes along the longitudinal depression of the Rhône/Rhine.

- Switzerland has a wealth of water power (page 154). It is the country's only native energy resource and the widespread location of its HEP plants (Fig 8.4) has led to the dispersal of manufacturing industry throughout the country.

- Because of the lack of coal and iron ore deposits, the Swiss, in the words of one geographer, 'have been saved from the temptations of mass production and condemned to superiority'. Over the centuries they have developed their skills in various craft industries. Today these traditional skills are concentrated in the production of quality goods of small weight but high value, e.g. watches, optical instruments, precision tools. The skills of Swiss craftsworkers thus compensate for the necessity of importing most of its raw materials over long distances and of selling its manufactured products in foreign markets. The Swiss export their skills.

- Switzerland is the source of the Rhine, the industrial lifeline of Europe, which is navigable from Basle to Rotterdam.

- Switzerland's traditional neutrality and political stability have helped its development as a major centre for banking and insurance and for such international agencies as the Red Cross, the World Health Organisation and the Telecommunications Union. Its reputation has attracted foreign investment on a huge scale.

Manufacturing industry

Switzerland is one of the most industrialised of the world's small countries. It manufactures and exports a wide variety of high-quality, high-value products. The major products are:

- Textiles
- Chemicals
- Food processing
- Watchmaking
- Metallurgy and engineering.

Textiles

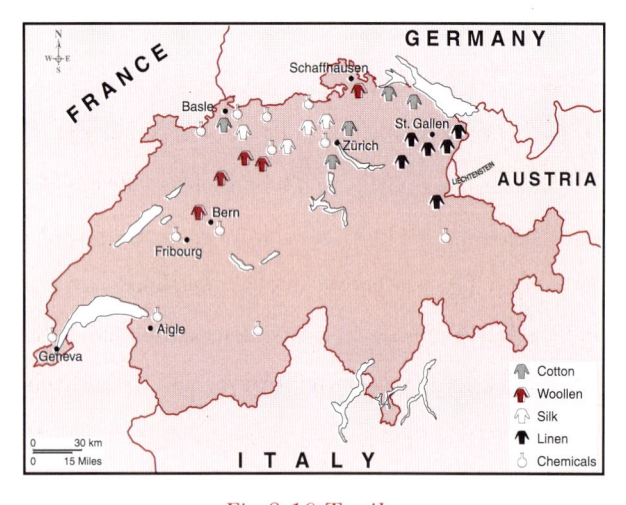

Fig 8.10 Textiles

In Switzerland the textile industry is closely linked with history. It originated as a cottage industry which made high-quality silks, lace and embroidery. As it developed, it kept its decentralised structure: it consists basically of small and medium-sized production units. It is concentrated mainly in the north-east part of the country, in the zone from Solothurn to St. Gallen. In recent years, the industry has concentrated on the production of high-fashion, high-quality textiles for export to Germany, France, USA and Britain.

Chemical Industry

The chemical industry originated in Basle with the manufacture of dyes for the city's main textile factories, and is now the second most important industry in Switzerland. It employs over 75 000 people and its products include agricultural chemicals, dyes, detergents, cosmetics, perfumes, plastics and most especially, pharmaceuticals. Swiss firms (Ciba, La Roche, Geigy, Sandoz) now dominate world markets in industrial pharmaceuticals and agrichemicals. Basle is the centre of the industry, producing dyes and pharmaceuticals. Geneva specialises in perfumes. Electro-chemical plants are located also in the Alpine region to avail of the abundant hydro-electric power.

Food processing

Food processing industries are widely dispersed throughout Switzerland and reflect the importance of dairying. Most of the milk is processed into butter, cheese and chocolate. The industry serves not only the home market but has achieved international fame with such products as cheese (Gruyère, Emmenthaler), chocolate (Suchard), baby and invalid foods (Nestlé) and soups (Knorr, Maggi).

Watchmaking

Watchmaking began as a cottage industry over two centuries ago in the small farming villages nestling in the mountain valleys of the Jura. It provided extra income for the small farmers and the forest workers of the region. Today the making of watches and clocks is one of Switzerland's most important industries and Swiss watches have won international acclaim. Competition from Japanese and American electronic watches has only served to spur Swiss watchmakers to greater heights of precision and ingenuity. The towns and villages of the Jura valleys still make the various components for the industry, but the major assembly factories are along the Jura foothills at Neuchatle, Le Locle and La Chaux de Fonds. Geneva is the main centre for the industry.

Metallurgy and engineering

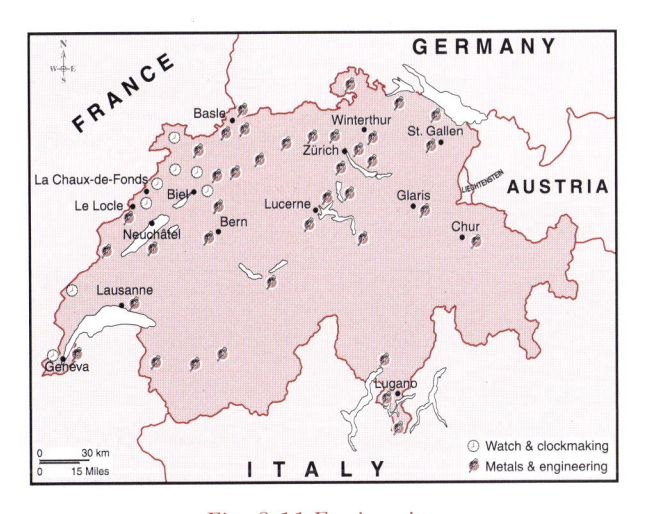

Fig. 8.11 Engineering

Metallurgical and engineering industries form the most important sector of Swiss industry in terms of employment and exports. The metalworking industries resulted from the development of HEP plants which provided abundant supplies of cheap electricity. A wide range of metal ores and refined metals is imported through Rotterdam, brought by barges to the port of Basle and thence distributed to the metallurgical centres where the ores are processed into copper, aluminium, zinc and lead. Most of Switzerland's steel is imported, but there are major steel plants at Schaffhausen, Biel and Winterthur operating electric furnaces.

The engineering industry has developed from the metallurgical operations and it is varied, sophisticated and highly specialised. It is centred on Zurich and stretches right across the Swiss Plateau from St Gallen in the east to Geneva in the west. Heavy engineering plants are concentrated in the larger cities of the Plateau and produce hydro-electric turbines, turbines, generators, textile machinery and marine diesel engines. Light engineering factories manufacture a wide variety of precision goods, e.g. machine tools, calculators, sewing machines, optical goods, medical and scientific instruments.

URBAN SETTLEMENT
Zurich

Zurich is the most important city of Switzerland and the centre of its commercial, banking and industrial activities. It is the focus of the country's road and rail networks. It is sited where the north-south route from Basle to the St Gotthard pass crosses the east-west route across the Plateau. Its status as a financial centre is internationally recognised. Its wide range of industries includes engineering, textiles and food processing.

Fig 8.12 Zurich

Basle

Basle has long been the second city of Switzerland. It is situated on the right-angle bend of the Rhine at the head of the Rift valley. It is the port of Switzerland. Basle derives its importance from these two factors; its location at the head of the Rift valley makes it a focus for rail and road routes from France and Germany, while its position on the Rhine at the limit of navigation makes it the funnel for imports and exports via Rotterdam. It is Switzerland's window on the Atlantic. Apart from its port activities, Basle is a major industrial city with special emphasis on pharmaceuticals, textiles and chemicals.

Geneva

Geneva, the third city of Switzerland, derives its importance from its location in a gap between the Alps and the Jura mountains. Here Lake Geneva, the largest lake in western Europe, narrows into the foaming torrents of the river Rhône. The Romans conquered the town in 120 BC and Julius Caesar fortified it for his wars against the Gauls. Today a stone fountain marks the place where the Roman road from Italy once crossed the road to southern France. Geneva is truly an international city. More than 35% of its 160 000 population are foreigners and foreign tourists total two million a year. It hosts some 30 000 conferences annually. Geneva is not only the European headquarters for the United Nations, but world headquarters for the World Meteorological Association, the International Commission of Jurists, the World Health Organisation, the World Council of Churches, etc. Geneva is a world diplomatic and conference centre not only because of its scenic location and its convenience but also because of its unique traditions and style. It is dedicated to neutrality like the rest of Switzerland. It is also an ideal place to talk, with its luxurious hotels, myriad telex lines, multilingual interpreters and beautiful lake in the shadow of Mont Blanc. It is also the centre of the Swiss watch and jewellery industries and has extensive printing and publishing industries.

Berne

Berne is the federal capital and occupies a defensive site on the river Aar. It is a route centre and has clothing, engineering, printing and food processing industries.

Questions

1. Draw a sketch map of Switzerland and on it show and name (a) three bordering countries, (b) the Alps and Jura mountains, (c) the rivers Rhine, Rhône and Ticino, (d) the lakes Geneva, Constance and Zurich, (e) cities Geneva, Berne, Basle and St Gallen, (f) passes St Gotthard, Simplon.

2. (a) Explain why hydro-electric power is important in Switzerland.
   (b) Describe the industrial uses to which it is put in Switzerland. (L.C. Higher Level)

3. Discuss the influence of the physical environment on the economy of Switzerland.

4. Examine each of the following statements in detail:
   (a) Switzerland houses the headquarters of many international organisations.
   (b) The Alpine region is very important to Switzerland.
   (c) Although Switzerland has a large export trade, it does not balance its imports. Yet is has a positive balance of payments.

(d) Switzerland has the highest standard of living in western Europe.

5. Discuss the importance of tertiary industries to the economy of Switzerland.

6. Identify Switzerland's main natural resources. Write an account of one resource and its importance to Switzerland.

7. (a) List the factors that have helped in the development of manufacturing industry in Switzerland.

   (b) Write an account of one manufacturing industry.

8. Discuss (a) Switzerland's tourist resources and the distribution of the industry, and (b) the impacts of tourism on the country's economy, society and landscape. (L.C. Higher Level)

9. Write an account of manufacturing industry on the Central Plateau.

10. 'Specialisation is the secret of Switzerland's success.' Discuss.

11. 'The harder the environment, the greater the stimulus to economic development.' Discuss, with reference to Switzerland.

12. Describe and explain the distribution of population in Switzerland.

13. 'The Alps are a major natural resource.' Discuss.

14. Write geographical notes on each of the following: (a) the watch-making industry, (b) the importance of the Alpine passes, (c) agriculture in the Alpine valleys, (d) the Föhn wind.

15. Describe the drawbacks to industrial development which Switzerland has to face and outline the efforts made by the Swiss to offset these disadvantages. (L.C. Ordinary Level)

16. 'Nowhere are the varied influences which mountains exert on human activities more in evidence than in western Europe.'

    Using suitable examples from your study of western Europe, examine the influence of areas of high relief on each of the following:
    - Settlement
    - Transport
    - Farming patterns
    - Tourism. (L.C. Higher Level)

17. Examine in detail the economic development of Switzerland under each of the following headings:
    - Primary activities
    - Secondary activities
    - Tertiary activities. (L.C. Higher Level)

18. (i) Draw a sketch map to show how you would divide Switzerland into its regions.

    (ii) Select two of these regions and, in the case of each, describe its main characteristics under the following headings:
    - Physical geography
    - Agriculture
    - Manufacturing industry and services.

    (L.C. Ordinary Level)

mediterranean europe

italy

iberia

spain

portugal

chapter nine
italy

Fig. 9.1 Italy – Relief and drainage

INTRODUCTION

Area:	301 300 sq km
Population:	56.6 million
Density:	188 per sq km

Italy is the central peninsula of the Mediterranean Sea, dividing that sea into the eastern and western basins and commanding the sea routes that join them. It joins the snows of the Alps in the north to the sands of the Sahara in the south and penetrates to central Europe by means of

Fig. 9.2 Italian renaissance painting

the Alpine passes. From the days of the Roman Empire and the early Christian church, Italy has played a significant role in the life and development of Europe. Its greatest input has been inspired by the Renaissance whose influence on art and culture has been felt throughout the world. The Unification of Italy took place in 1861 and since the beginning of this century it has experienced an economic boom. The lack of coal and significant iron ore deposits meant that it developed much later than Britain and Germany and came late in the industrial revolution timescale.

CLIMATE

As Italy stretches through more than 10° of latitude, it is not possible to identify a single climatic regime through the whole country. There are many other factors which influence climate - altitude, distance from the sea, aspect - and with latitude, these give us a multi-climate state. It is easy to break Italy down into three major physical divisions and to identify a distinct climate for each region. The physical division gives the Alps, Plain of Lombardy and the Peninsula (and islands).

The Alps

The Alps run north from the Gulf of Genoa before turning east in a wide arc across the north of the country. They are not as formidable a barrier as they look and are breached in places by a number of valleys and passes that lead to central Europe. The climate of any part of the Alps depends on altitude and aspect. Generally winter temperatures are a few degrees below freezing point with summer reaching a maximum of 14°C. Sheltered south-facing villages have a less severe winter. Precipitation is well distributed throughout the year and averages 1 250mm. There is much winter snow.

Plain of Lombardy

The Lombardy plain was once an arm of the Adriatic and was filled by the deposits of melting glaciers and the rivers flowing down from the Alps and Apennines (see page 167). The climate is continental in character but has not the extremes of the interior continental climates. Winters are cold, with frost and snow. Temperatures average 0°C or below, depending on location. The summers are very hot, sometimes rising to 30°C. The total precipitation averages between 800mm and 1 000mm and is well distributed throughout the year. There is usually a late spring/early summer maximum, a factor which is of great benefit to agriculture.

Peninsula

The peninsula and islands enjoy a Mediterranean climate which is a two-season climate. Summers are hot while winters are mild and moist. In summer the region comes under the influence of the north-east trade winds and experiences the hot North African conditions. Temperatures are in the high twenties and there is no rain. In winter the influences of the south-westerlies are felt. These winds bring the rains, but precipitation is only about 750mm in the west, falling to about 450mm in the east which lies in the rain shadow of the Apennines. Temperatures in winter rarely fall below 8°C. The length and severity of the summer drought increases as one travels south. High evaporation, caused by the high temperatures, is an added problem in a region with limited rainfall.

ENERGY

Italy uses a variety of sources to supply its energy needs. There are small deposits of oil in Sicily and along the central Adriatic coastline, but Italy imports most of its oil from the Middle East and North Africa. Genoa, Venice and Trieste are important oil ports in the north with pipelines across the plain and into central Europe. Naples and Syracuse (Sicily) have refineries in the south.

Natural gas was first discovered near Milan in 1946. Today, there are gas fields spread across the northern plain and along the Adriatic coastline, both on-shore and off-shore. Gas is also imported from the Netherlands, Russia and Algeria (in North Africa). Over 10 000km of pipelines distribute gas across the country. The gas is used for domestic purposes, for power production, for industry and as a raw material.

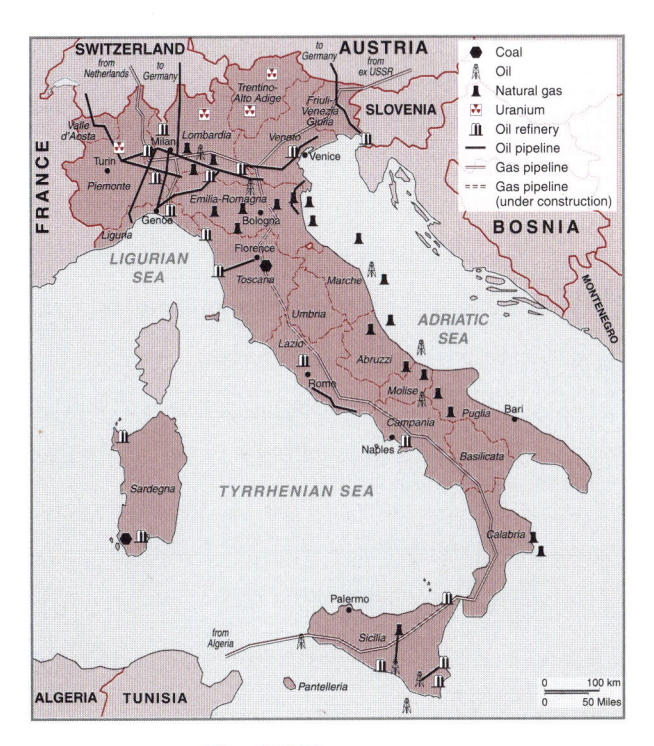

Fig. 9.3 Energy sources

Hydro electricity is an important element in the energy equation and was the instrument responsible for the rapid industrialisation of the north at the start of the twentieth century. Hydro provides a large share of the electricity needs and about 20% of total energy consumption. The Alps are the main source of hydro production where the conditions for generation are much more favourable than in the Apennines.

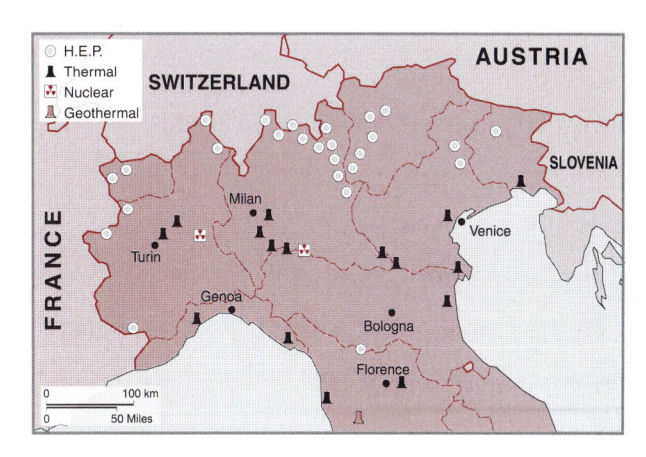

Fig. 9.4 Energy

The north of the country is particularly well suited to the development of hydro power. Note the following factors:

1. The Alps provide a large catchment area for rain and snow and so the supply of fuel is guaranteed.
2. Numerous rivers are fed by this rain or melting snow.
3. Glaciated highland lakes act as reservoirs and so the flow of water can be regulated.
4. The steep slopes of the Alps provide high heads.
5. There is great demand in the industrialised north for cheap HEP.

By contrast, the peninsula does not enjoy the same conditions for production. The rainfall is seasonal, rivers can run dry in summer, there is an absence of suitable reservoir lakes and the heads are not as steep as in the Alps. There is a good grid within Italy which is also connected to the European Grid. Electricity feeds the domestic and industrial demands and provides the power for the electrification of some stretches of railway.

Italy is very dependent on external energy supplies and imports over 70% of her energy needs.

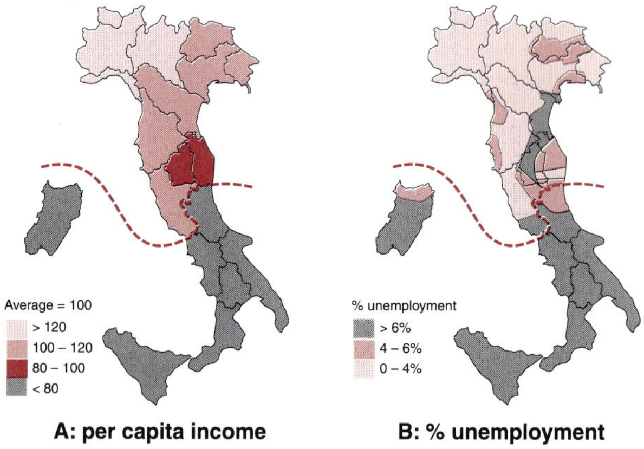

A: per capita income
Average = 100
> 120
100 – 120
80 – 100
< 80

B: % unemployment
> 6%
4 – 6%
0 – 4%

Fig. 9.5 Contrasts

LAND OF CONTRASTS

Core - Periphery

The idea of core periphery within a country is well exemplified in Italy. Italy is a land of contrasts between the forward looking, well developed, prosperous north and the less developed, poorer Mezzogiorno, south of Rome. Examine the summary table below and in the rest of this section we will examine the contrasts between north and south with regard to agriculture and industry. Many of the problems of the south have their origins in historical, physical, social and economic factors. The charts below highlight some of the contrasts between the two.

	The 'North'	The 'South'
Population	35,140,000	19,961,000
Total births p.a.	c 209,000	c 264,000
Agricultural workers	2,057,000	1,966,000
Cultivable land	172,000 km²	104000 km²
Employed in manufacturing	6,219,000	1,829,000
Employed in service trades	4,787,000	2,013,000
Unemployed	357,000	306,000

Fig. 9.6 Italy: statistical contrasts, north and south

Lombardy	Mezzogiorno
1 A fertile plain surrounded by mountains	1 A backbone of mountains with narrow coastal plains
2 Continental climate	2 Mediterranean climate
3 Abundance of power	3 Few local power resources
4 Productive agricultural plain	4 Problem agricultural region
5 Thriving industry and skilled workers	5 Little industry or skilled workers
6 Good communications and infrastructure.	6 Poorly developed infrastructure.

The Plains of Lombardy and Veneto

Agriculture

The plain of Lombardy is bounded by the Alps to the north and the Apennines to the west and south. It stretches in a wedge shape for about 400km to join the Venetian plain at the Adriatic and varies in width from about 100km in the west to 200km near the Adriatic. It is the prime agricultural area of Italy and one of the main food-processing areas of western Europe.

Agriculture in the Lombardy plain has contributed significantly to the economy of the whole country and in particular to the industrial and economic growth of the plain itself.

This is the most extensive lowland plain in Italy. Retreating glaciers and alluvium deposited by the Po and its tributaries have endowed this basin with a mixture of deep, fertile, high yielding soils.

There are many factors combining to make this plain one of the most productive agricultural regions in western Europe. Consider the following:

Rich soils. Deep fertile soils, improved with fertilisers, developed on the alluvium of the Po and on the glacial tills. The richest areas are Piedmont, Lombardy and Emilia.

Climate. The plain has a continental type climate. The late spring rains encourage growth and the hot sunny summer days are ideal for ripening and harvesting. The mountains provide shelter. These weather conditions ensure a variety of crops.

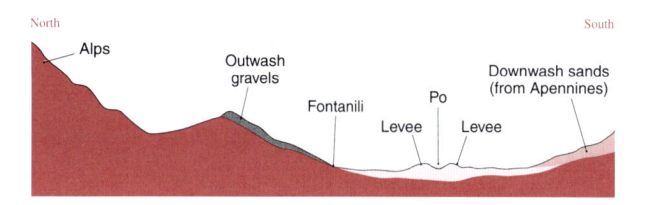

Fig. 9.7 Lombardy cross-section

Water. Water running down from the Alps and Apennines soaks into the ground through permeable sands and gravels and continues underground until it meets a band of impermeable silts. Here the water comes to the surface in a line of springs called fontanili. These springs, the water of the Po and the late spring/early summer rains ensure a plentiful supply of water for irrigation.

Transport and Markets. The level nature of the plain allows for easy transport of products from the farms to the urban markets and processing plants. This is the primary market. The many passes through the Alps allow for easy entry to the affluent markets of central and western Europe.

Agriculture and Industry. There is a well established partnership between agriculture and industry in northern Italy. Industry processes the farm products and in turn supplies machinery, fertilisers, chemicals, etc., to the farmers.

The agriculture in this northern plain is intensive mixed farming, with most of the crops associated with Italy being produced here. Modern scientific farming methods are employed, irrigation and the heavy use of fertilisers give high yields and the co-operative movement is well established. Wheat, maize and barley are widely grown for use in industry and as fodder for cattle. Yields per acre are nearly double those in the south. An unexpected cereal of great importance is rice, centred in Vercelli to the west of Milan. Grass, silage and hay are important everywhere with roots in the lower flood plain of the Po.

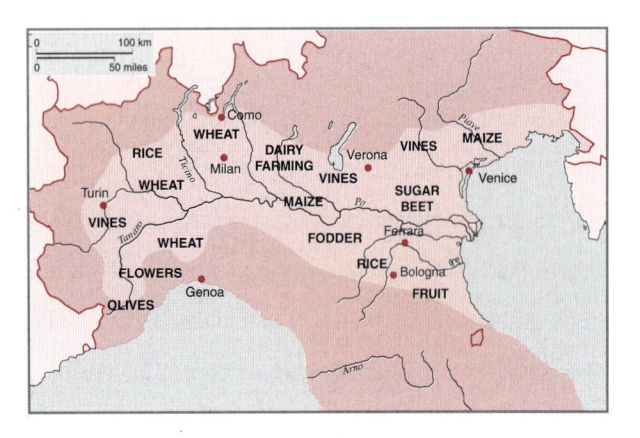

Fig. 9.8 Lombardy agriculture

Dairy farming is the main pastoral activity but especially so in Lombardy and Emilia with its well watered meadows and pastures. A large urban population provides the market and there is a heavy processing industry. Parmesan and Gorganzola are well known cheese varieties from the area. Fruit and vegetable growing is widespread and an indication of the intensive nature of the farming may be gleaned from the custom of bordering the fields with lines of fruit trees. Asti, to the east of Turin, is a world famous producer of wines. The Ligurian coast, with a southern aspect and shelter from the north, is renowned for the cultivation of vines, fruits, vegetables and flowers.

Mezzogiorno - Agriculture

The Mezzogiorno - *land of the midday sun* - is the peripheral area of Italy. Italy, including the south, is very much part of modern Europe and one of the seven richest nations in the world. Economically, the south lags far behind the north and behind the rest of the EU. As recently as 1950, the south displayed many of the features of Third World Countries - overpopulation, unbalanced employment structure, poor housing, low economic activity and heavy dependence on agriculture. In 1950 the average per capita income was below that of Latin America.

The Mezzogiorno - south of Rome - contains 40% of the land, 37% of the population but only 25% of its GDP. Incomes are still only about half those in the north. A combination of physical, social and economic problems have combined to make the region a major problem area both in Italy and the EU. The problems are listed here:

Climate. The peninsula and the islands experience the true Mediterranean climate. Summer temperatures are sometimes as high as in the hot desert and the average is around 27°C. Added to the heat is the fact that the summer is a drought season and the length and severity of the drought increases as one moves south. Rainfall totals range between 450mm in the east and 750mm in the west. In addition, there is a very high evaporation rate. The lack of water is one of the greatest handicaps to agriculture.

Fig. 9.9 Agrarian crops

In summer, with water, it would be possible to grow crops that cannot be grown anywhere else in the EU, but irrigation is difficult because many of the rivers run dry in summer. This leads to under-utilisation of the land with over-reliance on wheat and olives. Cattle rearing is difficult because of the lack of grass.

Difficult Topography. About 40% of the land is classified as mountain, too steep for cultivation. Another 40% is hill country with very limited potential. The plains are limited to Foggia, Naples and Taranto. Most of the Apennines are formed from limestone which indicates a dry surface and poor thin soil.

Land Tenure. Up to the middle of this century most of the farmland in the south was held in large estates **(latifundia)**, controlled by absentee landlords and worked by peasant tenant farmers and share croppers. It was not a system conducive to agricultural progress. The landowners had no interest in investing money in their estates while the peasants, who might have had the interest, had no money. A rising population added to the pressure on the small holdings. Subdivision within families meant that most peasant farmers had holdings of only 2-3 hectares - **minifundia**. Under this system it was impossible to grow enough to support a family, let alone specialise in one crop. In 1950 only 27% of the agricultural workers owned their own land.

Uneducated Workforce. The peasant population of the south were for the most part unskilled and uneducated. Many were only part-time day labourers, with little or no interest in the land, accustomed to taking orders, rarely making decisions. This gave rise to very poor agriculture based on traditional products, unemployment and poverty.

Lack of Markets. Physical distances from the great industrial markets of central Europe were made worse by the lack of any infrastructure of roads and railways.

Out-migration. Out-migration has persisted since the end of the nineteenth century. Over 8 million people have left since 1900.

Since the Unification of Italy in 1861, the agricultural climate in the south has been harsh, inferior and marked by low productivity. Distance from markets and an unskilled labour force have added to the problems. Most of the latifundias were devoted to the extensive production of wheat, alternated with fallow. This was under-utilisation of the land. Crops of olives, vines and some citrus were also grown. Some cattle rearing was carried on but a lack of rainfall led to a scarcity of grass. Sheep and goats were reared on the hillsides.

Reform and Development of the South

There had been many small-scale attempts to develop the agriculture and improve the economy of the south. Between the wars, there was some attempts at drainage and irrigation to improve agriculture but that achieved very little. After World War II, high unemployment and pressure on the land from a rising population, forced the government to take serious and radical action to develop and improve all sections of the economy of the south. In 1950 the Italian government established the ***Cassa per il Mezzogiorno*** to re-organise and develop the south. This was a long term regional development plan embracing all areas of the economy. The initial funds came from the government and were supplemented by private investment from home and abroad, by the World Bank and, later in the decade, by the European Investment Bank. Initially, the plan was to run until 1960, but as the enormity of the task was realised, the plan was extended to 1980. The initial £600 million investment grew to a total of £8 000 million. A time-frame of three stages, investments and objectives was envisaged:

1 **Agricultural and Infrastructural Reform**
2 **Industrial Development (page 180)**
3 **Tourism (page 182)**.

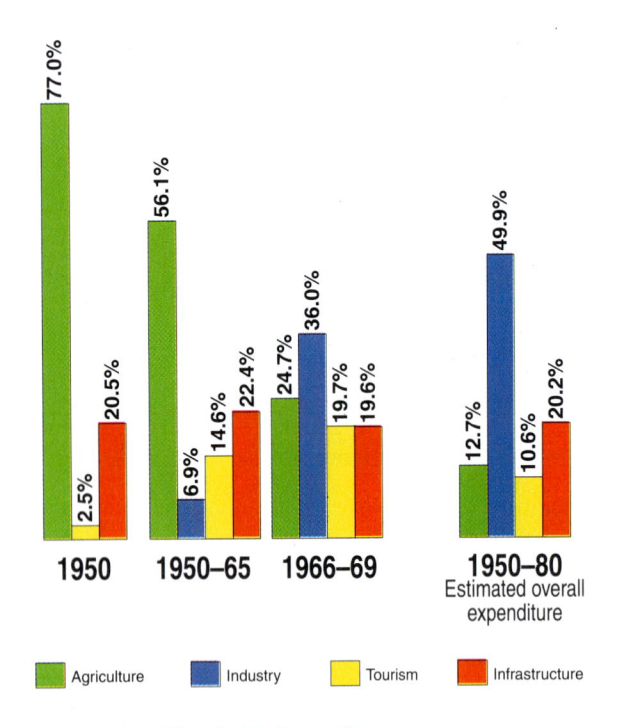

Fig. 9.10 Cassa Investment

Agricultural Reform

In the early years much of the work and most of the money was invested in agriculture. Two main methods of agricultural reform were concentrated on: land reform and improved farm techniques.

The latifundias were acquired from the landlords and were redistributed among the tenant farmers in viable holdings. Irrigation and drainage schemes (where necessary) were initiated and afforestation was carried out on the hills and mountain slopes to prevent further soil erosion. Agricultural schools were established, co-operatives introduced and service centres set up to supply the needs of the farmers and to guarantee markets. Food-processing and refrigeration plants were etablished in these centres. New houses and farm buildings were built on each new farm unit and the co-operatives provided machinery either on a purchase or hire basis.

The extensive cultivation of wheat and olives was changed to a cash crop economy of citrus, vegetables, stone fruits, vines, sugar beet, tobacco, salads, etc. There was a ready market for these products in Europe and many had guaranteed prices under CAP. Irrigation improved the pastures so livestock numbers increased.

Villages were established on the lowlands replacing the mountain-side settlements. Thousands of kilometres of new roads were built, linking the farm settlements and the markets. The new motorways brought the rich markets of Europe much nearer.

The problems of the south were not solved overnight, but a steady improvement came about in the life of many farmers. The purchasing power of the population was increased, creating a better market for consumer goods.

The inefficient latifundias disappeared and many tenant farmers and share-croppers became settled farmers in charge of their own farms and futures.

Lombardy Plain - Industrial Development

As well as being one of the most important agricultural regions in western Europe, the Lombardy Plain is second only to the Ruhr in industrial development, expansion and importance. Industry is well dispersed all across the north but the major concentration of industry lies in the south western corner of Piedmont, Lombardy and Liguria and their capitals, Turin, Milan and Genoa. Between them they provide roughly 30% of the industrial workers and 40% of the industrial exports.

This region has no worthwhile deposits of coal or iron ore so it came late to the industrial revolution. Because of its late start, it developed a wide range of industries spread across many centres. Many factors have contributed to the growth, including:

Agriculture. A high yielding agriculture provides the raw materials for the food processing industry and, in its turn, creates a market for farm machinery, fertilisers and chemicals.

Power Supplies. The district, lacking coal and oil, made a great leap forward with the development of cheap HEP in the Alps. After the war, in 1945, major deposits of natural gas were discovered for use as a power resource and as a raw material for chemicals.

Good Communications. The level plain, with thriving ports Venice and Genoa at either end, facilitated the building of a good communications network of roads, railways, canals and pipelines. The many Alpine passes allow entry to Europe bringing the north of Italy into closer contact with the core area of north-west Europe, its major market.

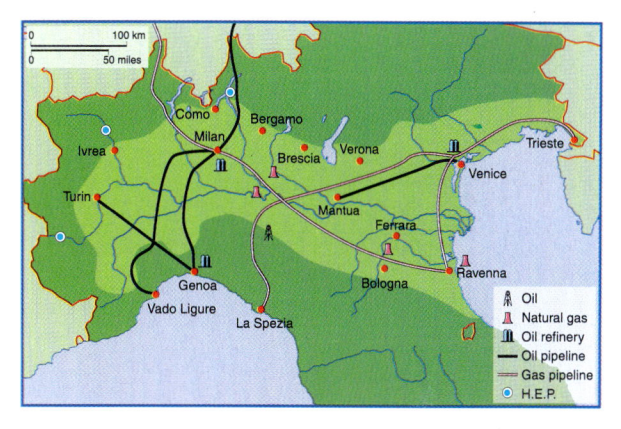

Fig. 9.11 Industry in Northern Italy

Skilled and Unskilled Labour Force. The north of Italy has developed skills in engineering, food and textiles since the Renaissance period, and these skills are continued today. The immigration from the south provided the unskilled labour.

We have noted that manufacturing in the north of Italy is characterised by a wide range of industries. Four branches, in particular, are worth noting:

Food Processing

This industry is found in many centres right across the plain from Turin to Venice. The high-yielding crops provide the raw materials and the industrial towns provide the markets. In addition there is a large export market. Cheese, pasta, confectionery, wine, meats, sugar, milling, and vegetable canning are some of the food-processing industries. There is also a large segment which processes imported foodstuffs. Food-processing centres include Turin, Milan, Genoa (imported raw materials).

Metallurgy and Engineering

Fig. 9.12 Steelworks

Italy has very limited iron ore supplies (Elba and Val d'Aosta) and no coal. Both have to be imported for the steel industry. This has led to the production of steel in integrated steelworks at coastal sites where trans-shipment of the raw materials is not necessary. Cornigliano (near Genoa), Savona and Venice have large steel mills, supplying their own industries and the towns of the northern plain, but there are older branches of the industry still to be found in Milan and Turin. The steel industry supplies the raw material for a highly diversified engineering industry. Shipbuilding yards at Genoa and Venice use local steel, as both industries are linked under state control.

The manufacture of motor vehicles is an industry that has built up a worldwide reputation and Italy is now regarded internationally as the pioneer of new designs and developments in this industry. Turin is the headquarters, with Fiat, Lancia, Lambretta and Alfa-Romeo all located there. The products range from scooters to cars, trucks, agricultural and earth-moving equipment and aircraft engines.

Light engineering is widespread. Requiring only small amounts of raw materials but great technical skills, these industries form one of the pillars on which the Italian economy is built. The products are wide ranging and include electrical goods, domestic appliances, textile machinery, tools, office equipment, computers, radios and televisions. Turin, Milan, Brescia, Bologna, Como and Verona are the chief centres.

Textiles and Clothing

The textile industry is probably the oldest in the plain and the modern skills can be traced back to the time of the Renaissance, when the patron families demanded the finest in textiles and workmanship. Wool and silk were the early industries, using local raw materials. Cotton, linen and jute were added later. With the development of hydro power, the industry became factory-based and widespread. In the second half of this century the synthetic fibre branch developed rapidly, replacing the traditional fibres. The petro-chemical industry (using native gas), supplies the synthetic trade with its raw material.

While the industry is widely spread, some towns have developed a reputation for specialisation. Como is noted for silk, Bologna for hemp and Biella for wool. Turin, Milan, Padua and Cremona are still the main centres. Associated with the textile industry is the clothing trade. The Italians have developed a worldwide market for their clothes, based on the quality of the cloth and on the design, workmanship and finish of the garments.

Chemicals and Petro-chemicals

This is one of the growth industries in the twentieth century and Italy has kept pace with the rest of the EU. The Lombardy Plain is again the main growth centre within the country.

The Plain provides a number of the requirements of the industry, notably:

1. cheap HEP - especially for the electro-chemical branch
2. raw materials - from natural gas
3. suitable coastal sites for the import of oil and the export of finished products
4. an affluent market
5. technology
6. investment capital.

THE INDUSTRIAL TRIANGLE

While there are a number of industrialised areas across this core area of Italy, the centre of the core lies in the industrial triangle of Milan, Turin, Genoa and this triangle dominates the economic life of the country.

Milan

Milan is the capital of Lombardy. It dates from Roman times and was a Renaissance city of note. After the

Fig. 9.13 The industrial triangle

Unification of Italy in 1861, Milan emerged as the financial and industrial capital of both the north and of Italy itself. Between the wars the city expanded to absorb many of the nearby towns and now has a population of 1.8 million people.

Milan dominates Italian industry and the city is the centre for heavy engineering, oil, gas, chemicals, cars, tyres and textiles. As well as the larger industrial units (ENI, Alfa Romeo, etc.) there are 100 000 small engineering and

Fig. 9.14 Milan Cathedral

component firms in Milan and its hinterland. The clothing and fashion industry employ 120 000 workers and famous names include Benetton, Armani and Gucci.

The city is the focus of the road and rail routes within and across the plain, across the Alps and south to Genoa. This focuspoint brings trade and commerce to Milan.

Despite the importance of manufacturing industry, over 60% of the working population are involved in the service sector with banks, finance and insurance. Italy's main Stock Market is in Milan.

Turin

Turin controls many of the important routes west and north through the Alps, south to the Ligurian coast and Genoa and east through the Lombardy Plain. The development of roads, railways and autostrada during this century underlines the importance of Turin's focal position.

Turin is the capital of Piedmont and the second industrial city of Italy. It has a population of 1.2 million. The car companies of Fiat, Lancia and the office equipment giant Olivetti were established early in this century. These firms confirmed Turin as a centre for engineering. The good communications and the availability of cheap HEP from the Alps helped.

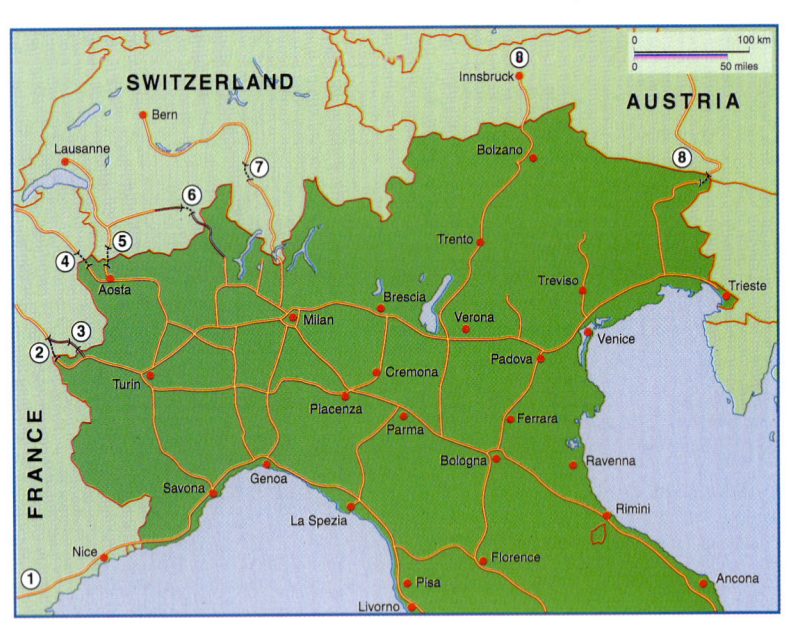

① Riviera coastal motorway to Marseilles and the Rhône valley
② Fréjus tunnel to Chambéry, Grenoble and Lyon
③ Mont Cenis pass to Chambéry and Lyon
④ Mont Blanc tunnel to Chamonix and upper Rhône valley
⑤ Grand St. Bernard pass to Lake Geneva
⑥ Simplon pass to Switzerland
⑦ St. Gotthard pass to Zurich
⑧ Brenner pass to Innsbruck and Munich
⑨ Villach (Austria) Salzburg–Munich route

Fig. 9.15 Italy – Routes

Turin has been described as a company city, as much of its industrial development is due to Fiat, which employs nearly 150 000 workers. It produces many products besides cars - electrical goods, marine and aircraft engines, earth moving equipment, farm machinery and domestic appliances. There are hundreds of ancillary plants - sheet steel, machine tools, rubber, engineering, etc.

The local industries have created a large banking and financial market in Turin.

Genoa

Genoa is the third apex of this industrial triangle. It was an important port up to the 17th century when it went into decline following the rise in trade of the Atlantic ports. With the industrialisation of Lombardy and the opening of the Suez Canal, its importance grew again.

Genoa is the second port of the Mediterranean after Marseilles. It has a fine natural sheltered harbour but its growth inland is restricted by the Ligurian Apennines. Instead the harbour has been extended along the western coastline and several new quays and docks have been built. The mountains stretch down to the coast but Genoa is fortunate in that there are a number of low passes - Altare and Giovi - through the mountains giving easy access to the Lombardy Plain and so to Switzerland, Germany and beyond. Genoa is a natural outlet for Turin and Milan.

Genoa is unusual as a port in that 90% of its trade is made up of imports. Oil is by far the chief import and the port is the terminus for the Central European Pipeline (CEP) which runs through Italy to Switzerland and Germany. It also imports coal, iron ore, chemicals, grain and foodstuffs.

The list of industries is impressive. There is an integrated steel works at Cornigliano, marine and electrical engineering, shipbuilding, oil-refining and petrochemicals.

SMALL INDUSTRIES, HUGE SUCCESS

Italy is not a land of industrial giants. Only four Italian industrial companies - Fiat, I.E.I., E.N.I. and Feruzzi - make the list of the world's 500 largest corporations. Even adding in such familiar names as Pirelli and Olivetti, both too small to make the top 500, still leaves Italy short of industrial giants.

Italy is no longer the industrially backward country of fifty years ago. Italian industry has developed a new strength in the thousands of sophisticated small and medium-sized companies whose factories dot the landscape of northern Italy. With exports of almost £115 billion a year, Italy ranks 6th in the world table. 98% of these exports are manufactured products. A large share of these products comes from the horde of smaller companies, busily turning out a wide variety of goods: textiles, shoes and fashion of course, but also ceramics, jewellery, furniture and precision instruments. One quarter of Italy's exports comes from companies with only 11 to 100 employees.

How do we explain the success of these small businesses? Much of it is due to a strong sense of *localismo* - local pride and self-reliance - allied to close family ties and a healthy handicraft tradition. This encouraged the creation of small family companies. Add in Italian technical ingenuity and individual enterprise to produce success. In general, Italian companies are smaller than their counterparts in the rest of

Europe. For example, the average Italian metalworking company employs 127 people, compared to 194 in France, 216 in Britain and 264 in Germany. Similar ratios apply to textile and footwear companies and to other manufacturers.

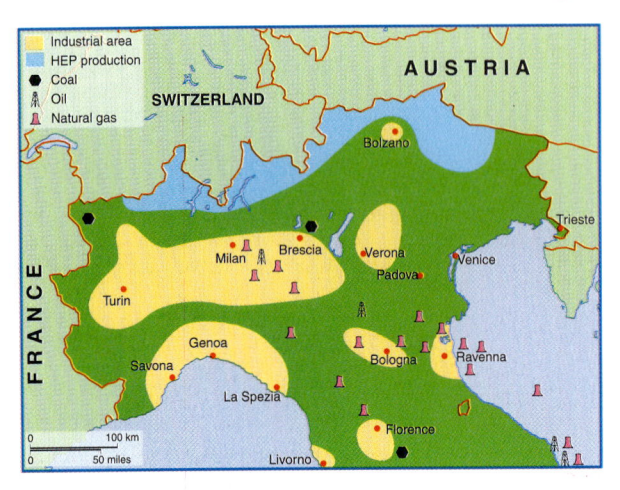

Fig. 9.16 Energy production

Most of these small companies are located in the north of Italy. A typical company is 'Alessi', located in a small village. Founded by the grandfather of the present owner, it has gained an international reputation for stylish kitchenware. With 450 employees and annual sales of around £50 million, and by engaging top designers of many nationalities, the company has made kettles, teapots, coffee sets and lemon squeezers glamorous the world over. In Italy, small is not only beautiful, but successful.
TIME magazine

Mezzogiorno - Industry

As with agriculture, industry in the Mezzogiorno also fell behind that of the north. The southern peninsula and islands had a poor agricultural economy, an unskilled illiterate workforce (90% illiteracy rate in 1870), very poor communications, no infrastructure worth noting and was located a considerable distance from the flourishing markets of northern and western Europe. In addition to these problems, the south had very few mineral resources and neither power nor the potential to generate it. The limited amount of industry was small scale, undeveloped, with poor production methods and geared to the needs of a small, poor, local market. Emigration was rife.

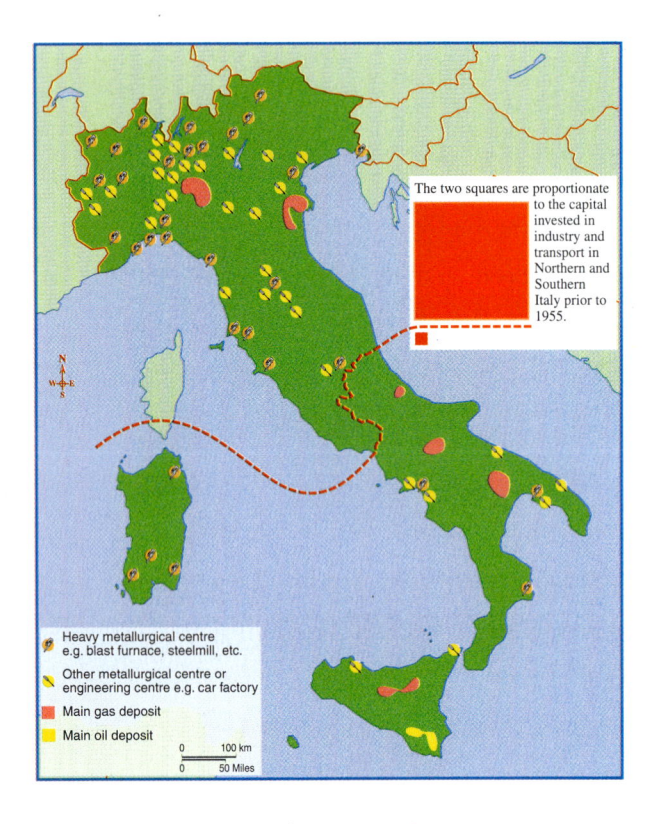

Fig. 9.17 Industrial sites

The investment chart (page 174) noted earlier in the chapter highlighted the fact that most of the early *Cassa* funds were invested in agriculture, some in infrastructure and little or none in industry. The 22.4% invested in infrastructure was shared between the social infrastructure and the physical one. The establishment of schools, training centres, co-operatives, hospitals, processing and market centres contributed to social improvements. But

Fig. 9.18 Naples

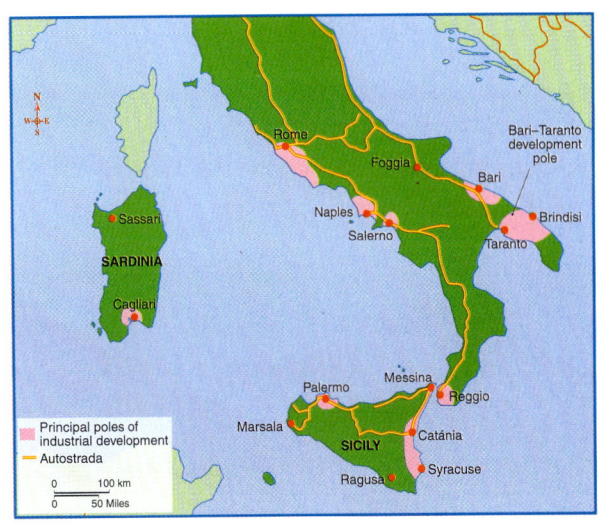

Fig. 9.19 Growth poles

the building of roads, railways, ports, airports, power stations, telephone services, etc., made the south more accessible and brought the European markets so much nearer. These improvements were of great help in Stage II - industrial development (page 174).

The shift to industrial investment came in 1965. Three main methods were employed to promote industry:

(i) The Stage I improvements were designed to create a market for consumer products and to make the south more attractive for industry. To encourage industrialists, generous building and training grants, subsidies, tax exemptions and subsidised transport were granted to those who set up in the south.

(ii) State controlled companies were required by law to place 40% of all new investment in the south. These concerns were generally involved in heavy capital intensive industries - iron and steel, shipbuilding, oil-refining, chemicals, petro-chemicals, heavy engineering. These industries would create employment and also create a market within themselves for other goods and services. In this way a multiplier effect would be created.

(iii) Certain areas, capable of rapid growth, were selected for initial investment and from these, five growth poles were designated (see Fig. 9.19). The growth poles received the bulk of the investment as they were perceived to have the greatest potential for industrial expansion and job creation. Among the plants established were steel, shipbuilding, aircraft and chemicals at Naples. The new industrial triangle at Bari, Brindisi and Taranto shared steel (the largest integrated plant in Europe), engineering, oil-refining, shipbuilding and cement. Sicily has deposits of oil, gas, sulphur and potash so the oil, chemical and petro-chemical industries were encouraged around Augusta and Syracuse, using home produced and imported raw materials. Port facilities have been improved to take the largest tankers.

Obviously not all the plans of the *Cassa* have worked, but nevertheless considerable progress has been made. The table below shows the change in employment structure between 1950 and 1990. Agriculture has lost over two million workers and many have been absorbed into the secondary sector. The growth in this sector has stimulated growth in the tertiary sector or service zone. This has produced a more balanced economy and has brought income levels in the south nearer the national average. Yet income levels in the north, which surged ahead during the boom period of the 70s, are still double that of the south.

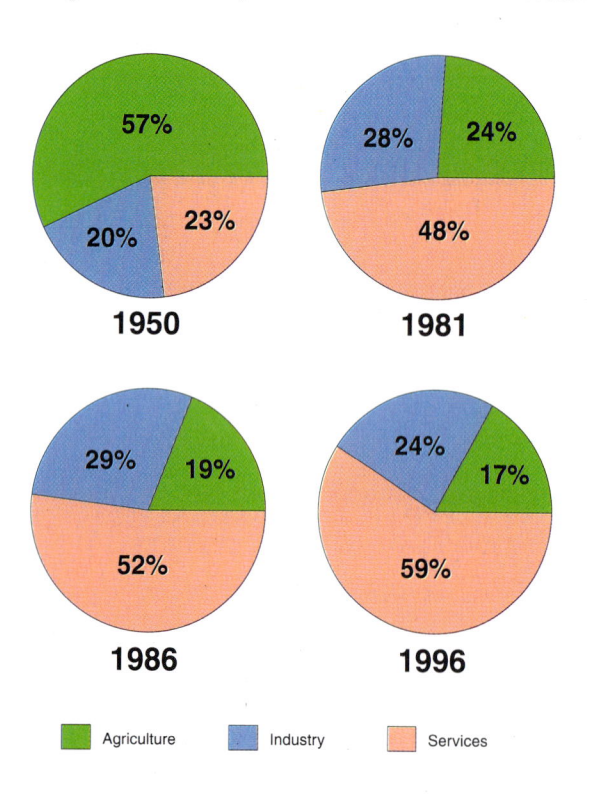

1950: Agriculture 57%, Industry 20%, Services 23%
1981: Agriculture 24%, Industry 28%, Services 48%
1986: Agriculture 19%, Industry 29%, Services 52%
1996: Agriculture 17%, Industry 24%, Services 59%

Fig. 9.20 Employment structure in the Mezzogiorno

Emigration is still a problem in the Mezzogiorno, but it is a necessary one. Secondary and tertiary industry cannot absorb all the unemployed or redundant agricultural workers. However, as the income of the gainfully employed workforce increases, their spending power also increases. This in turn creates a demand for consumer goods and services and so creates more jobs, thereby reducing the need for emigration.

TOURISM

Each year Italy attracts up to 50 million visitors, who spend about $15 000 million. This is a major source of income which brings in much needed foreign currency and helps in the balance of payments.

Why does Italy attract so many tourists?
Initially it must be recognised that, unlike some of the other Mediterranean countries, Italy has a **year round** industry. In addition, it has a wealth of tourist resources, both natural and man-made. It has impressive scenery, more historical features than the rest of the Mediterranean, and weather to suit the tourist in both summer and winter.

The **scenic Alps**, with the attractive lakes, Como, Garda and Maggiore are obvious summer attractions. The rugged peaks, forested slopes, Alpine plants and mountain villages combine with the sheltered south-facing slopes to make the area an attractive destination for many summer visitors. The **Apennines** also provide a magnificent setting for tourists, and the new road systems open up the potential for the motoring tourist. The fact that the Mezzogiorno is relatively new, undiscovered and uncrowded is of benefit to the tourist and offers an opportunity to the industry for expansion.

The fastest expanding sector of the industry is that of **winter sports** holidays. These are concentrated in the Alps where up to four months of winter snow provides the resources. The infrastructure of small airports, mountain railways, ski lifts, hotels, etc., has been developed to provide the facilities for the tourists. Obviously tourism is a major contributor to the economic life of the Alps.

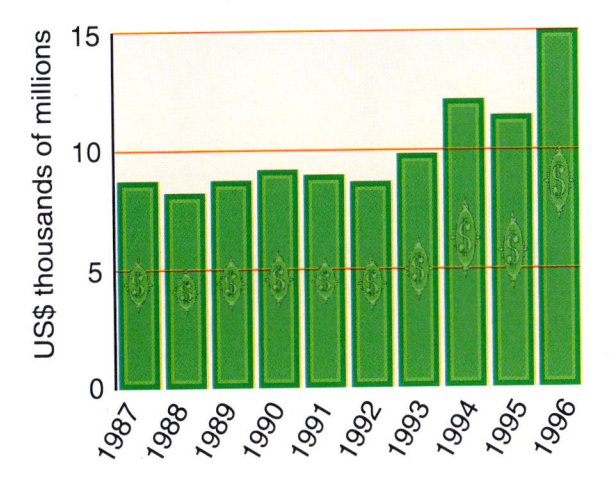

Fig. 9.21 Receipts

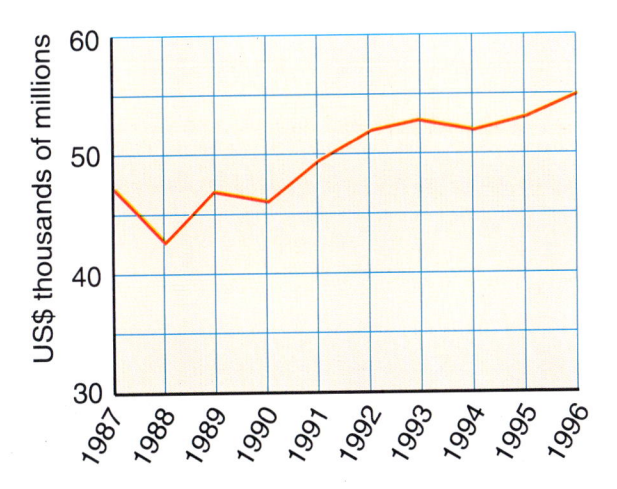

Fig. 9.22 Visitors

Italy has probably more **historical wealth** than any of the Mediterranean lands. Dotted around the country are numerous features recalling the civilisations, cultures and history of Greek, Roman, Phoenician, Byzantine and Norman occupations. The main cities - Rome, Florence, Venice, Naples, Turin and Milan - are treasure houses of Renaissance scholarship and art.

Rome, as the centre of the Catholic church, is a focal point for tourists. The excavated towns of Pompeii and Herculaneum, nestling at the foot of the still active Vesuvius, are grim reminders of the destructive power of that volcano. With nearby Naples, Salerno and Capri, they create another focal point. The historical features alone are enough to maintain a vibrant industry.

Fig. 9.23 Tourism

In the section on the work of the *Cassa* (pp 173-174), tourism was identified as the third arm of the development plan with a vast potential for expansion. There are miles of empty beaches, historic ruins, magnificent scenery, lemon and orange groves, hot summer weather and a wealth of new foods and wines.

The main reason for the lack of development of the industry in the south was the remoteness and inaccessibility of much of the region. The *Cassa* immediately recognised the important part tourism could play in the development of the Mezzogiorno. In the early years of the *Cassa* involvement, there was an overlap between agricultural and tourist development as both shared in the benefits of infrastructural reform. The new autostrada to the toe and heel are supplemented by many new and resurfaced roads and specially constructed scenic routes within the south.

About 30 000km of new or improved roads have made the south more accessible. In addition, a new airport in Calabria has opened up the extreme south and Sicily. Nearly 15% of the total *Cassa* money has gone directly to the industry and much of this money has been channelled into the building of new hotels or the refurbishing of existing ones. Up to 3 000 hotels and *pensions* have benefited from this investment and many tourist villages have been established. With improvements in accessibility and accommodation, the third element of the industry - amenities - was developed by the management teams of hotels and resorts.

The Italian Tourist Board has launched both a national and an international campaign to attract people to the south, pointing out its obvious advantages. The tour and package operators have been quick to see the advantages for themselves and have marketed it strongly. The number of tourists to the south has quadrupled in the last twenty years and the industry has contributed substantially to the socio-economic development of the Mezzogiorno.

URBAN SETTLEMENT

Rome

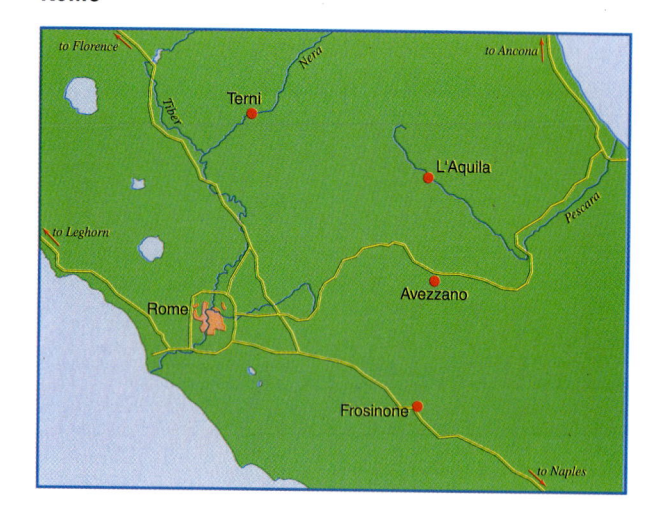

Fig 9.24 Rome

Rome is the capital of Italy. It is an ancient city dating back to the eight century BC. It first reached importance as the centre of the Roman empire - an empire that created wealth and importance for its capital. It was the focal centre of that empire which stretched from Britain to the Middle East – 'all roads lead to Rome'.

With the collapse of the empire and the sacking by the Vandals and Goths, Rome went into decline and for a time was outstripped by Naples and Milan. Its development as the primate city of the Catholic church helped its revival as did the Renaissance. Its central position on the peninsula as well as its historical and ecclesiastical importance were responsible for its selection as capital.

Rome is situated on an easy crossing point of the Tiber about 25km from its mouth. It has little port activity and few of the traditional port industries. It is essentially a service and administrative city with a large tertiary sector. Tourism is a major industry. The attractions include the

Roman and early Christian ruins, the Renaissance riches and the Vatican.

Fig. 9.25 The Spanish Steps, Rome

The Vatican city is contained within Rome. It is a small independent city state (60 hectares) on the right bank of the Tiber and is the religious centre of the Catholic church.

Naples

Naples is sited on the best natural harbour along the west coast of peninsular Italy. It has developed into the second port and third city of Italy with a population of 1.3 million. Manufacturing industry is important and the industrial base has been expanded with the help of *Cassa* funds as Naples is one of the selected growth areas. HEP has been developed in the Apennines behind the city and this provides the power for industry. Among the industries are iron, steel, shipbuilding, repairs, marine engineering, aircraft, cars, chemicals, textiles and food processing. Food processing is a well-established industry because Naples is the centre of a fertile agricultural plain with rich volcanic soils.

Naples is the administrative and commercial capital of the Mezzogiorno and so the tertiary sector is expanding. The situation of the city on the magnificent bay, beside Pompeii, Herculaneum, Vesuvius, Sorrento and Capri makes Naples a Mecca for tourists.

Venice

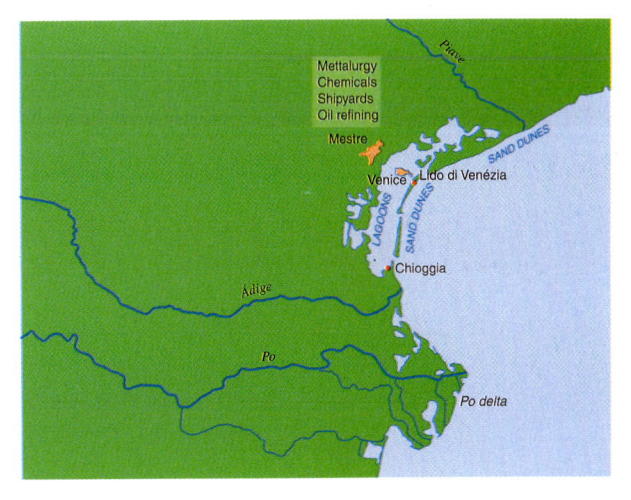

Fig 9.26 Venice

Venice, as *Queen of the Adriatic*, was in its time one of the world's great trading cities. It had an impressive fleet and its traders carried on a lucrative trade with the Middle East, the Far East and India. This trade went into decline during the sixteenth century, when western Europe opened up the sea routes to India, the Far East and the Americas.

The city is built on a series of islands which are connected by nearly 400 bridges. The islands are connected to the mainland by a road and rail causeway. The city is unique in Europe in that intercity transport is dependent on waterways and boats.

New large-scale industry has been introduced and now iron, steel, shipbuilding, heavy engineering and oil-related industries are important. Its development as an oil terminal has also helped. As part of the Venetian and east Lombardy plains its trade has grown alongside that of the plains. Many of its industries are based on the old craft trades of glass, pottery, lace, textiles and silverware. Because of its beauty, history and uniqueness the tourist industry is vibrant.

Population distribution and density

Fig 9.27 Population distribution and density

Italy displays wide variations in population densities, ranging from isolated mountain villages to teeming industrial cities. The variety of physical landscapes, the degree of fertility of the soils, the affluence of Lombardy, the poverty of the Mezzogiorno and the out-migration from south to north have all contributed in some way to the population pattern. At the same time it should be noted that there are very few areas with a very low density.

The industrial triangle of Milan, Turin and Genoa embraces a region of very high density. This is the affluent region of Italy, rich in agriculture, industry and commerce and well able to support a large population.

The eastern Lombardy plain and the adjoining coastal lands stretching from Venice to Rimini is a second area of high density. Again, successful agriculture, thriving industry and a well organised tourist industry are the main reasons.

The three fertile lowland basins and the southern industrial triangle of Bari, Brindisi, Taranto are the notable areas of high density in the south. The well established cities and the port industries provide the key. The rural areas surrounding the cities are also densely populated. It must be remembered, however, in dealing with the Mezzogiorno, that high densities are associated with poverty and not with wealth as is the case in the north.

Areas of moderate density include the rest of Lombardy, much of the rest of the coastal lowlands of the peninsula and the island of Sicily. These are areas of moderate agricultural quality but they have not developed commercially or industrially like the areas of high density.

Sardinia, the Alps and the upper Apennines have a low density. The steep slopes and infertile soils do not attract settlement. Summer drought in the south is also a handicap.

SAMPLE QUESTION

Divide Italy into regions and justify your subdivisions by reference to physical, social and economic geography.

It is usual to divide Italy into three main regions, the division being based on relief, climatic, economic and social characteristics. On this basis, Italy divides easily into the Alps, the Lombardy Plain and peninsular Italy. The Plain and the Peninsula have been dealt with earlier in this chapter.

The **Alps** swing in a great arc across the north of Italy down to the Gulf of Genoa. They form the frontier with France, Switzerland and Austria. The Alps are drained by numerous streams and rivers flowing to the Po or the Gulf of Venice. Heavy glaciation has left a deep imprint on the mountains with jagged peaks, glaciated valleys, corrie lakes, moraine-dammed lakes and waterfalls. The Alps are not an impenetrable barrier as they are cut through in many places by passes. Roads and railways have been built through the passes providing an important economic link between the north of Italy and the affluent markets of Europe. The northern plain benefits from the protection afforded by the Alps. *Revise the distinctive climate of this mountain region which has been treated at the start of this chapter.*

Agriculture is important, particularly on the south facing slopes and on the valley floors. Barley, rye, maize, roots and grass are the main crops. Much of this produce is converted to fodder to winter feed the dairy cattle. There is some sheep rearing. Fruit, vines and vegetables are cultivated, but aspect and shelter determine the fruits and their location. The upper slopes of the mountains are covered in forest.

The numerous rivers fed by the abundant rainfall and melting snows are harnessed for hydro production. There is a ready market for the power in the many industrial cities and towns of the plain, but also in the varied industries of the mountain towns and villages. The cheap power has attracted the electro-chemical and electro-metallurgical sectors. Textiles, food processing and timber are traditional Alpine industries which have expanded in recent years.

The attractive glaciated landscape provides the physical resources for a thriving tourist industry. The industry is a year-round one with attractive summer scenery and the opportunities for walking, climbing and viewing. With abundant winter snow the Alps convert easily to winter sports arenas. The industry is of vital economic importance to the many Alpine towns and villages, providing jobs and halting rural depopulation.

Questions

1. Draw a sketch map of Italy and on it show and name: (a) the Apennines, (b) the rivers Po, Arno and Tiber, (c) the lakes Maggiore and Garda, (d) the volcanoes Vesuvius and Mt Etna, (e) the cities Genoa, Turin, Milan, Venice, Naples, Rome and Taranto.

2. Examine each of the following statements in detail:
   (a) The north of Italy is very suitable for the development of hydro-electric power.
   (b) There is a significant difference between the soils on the plain and those in the peninsula.
   (c) Italy may be divided into three main climatic regions.
   (d) The Alps, the coast and culture attract most of Italy's tourists.

3. Write an explanatory note on the development of agriculture in the North Italian Plain. (L.C. Ordinary Level)

4. Analyse the factors that have contributed towards the growth and development of settlement and industry in the Po Basin. (LC. Higher Level)

5. 'A number of factors have combined to make the Mezzogiorno a major problem area.' Discuss.

6. Study the population map of Italy (Fig. 9.27) and answer the following questions:
   (a) Which areas are most sparsely populated? Account for their lack of population.
   (b) Describe and account for the distribution of the major towns of Italy.
   (c) Account for the contrast in population distribution between the north and south. (L.C. Ordinary Level)

7. 'If the problem of underdevelopment within the EU is to be tackled with any chance of success, the crucial testing ground will be southern Italy.' Discuss the efforts of the *Cassa per il Mezzogiorno* to develop industry in the south.

8. What are the chief attractions of Italy for tourists? Discuss the efforts being made to attract tourists to the south of Italy.

9. Over 10% of migrant workers within the EU come from Italy.
   (a) Name two countries to which Italian workers migrate.
   (b) Give reasons for the migration.
   (c) Discuss some of the social and cultural problems of these migrant workers.

10. Discuss the physical and social problems that affect agriculture in the Mezzogiorno.

11. Discuss the factors that have contributed to industrial development in the Plain of Lombardy.

12. Three major climate types can be recognised in Italy.
    (a) Name and locate these climate types on a sketch map.
    (b) Choose two of the climate types and describe the climatic conditions there and the economic activities associated with them.
    (c) What are the main energy resources of Italy and what is their effect on industrial development?

13. The republic of Italy is physically a well-defined geographical entity, yet of all the countries in western Europe it is one of the most diverse. With the aid of

the information given below make a comparative study of northern Italy and southern Italy (Mezzogiorno). In your answer account for the major differences of population density, agricultural production and the economy of each.

(L.C. Higher Level)

	N. Italy	S. Italy
Population (millions)	34.19	18.96
Area (000 sq km)	178	123
Agr. land (000 sq km)	172	104
Agr. workers (millions)	2.05	1.96
Indus. workers (millions)	6.2	1.8
Unemployed (000)	357	306

14. Write geographical notes on each of the following:
    (a) The importance of the port of Genoa.
    (b) Textile industries in the Plain of Lombardy.
    (c) Land reform in the Mezzogiorno.
    (d) The high population density in the Plain of Lombardy.

15. Southern Italy - a problem region.
    (a) What are the main problems and their causes which distinguish this region?
    (b) Discuss the efforts which have been made and suggest other efforts which should be adopted to help solve the problems of the region. (L.C. Higher Level)

16. Outline the main contrasts between the north and south of Italy under the headings:
    (i) physical environment, (ii) agriculture and (iii) industry.

17. Identify and explain the differences between Norway and Italy under the headings:
    (i) climate, (ii) agriculture, (iii) tourism.

18. Write an account of one of the three major cities of the Italian Industrial Triangle under the headings: situation, communications, industrial base.

19. With reference to Italy, examine the ways in which the development of transport links has encouraged economic growth.

20. Describe the economic and social benefits of the tourism industry in Italy.

chapter ten
iberia - spain & portugal

INTRODUCTION

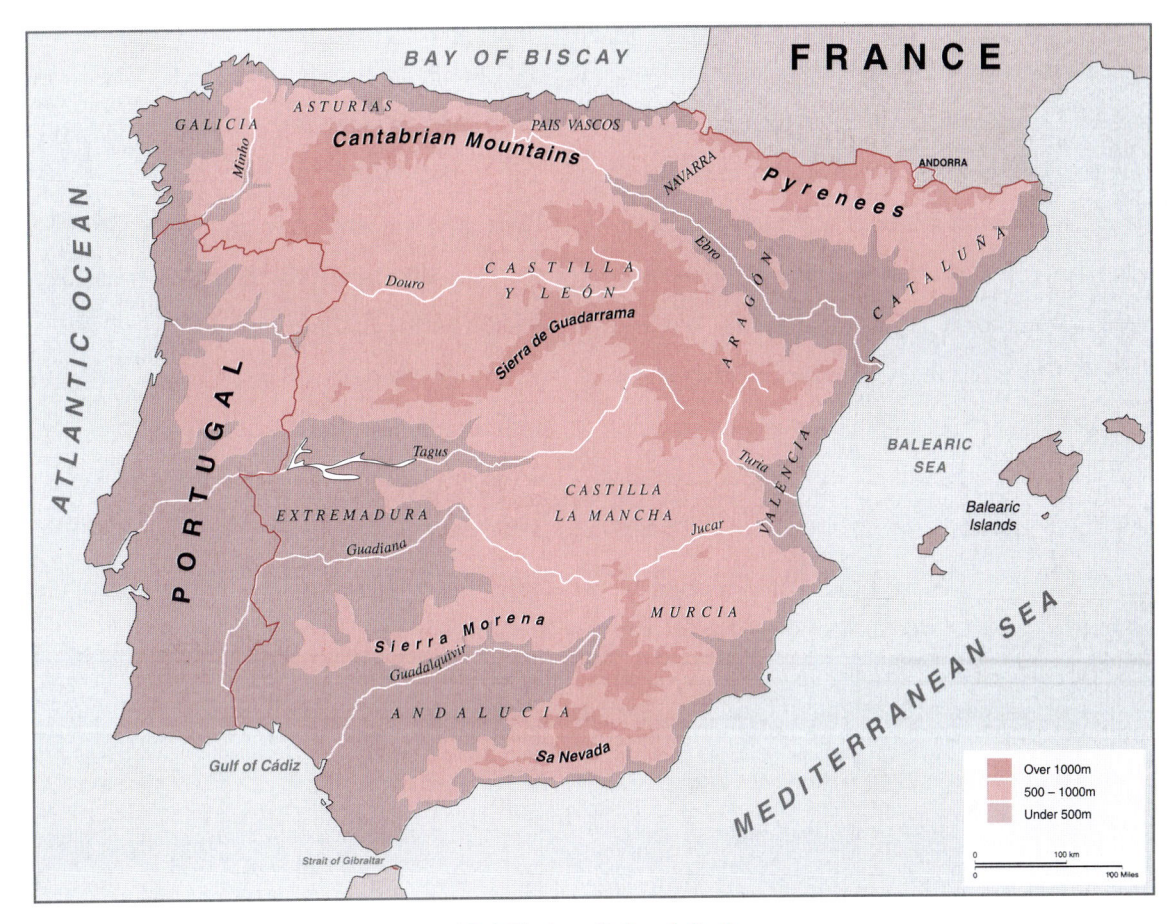

Fig. 10.1 Iberia relief and drainage

Iberia is the most westerly of the three peninsulas that penetrate the Mediterranean from Europe. It contains the two kingdoms of Spain and Portugal and the British protectorate of Gibraltar. For comparison purposes, Spain has 505 000 sq km and Portugal 92 000 sq km. Iberia is a well defined rectangular block cut off from the rest of Europe by the Pyrenées. This barrier inclined the Iberians to look south to Africa rather than north to Europe. This presents us with a modern day Iberia which is a mixture of both African and European influences and cultures.

From the earliest times, Iberia, sitting on the south-west of Europe and on the western edge of the Mediterranean, has attracted traders and settlers from many lands. The Phoenicians and Carthaginians were probably the earliest visitors but they were more interested in trade than in settlement. They crossed through Gibraltar to the Atlantic and established Cadiz as a major trading port.

The Romans conquered Iberia from the east, established many settlements and linked them with fine roads. They also established the first irrigation schemes.

With the decline of the Roman empire, the Vandals and Visigoths moved in from the north and quickly spread their influence over all Iberia. Later, in the eight century, the Moors moved across from North Africa and established themselves everywhere except along the north and north-west coasts which they found too damp. It was from this northern area that the Christian re-conquest took place. The Moorish influence was a great factor in developing Iberia. The Moors were expert at the use and control of water (North African influence), and re-organised and refurbished the old Roman irrigation works as well as building new schemes. They introduced new crops and plants like oranges, dates, sugar cane and cotton. Generally, the Moors improved the commerce and trade of Iberia and fostered agriculture, education, science and architecture. They were finally expelled after the marriage of Ferdinand and Isabella in 1492. Portugal developed from the groups of people who had originally settled in the north-west during the Moorish occupation. They gradually moved south along the Atlantic coast and established a capital first at Coimbra and later at Lisbon. Portugal has been recognised as an independent state since 1147.

The late fifteenth, sixteenth and seventeenth centuries saw the rise of Spain and Portugal into major colonial powers. Their ideal position on the western edge of the Mediterranean gave them an advantage over the rest of Europe in respect to the Atlantic and the Cape route to India and the Far East (in 1488 Diaz rounded the Cape, in 1492 Columbus discovered America, in 1498 Vasco da Gama reached India). From this period onwards, colonies were established in the Far East, India, Africa, Central and South America. Food, spices, raw materials, fabrics, gold, silver and precious stones poured into both countries, enriching the Iberians and providing cheap raw materials for indigenous industry. In addition, the great trade routes and trading links were established. During this period, Spain and Portugal were the envy of the rest of Europe.

These great empires, however, did not last. Portugal did not have the population to service great colonies and Spain expelled the Jews and the Moors, who were the experts in commerce. Both countries went into rapid decline and lost many of their colonies during the eighteenth and nineteenth centuries. With the colonies gone, the sources of much of the wealth were gone and Iberia degenerated into backward, poverty-stricken countries.

Both countries have experienced major changes since the 1970s when European-style democracies replaced the dictatorships of Franco and Salazar. Spain developed faster than Portugal with tourist revenue being invested in the total economy. Both joined the EU in 1986 and are in receipt of substantial EU funding.

CLIMATE

Three major climate zones may be identified in Iberia and these climates reflect many influencing factors including location, high relief inland, Atlantic air masses and depressions, coastal mountain barriers and distance from the sea.

Cool temperate maritime. This climate is experienced along the north and north-west coasts of Spain and in

Portugal to south of the Douro valley. Summers are warm, with temperatures averaging 20°C, and winters are mild. Winter temperatures rarely fall below 8°C. Rainfall is well distributed throughout the year but there is a definite winter maximum. Totals vary between 1 000mm and 1 500mm. There is much cloud which limits the amount of sunshine but there is compensation in the fact that the region has only 10 – 15 days frost on average. The main influences on this climate include location, the south-westerlies and the Atlantic depressions. The mild damp climate favours the growth of grass and is thus an important factor in the beef and dairy industry of the region.

Continental type. The continental type climate is experienced on the Meseta of both countries. Winters are cold with many days of frost, and January temperatures in the interior average about 2°C. High pressure forms over the Meseta and this prevents any moderating influences from the sea penetrating inland. In addition the high relief along the coast creates a barrier. The summers are hot with July averaging 27°C. Summers are for the most part dry, with rainfall decreasing from north to south but nowhere exceeding 500mm. Autumn and winter are the seasons of heaviest fall. The major influences on this climate are height, distance from the sea, coastal relief barriers and local high pressure in winter.

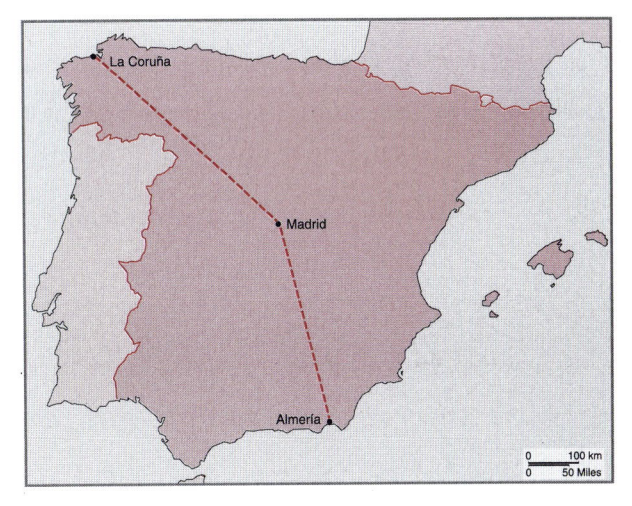

Fig. 10.3 Spain

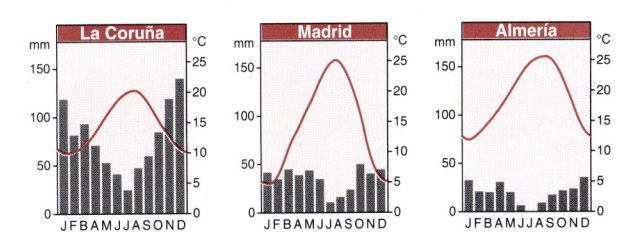

Fig. 10.4 Climate

Mediterranean. The true Mediterranean climate is found along the east and south coasts of Spain and a modified form of it along the coast of Portugal. The summers are hot, dry and sunny with temperatures in the high 20s. The sea has a moderating influence on these coastlands, keeping the temperatures down slightly. Winters are mild and moist and temperatures rarely fall below 9°C. Frosts are rare especially along the coast. Rainfall varies

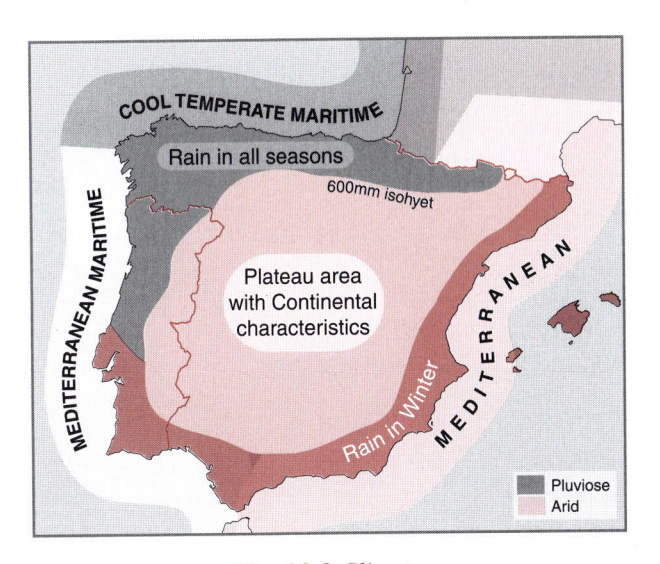

Fig. 10.2 Climate

with location, relief and shelter but is never more than about 500-600mm. Summer is a season of drought and the length and severity of the drought increases as one moves south. The major influences on this climate are proximity to the sea, the south-westerlies in winter (rain) and the north-east trades in summer (drought).

chapter eleven
spain

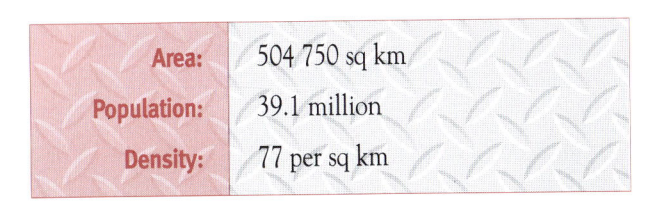

Area:	504 750 sq km
Population:	39.1 million
Density:	77 per sq km

Fig. 11.1 Barcelona

Minerals and Energy Production

Spain is a country with good resources and therefore great potential, but wide-scale industrialisation was late coming. However, today Spain ranks second only to Italy in the Mediterranean and ranks in the top twelve industrial nations of the world.

There are extensive coalfields in the provinces of Asturias and Leon along the Cantabrian coastlands. Oviedo is the centre of the coal mining and still produces nearly 20 million tonnes per annum. The coal is used in the steel mills for electricity generation and as a raw material in the chemical industry. Lignite burned in thermal power stations is mined south of Barcelona. Output has increased in recent years and now reaches about 15 million tonnes. However, it is hoped to increase this over the next ten years.

Spain has long been recognised as one of the chief mineral producers in Europe. The minerals are varied as are their locations, but three regions stand out – Cantabrians, Sierra Morena, Sierra Nevada (see Fig. 11.2).

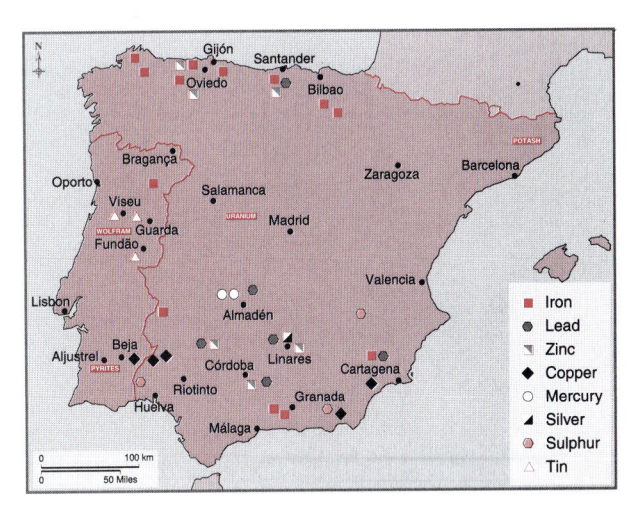

Fig 11.2 Minerals

The Cantabrians have provided iron ore for centuries for the smelters of Europe. Now the more accessible mines are near exhaustion and what is produced is used in local steel mills. Bilbao, Santander and Oviedo are the main production areas.

A whole cocktail of ores – copper, lead, zinc, silver, mercury, uranium – are mined at Rio Tinto, Linares and Almaden in the Sierra Morena. Much of this production is exported through Huelva.

In more recent years good deposits of iron ore, copper and lead have been worked in the Sierra Nevada near Granada and Almeria. Potassium salts, used in the manufacture of fertilisers, are found in the foothills of the Pyrenées. Uranium is mined in Salamanca.

Thermal power stations use coal, lignite and imported oil, and nuclear plants now produce about 10% of the energy needs. There is an increasing production of hydro power (HEP). The major areas of production are the Pyrenees, the Cantabrians and the province of Galicia. All three areas have a regular well-distributed rainfall regime which ensures adequate water supplies. There is also a steady market along the industrial north coast. The Ebro receives a good water supply from the surrounding uplands and electricity is generated at many points along its course. Again the northern and Barcelona regions provide the market.

The Douro and Tagus are harnessed where they fall across the Meseta near the boundary with Portugal, but limited summer water creates difficulties. There are numerous smaller stations in the Sierra Morena, the Sierra Nevada and along the small rivers emptying into the Mediterranean, but again the lack of sufficient water limits production. In recent years the control of rivers has been better organised with multi-purpose schemes for hydro production, irrigation and domestic supplies. The very high summer evaporation remains a problem.

The Fishing Industry

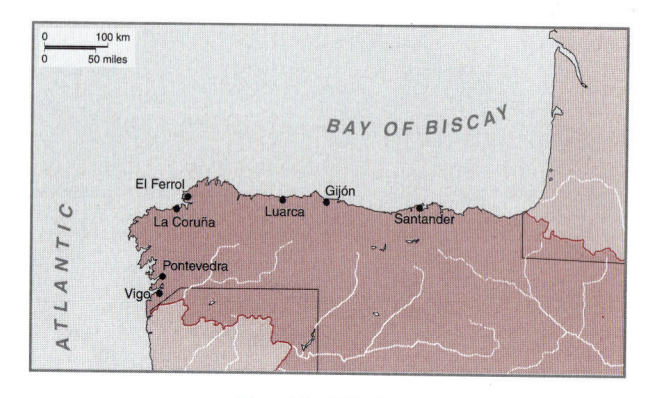

Fig. 11.4 Fishing

The fishing industry in Spain is very important as it provides an alternative food supply and is a large employer. Spain has the largest fleet within the EU but the total catch at 1.1 million tonnes is not as great as Denmark's. Spain has 18 000 boats and 90 000 fishermen, but there are tens of thousands of other workers employed indirectly. The industry does not mean as much to the economy, however, as that of Norway or Denmark.

Both the Atlantic and the Mediterranean are fished, but over 80% of the catch is taken in the Atlantic waters. There is both coastal and deep sea fishing from the Atlantic ports. Like Norway, the limited land resources along the coast have driven people to the sea for their livelihood.

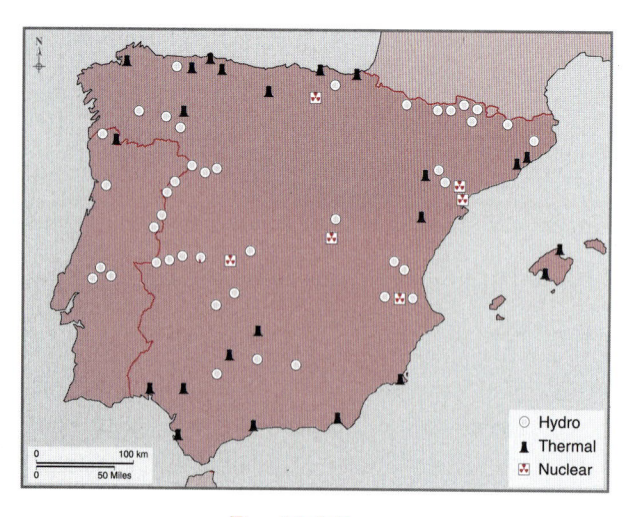

Fig. 11.3 Energy

The Spanish fishing industry has run into some difficulties in recent years. Since entry to the EU, Spain has been restricted in its activities in both the Celtic Sea, between S.E. Ireland and S.W. England, and the coastal waters around Ireland – the *Irish Box*. Spain also had a dispute in the 1990s with Canada with regard to the diminishing stocks around Newfoundland.

Vigo and Corunna are the main ports, but all the smaller ports along the coast have fleets. Tunny, anchovy and sardines, with the normal deep sea varieties of cod, haddock, plaice, etc., make up the bulk of the catch. Shellfish are caught in-shore. Well over half the catch is eaten fresh (compare with Norway) but Spain is expanding its processing, canning and freezing industries. Fish farming is carried on in the sheltered rias of Galicia in the north west.

The **Mediterranean** is not as rich a fishing ground as one would expect. It has a high saline content, is low in oxygen and poor in nutrients. Therefore it is poor in plankton and so poor in fish. It is becoming increasingly polluted, which causes damage to the breeding grounds. There are a number of richer areas including:

- Off the mouth of the Rhone, Po and Nile
- The wider continental shelves of the Gulf of Lions and the north Adriatic
- Between the North African coast and Sicily.

The chief varieties from the Mediterranean include anchovy, sardine, cod, haddock and tuna.

Agriculture

Agriculture in Spain suffers many of the traditional Mediterranean problems already encountered in the Mezzogiorno in Italy and are summarised briefly.

Climate

Galicia in the north west and the Cantabrian coastal plains are the only parts of Spain that receive anything approaching an adequate rainfall. Over the rest of the country rainfall is seasonal and limited. High evaporation is another problem. The Mediterranean coasts get winter rain only, amounting to about 600mms. The Meseta has extremes of temperature and about 500mms of rain. Rainfall is limited on 85% of arable land.

Soils

The best soils are confined to the Mediterranean coastlands and the lower flood plains of the rivers. Much of the Meseta has poor thin soils suitable only for sheep grazing without the aid of irrigation.

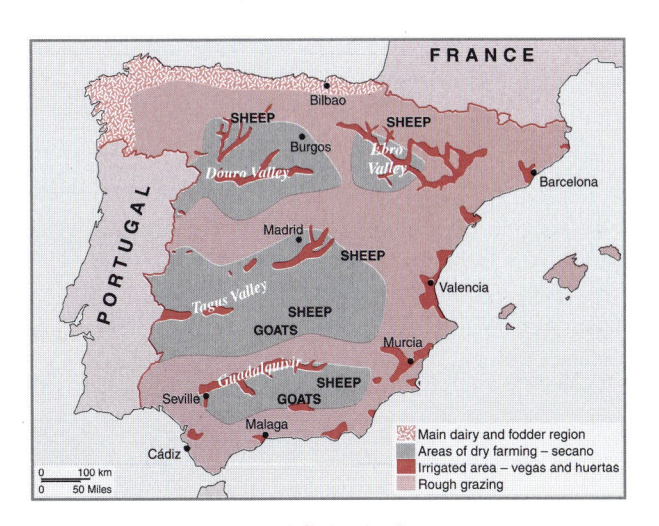

Fig. 11.5 Agriculture

Land Tenure

Spain suffers from the twin evils of *latifundia* in the south, often in the hands of absentee landlords, and *minifundia* in the north because of sub-division among a dense rural population. The latifundia are underworked, giving low yields while the minifundia are too small to be viable in the EU context.

Lack of investment

There is a lack of both capital investment and training investment in agriculture.

Distance from markets

Much of the centre and south is at a disadvantage with regard to the lucrative EU markets.

Reforms

However, over the last 25 years improvements have taken place. The tourist boom from the 1970s has provided much-needed capital for the infrastructure and for agriculture. Some of the latifundias have been subdivided into viable units and given to the previous tenant farmers, and much amalgamation and consolidation have taken place in the north. Mechanisation has replaced labour and the numbers employed in agriculture have fallen by over 1 million over that period. The guaranteed prices of CAP have also given a new impetus and a new confidence to Spanish agriculture. The greatest single factor in the expansion of agriculture has been the development of irrigation schemes. Irrigation brings new land into production and increases yields when used as a supplement to the rainfall.

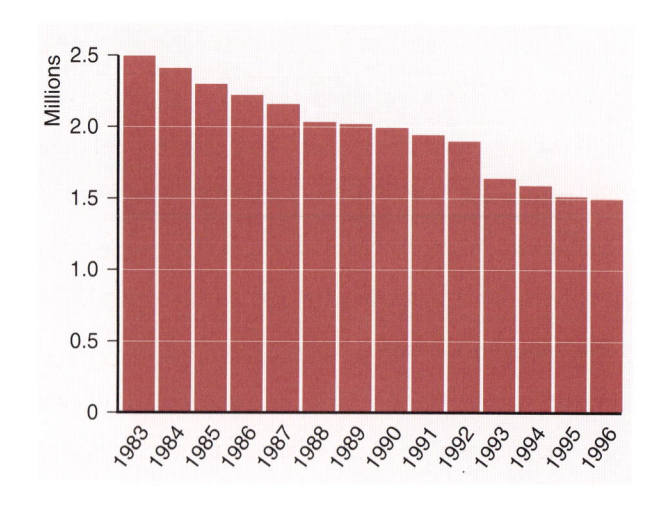

Fig 11.6 Employment in agriculture

The more affluent home market and the substantial tourist market have also helped farming.

TYPES OF FARMING

Fig. 11.7 Spanish agriculture

With a variety of climates, soils and landscapes, Spain has a variety of farming types and products, ranging from sugar beet in the north west to sugar cane in the south east.

The north west and north, with the temperate maritime climate, has a mixed farming economy. Cereals, sugar beet and potatoes are the chief arable crops, and both beef and dairy cattle are reared. These areas feature the minifundia land tenure system and it is difficult to earn a decent living.

As a result many young people have left farming, which is now left to the older, less skilled, more conservative family members. As a result farming has changed little and is slow to adapt to the demands of the modern European systems. The Meseta has problems of climate and soil deficiency. Farming is difficult and low yielding with much wasteful fallow. There is the extensive growing of wheat across the northern half. South of Madrid lies the province of New Castile known as La Mancha – the desert. Here the grazing of Merino sheep, for their wool, is the main activity. There are about 25 million sheep reared. Pig meat is the most popular meat in Spain, so pig rearing is carried on, all across the Meseta.

Over the years irrigation schemes have been improved and extended on the Meseta and EU funds have recently helped. In the irrigated areas more intensive agriculture can be carried on, but overall, many parts of the Meseta have still a low yielding primitive agriculture, characterised by large estates.

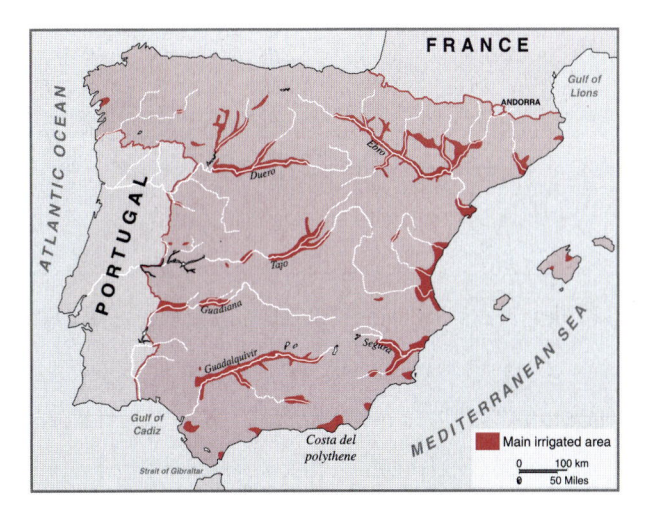

Fig. 11.8 Irrigation

Mediterranean agriculture

The most important agricultural area in Spain is along the Mediterranean coast from the Pyrenées down and into the Guadalquivir valley. Here polyculture dominates. The Ebro valley and its coastal lands have a constant supply of water from the surrounding mountains and are major farming regions. The central coastlands are fed by many small rivers coming off the Meseta but the supply is unreliable. New irrigation schemes and reservoirs are helping to maintain the flow. The Guadalquivir collects from the Meseta and the Sierra Nevada and so has a good supply. Water is the key to the variety and richness of agriculture over the whole area.

Some of the problems affecting agriculture have already been noted but there were others affecting this area as well. There was a limited amount of lowland along the coast and too many people, attracted by the climate, working that land. In addition there was a limited local market because of low incomes. Farming, therefore, tended to be traditional and conservative.

But changes have taken place. The most significant change has been the guarantee of water through the new irrigation schemes. With hot summer and warm winters there is a year-round cultivation of many crops with many areas producing two or three harvests over the year. Very often a number of crops are grown on the same piece of land.

Modern refrigerated container trucks deliver the products fresh to northern and central European markets, particularly when the products are out of season in these areas. New motorways, funded by the ERDF link the

Mediterranean coast with the EU. Improved roads reduce costs. Membership of the EU has helped in providing capital grants to modernise farming and the infrastructure. New markets have been opened to Spain with higher prices and guaranteed prices under CAP.

There is a distinct pattern to agriculture along the Mediterranean coast, although differences do occur from region to region. There are three distinct farming areas – (1) reclaimed lagoons, (2) coastal plains, (3) terraced slopes. The reclaimed lagoons are ideal for the cultivation of commercial crops of rice, cotton, tobacco and sunflowers. Along the coastal plains are the *huertas*, which are irrigated market gardens for the production of vegetables and salads – peas, beans, onions, potatoes, lettuce, tomatoes, etc.

The coastal plains slope up to the Meseta and here the slopes are terraced. On the terraces are irrigated orchards called **vegas.** The vegas are the most intensively cultivated areas along the Mediterranean, often with three crops growing on one parcel of land – citrus and olives, vegetables on the ground and vines on trellises between the trees.

A recent development is the cultivation of crops in glasshouses. Almeria in the south east is now regarded as the glasshouse of Europe – (*Costa del Polythene*) with thousands of hectares of irrigated glasshouses. The output from the Mediterranean areas now has three major outlets:
1. The local urban population and the huge tourist market
2. North and north-west Europe, with a single annual harvest, anxious for out of season products
3. A fast growing fruit and vegetable canning industry in the cities of Valencia, Cartagena, Almeria, etc.

INDUSTRY IN SPAIN

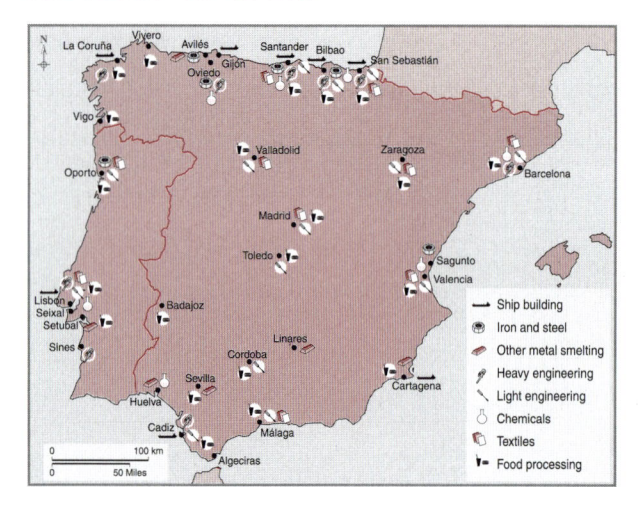

Fig. 11.9 Manufacturing

Spain is rapidly catching up with the main west European countries as regards industrial expansion and has made remarkable progress over the last forty years. It is worth taking a glance at the industrial history of Spain in this century. The world depression of the 1920s and 1930s had a serious effect on the economy, as Spain is peripheral to the industrial heartland of western Europe. The failure of the economy at this time was later compounded by the effects of the Civil War in 1936 and the World War of 1939-45. Spain remained neutral during this war but in 1945 was virtually ostracised by Europe and the USA. In 1953 however, agreement was reached with NATO which allowed for the building of NATO bases at Cadiz and Cartagena and of air bases at Zaragossa, Madrid and Seville. This concession to NATO opened the way for massive overseas investment and Spain's recovery was on the way. In 1956 Spain became a member of the United Nations and this also helped attract foreign investment. A state-sponsored industrial development plan was also put into operation at the time.

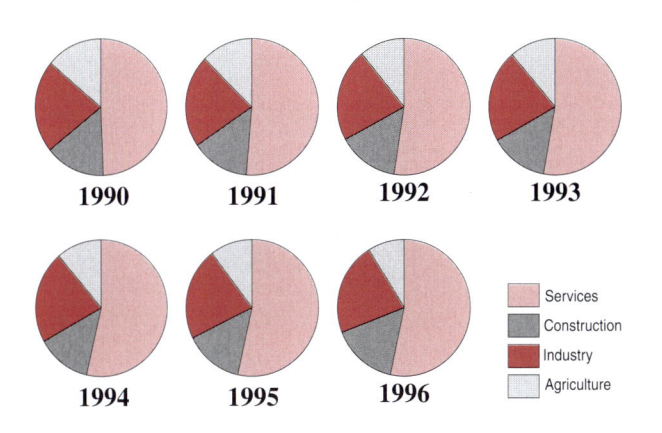

Fig. 11.10 Employment Structure

Two other sources of capital came onstream during this period. Europe began to discover Spain as an attractive tourist centre and the number of tourists soared from less than 200 000 in 1946 to over fifty million in 1996. This brought much needed capital and stimulated the construction, manufacturing and service industries. Substantial sums of money were also sent back to Spain by the 3 million emigrant workers in the USA and Europe. In addition, many of the returning emigrants brought back with them new ideas, techniques and skills which were an invaluable asset in generating industry.

This industrial movement was also helped by the development of power resources. There was a great expansion of HEP particularly in the north, where the greatest demand lay. However, the industrial expansion was not evenly balanced, as industry seemed to gravitate towards the regions which were already well established while others did not generate growth. Thus the south of Spain is still under-industrialised, poor, over-dependent on agriculture and has a high outward migration rate. The important industrial regions are:

Madrid

Catalonia

The Cantabrian coastal plain.

Madrid

Madrid, the capital, is built on the Manzanares, a tributary of the Tagus. It was selected by Philip II in 1561 as the capital and permanent seat of government. The chief consideration at the time was the unification of the country and so the centrality of Madrid was important.

Madrid is situated in the centre of the Meseta and is the focus of road, rail and air routes. There are easy routeways across the Meseta and the Sierras to Galicia, the northern coastlands, Barcelona, the Ebro basin, Valencia and Andalusia. This focus and ease of communications has established Madrid as the chief collection and distribution point in Spain.

Fig. 11.11 The chemical industry

The hinterland of Madrid is not itself very productive because of poor soils, arid climate and lack of minerals. Nevertheless, because of its importance as a government, financial and administrative centre, Madrid has grown into a city of 3·5 million people. A large in-migration from the provinces has aided this growth.

Modern industrial developments include vehicles, aircraft, electronics, electrical equipment, chemicals, food processing.

As national capital, Madrid has a thriving service sector with the major institutions and ministries situated there. Entry to the EU increased this sector and most of the MNCs located in Spain have their headquarters in Madrid. While the recession of 1975-85 cost industrial jobs, that position has now been reversed and Madrid now attracts 40% of all foreign investment.

Fig. 11.12 Madrid

Catalonia

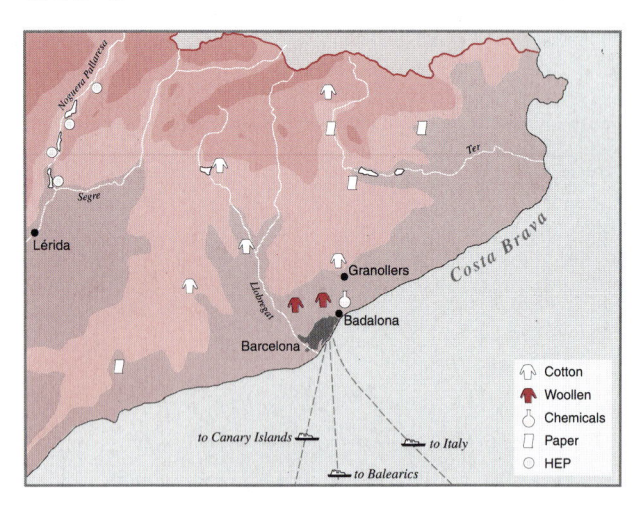

Fig. 11.13 Barcelona

The Catalonian coastlands are centred upon Barcelona which is the chief port and second city of Spain. It is the single most important manufacturing city and its industrial influence has spread to many of the surrounding towns and cities.

Consider the following factors which have helped Barcelona to attain its prime position:

- It has a well developed deep artificial harbour where fuels and raw materials can easily be imported. Its chief advantage lies in its strategic location in the western Mediterranean.
- It has a history of commerce and trade with the Mediterranean and Middle East, built up over the centuries.
- Its early industrial life was based on textiles, using local wool and water power.
- Supplies of HEP are now available from the Pyrenees, the Ebro and the Catalan mountains behind the city.
- There are good transport links with the capital, Madrid, and the northern industrial zone and the

other cities along the Mediterranean. It is the centre of a region that extends across the French border, through Toulouse and Marseilles and into the Lombardy Plain.

- There is a plentiful supply of both skilled and unskilled labour with an in-migration from rural Spain. The population of Barcelona has risen from 175 000 in 1850 to 2 million today.
- In this half of the twentieth century, growth capital has come from the booming tourist industry. The 1992 Olympics provided Barcelona with the opportunity to present itself to the world as a thriving, prosperous city.

Fig. 11.14 Shipbuilding in Catalonia

The textile industry is the single most important employer, with 200 000 involved in all aspects of the industry. Cotton is the dominant textile, followed by wool and synthetics.

The other growth industries are shipbuilding, railway stock, cars, oil-refining, chemicals and food processing.

Since the late 80s industrial Catalonia has developed dramatically, attracting many international companies. The skilled workforce, good transport and proximity to the rich urbanised markets of Europe are the attractions. Japan leads the way with well over 100 manufacturers.

Barcelona is the centre of the Costa Brava tourist region. This is only one of the major service sectors in the region.

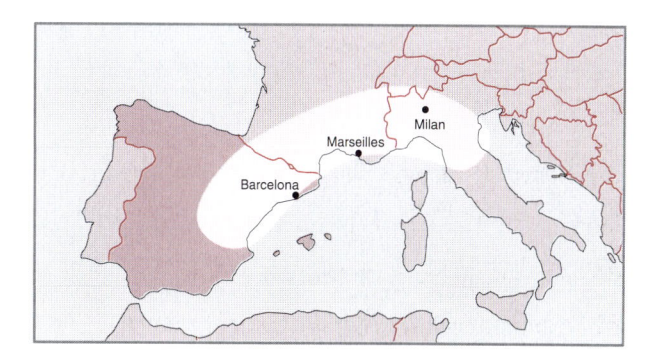

Fig. 11.15 Second banana

The Cantabrian Coastal Plains

This rich industrial area stretching across the northern lowlands has many advantages which gave it a head start over the rest of the country as regards industry. There are rich deposits of iron ore and coal in the Cantabrians and abundant supplies of cheap HEP. Good deep-water natural harbours also played their part in the development of this region, which is the part of Spain most accessible to the European markets. The cities along this coast have a tradition of trading with Wales, England, France and the Low Countries. Early industry used water wheels as a source of power, so there is a tradition of industry in the area. Labour is plentiful and by western European rates, comparatively cheap.

Iron and steel are the most important industries, using both native and imported ores and local coal. There are integrated works along the coast at Aviles, Gijon, Oviedo, Santander and Bilbao.

This whole region, stretching from Gijon to Bilbao, was Spain's most important industrial region before the recession of 1975 to 1985. Like other European traditional coal/steel regions it suffered the full force of the recession. Many jobs were lost in the coal, iron, steel and ship-building industries and the region went into decline.

But from the late 80s the region fought back. Heavy industry was modernised and revamped and new small and medium sized high-tech companies were established. The whole infrastructure was up-dated with new motorways, built with EU funds, extending along the coast and into France. New port facilities at Bilbao include roll on-roll off ferries to Britain and mainland Europe.

The availability of steel has led to a diverse engineering sector and shipbuilding remains the main market for the steel. Spain has invested heavily in shipyards and modern equipment and has a flourishing industry from Corunna to Bilbao. It now ranks in the world's top five shipbuilding nations. Other branches of engineering include railways, rolling stock, marine works, armaments, hydro machinery, agricultural equipment, electrical and industrial machinery.

New aircraft components factories have been set up and Volkswagen have established car plants. All branches of the chemical and petro-chemical industries are present, using the coke by-products, potash from the Pyrennées and imported oil.

ANDALUSIA — PROBLEM AREA

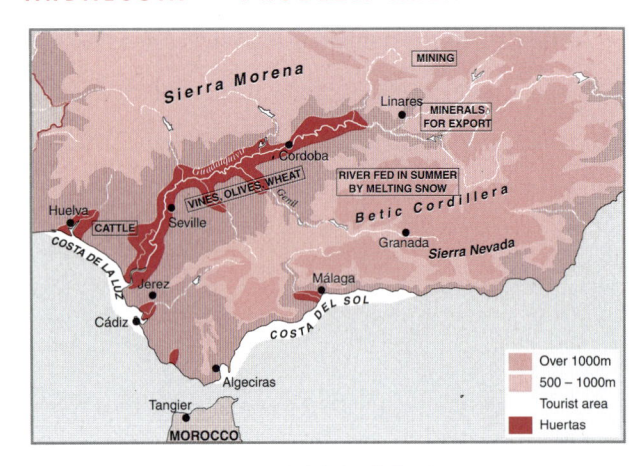

Fig. 11.16 Andalusia

SAMPLE QUESTION

Discuss the problems of Andalusia. How are these problems being solved?

Andalusia, lying to the south of the peninsula, is one of the largest of the old Spanish provinces. The Sierra Morena lie to the north, Murcia to the east and Portugal to the west. It runs from Almeria on the Mediterranean through Gibraltar to the Gulf of Cadiz on the Atlantic. The river Guadalquivir flows through the heart of the region and is the only Spanish river navigable for any distance. Andalusia contains about 17% of the population – about 6 million. It is a peripheral region in Spain.

We noted earlier that regional development in Spain was not balanced and that some regions had made great progress, but that others lagged far behind. Andalusia is one of the most backward and less developed of the poorer regions. It contains one in six of the population and has a birth rate nearly as high as that of India or China. It has therefore a large, young population with over 50% of the people under the age of 25. It is this young population which holds the key to the future of the region.

Problems

Since medieval times Andalusia has been a region of rural mismanagement, latifundia and absentee landlords. Farming has always been extensive (wheat and olives), limited and low yielding. Peasant farmers practised backward methods and there was little mechanisation. The landlords encouraged this tradition as it gave them a vast pool of cheap labour. Casual or seasonal work provided little training or education for the work force.

The untrained work force was not an inducement to investment in either agriculture or industry, so the more developed regions in the north benefited at the expense of Andalusia. It also suffered an out-migration of its young people leading to the decay of many villages and towns and to the deterioration of the infrastructure. Many areas have less than 30 people per km^2.

Andalusia lacks coal and has only limited HEP. Industry tends to concentrate in the larger cities and along the coast, leading to further depopulation of the interior. At 27%, it has the highest unemployment rate in Spain.

We see Andalusia then as the classical backward rural region with an out-migration of capital, resources and labour, a poor home market, scattered industrialisation and little technical know-how.

However there is hope when we consider the potential of the region. Consider the following:

Resources of Andalusia

- The very fertile lowlands of the Guadalquivir valley.
- A young workforce eager for education, trainig and skills.
- A hot sunny climate provides good growing conditions where irrigation waters are available.
- A great tourist potential – the Mediterranean sea, spectacular scenery, Moorish architecture.
- Easy communication across the valley and good ports.
- EU structural, regional, social and cohesion funds are available.

Already some development of the region has been undertaken. Some of the latifundias have been taken over and subdivided among the tenant farmers. Training has been provided and advice, service and market centres established. Many irrigation schemes have been completed so farming yields and returns are significantly higher. Many of the remaining latifundias have been irrigated and the owners are turning to modern methods and new crops. These changes constitute a permanent improvement in agricultural output.

There is now a new generation of farmers concentrating on the cash crops of fruit, salads and vegetables, in addition to the traditional citrus, vines and olives. The delta and lower flood plain of the Guadalquivir are devoted to rice, sugar cane and cotton. Thousands of hectares of greenhouses are adding to the output and Spaniards now boast that Andalusia will become the California of Europe over the next number of years.

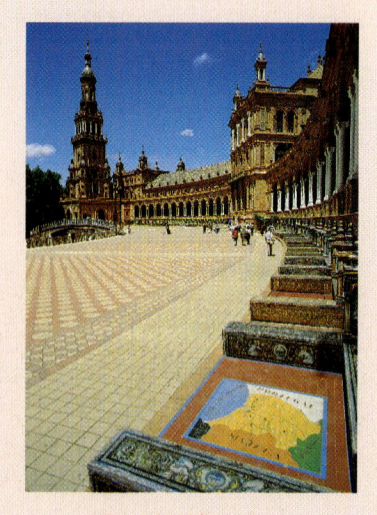

Fig. 11.17 Seville

Industry has also attracted attention. The National Industrial Institute (INI) was established to promote new and heavy industries which private companies could not afford to create. Andalusia, with its good ports and its location at the entrance to the Mediterranean, has got its share of the INI investment. The most spectacular success has been that of the shipbuilding industry. Seville and Cadiz now have the busiest yards in Spain and have helped place Spain fifth in the world of ships. Other industries initiated by the INI include metallurgy, aircraft and armaments, cement, paper, electricals, telecommunications and machine engineering.

The second arm of industrial expansion has been the selection of **growth poles** (as in the Mezzogiorno). By establishing capital intensive industries at the growth poles it was hoped that ancillary and consumer projects would follow naturally as downstream industries. Five major growth centres were selected – Huelva, Seville, Cordoba, Granada and Algeciras. Generous loans, grants and tax concessions were made available to industrialists establishing at these centres. Much foreign capital was attracted by the prospects of tax concessions, cheap labour and a large market. The investment also brought new skills and techniques and good management. Huelva has developed chemical and fertiliser plants, while Seville has iron and steel, cars, armaments and textiles. Cordoba and Granada have textiles, paper, chemicals and food processing. Algeciras has oil, chemical and fertiliser industries.

But problems still persist. The development of the industrial sector and the growth of tourism have further increased the differences between the coast and the interior, for most of these activities are concentrated in the coastal zone. Some of the interior regions still have a GDP 50% lower than the coastal provinces.

Tourism is the single most important source of foreign currency in Spain and Andalusia has used all its natural advantages to earn for itself a large share of the tourism bonanza. The whole coast from Almeria to Huelva is involved and the industry is developing into a year-round one by the promotion of cheap long-term winter *retirements*, golf, fishing and water sports activities. Andalusia offers miles of golden beaches and 3 000 hours of sunshine per annum (Costa del Sol). Inland from the beaches, Andalusia boasts of rugged, unspoiled scenic beauty and a landscape rich in Moorish architecture. The tourism industry is vital, as it generates immediate capital and has important effects on the construction, horticultural, service and consumer industries.

We see then that Andalusia has the potential to create growth in many areas. New farming and new industry will create new employment, which in turn will create a new market. This market will provide the stimulus and impetus needed to gain maximum benefit from Spain's entry to the EU.

TOURISM

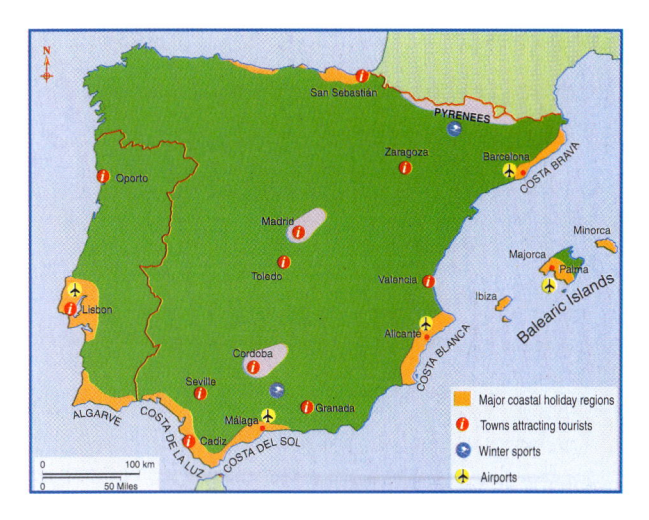

Fig. 11.18 Tourist attractions

The modern tourist industry is one of the great growth industries of the twentieth century. This growth has been particularly significant since the end of the 1939-45 war and its expansion is linked to the cultural and technological developments that have taken place since then.

There is a big increase in world population and people now have longer holidays, more disposable income and a better education with a consequent desire to visit foreign places. Modern day living in highly urbanised societies creates a necessity for people to get away for some time to a different environment. Improved air transport has made this possible. All this means more people taking more holidays. Spain has exploited this market.

Over 180 million international tourists visit Europe each year and Spain is one of the chief destinations, attracting nearly 50 million visitors, who spend well over $12 000 million. This accounts for 20% of exports and 50% of Spain's foreign currency. About 90% of the tourists come from western Europe.

The Spanish tourist industry has seen a remarkably rapid growth from 250 000 tourists in 1950 to 50 million in 1996. What factors have influenced this development?

- Proximity to the affluent European market and the rapid development of air transport.
- A guaranteed hot and sunny climate with miles of golden beaches along the Mediterranean.
- An initial period of cheap holidays to establish the industry.
- The introduction by tour companies of charter flights and package holidays.
- The support of the Ministry of Tourism from 1962.

The Ministry helped in developing the Mediterranean coastal regions initially. It provided cheap loans and grants to facilitate the building of hotels, apartments, villas, camping sites and amusement amenities from the Pyrenees to Gibraltar. It extended credit facilities to hoteliers and tourism investors. It also planned and built a string of national tourist hotels across the country. As far as possible in the initial years, the ministry monitored and controlled hotel prices so as to preserve the cheap holiday idea. At the same time the idea of the *package holiday* emerged. This also helped in keeping prices down as the competition between the operators increased.

Tourism has been of major significance in the economy of Spain and tourist revenue has been the tool that broke the vicious circle of under-development. The revenue generated has been used to finance many other sectors of the economy, particularly the infrastructure. But not all regions have experienced the benefits. Over 50% of tourist accommodation and revenue is generated and concentrated in only five areas – Costa Brava, Costa Dorada, Costa Blanca, Costa del Sol and the Balearic Islands. The major centres are Barcelona, Valencia, Alicante, Benidorm, Malaga and Palma. All these areas are along the Mediterranean and Madrid is the only area in the rest of Spain to benefit directly.

Fig. 11.19 Scenic view

As the Mediterrranean resorts are overcrowded for the short summer season, the Ministry of Tourism is actively promoting the interior of the country. Here there is a variety of scenery, interesting cuisine, traditional customs and festivals and widespread historical monuments, particularly those associated with the Moors. It is hoped that this will draw people away from the coast, protect the coastal environment and offset the seasonality of the industry as well as spreading the benefits of the industry more widely. Special activity holidays – golf, water sports, deep sea fishing, cruising – have been introduced to lengthen the tourist year as has the development of winter sports in the Pyrennees and Sierra Nevada. Interior Andalusia was not part of the package boom of the 60s and 70s but has since developed to serve the needs of the more exclusive tourist.

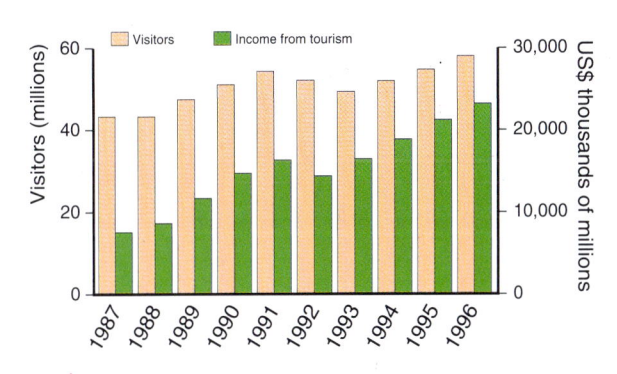

Fig. 11.20 Visitors

Tourism – Problems

The Spanish tourist industry is not without its problems.

- In the early days much of the building along the coast was haphazard and unplanned. The result is a linear high rise development of hotels and apartments blocking the view of the scenic background and leading to congestion, traffic problems and pollution along the coast.
- Seasonality is a major problem. Nearly three quarters of the tourists come in July, August and September. This creates long periods when both the labour force and the physical amenities are unemployed or under-employed. It also means extraordinary pressure on resources during the high season.
- Agricultural land is being taken over for villas, hotels, apartments, etc., leading to the loss of productive farmland and the local economy is being changed. Traditional farming, on which the local community totally depended, is being replaced by a tourist economy. Very often the local community is now dependant on an economy over which they have no control, as the marketing (and therefore the success), of the local tourist industry is in the hands of tour operators in Europe.
- In very dry years scarce water supplies can cause problems and disputes between hoteliers and local farmers who need water for irrigation.
- With mass tourism, standards fall. Crime, drugs and vandalism are inevitable. Competition from elsewhere in the Mediterranean follows.
- A high quality environment, clean air and water, attractive landscapes and restfulness are the qualities which attract tourists. However, these qualities are threatened by both the number of tourists and by the developments necessary to attract them. Spain's Mediterranean coast suffers from the dilemma of balancing both.

Fig. 11.21 Spanish attractions

Benefits of Tourism to the Economy

- Spain is very dependent on the tourism industry. It is a labour intensive industry, so obviously the main consideration is that of employment, with tourism providing jobs for nearly 12% of the total workforce.
- Tourism accounts for over 20% of export earnings.
- There are many thousands of seasonal and part-time jobs created.
- Tourism offers a rapid return on the investments made in it and so makes an immediate impact on Spain's finances. In this way it has contributed to the development of other sectors of the economy and so to the overall economic growth of the country.
- Many industries have benefited from the growth of tourism. They include cement, steel, construction, farming, food processing, carriers and transport, etc.
- Infrastructural and service improvements have developed rapidly. Roads, rail, airports, water and sewage structures have had to be improved. In the resorts, shops, bars, restaurants, etc., have had to be provided and these improvements have been of enormous benefit to the Spanish people themselves.

CITIES OF SPAIN

Valencia

Valencia is the third city of Spain lying in a huerta which is said to be the most fertile and beautiful garden area in Spain. It is situated on the Guadalaviar about 5km from the Mediterranean and it uses El Grao as its outport. It is a leading industrial and commercial centre where the products of the region are processed and marketed. The most important of these are cereals, flour, tobacco, wine, citrus fruits and vegetables.

Fig. 11.22 Orange picking in Valencia

There is also a wide variety of manufacturing industry, including textiles, pottery, glass, ceramics and the heavier industries of shipbuilding, engineering and chemicals. There is a large integrated steel mill at Sagunto about 25km north of Valencia, which supplies the steel for shipbuilding.

Valencia is an important port with good road, rail and air links with Madrid, Barcelona and the northern industrial region.

Seville

With a population of over 600 000 Seville is the chief city of Andalusia. It is situated on the Guadalquivir about 120km from its mouth, but with the aid of canals ocean-going ships can reach Seville. It is thus an important port for the south of Spain. It is the centre of the orange and wine (sherry) districts and these items form an important part of its trade. It also exports the minerals from the Sierra Morena mines.

Seville has the traditional food-processing, textile and ceramics industries based on the local raw materials but it has also, over the last number of years, developed steel, engineering, armaments and cars. It is one of the growth poles of the Andalusian industrial revival and capital is available for further industrial expansion. The most important single industry is probably tourism, because Seville is an ancient city with a glorious architectural treasure house. It was the old Roman capital of southern Spain before being captured by the Visigoths. In 712 it fell to the Moors, who used it as a capital for over 500 years. The Moors were expelled and Seville went into decline, but its revival began when it was granted, with Cadiz, a monopoly of trade with the newly discovered Americas in the early 1500s. This was a period of great prosperity making Seville, at the time, one of the richest cities of Europe.

Modern Seville has managed to retain many of its architectural treasures. Parts of the old Moorish walls remain as does the Alcazar, the Moorish palace. The magnificent cathedral, adorned with paintings by Murillo and El Greco, is a focal point for tourism.

SAMPLE QUESTION

Divide Spain into its regions and select three for discussion.

The three regions selected for discussion are:

1. The Mediterranean coastlands – an emerging prosperous agricultural area
2. Catalonia – the core area of industry
3. Andalusia – a problem region.

For your answer, refer to the text.

Questions on Spain are combined with those on Portugal on page 221.

chapter twelve
portugal

INTRODUCTION

Area:	92 000 sq km
Population:	9.5 million
Density:	103 per sq km

Portugal is the second country of the Iberian Peninsula. It has been recognised as an independent state since 1147 and its boundaries with Spain have hardly changed since then.

Portugal has a long coastline facing on to the Atlantic. Inland, the Spanish Meseta crosses the boundary and extends into Portugal in a series of upland ridges. These uplands gradually slope down on to the coastal plains which run the whole length of the coast. The lower flood plains of the Douro, Tagus and Guadiana occupy part of these plains.

Climate

The cool temperate maritime climate stretches to south of the Douro valley. Summers are hot (20°C) and the winters warm (10°C) with an abundant rainfall from the Atlantic depressions (1 250mm). South of here the country enjoys a Mediterranean type climate similar to the south of Spain – 11°C in winter, 25°C in summer. Relief and distance from the sea both become important away from the coast, so that winters are colder in the uplands and summers are warmer. The south has less rainfall than the north and suffers summer drought, e.g. Oporto (1 210mm), Lisbon (755mm).

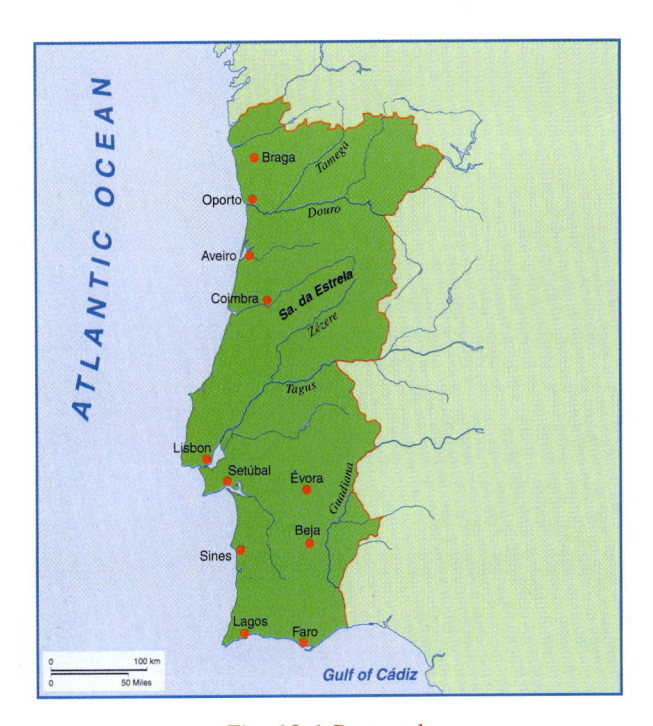

Fig. 12.1 Portugal

Fig. 12.2 Portugese hill town

Minerals and energy

The minerals in Portugal are varied both in quality and quantity and are in widely scattered locations. Iron ore is mined in the upper Douro valley and supplies some of the needs of the home market. Tin is found to the south of the Douro around Guarda and Viseu. Copper is the most important mineral. The chief copper mines are at Beja and Aljustrel and much of the ore is exported through Setubal. Some of the copper is processed in Lisbon. Portugal is hindered by a lack of capital to finance a full and detailed geological survey and by the poor communications in the highlands.

Fig. 12.3 Energy and minerals

Energy

Very limited power resources are available in Portugal and this has hindered economic progress somewhat. There are small coal mines north of the Douro and near Setabul, but most of the country's needs are met by imports from Britain and the USA. There is neither gas nor oil of any significance, but exploration is still continuing off the coast. As in Spain, **hydro electric generation** is hindered by the irregular flows of the rivers and by the low summer supplies of water. Nevertheless, there are major schemes on the rivers Zegere and Tamega – tributaries of the Tagus and Douro.

As Portugal continues to expand its industries and economy, more and more reliance is placed on imported oil and coal for thermal stations. At present, HEP contributes about 20% of the electricity needs.

Fishing

The sea plays an important part in the economy of Portugal, which is a traditional maritime nation. Because of its limited land resources, Portugal has always looked to the sea for much of its food. There is a well-indented coastline along the Atlantic, so that there are numerous fishing ports both large and small from north to south. The benefits from fishing are therefore felt along the whole coast.

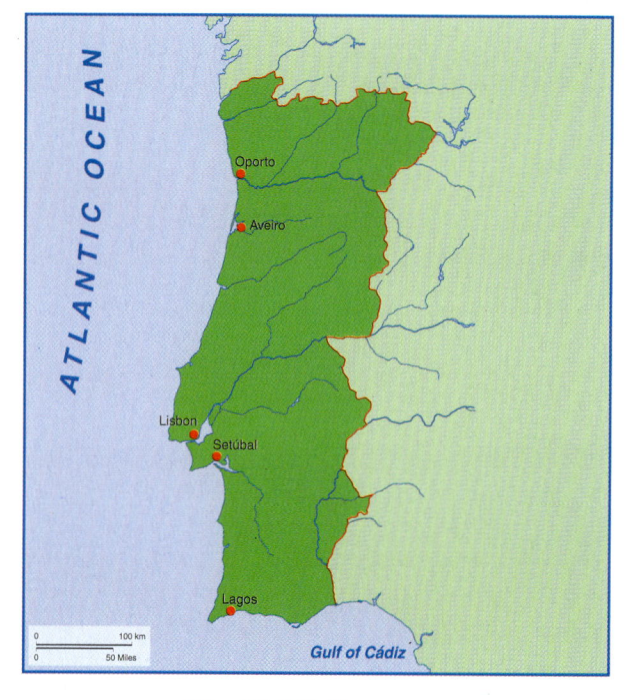

Fig. 12.4 Fishing ports

Both coastal and deep sea fishing are carried on in the Atlantic waters. The chief varieties of catches are anchovy, sardines and tunny in the coastal waters and cod, hake, haddock, plaice etc. in the deeper waters. Portugal has about 5 000 boats and 40 000 fishermen, though some of these are part-time. In addition, back-up industries on land provide considerable employment.

Well over half the catch is consumed fresh, with only a small percentage used for industrial purposes (oils, fertilisers etc.). However, in the last ten years an increasing amount is being cured, canned or frozen. The opening of the EU market has stimulated this section of the industry. Setubal is an important canning centre, but there are processing plants also at Lagos, Lisbon, Averia and Oporto.

EU aid has been provided over the past ten years to upgrade the fishing ports, modernise the processing plants and restructure the fishing fleet. But Portugal now faces the same problems as the other fishing states in the EU. Some of the small-time fishermen (2/3 man boats) are leaving the industry, with compensation from the CFP (Common Fisheries Policy). Quotas and restrictions are making life difficult for the Portuguese fishermen. There are really too many boats chasing too few fish in European waters.

Tourism

The tourist industry in Portugal enjoys many of the natural advantages that were noted in Spain – sandy beaches, warm seas, many hours of sunshine, rainless summers, warm winters and attractive scenery. The major centre of the industry is along the Algarve, with Lisbon/Estoril also important.

Portugal's tourist industry started later than that of Spain. In this way, they avoided many of the mistakes made by Spain in its early years. Growth in Portugal was slower, so the building of apartments, hotels, villas, etc, was better organised, more controlled and better planned. At the same time, much of the development was confined to just one coastal area – the Algarve. There is a very limited amount of land in the Algarve as 60% of the land is classified as upland. Inevitably, disputes arose as to the best use of the available land and water resources – farming or tourism.

Portugal has built up the number of tourists from 2.5 million in 1980 to 10 million in 1996, with over 4 100 million dollars in tourist income in that year. 80% of the tourists come from Europe.

For Portugal, the accessibility factor is important, as is the expansion of the airport at Faro in the Algarve. Portugal differs somewhat from Spain in its market strategy. It targets the more affluent up-market tourist so as to avoid the problems of mass tourism. It appeals to the higher-

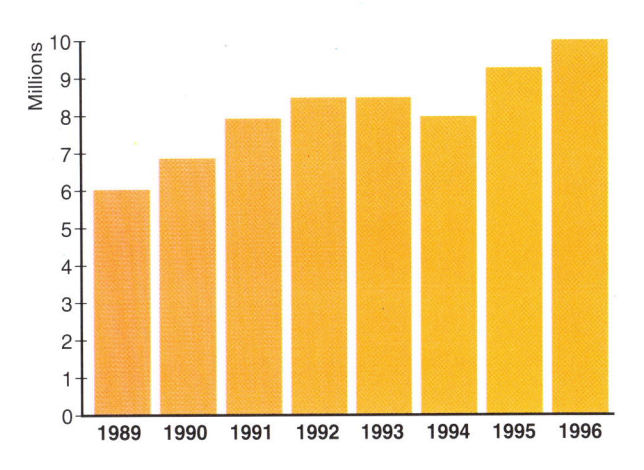

Fig. 12.5 Tourism

spending tourist by developing special activity holidays – golf, cruising, deep-sea fishing, water sports, cultural holidays and winter specials.

Benefits

The major benefit is that of job creation – either directly in hotels, restaurants, accommodation, etc., or indirectly in services, amenities, carriers, entertainers, etc. The list of job opportunities is impressive. The cement and construction industries enjoy ongoing support and benefits. Farmers along the Algarve enjoy the same advantages as those in Mediterranean Spain, so they are specialising in the intensive production of fruit, vegetables, salads and flowers. Tourism provides a ready market for both farmers and food processing industries.

Many of the problems associated with Mediterranean tourism are also found in Portugal. The seasonality of the industry and the associated winter under-utilisation of human and natural resources are very evident. There is also the problem of water supplies. Which has priority, irrigation or tourism? The attractive landscape also suffers from high-rise building. Inevitably, the way of life of a once rural society is being changed forever.

PRIMARY ACTIVITIES

The main primary activities in Portugal are fishing, mining, forestry and farming. Fishing and mining have been treated earlier in this section.

Forestry

Portugal is dominated by maritime influences from the Atlantic Ocean. Most of the country, particularly the centre and north, has an equable climate with adequate rainfall. The abundant rainfall is a major influence on the natural vegetation. The original vegetation cover was forest of cork oak, pines, chestnut and evergreen oak. About 30% of the country is still forested. Portugal is unique in Europe because it is here that the tropical palms of Africa meet the deciduous varieties of Europe.

The forests are found up to an altitude of 1 500m but this tree line varies with different regions. While much of the forest is in private ownership, there is an increasing state involvement in the planting and management of coastal sand dunes and mountain slopes. The timber is used for fuel, construction, furniture and pulp. The pinewoods are also an important source of resin and turpentine.

By far the most valuable forests are the cork oaks which are spread wide across south Portugal. This is the world's chief producing area for cork with an annual production of over

Fig. 12.6 Scenic attractions

half a million tonnes. Sheet production is the most important section, but the shavings and granules are also used for fruit packing or as insulation material. The cork is also manufactured into linoleum or cork floor covering. There are over 300 factories involved in the processing of cork with the chief centres at Evora and Beja. The cork oak acorns are used for pig feeding.

The **pine forests** of the north and of the sand dunes are next after the **cork oak forests** in importance as a forest resource. The plantations cover about 1.5 million hectares. The timber is used for pit props, railway sleepers, construction and furniture. Forest thinnings are used for fuel. Other important products include gum, turpentine and resin which are obtained by tapping the pines. About 100 factories process these products, mainly for export.

Farming

For a study of farming practices, Portugal may be conveniently divided into (i) the **interior** where the Meseta slopes down to (ii) the **coastal and river lowlands**. Within that division it is also important to distinguish between the damp **north** and the drier **south**.

Much of the interior lies between 600m and 2 000m in height and is crossed by the Douro, Tagus and Guadiana as they make their way to the Atlantic. The **north interior** is covered with forests of chestnut, pine and evergreen oak. This area is sparsely populated but there is some cultivation of rye, oats, potatoes, etc. Sheep and pigs are reared. Agriculture here is generally backward. There is an outward migration of the young, who find that the farming

Fig. 12.7 Farming

of the minifundia (small uneconomic farms) is not competitive in the context of EU farming. Very little amalgamation has taken place here.

The upper slopes of the **southern interior** are covered in scrub and poor pasture with forests of cork oak, but the lower slopes are quite productive with olives, cereals and extensive cork oak forests. Again, sheep and pigs are reared.

The **main agricultural areas** of Portugal are the coastal lowlands and the river flood plains. They can generally be divided into those north and south of the Sierra del Estrella, which runs south-west across the country to reach the Atlantic just north of Lisbon. The north coastal area is closely cultivated with cereals and root crops. Cattle rearing is important. This is an important vine-growing area, especially on the south-facing slopes of the Douro valley. It is the home of **port wine** exported from Oporto for centuries.

The **Coimbra plains** lie between the Douro and Tagus valleys and comprise some of the richest agricultural lands in Portugal. There is intensive cultivation of cereals, fruit, vines, olives and other tree crops. Extensive pine forests lie along the coast, with cork oak forests further inland.

The lower Tagus and the area around Lisbon have similar type crops. The vine is particularly important here and this region accounts for over 40% of Portugal's wines. Salads and vegetables are intensively cultivated also with many thousands of hectares of greenhouses. Inland from the coast and south of the Tagus many large estates grow wheat. This is **latifundia** country and is called the *bread basket* of Portugal. Over the last 20 years many of the latifundia have been taken over and subdivided among the tenant farmers.

The **Algarve coastal plains** have the lowest rainfall in the country, but these fertile coastal soils are irrigated by the many streams flowing from interior uplands. The high temperatures, the sunshine and the irrigation waters allow the cultivation of fruit, flowers, vegetables and salads. Figs and almond crops are a speciality of the Algarve. There is a large tourist market for all the products.

The number of people in farming has dropped from 25% of the labour force in 1980 to 12% in 1996. Amalgamation and mechanisation together with the rural-urban migration have been responsible. Farming in the coastal area has improved significantly with EU help over the past ten years, but in interior Portugal progress is slow. Productivity is low and unemployment is high. In fact, since entry to the EU, the inequalities between coast and interior have increased.

Manufacturing industry

Portugal has not a well developed industrial base as it is lacking in coal and oil and has only a small supply of minerals. Most industry is small and there are no large industrial centres except for Lisbon and Oporto. Over the rest of the country industry is small and localised, mainly concerned with the processing of local raw materials – fish curing and canning, wine, fruit and vegetable processing, cork, pottery and textiles. These industries are **labour intensive**, using the plentiful but poorly paid local workers, many of whom are part-time farmers. This is the industrial pattern particularly north of the Tagus.

Lisbon and Oporto are the major industrial bases combining both traditional and new industry. **Lisbon** has shipyards, oil refineries, petro-chemical works, iron and steel, marine engineering and a giant food-processing industry based on the products of its rich hinterland and

Fig.12.8 Sheep farming

imported 'colonial' foodstuffs. With a population of nearly two million, Lisbon has the usual consumer industries associated with a capital city. **Oporto** is the second city of Portugal and the port of the north. It is the traditional home of the port wine industry, drawing its supplies from the Douro valley. It is the largest textile centre with cotton, woollen and synthetics. Other industries include steel, engineering, electricals, shipbuilding and food processing.

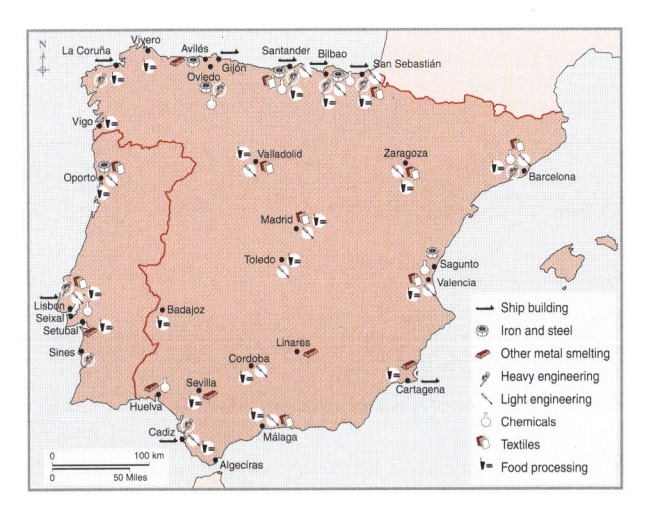

Fig.12.9 Manufacturing

Seixal has many advantages as an industrial base. It has a good harbour and water transport, local power supplies and a plentiful supply of cheap labour. Investment capital and technical assistance and training have been provided by the foreign firms who have established in the area. Like the heavy capital intensive industries of south Italy, Portugal sees this investment as a magnet to attract and create new ancillary and consumer industries.

From 1974 onwards the government of Portugal started a policy of **nationalisation** of the important basic industries – oil, chemicals, cement, steel, pulp and electricity. With direct state involvement in finance, management and marketing the basic industries started to expand. In the late 1970s the largest Portuguese industrial enterprise was begun with the establishment of a new industrial enterprise at Sines. The plan provided for a new port and city and the establishment of heavy industries like oil, chemicals, fertilisers, cement, steel and copper processing. In addition the authorities created industrial parks for light engineering, electronics and consumer goods. Sines has grown rapidly, handles most of Portugal's oil and in terms of tonnage is now the busiest port in the country.

Restructuring of industry has been taking place since Portugal joined the EU in 1986. A whole new market has opened up in Europe. EU grants are being directed towards industries which will succeed in the export market. The older, traditional industries, such as textiles, clothing, leather and footwear, are not able to compete with the European giants and the cheaper Third World products. They are in decline and jobs are being lost. However, the decline has now steadied as Portugal is concentrating on high-quality products with an emphasis on design and skills. These industries account for 20% of exports.

Since 1986, foreign investment has substantially increased. This, allied to EU funding, has created industrial expansion. Setubal, south of Lisbon, is an example. It has been transformed from a small canning town into a major industrial centre with shipbuilding, electronics, machinery, tractors and a giant Ford VW car plant (producing 200 000 units a year) along with dozens of smaller supply factories for all of Setubal's industries.

Many of the MNCs (multi-national companies) are now investing in Portugal to avail of the relatively cheap labour and the generous government aid packages. Among the investors are General Motors, Ford, VW, Texas Instruments, Nestle, Bendix, Siemens, Mitsubishi, Samsung and Pepsi. The most significant advances in the country's industries have been in chemicals, electronics, vehicles and machinery. The chief centres for industrial expansion have been Liston, Oporto, Setubal, Coimbra and Sines.

URBAN SETTLEMENT
Lisbon

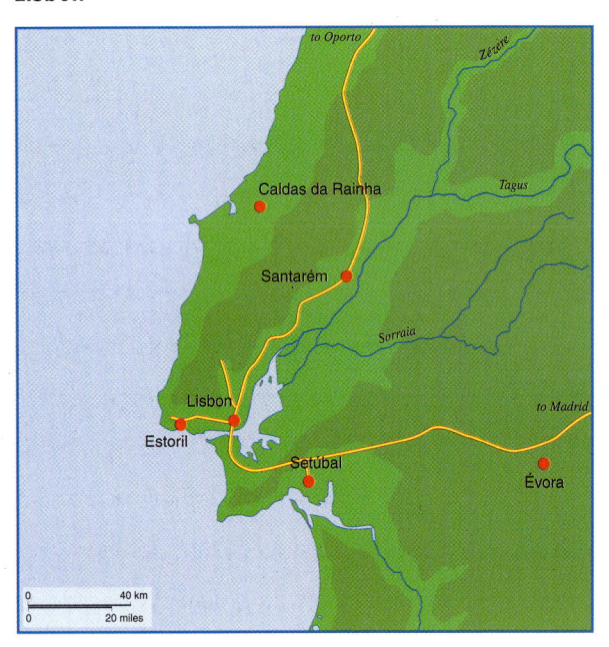

Fig.12.10

Lisbon is situated on the north bank of the river Tagus 20km upstream from the open sea. It has one of the world's great natural harbours. It was established as the capital city in 1260, but reached its greatest wealth during Portugal's Golden Age when it established vital markets and trade links with Africa, India and the Americas. The trade with these markets still persists today, providing valuable raw materials for long-established industries. The original city was destroyed by an earthquake in 1775 and was replaced by a very beautiful carefully planned city with wide avenues and broad squares.

Lisbon is the state capital, important port, passenger port of call and air terminal. It is the government, administrative and commercial centre and so has an impressive tertiary sector. It has a wide range of manufacturing industries including iron, steel, engineering, shipbuilding, oil, chemicals and food processing. The rich agricultural hinterland and the colonial imports provide the raw materials for sugar, tobacco, milling, oil pressing, chocolate, fruit and vegetable processing industries.

Fig.12.11 Lisbon

Oporto

This is the second city of Portugal. It is situated on the north bank of the Douro about 8km from the sea. There is a large sand bar at the mouth of the Douro so an artificial harbour has been created at Leixoes and this acts as an outport for Oporto.

Oporto is the capital and chief port of the northern region. It is the headquarters of the wine trade, with port wine the chief export. Industry has been developed since the early 50s with many new industrial estates ringing the city. The traditional industries of wine, food processing, textiles, glass and ceramics are still dominant but iron, steel, engineering, shipbuilding and chemicals are growing rapidly. Oporto has a population of 1·2 million.

Questions

1. On a sketch map of Iberia, show and name the following: (a) mountains: Cantabrian, Sierra Morena, Sierra Nevada, (b) rivers: Douro, Tagus, Ebro, (c) two areas of irrigated lowland, (d) an area noted for orange production, (e) an area noted for lemon production, (f) the major sherry production area, (g) cities: Bilbao, Oporto, Lisbon, Madrid, Seville, Barcelona.

2. Three major climate types can be recognised in the Iberian peninsula.
   (a) Name and locate on a sketch map these types.
   (b) Choose two of the climate types and describe the climatic conditions there and the economic activities associated with them.
   (c) What are the main mineral resources of Iberia and what effects has their location on industrial development? (L.C. Ordinary Level)

3. Write notes on each of the following:
   (a) The fishing industry of Portugal.
   (b) Hydro-electric power in Spain.
   (c) The mineral resources of southern Spain.
   (d) Agriculture on the coastal plains.

4. Show how physical features influence (i) agriculture, (ii) settlement and (iii) routeways in the Ebro Basin. (L.C. Higher Level)

5. 'The rugged terrain and poor communications are major obstacles to industrial progress in Iberia.' Discuss.

6. Discuss the major problems affecting the development of agriculture in Iberia.

7. (a) Describe and account for the distribution of manufacturing industry in Spain.
   (b) Explain the factors responsible for the undeveloped nature of Spanish agriculture.
   (c) Apart from climate, outline some of the factors responsible for the growth of tourism in Spain. (L.C. Ordinary Level)

8. 'The uneven social and economic development has produced an industrialised and advanced Iberia alongside a rural and backward one.' Discuss, with reference to particular regions.

9. Explain what you understand by the term 'region'. Illustrate your answer by referring to examples drawn from your study of Spain. (L.C. Higher Level)

10. 'Though Iberia is surrounded almost entirely by seas and its general slope away to the west apparently favours penetration of Atlantic influences, it suffers from deficiencies and uncertainty of rainfall over the whole interior and Mediterranean coastlands. Less than a quarter of the entire area, and that mostly mountainous, receives a precipitation of 750 to 1 000 mm, the minimum adequate amount in view of the generally high rate of evaporation. Several factors combine to cause this fundamental disability.'
    (a) Explain briefly what is meant by 'Atlantic influences'.

(b) With the aid of a simple map outline clearly the areas which have a precipitation of 750 to 1 000mm.

(c) Name and explain two of the 'several factors which combine to cause this fundamental disability'.

(d) Climatically, Spain may be divided into three broad regions, the Atlantic, Sub-Continental (Meseta) and Mediterranean. Outline the distinguishing characteristics of each of these climatic types and indicate their location on your map.

11 Describe the type of agriculture practised along the Mediterranean coast of Spain.

12 Describe how the sea has influenced the economy of Portugal.

13 Select one important manufacturing region in Spain. Explain in detail why the region has attracted so much industry.

14 Write a note on the tourist industry in Portugal.

european topics

core growth regions

the decline of coal

energy in the EU

the iron and steel industry

europe's environmental problems

the influence of the sea on europe's economy

european migration

aspects of tourism

common agriculture policy (CAP) & common fisheries policy (CFP)

economic & monetary union

european topics
core growth regions

Fig. 13.1 European Union flag

In many European countries there are areas which, due to a number of favourable factors, both natural (relief, climate, natural resources) or acquired (industrial development, communications) become highly developed core regions.

Characteristics

These core regions:

- Are the focus of economic activity
- Contain the main centres of employment
- Have concentrations of skills and expertise
- Have high population densities
- Are very accessible with efficient communication networks
- Are centres of decision making and financial capital
- Attract migrant workers
- Have a high degree of urbanisation
- Are often cultural centres.

Examples

Brussels-Antwerp axis

Paris Basin

Milan-Turin axis

South-east England

German Rhinelands

North-east Spain.

Old industrial regions in decline

The majority of European countries have experienced a steady decline in such traditional industries as coal mining, iron and steel, shipbuilding and textiles.

Characteristics

- High unemployment
- An unsightly, neglected environment
- A run-down infrastructure
- A declining population with younger people moving out of the region because of the lack of jobs
- Little investment in the region
- A steady deterioration in educational, social and transport facilities.

Examples

Sambre-Meuse region (Belgium)

Nord (France)

South Wales

North-east England.

Peripheral regions

Within the EU there are relatively under-developed regions which are remote, have a harsh environment, a marginal agricultural base and a lack of industrial employment.

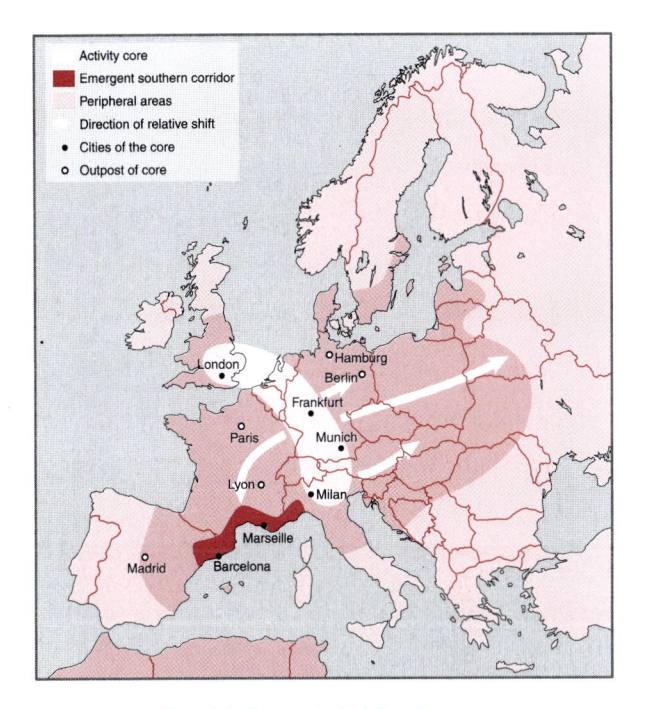

Fig. 13.2 Europe's Hot Banana

Characteristics:

These peripheral regions:
- Have much slower growth rates
- Have fewer job opportunities
- Have lower wage rates
- Have a lower standard of living
- Are more poorly served by communications
- Suffer from persistent out-migration, leaving an ageing population
- Are dependent on and dominated by the core region.

Examples

The Mezzogiorno (Southern Italy)

Massif Central (France)

Norrland (Sweden)

The Highlands of Scotland

Andalusia (Spain).

Factors which make it difficult for a peripheral region to compete economically with the core region:
1. Poor management skills in the peripheral region
2. Higher interest rates
3. Lack of local skilled labour
4. Poor infrastructure (lack of roads, airports, etc)
5. Low expenditure on research and development.

european topics
the decline of coal

Coal provided the energy for the Industrial Revolution in western Europe. It powered the steam-driven machines, the railways and the ships without which the Industrial Revolution of the eighteenth and nineteenth centuries could never have happened. Since it was the primary source of energy, it led to the development of industrial regions on the coalfields. Coal was also extremely versatile and was used as a domestic fuel, as coke in the smelting of iron ore and in such basic processes as the production of pottery and glass. Countries with extensive coal deposits became the giants of the industrial world. However, since World War 2, coal has been replaced as Europe's main energy source.

Since the mid-1950s the role of coal has dramatically declined. The causes of this decline may be noted as follows:

- The richest and most easily accessible coal seams have been exhausted. Mining the deeper seams has become more difficult and more expensive.
- Coal-mining is a labour-intensive industry, with high production and transport costs. Smaller, uneconomic mines were closed.
- New alternative sources of energy (oil, natural gas, hydro-electric power, nuclear, solar, wave-power, wind-power and the secondary energy source, electricity) were introduced and rapidly reduced the role of coal.
- The alternative forms of energy now available (oil, natural gas, electricity) are much more easily distributed by tankers, pipeline or cable and are cheaper to transport. In comparison to these, coal is a high-cost, inconvenient source of energy for modern industry.
- The increasing concern of people and governments worldwide for protection of the atmosphere against pollution caused by factories burning coal is another factor in the decline of coal.

Fig. 13.3 Coalyard

Coal-mining in Britain

Coal-mining in Britain illustrates the changes which have resulted from the decline of coal:

- The **demand** for coal has declined dramatically since 1947. Since then nearly 900 of the small, less productive mines have been closed.

- Production has fallen from 191.2 million tonnes in 1961 to 61.3 million tonnes in 1993.
- Improvements in technology and mechanisation have reduced the workforce from 410 000 in 1967 to 20 000 in 1993.
- While the oil crises of 1973 and 1980 created a short-term demand for coal, it increased the government's determination to develop North Sea oil and gas as cheaper sources of energy than coal.
- The coal industry was modernised and privatised to make it more efficient and productive.
- Areas facing social and economic problems resulting from mine closures have been helped by EU funds. Grants have been provided for retraining redundant miners and for attracting new industries to replace mining.

Socio-economic problems caused by the decline in the coal industry

The closure of coalfields and the rationalisation of the industry have resulted in massive unemployment in coal mining regions. In Britain, the closure of some of the smaller uneconomic mines led to political unrest with the miners' strike of 1984-85.

The decline of the coal industry seriously affected ancillary industries such as the manufacture of mining equipment, as well as service industries affected by the downturn in the local and regional economy.

Out-migration became a feature of coalfield regions as people moved away in search of jobs. Industrial activity moved away from the coalfields to coastal locations. The strong, social links of mining communities were broken as the coalfields contracted or closed, leaving behind a scarred and abandoned landscape.

ANGRY MINERS BESIEGE BONN

March 1997

Riot police swinging batons yesterday struggled to head off angry German coalminers as they broke through cordons and tried to storm the offices of Chancellor Helmut Kohl.

'We want to work', chanted the miners as they elbowed their way into the no-go area around the parliament and chancellery. The brawny pit workers, many wearing safety helmets to protect them from batons, were eventually thrust back.

Some 20 000 miners, furious at government plans to cut coal subsidies, have been laying siege to Bonn since Monday; buses from the Ruhr and the Saar are swelling the numbers of demonstrators, and the mood is turning ugly.

Chancellor Kohl yesterday refused to hold talks with a miners' delegation, led by Hans Berger, the coal union chief, saying he would not negotiate in a 'blackmail-like' atmosphere. The talks have been postponed until tomorrow, and Herr Berger will try to persuade the miners to lift the blockade of Germany's political capital.

In Hamm, a critical rail junction in the Ruhr, 1 000 miners blocked the station and several town halls in the industrial region were paralysed. The motorway leading to Luxembourg was blocked for the second day in succession.

Gunter Rexrodt, the Economics Minister, says that each mining job now costs the Government £50 000 a year. Some 50 000 redundancies – out of a total workforce of 90 000 – are scheduled over the next seven years.

© *The Times, London*

Strategies

1. The EU has recognised that regions suffering from mine closures face special problems and has created a fund called **Rechar**. It re-trains redundant miners, provides housing grants and attracts new industries to industrial estates in these areas.

2. Modernisation of the coal industry has been undertaken by private or state companies. In Britain, RJB, Europe's largest independent coal mining company, now controls most of the coalfields. Ruhrkohle, the German coal company, has launched schemes to develop new technologies and attract new high-tech industries to the area.

3. Diversification of energy sources is the primary aim of EU energy policy. The fossil fuels (coal, oil, natural gas) are now the main energy sources in the EU. In recent years, the search for alternative energy supplies has focused on the development of renewable energy sources (RES) – HEP, tidal, wave, wind, solar power and geothermal energy. These are obtained by harnessing energy in the natural environment and have the additional advantage of being non-polluting.

european topics

energy in the EU

The economy of most EU countries is based on manufacturing industries and these in turn are based on the availability of energy. There are five major sources of energy – coal, oil, natural gas, water power and nuclear energy. These are termed primary sources, and are generally used to generate heat which is converted immediately into electricity. So electricity is a secondary energy. It is the most significant of all forms of energy because of its efficiency and ease of transmission.

With the decline of coal over the last few decades, the coal industry has been rationalised and restructured. Uneconomic mines were closed and the coal mining industry across Europe was concentrated into fewer, but more modern and efficient units. The discovery of a huge natural gas field in Gröningen (Netherlands) in 1959 and of significant deposits of oil in the North Sea in 1965, gave further impetus to diversification of energy sources. From 1970 on, natural gas and HEP began to play an increasing

Fig. 13.4 Natural gas platform off Kinsale

Fig. 13.5 Nuclear power station

role in energy supply. Nuclear power stations for the generation of electricity were built in Britain, France and Germany. The great advantage of nuclear fission is the tremendous amount of energy released from the use of very small amounts of fuel – 30 grammes of uranium have the energy equivalent of 100 tonnes of coal.

Nuclear reactors require extensive areas of land and large supplies of water and are usually located away from major centres of population.

France leads the EU in its production of electricity from nuclear power. Coal, oil, thermal power stations and HEP contribute the remaining 22.3%.

France	Belgium	Germany	Britain
77.7%	59.2%	20.8%	26.7%
Electricity produced by nuclear power, 1993			

However, there are major and serious health and environmental risks attached to nuclear plants and to the disposal of nuclear waste. The accident at Chernobyl in 1986 created immense controversy as radioactive particles were carried by the wind as far as remote hillsides in Scotland and affected livestock. The disposal of nuclear waste, which remains radioactive for periods up to 200 000 years is a serious cause of concern, as evidenced by the concentrated attacks on the train carrying nuclear waste in Germany in March 1997. Environmental groups in Ireland constantly protest at the pollution of the Irish Sea by waste emmissions from the British nuclear plant at Sellafield and by the dumping of nuclear waste in the Irish Sea.

The reduction in the importance of coal, the rise in oil consumption, the increasing use of nuclear energy and natural gas – all these factors provide a greater choice of energy sources in the EU today. In addition, the focus on **renewable energy** resources – tidal, wind, solar power – is expected to lessen dependence on the fossil fuels such as coal, oil, natural gas which will sooner or later be exhausted.

EU energy policy has three objectives:

1. To maintain security of supply
2. To develop alternative sources of energy, so as to minimise the impact on the environment
3. To develop a single energy market so that countries may buy their energy from wherever they choose.

european topics
the iron and steel industry

The iron and steel industry is an important index of a country's wealth and development. It is a major employer and requires high capital investment. Steel is a basic material which is required in many sectors of manufacturing industry.

Like coal, the steel industry has been in decline in recent years. The main factors in the decline may be noted as follows:

- The oil crisis of 1973 seriously affected the European steel industry which used large amounts of energy
- Third World producers of steel, because of their cheaper labour costs, were able to sell steel at a much lower price than their European rivals
- New raw materials and substitutes for steel (aluminium, plastics, etc.) reduced the demand for steel in the economy of developed countries
- High-technology industries require less steel than the older industries.

To halt the decline, the EU introduced the **Davignon Plan**, which was a mixture of production quotas, minimum prices, government subsidies and mergers of steel companies – all aimed at protecting the EU steel industry from foreign competition. When the Plan expired in 1988, the EU steel industry was exposed to competition from South Korea, Japan and eastern Europe. Meeting this challenge in the 1990s has resulted in:

- Considerable reduction in the quantity of steel produced
- A 40% reduction in the workforce
- Modernising the steel industry by using new technology
- Mergers of the numerous steel companies into a few major producers
- Control of steel imports from central and eastern Europe
- Government subsidies.

The steel industry is an excellent example of an industry where changing technology has strongly influenced location. Thus, in response to changing techniques, different locational factors have become important at different times. And since iron and steel supplies are vital to a wide range of industries, changes in location have inevitably affected entire industrial regions, for better or worse.

We may note three major locations of the steel industry in western Europe: **coalfields, orefields, coastal sites**.

Coalfields. Ruhr, Nord, Sambre-Meuse, Britain. Coalfield locations for the industry in the late eighteenth and nineteenth centuries had three advantages: (a) there was a tradition of iron working, based on the forging of smelted iron; (b) in some coalfields iron ores were found interbedded with the coal seams and could be mined at the same time as the coal; (c) the most important advantage was that, with the existing techniques, eight times as much coking coal as iron ore was required to produce a given amount of iron. It was therefore much cheaper to bring the ore to the coalfields than to bring coal to the orefields.

Orefields. Lorraine, Salzgitter, northern Spain, northern Sweden. The exhaustion of iron ore supplies in many of the coalfield regions directed attention to the orefields.

Fig. 13.6 Coalfields

Fig. 13.7 Coal stacker

New techniques in the smelting process meant that iron ores which were formerly unsuitable, such as the phosphoric ores of Lorraine in north-eastern France, could now be used. Steelworks were built in Lorraine, southern Luxembourg and north-east England.

Coastal sites. In recent times, the iron and steel industry has again changed its location. The centre of gravity of the industry is today being pulled away from the coalfields and the orefields to coastal locations. In 1938, western Europe did not possess a single coastal integrated iron and steel plant. By 1966 there were eight and today there are twenty one.

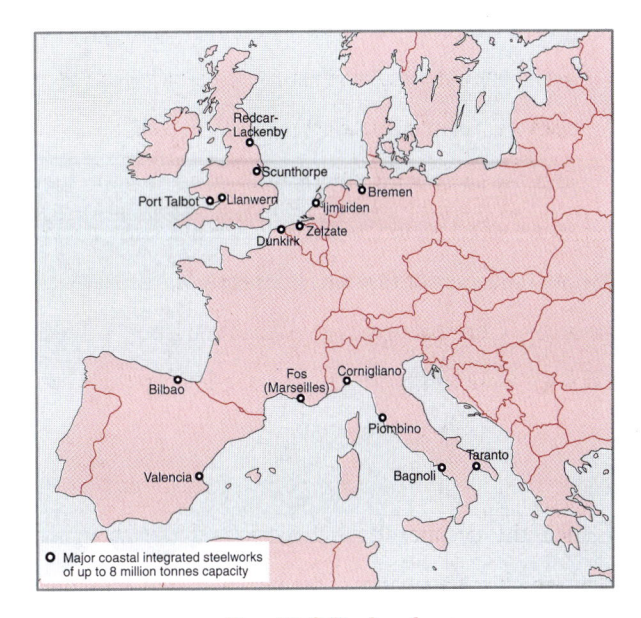

Fig. 13.8 Steelworks

Coastal steelworks have developed for the following reasons:

(a) Modern techniques such as the oxygen-blown process and the electric arc method produce high-quality steel using little coking coal.

(b) Good quality coking coal from the USA and high-grade iron ore from Sweden, Canada and West Africa replaced local coal and iron ore.

(c) These foreign supplies of coal and iron ore were imported in bulk at deep-water coastal terminals.

(d) The continual expansion of the steel industry demanded huge supplies of high-quality ores. All the major steel producers today, including Britain, Italy, France and west Germany, depend on imports of iron ores.

(e) Government policy in some European countries has encouraged the location of steelworks at coastal sites in areas of high unemployment. The coastal steelworks at Taranto was the result of government policy to provide a growth centre for the south of Italy.

Among the most important coastal sites are Mo i Rana (Norway), Oxelosund (Sweden), Ijmuiden (Netherlands), Zelzate (Belgium), Bremen (Germany), Dunkirk, Fos (France), Genoa, Naples and Taranto (Italy), Margam (Wales), Sines (Portugal), Sagunto (Spain).

Movement to the coast has been a major trend in the European steel industry in recent years. Countries like Belgium and Italy, which have modernised their steel industries around coastal locations, are gaining ground on the traditional steelmaking giants, many of whose steelmills are located on the coalfields and orefields.

european topics
europe's environmental problems

Fig. 13.9 Land usage

From the Arctic to Italy and from Connemara to the Balkans, Europe is characterised by a landscape of immense beauty and variety. For the most part Europeans enjoy a comfortable way of life and standard of living. But we are now beginning to realise that there is a price to pay for our high standard of living and that future generations may not thank us for the legacy of the twentieth century.

Natural resources are being used up at an alarming rate. Pollution of air, land and water is on the increase. Valuable agricultural land and its habitats are being swallowed up by cities, industries and routeways. Much of the urban heritage, stretching back to medieval times, is decaying or being destroyed. Why?

Industrial revolution

The **Industrial Revolution** of the nineteenth and twentieth centuries initiated environmental problems on a major scale. Coal and iron ore originated the revolution and much of western Europe was soon marked by mining scars as mining companies extracted the coal or ore, abandoned exhausted sources and moved on to new sites. Spoil heaps and slag mounds ruined the approaches to the towns and collieries. Coal-burning factories, homes and trains emitted huge volumes of poisonous pollutants into the atmosphere, as well as blackening and disfiguring public buildings and people's homes. Black smoke and soot filled the sky at night. Rivers, lakes and the seas were used as dumping grounds for untreated wastes and poisons.

Industrialisation

Parallel with the industrial activity came rapid **urbanisation**. Cities and towns grew at an alarming rate with little or no planning for their growth. This caused more coal burning, more waste, more traffic, more pollution. This was an era of great wealth for mine and factory owners, poor working conditions for the workers and a total disregard for the environment.

This century, and particularly since 1945, has seen a **massive increase in industrialisation**. New industrial countries (Netherlands, Italy, etc.) have emerged and motorised transport has led to an increase in environmental pollution. Sulphur dioxide and oxides of nitrogen are discharged daily into the atmosphere from thermal power stations, smelting plants and industrial boilers. These gases combine with water vapour to form sulphuric acid. The lethal mixture is carried by the westerlies from the industrial zones of western Europe to central Europe and Scandinavia where they fall as **acid rain** or **acid snow**. Acid rain causes immense damage to lakes, rivers, fish life and forests. There is also the danger to the health of Europe's population who breathe the polluted air or drink the contaminated water.

Energy sources

New energy sources – oil and gas – came on stream in the mid 1920s. They have caused their own problems. Oil spillages and accidents have destroyed fish and bird life, their breeding grounds and habitats. Untold damage has been caused to the beaches and coastal wildlife of Scotland, south-west England and Brittany from accidents to oil tankers (such as the Braer, Torrey Canyon and Amoco Cadiz). The Mediterranean is the main transport route for much of the oil used by industrial Europe. It is becoming increasingly polluted from leaks, spillages and tanker wash-outs. In 1976, the **Blue Plan** was put in place to prevent chemical dumping and oil spillages. Norwegian and Danish fishermen are concerned about the dangers to the rich fishing grounds of the North Sea from the exploitation and transport of oil and gas.

Greenhouse effect

Continued reliance by industry on fossil fuels (coal, oil, natural gas) is raising the carbon dioxide level in the atmosphere, where it acts like a thermal blanket around the planet, allowing the sun's rays to pass through it, but blocking the heat waves given off by the earth's surface from radiating back into space – somewhat in the manner of glass in a greenhouse. Result – the temperature of the earth's surface rises, giving the **greenhouse effect** and leading to *global warming*. The United Nations issued a stark warning that millions more people in rich and poor countries could die from once purely tropical diseases in the coming decades, unless action is taken to stop global warming.

The shocking report from the World Health Organisation (WHO), the World Meteorological Organisation (WMO)

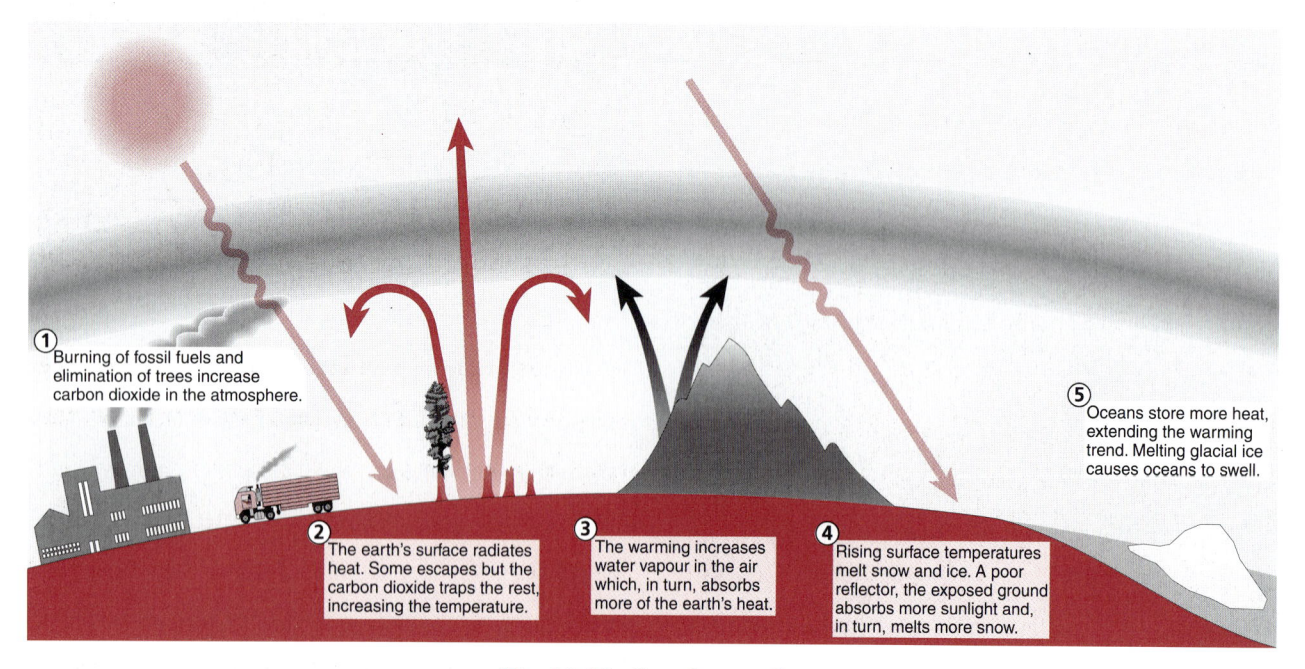

Fig. 13.10 Greenhouse effect

and the UN's Environmental Programme (UNEP) said warming could also cause food supplies to dry up while rising seas contaminate fresh water sources.

'Current models indicate that by around 2050, many major cities around the world could be experiencing up to several thousand extra heat-related deaths annually, independent of any increases due to population growth', the report declared.

Rising temperatures around the globe, widely blamed on emissions from fuels like coal and oil, would increase the global incidence of malaria by one third and extend it and other killer diseases from hot countries into now temperate areas.

"In the next century, climate change is expected to increase the global incidence of malaria by 50-80 million additional cases each year', said the report.

Urbanisation

Urbanisation also creates environmental problems. Transport networks are vital to move people, raw materials and finished products. Lead, carbon dioxide and nitrous oxides pour from the exhausts of buses, trucks and cars adding to the greenhouse effect, poisoning citizens' lungs and disfiguring historic buildings.

Urban lifestyles and industrialisation are not the only causes of environmental degradation. The emphasis in **farming** today is on high yields. There is less land on which to achieve this, so there is an increasing use of fertilisers, chemicals, pesticides, etc. Many of these chemicals eventually find their way to the streams and rivers. When added to the slurry and silage effluents, they are a serious hazard to fish life.

SLURRY KILLS FISH

A major slurry escape has wiped out all fish life over a three-mile stretch in a west Cork river.

An estimated 20 000 gallons of highly toxic slurry escaped from a farmyard holding area into a tributary of the highly stocked Argideen River. A full investigation was underway yesterday.

18 April 1997

In addition, to obtain more land, woods and hedgerows are being cleared and with them, the habitats of the flora and fauna are disappearing.

Responses

Individual governments and the EU are well aware of the harmful effects on people's health and the environment of

13.11 Urbanisation

Europe's economic progress. But responses to the problems have been slow, because of the difficulty of getting a general agreement on solutions since individual governments are fearful of the effects that some proposed solutions would have on their own economy.

A recent survey (1995) by the EU showed that 82% of Europeans viewed environmental protection as 'an immediate and urgent problem' and 72% considered that 'economic growth must be ensured, but that the environment should also be protected'. A number of measures by individual governments and the EU are already in place:

- All cars are now built to take unleaded petrol.
- Eventually, catalytic converters will be compulsory on all cars.
- Research is taking place into non-polluting renewable energy resources (wind, solar, tidal, etc.)
- Smokeless fuels are encouraged in homes.
- Homes, factories and cars are to be more energy efficient.
- The European Investment Bank provides finance for a whole range of environmental schemes – water treatment, sewage disposal, collection, processing and recycling of domestic and industrial waste.

People in many countries have become increasingly concerned about the dangers to their health and the environment. *Green* political parties and concerned voluntary groups like Greenpeace and Save the Earth highlight the problems. The European Environment Agency (EEA) has been established at Copenhagen to inform the public and to monitor and evaluate environmental policies. All major farming, transport and construction projects now need an environmental impact assessment (EIA), before planning permission for the project is issued.

The EU realises that environmental protection must be carried out across the whole of the EU and that the EU problems are, in turn, part of a **global problem**. It is rightly concerned about global warming, the greenhouse effect, depletion of the ozone layer and the fact that the EU itself is a contributor to these problems. Formerly the emphasis was on **remedial measures**, but this has now changed to an **active** programme of enforcement – i.e. that prevention is better and cheaper than cure. It also insists that the polluter must pay.

The emphasis is not solely on **industry** and **transport**. **Farming** also must play its part. Governments are encouraged to preserve areas of natural beauty, to open National Parks, to provide rural areas of special educational or recreational interest and to provide grants to farmers to preserve the environment. Environmentally Sensitive Areas (ESA) are to receive special attention.

Efforts are also being made to preserve and restore buildings of outstanding beauty or historical significance. With this aim in mind, 1975 was declared European Architectural Heritage Year. The impetus this generated has lasted right through to the present day.

european topics

the influence of the sea on europe's economy

SAMPLE QUESTION

Examine, with reference to appropriate examples, the extent to which the sea has influenced the economic geography of Europe.

The sea plays an important role in the economic geography of Europe. The following examples illustrate both the direct and indirect effects of its influence.

Fishing (Norway): Norway has a long, deeply indented fiord coastline. The long coastline means that fishing is possible from north to south and benefits most of the coastal communities. The lack of good agricultural land in this narrow country has influenced people to turn to the sea for a livelihood and for food.

Norway has an extensive continental shelf which is rich in plankton. This ensures a good supply of fish. Norway is also influenced by the North Atlantic Drift which keeps the ports and coastal waters ice-free throughout the year and thus allows for a year-round fishing industry. In addition, the mixing of the warm North Atlantic Drift waters and the cooler Atlantic waters ensures a wide variety of fish species.

The benefits to Norway's economy are very great. Over 30 000 jobs are created directly at sea. This is of considerable importance, especially to northern Norway where alternative sources of employment are few. Hammerfest, Tromso and other fishing ports benefit. On land, thousands of people are employed in shipbuilding, net making, marine engineering and in repair yards, for example in Bergen and Stavanger. Norway has a very small population, so only 5% of the catch is consumed fresh. The remainder is either filleted, frozen and canned for human consumption or reduced to oils, fertilisers, animal feeds, etc., at many of the ports. Fishing not only creates jobs, it forms a valuable export in fish and fish products that account for 15% of Norwegian exports.

Tourism (Spain): Spain receives about 50 million tourists each year, but the main concentration of tourists is along the **Mediterranean coast** and the **Balearic islands**. In fact, Madrid is the only inland location that attracts tourists in any great numbers. Tourists come to the Mediterranean coast for its miles of sandy beaches, warm waters and long hours of sunshine. Tourism creates thousands of jobs (12% of the workforce) directly in hotels, apartments, restaurants, etc. Tens of thousands of people are affected indirectly – farmers and market gardeners who supply fruit, vegetables, meat to the industry. Over the past few decades, the construction industry has prospered with the building of hotels, villas and apartments. The sea has obviously influenced the siting of airports and coastal routeways for ease of access.

All the above activities have contributed over £8 000 million per annum to the Spanish economy and pay for water schemes, farm improvements, routeways, etc. Tourism in Spain accounts for 50% of foreign currency, 20% of exports and is essential to the balance of payments – all thanks to the Mediterranean Sea.

Oil and Natural Gas (Norway): The discovery of oil and gas fields in the Norwegian sector of the North Sea from 1969 onwards has been of enormous benefit to the economy, especially since new techniques in the late 80s enabled the oil and gas to be piped ashore. The major fields are Statfiord, Ekofisk, Sleipner and Troll. With a small population and abundant HEP, Norway is able to export 80% of the oil and gas. Oil and gas form 30% of the country's total exports and are to European countries.

As a result of the North Sea oil and gas finds, Norway's national debt has been cleared off, 8 000 offshore jobs and 50 000 land jobs have been created. **Bergen** is the chief supply centre and service base for the North Sea. **Stavanger** is now a major world centre in the design and construction of rigs, platforms, tankers, pipelines, etc. The refining and chemical industries now have a native natural resource and have expanded at Oslo, Bergen, Stavanger, etc. The sea has ensured a high standard of living for Norwegians well into the next century.

Fig. 13.12 Fishermen with their catch

Fig. 13.13 The Aran Islands

european topics
european migration

13.14 Movement within Europe

In Europe before the Industrial Revolution, rural populations were tied to their native villages because of ignorance of the outside world, the lack of opportunity for self-advancement and the lack of transport facilities. There was very little migration because migration depends on a changing economic climate and there was very little change in the economy of Europe up to 1750. Thus settlement, migration and economic activity are interdependent.

At the time of the Industrial Revolution, Europe was experiencing a rapid population growth. Industry grew rapidly in the towns and cities. Europe was changing from an agricultural economy to an industrial one. Rural workers drifted to the cities in search of work. As a result, settlement in Europe changed from a dispersed rural settlement to one dominated by large urban centres with concentrations of population around industrial complexes.

That pattern has continued to the present day so that now the great majority of people in modern Europe are urban dwellers – in complete contrast to their ancestors in 1800. Thus was established the **core-periphery** model which has persisted throughout this century.

Migration redistributes population, moving people from areas of surplus labour to areas where it is in short supply. This introduces the classic migration theory of **push and pull** factors. We will examine how they operated in Europe.

Push

During the nineteenth century Europe experienced rapid population growth. Birth rates were high and death rates were falling, because of improvements in health, hygiene, clean water, etc. In rural Europe farms were divided and sub-divided, and competition for work increased. There were simply not enough jobs in rural Europe for the expanding population. In addition, two other factors made the situation worse.

Small-scale rural handicraft industries could not compete with the large-scale mechanised industries of the towns. So **de-industrialisation** took place in the countryside. Then came the **mechanisation** of agriculture and machines replaced workers. The only response for the rural workers was to migrate to the towns and cities in search of jobs. This rural depopulation has persisted to the present day and is a feature of most European countries.

Pull

The balancing 'pull' factors were associated with the rapid advancement of the industrial revolution. Coal and iron were the cornerstones of the revolution. Industries like steel, textiles and chemicals were quickly mechanised and grew rapidly. Technology at that time was low-level, so plenty of jobs were available. With no mechanised transport, workers had to live near the factories and mills so towns grew rapidly. Thus the **industrial towns** became the first focus of the migrants. Growth in trade, commerce and services accompanied the growth in manufacturing. As a result the ports, large provincial towns and capital cities also expanded. In this initial phase, most of the migration was **internal**.

As the nineteenth century progressed, Europe's population continued to rise as the death rate slowed even further. Even though industry continued to expand, the population numbers grew faster. Industrialised cities could no longer supply the demand for jobs. **International** and **intercontinental migration** replaced the old internal movement.

Europe looked to North America where the small population was unable to fully exploit the natural resources. Land overseas was cheap or free - a great 'pull' for Europe's rural population. Industry was establishing and there were also thousands of jobs in construction, in the mines and in the building of railroads.

Between 1820 and 1920, 60 million Europeans migrated to the USA (40 million) or Canada (12 million) or Argentina (8 million). Most of the early migrants were from rural Britain and Germany, but countries with little industrialisation in the towns to absorb the redundant labour force also had high emigration. Ireland is a case in point. Early waves of emigrants were from north west Europe, but in the late nineteenth and early twentieth centuries the main supply source was from east, south-east and south Europe. Since the end of World War II, economic factors again created a steady movement of migrants **within** Europe.

At the end of the 1939-45 war, much of north-west Europe lay in ruins, industrial production was shattered and consumer goods were in short supply. Some countries, e.g. Switzerland and Sweden, had escaped the full ravages of the war and their economies were sound enough to enable them to meet some of the consumer demand. However, they had not enough workers and so opened their gates to receive migrant workers. Gradually the economies of Belgium, The Netherlands, France and Britain built up towards full production, but they all experienced acute labour shortages and were more than willing to accept labour, mostly unskilled, from Ireland, Spain, Portugal, Italy, Greece and Turkey. In the 50s and 60s the north-west industrial countries were each taking up to 1000 migrants per week. From the late 50s onwards west Germany became a major importer of foreign labour, taking in over 250 000 in 1960 alone. With its rapidly expanding industrial economy, it soon became the main focus of all the sending countries.

Both pull and push factors were responsible for the movements. Most of the early migrants shared a common background in that they were from rural, less developed regions.

The donor countries of south Europe and north Africa were overpopulated, underdeveloped with high unemployment and very slow economic growth. Migration was a safety valve for these countries or regions.

The **effects** of this cross-frontier migration benefited both the immigrants and the destination countries:

- Industry and services benefited from a plentiful supply of cheap labour.
- The native labour force refused to work the menial, lowly paid jobs and so were able to climb the labour ladder.
- The unskilled migrant gladly accepted any job, even for low wages which were often higher than he could ever hope to earn in his own country.
- The temporary immigrant often became a permanent one and brought family members over to join him. This, in turn, created many large foreign communities who married within their group, leading to further increases. This gave rise to ghettos, as most migrants like to live within their own ethnic group. Ghettos create the 'them and us' mentality leading to segregation and racial intolerance.

Another problem concerned housing and on mainland Europe the migrants were housed in hostels or drifted into *shanty towns* on the outskirts of the cities. This was another form of segregation and led to problems in integration, education and policing. When the recession hit Europe in the late 70s and early 80s, the immigrants were the first to feel the effects. Unemployment, poor housing and inadequate social welfare led to violent riots on the streets of cities such as Berlin, Paris, Amsterdam and Zurich. Between 1981 and 1985 several cities erupted in Britain, highlighting the problems of immigrants and their British-born children. Toxteth, Brixton and Handsworth became household names overnight.

At the same time the destination country held the right to re-patriate migrants when their labour was no longer needed. This occurred in both France and Germany during the recession 1975-85.

At present, the flow of migrants from Europe has slowed down significantly. However, within the past 15 years a new movement of people has emerged – migration from the cities to the surrounding towns and villages. This migration has nothing to do with jobs or money (the factors which brought people to cities in the first instance). Rather it is a desire for a better quality of life, better houses, less noise and more space.

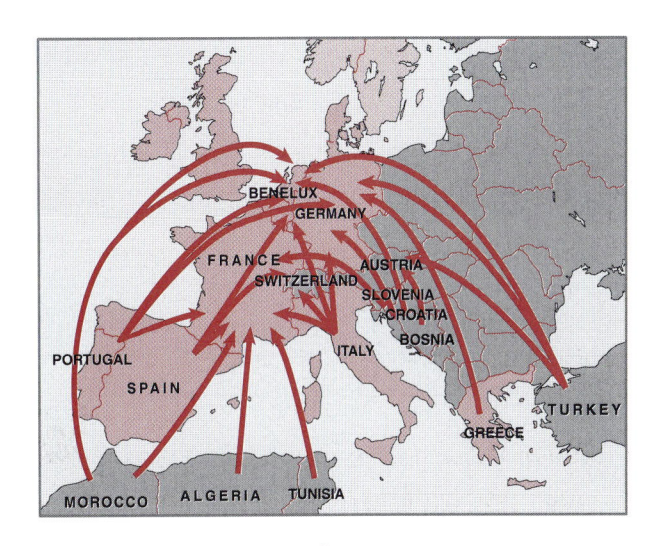

Fig. 13.15 Migration

european topics
aspects of tourism

Fig. 13.16 Malaga, Spain

exports. The following notes provide an overall look at the various aspects of tourism in western Europe.

The growth of tourism

- Tourism is one of the most important growth industries in Europe. It is closely related to social and economic improvements, especially in the industrialised countries. Higher incomes, higher standards of living and increased leisure time have given a tremendous impetus to tourism in recent decades. More money and more time are now available for holidays at home and abroad.

- The growth of urban areas has led to the vacation movement of people who need to escape, even briefly, from day-to-day pressures of urban living – the traffic congestion, the air and environmental pollution, the increasing crime and violence in towns and cities.

- The range of leisure activities has widened enormously in recent years from the traditional family holiday at the seaside. Winter sports, yachting, the cruise, the cultural tour, the historic tour, the holiday camp – all these are now available to many people. In addition, a whole new range of physical and adventure activities – trekking, mountaineering, scuba-diving, potholing, sailboarding, etc. – have widened the horizons of prospective tourists.

- However, the single most important factor in the growth of tourism is increased access. Private car ownership has seen an explosive growth. In 1950 there were only 6.1 million cars on the roads of western

Tourism is a service industry that is of relatively modern origin. People have always travelled to explore and discover, to enjoy and delight in new lands and new experiences. But the modern tourist industry is different. It refers to the large-scale movement of people from their homes to a different location for a definite limited period. This movement is usually on an annual basis. It is both national and international in character.

Tourism now plays a significant part in the economy of every west European country. In some, it is a seasonal operation, but in others it continues all year round. In all countries, however, it is a valuable *invisible export* which helps to balance the difference between imports and

Europe, compared with some 150 million today. The family car has made people more mobile and faraway places more accessible. The European highway network, cross-channel ferries, the Channel Tunnel and the *fly-drive* services have all helped to open up new vistas for motorists. Air travel has also helped in the growth of tourism with the development of charter flights and package holidays offering sun, sea and sand at affordable prices.

The organisation of the tourist industry has been very efficient. Individual governments sell their country's attractions at home and abroad through tourist boards (e.g. Bord Fáilte in Ireland) which organise and market tourist facilities in a highly professional way. Charter flights, group travel and special offers have all helped to make holidays cheaper and travel easier. Mass advertising and resort promotions attract the intending tourist.

Tourist locations

Fig. 13.17 Irish scenic view

The tourist attractions of western Europe are many and varied. They range from the natural attractions of scenic beauty, climate and coastline through the fascination with religious, historical and cultural places to the amenities provided: accommodation, food, entertainment and sport. What the tourist wants is essentially a change of environment. Since most of the population of western Europe live in urban areas, they tend to seek out places far removed from the congestion and stress of population and industry.

A number of areas stand out as major tourist destinations:

- Coastal resorts, especially in the Mediterranean
- Mountainous areas, notably the Alps and Pyrénées
- Scenic areas, such as the west of Ireland, Killarney, the Highlands of Scotland
- Capital cities and cultural centres, such as Seville, Paris, Rome, Edinburgh and Dublin
- Leisure parks, such as EuroDisney.

To some of these areas, tourism has brought many benefits by using resources that have no apparent economic use, e.g. snow, scenery, mountains and beaches.

Economic effects of tourism

Benefits

1. Tourism, where it is well-developed in a region, provides employment on a large scale since it is a **labour-intensive** service industry. This direct employment is in the services that provide accommodation, food, entertainment and transport.

2. The indirect effects of tourism are no less important. The **multiplier effect** involves the construction industry, farmers, food-processing industries, craft industries, furniture manufacturers and many others.

3. Earnings from foreign tourists play a vital part in the **balance of payments**. In Spain, Austria, Greece and

Portugal, the money earned by tourism is roughly 20% of their exports.

4. Tourism helps to **revitalise** a region's economy more speedily than other industries and, as noted already, its impact has mainly been on remote, isolated and undeveloped rural regions.

Disadvantages

1. Tourism challenges the dependence on agriculture in the local economy. In a short time, the local economy changes from being mainly dependent on agriculture to being mainly dependent on tourism. Eventually, the local population are as wedded to tourism as they were to agriculture, but have even less control over it.
2. The comparatively high wages paid in the tourist sector entice many workers away from agriculture. In the rural areas farms are abandoned as the owners have found better-paid jobs in the tourist towns.
3. Since the tourist season is usually highly concentrated into the summer months, much of the labour force in the tourist areas is either unemployed or underemployed for much of the year.

It must be remembered, however, that the tourist industry is intensely competitive. Spain, for so long the market leader, has seen a steady decline in its tourist earnings because of its rising prices. Currency fluctuations also play their part. The rise in the value of the dollar created an explosion of American visitors to Europe in the summer of 1985. This was not repeated in 1986 when the value of the dollar fell.

Social effects of tourism

Advantages

1. The development of a region's **infrastructure** (roads, water supplies, phones, etc.) for tourism will also benefit the local people.
2. The **service industries** (transport, shops, discos) are available to the local population, who would otherwise be unable to obtain them.
3. **Recreational** facilities (swimming pools, parks, nature walks) provided for tourists also contribute to the welfare of the local community.
4. **Cultural** contact with tourists broadens the attitudes of locals.

Disadvantages

1. Cultural contact may not always be for the better. Tourists and migrant workers may bring with them lifestyles that offend the local population.
2. Co-operation within the community is often replaced by competition.
3. There is a growing dependence on services. The local community aims at a higher lifestyle than that to which it was accustomed.
4. A previously isolated society is whirled into an urban-orientated one. The whole balance of the local society is thus altered.
5. The tourist industry is often dependent on social and economic factors over which it has no control.

Environmental effects of tourism

Benefits

- Scenic, unspoiled, rural landscapes are a major attraction for tourists. For environmental and economic reasons, governments throughout Europe have taken an active part in the conservation and protection of the **natural** and **cultural** landscape. Features of this conservation policy are national parks, historic houses and gardens, wildlife reserves and National monuments. In Ireland, the Heritage Service cares for the country's national parks, gardens and nature reserves.

- As part of the EU conservation policy, 500 000 hectares of the Irish countryside will be designated **special areas of conservation** (SACs). These areas are mainly boglands, heaths, uplands and limestone pavements (the Burren). Traditional farming will be allowed in the SACs and some 10 000 farmers will be compensated for the loss of some of their land to a SAC.

- Europe has an **urban heritage** stretching back to medieval times, and towns and cities are at the very heart of its culture. Tourists are always delighted to see the evidence of the past in the urban areas they visit – churches, historic buildings or medieval market places. Civic groups and local authorities have united to preserve particular townscapes. In retaining their cultural heritage, they at the same time attract the tourist.

Disadvantages

- The increasing popularity of coastal resorts along the Mediterranean coasts of Spain and France has had a serious **visual** impact. An unplanned, unattractive ribbon development of high-rise apartments, bars and hotels has all but destroyed the scenic beauty of the coastline.

- In addition, inadequate sewage treatment has led to **marine pollution** with resultant health problems for tourists.

- In the Alpine tourist resorts, although skiing and winter sports have transformed the local economy, they have also created environmental problems. Large apartment blocks have been built for Swiss people and foreigners. These **apartment blocks** are out of character with the traditional housing pattern of the Swiss villages. The ski resorts, once attractive and secluded villages, now have car parks, supermarkets, hotels, apartment blocks, discos and nightclubs. Erosion on mountain slopes by constant skiing can cause an avalanche.

TOURISM IN IRELAND

Tourism is a major growth industry in Ireland. It is a service industry which has become an important source of income for the country. For a small island, Ireland offers a wide **variety of attractions** for the tourist:

- Ireland is still a relatively quiet unpolluted retreat that offers a relaxed atmosphere for many people who spend the rest of the year in an urbanised industrial setting.

- A wide range of activities – golfing, fishing, motoring, boating, mountaineering, etc. – can be enjoyed in an uncluttered and scenic environment.

- Much of Ireland still has a rural environment which provides a pleasant contrast to that from which the

majority of tourists come.
- A notable percentage of American and British tourists are second or third generation Irish people who like to visit the home of their ancestors.
- Tourist surveys indicate that the friendliness and hospitality of the Irish people and the scenery are the major tourist assets which the country possesses.
- Ease of access is a vital factor in tourism today. Ireland is a small island, so tourists can reach all parts of the country by car or coach. This spreads the economic benefits of tourism to most parts of the country. The availability of the car ferries from Britain and France creates a mobile tourist and ensures a spread of benefits and activities outside the traditional tourist centres.

Tourist promotion

Bord Fáilte and the Northern Ireland Tourist Board are State bodies charged with the development and marketing of the tourist industry at home and overseas. This is done in co-operation with the international air carriers and the world travel trade. An extensive advertising campaign in the world's media promotes the merits of 'Ireland of the Welcomes' and major tour operators are encouraged to include Ireland in their itineraries.

Bord Fáilte closely monitors the standards of accommodation and amenities. It offers an advisory service to a wide range of tourist amenities. CERT, the State tourism training agency, is responsible for education, training and career development.

In 1997, Bord Fáilte signed a £150 000 advertising deal with British Airways in Australia, in an effort to increase the 40 000 Australians who came to Ireland in 1996. The airline agreed to support the TBI (Tourism Brand Ireland) campaign in Australia.

Fig. 13.18 Monasterboice, Co Louth

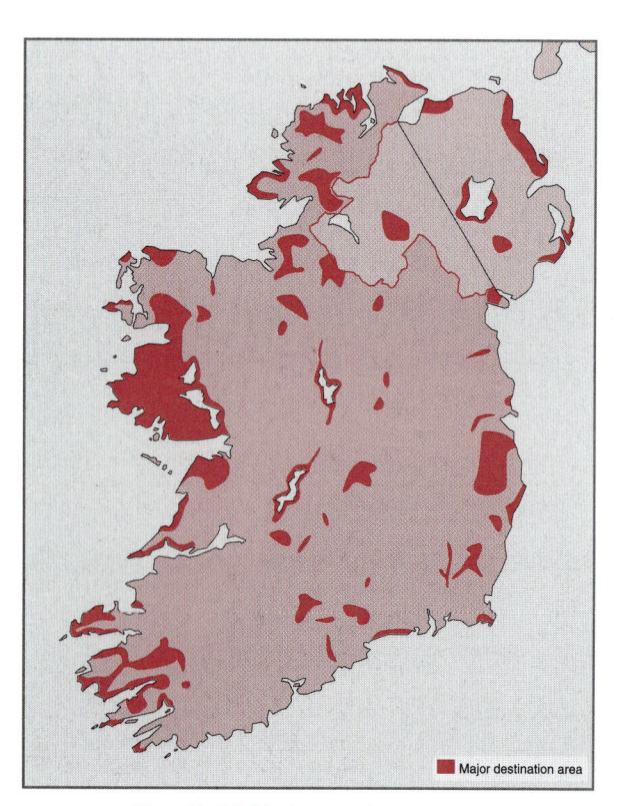

Fig. 13.19 Major tourist attractions

Economic benefits

- Tourism in Ireland is a £2.2 billion industry today in 1997, supporting almost 100 000 jobs throughout the country. These include jobs directly related to tourism and jobs created by the spin-off effects of tourist spending throughout the country.
- In 1996, 4.7 million overseas tourists visited Ireland, contributing £1.6 billion in foreign exchange revenues. Irish residents taking holidays in Ireland added a further £800 million.
- Tourism has brought revenue to developing areas of the country, especially along the western coast. In this way, tourism helps in balancing economic growth throughout the country.
- The tourist boom has sparked off a £200 million investment in new hotels and other holiday facilities in 1997. This includes investment in new river cruising craft, new B&B homes and sports facilities.
- Jobs in the tourism industry cover such areas as hotels, guest houses and catering as well as heritage centres, golf courses, tourist information offices, tour guides, historical sites, etc.
- Tourism contributes to Ireland's balance of payments and it is estimated that tourism revenue accounts for 7% of GNP (Gross National Product).
- Britain remains Ireland's biggest market for tourism. But there has been a significant annual increase in mainland Europeans visiting Ireland.

Where did Ireland's tourists come from?

A wide variety of attractions awaits the tourist in Ireland. As the Bord Fáilte brochure invites, 'Feast your eyes far and wide'. Dublin is the Mecca for most tourists with over 3 million annually. Certain coastal areas of Ireland remain focal points of tourist interest, ranging from Donegal through Connemara, the Burren to Kerry, Cork and the sunny south-east. But many inland counties are also sharing in the tourist harvest by providing a feast of attractions that range from band festivals, salmon festivals, harvest festivals, Fleadhanna Ceoil, storytelling festival, strawberry festival to a comedy festival and a flying pig festival!

Ireland's rich and varied heritage provides an endless source of fascination for the tourist. Early settlement (Newgrange), monastic settlement (Glendalough), Norman conquest (Nenagh castle) and stately homes and gardens (Powerscourt) attract thousands of visitors each year. In addition, there are many special interest/activity holidays available from angling to gourmet cookery to hill walking that whet the appetite of the tourist.

	1994 visitors (in thousands)
Britain	2,038
Europe	988
North America	494
Rest of world	159
Domestic trips	7,422

european topics

common agriculture policy (CAP) & common fisheries policy (CFP)

Fig. 13.20 Crop yields

SAMPLE QUESTION

(i) Describe briefly the main aims of the European Union's Common Agricultural Policy (CAP). (ii) Explain some of the problems associated with CAP. (iii) What reforms have been introduced to deal with these problems?

(i) **Aims:** The main aims of the Common Agricultural Policy were:

- To ensure a fair standard of living for farmers
- To increase agricultural production by promoting technical progress and making the most efficient use of labour
- To stabilise markets in a high-risk business
- To ensure that food was available to the consumer at a fair price.

At the centre of the CAP was the system of guaranteed prices for unlimited production. This price support system encouraged farmers to produce as much as possible since it provided a guaranteed market for their produce. This involved the removal of national and financial barriers to ensure the free movement of EU agricultural produce and to establish agreed prices throughout the EU. The improvement in farm production involved the merging of fragmented farms, encouraging elderly farmers to retire, promoting a fall in the farming population by encouraging people to move out of farming.

(ii) **Problems:**

- The price support system encouraged over-production and the creation of enormous surpluses – butter and beef mountains, milk and wine lakes – which were very costly to the EU which intervened to buy and store the surpluses.
- Countries such as Germany and Britain, with relatively small agricultural sectors, found that they were contributing more and more to an ever-increasing EU budget.
- The price support system began to be seen as wasteful, costly and unfair. The CAP was eating up 60% of the EU's total budget.
- Instead of helping peripheral regions, the

CAP had worked to the advantage of the more prosperous inner areas of the EU.

(iii) **Reforms:**
- The introduction of quotas limiting the amount which an individual farmer can produce, e.g. milk quotas were reduced by 2%.
- Price cuts. The price for cereals dropped by 29% and that for beef by 19%.
- The introduction of set-aside schemes to take land out of agricultural production and to use it for forestry, leisure and nature reserves.
- Development programmes in peripheral areas of the EU (Greece, Ireland, Spain, Portugal) aimed at improving transport, water supplies and energy distribution, farm modernisation and training in new skills.

Fig. 13.21 CAP debated in European Parliament

Is reform of the CAP working?

Although the proposed reforms are only now fully in place in 1997, there is evidence that the CAP reforms are working. Expenditure on agriculture continues to fall as a percentage of the EU budget. The butter mountain has virtually disappeared, the cereal mountain has been lowered from 25 million tonnes in 1990 to 5 million tonnes in 1995. Average farmers' incomes across the EU have risen by 6%.

Less fertilisers and pesticides are being used and the set-aside system is being used to extend woodland areas and to increase re-afforestations.

Fig. 13.22 Farm mechanisation

Renewable resources (fish, forests, etc.) are valuable only as long as they are carefully harvested and managed, so as to prevent over-exploitation and possible exhaustion. In recent decades, stocks in fishing grounds in close proximity to densely populated urban regions have come under increasing strain.

The European Union is the world's largest market for fish products and the third major sea fishing power behind Japan and China. Although fishing may appear to contribute comparatively little to the economy of most EU countries in terms of finance and jobs, it is of vital importance to certain coastal communities where it provides income and jobs directly and also in back-up industries, such as boatyards, processing, packaging and equipment suppliers. There are estimated to be around 300 000 full and part-time fishermen in the EU and every job at sea creates another four or five on shore.

Fig. 13.23 Quota fishing

Problems

- The development of new technology. Modern fishing fleets equipped with sonar can locate and sweep up fish irrespective of size or species
- Large numbers of fish which are too small or the wrong species are thrown back dead into the sea, with disastrous effects on the breeding stocks
- Severe over-fishing
- Destruction of breeding grounds, by the use of fishing gear with heavy chains
- Drastic reduction in the number of certain fish species (herring, sole, cod)
- Factory ships can catch, freeze and process hundreds of tonnes of fish before returning to port
- The European fishing industry also has an overcapacity of vessels. This leads to overfishing and depletes fish stocks even further.

The Common Fisheries Policy (CFP) created a **Blue Europe** in 1983 (as opposed to the **Green Europe** for agriculture). It was designed to create free trade in fish inside the EU, and also to conserve fish stocks.

The conservation element of the CFP consisted of three main strands:

- **Technical measures** to regulate the type of fishing gear, the size of catches and the areas closed to fishing
- **Reform measures** to reduce overall fishing capacity
- The setting up of **Total Allowable Catches (TACs)** for each species of fish in a given area. National quotas were assigned to each country for specific fishing areas.

Problems. After many years of 'Blue Europe', fishermen in the EU still have problems in catching fish economically and efficiently. The outlook for fish stocks is bleak. Fishing is still in crisis as a result of external and internal factors:

External factors

- Competition from non-EU countries
- Agricultural alternatives to fish (low-price meat products)
- Aquaculture (fish farming).

Internal factors

- Infringing territorial limits (each EU country has exclusive fishing rights within 12 miles of its shores). EU territorial waters were extended to 200 miles and any EU country may fish there
- Fishing quotas fixed by the CFP were not observed by some member countries
- Overfishing by fleets from member countries

- Misrepresentation of catch size
- **Quota hopping** – the registration of trawlers in another country in order to gain access to that country's quota.

The **New Common Fisheries Policy: Blue Europe** has not solved the problems of the fishing industry. It led to violent clashes between Spanish, British, French and Irish fishermen over the use of over-sized nets and territorial infringement of Irish and British fishing grounds by Spanish trawlers.

In 1994, the EU published 'The New Common Fisheries Policy' which suggested the following measures:
- Computer databases to follow the movement of fish from producer to consumer by logging catches, landings, transport and sales
- Satellites used to monitor and track trawlers
- Penalties to be standardised and strengthened between member states.

But many argue that these measures will do little to solve the real problem of the European fishing industry: too many fishermen are chasing too few fish.

Controversy continues to follow the CFP. In April 1997, EU ministers decided on a 30% cut in fishing quotas over the following five years. The number of days at sea was to be reduced as was also the size of the fishing fleets. These conservation measures were taken in order to preserve the ever-dwindling fish stocks. The biggest fishing fleets would suffer the biggest cuts. The British and French governments protested angrily at the cuts. Ireland would not be greatly affected by the decision.

CALAIS HIT BY FISHING BLOCKADE

Channel Tunnel services were last night called in to ferry passengers hit by a French fishermen's blockade in Calais.

Ferry services between Dover and Calais, Boulogne and Dunkirk, were suspended when trawlers blockaded the ports in protest at an EU directive which they claim threatens their livelihoods.

european topics
economic & monetary union

Fig. 13.24 Euro notes

On 1 January 1999, a number of countries in the European Union (EU) will adopt a single currency (the **euro**) which will replace the national currencies of francs, punts, deutschmarks, pounds, etc. The euro will be phased in gradually over a three-year period to replace the existing national currencies of member states.

Benefits

The aim of a single currency is to provide a foundation for a stable economic system. Within a single currency area, trade will no longer be disrupted by currencies moving up and down in value against one another, as happened in the currency crisis of 1992/3. The introduction of the euro will create an economic environment which encourages low inflation and low interest rates. Business people will no longer have to bear the cost involved in buying and selling foreign currency. The holiday traveller will also gain by no longer having to buy different currencies when visiting other countries in the euro area.

Euro countries

Countries expected to qualify for joining the single currency in 1999 are: Ireland, Germany, the Netherlands, Denmark, Austria, France, Luxembourg, Finland and Belgium.

Euro money

Euro notes will be issued in denominations of 5, 10, 20, 50, 100, 200 and 500 euros. There will be eight different coins, ranging from one-hundredth of a euro (eurocent) to two euros. At the moment, the euro would be worth eighty pence. This means that someone now earning £200 a week will be paid 250 euros, and a pair of shoes now costing £40 will cost 50 euros.